Framed in Death

Framed in Death

J. D. Robb

LARGE PRINT PRESS
A part of Gale, a Cengage Company

GALE
A Cengage Company

GALE
A Cengage Company

In Death.
Large Print Press, a part of Gale, a Cengage Company.

The text of this Large Print edition is unabridged.
Other aspects of the book may vary from the original edition.
Set in 16 pt. Plantin.

LIBRARY OF CONGRESS CIP DATA ON FILE.
CATALOGUING IN PUBLICATION FOR THIS BOOK
IS AVAILABLE FROM THE LIBRARY OF CONGRESS.

ISBN-13: 978-1-4205-3707-9 (paperback alk. paper)

Published in 2026 by arrangement with St. Martin's Press, an imprint of St. Martin's Publishing Group.

Nothing is really so poor and melancholy as art that is interested in itself and not in its subject.

— George Santayana

Some people's money is merited,
And other people's is inherited.

— Ogden Nash

Chapter One

Death was his art.

For too long he'd waited for recognition of his gift, even — yes — the adulation his extraordinary talent deserved. He wanted his due, and had worked and suffered to share his vision, his genius with the world, only to see lesser talents rewarded while he faced rejection.

Rejection, criticism, and worse, tepid, patronizing, infuriating advice.

He took some comfort knowing so many of the great masters had faced the same ignorance, the same blindness during their lifetimes, only to be lauded after death.

At times he fantasized about sacrificing himself on the altar of his art as others had before him.

Van Gogh, Maurer, Goetz, and more.

He wrote long, vituperative suicide notes, placing the blame for his death on the cruelty of art critics, gallery owners, art patrons, and collectors.

He considered hanging, swallowing pills, a leap from the rooftop. He considered, most seriously, slicing his wrists, then using his own blood to paint his final self-portrait.

It would serve them right, all of them.

The drama of it spoke to him. And oh, the copious tears that would fall over the tragedy. He envisioned that last, stunning portrait in a place of honor and wonder in the Metropolitan Museum of Art.

Millions would gaze at it, and weep for the incalculable loss.

But he didn't want to die. He didn't want fame and recognition after his death.

He wanted it now. He wanted to bask in it, bathe in it, luxuriate in it.

He would wait no longer.

Not his death, no, not that. But death and art would merge in their ultimate beauty and mystery. And he would give to others the gift of that beauty, others who found themselves ignored, overlooked, devalued.

He would, with his genius, immortalize them.

So he planned, and he planned, and he spent months on every detail of what would be his new period. And at last, with all in place, with all perfection, the time had come.

Wandering his studio, admiring paintings he'd created, he took a pill for energy, for clarity. He often wondered how anyone could create without that lovely boost.

Riding on it, he prepped his canvas.

He'd acquired all the costumes for his models, and now painted the background for the first, created the negative space for her head, her shoulders, the trail of the scarf from her headpiece.

By re-creating a masterpiece, improving on it, he would prove himself a master without peer. And the model he chose would become, fortunate girl, immortal. She would live on well beyond a September night in 2061.

Indeed, she would live forever.

Pleased, he cleaned his brushes.

He dressed carefully and without his usual flair. It wouldn't do to stand out. He chose black to blend with the night, and worked his fall of golden brown hair into a braid, then wound the braid into a tight circle at the base of his neck.

He studied himself in the triple mirror on the bedroom level of his home and imagined what she would see.

While the glass reflected an ordinary face, a man of small stature and slim build, he saw a young, beautiful man with a poetically pale, perfectly symmetrical face. He saw deep blue eyes he'd trained, when younger still, to telegraph innocence.

She, he thought, would see the beauty, and the opportunity.

He'd spotted her when he'd scouted the streets for the right one among the poor, the unfortunate, the ones who worked to eat, those who worked to simply survive another day.

He often wondered why they didn't just kill themselves and be done with it.

He'd never known that drudgery. But he had known despair. A despair pushed on him again and again by ignorance. He was an artist who used his innate talents to bring beauty to this dull, often dreary world.

He'd been born into wealth and privilege, and that afforded him the means to focus all on his art, and not have to fracture that focus on some mindless, miserable job.

He understood the power of money.

Tonight, he'd offer the one he'd chosen the kind of money she couldn't resist.

He took the elevator down to the garage, where he kept two vehicles. He thought the sleek black sports car would serve as another lure for her. He'd bring her to his studio in that.

When he took her out, he'd need the all-terrain.

Though the area she worked was several blocks away, he didn't want to draw too much attention. So he cruised by it. Sometimes the street-level licensed companions gathered in groups, other times they spread out. He spotted her, the short red skirt, the low-cut top with spangles that glittered in the streetlights.

He drove another two blocks to an automated lot where he flicked on the jammer that would prevent the scanner from reading his car.

He meandered his way down to her, made eye contact, then stopped as if unsure.

He watched her slow smile, and thought again: Perfect.

Hips swaying, she walked to him.

"Looking for a date?"

"Actually, I was just going to . . . You have wonderful eyes."

"The rest of me's even better. Standard rates, and I'll prove it."

"I . . . would you walk with me?"

"I'm working, handsome."

"I'll pay you." He reached in his pocket, took out a fifty. Bait for the hook.

"Fifty to take a walk?"

"Yeah, for that." He gestured the way he'd come. "And more if you agree to pose for me."

"What kind of poses are you into?" She took the fifty, then fell into step with him.

"I'm an artist."

"Yeah, what kind?"

"I paint. I'm working on a show for next spring. I don't actually know the standard rates for what you do, but if you'd pose for me tonight — and tomorrow night. At least two sessions? I'll pay you double. You've got the face I want for this portrait."

Her eyes narrowed. He wanted her eyes on canvas.

"Double?"

"It's important to me. It could be the centerpiece of my show. My car's in the lot right over there. My studio's not far."

She wasn't ready to buy it, he thought, so he offered what he believed would tip her over the edge.

"I can give you a thousand a session. It's probably going to take three, maybe four. Up to four hours each. After that a model, especially if she's not a professional, can get stale."

"Four hours?"

He could see her calculate. Yes, those who needed money often calculated.

"And any sex work's extra — standard rates."

"That's fine."

"Half now."

As they were nearly to the lot, he took out his wallet, made the payment.

"This is great. I'm right over here. I was just going to walk around, do some people watching, maybe hit a coffee shop or club, and there you were."

"This is your car?"

"Yes." He opened the door for her, and felt the next step click into place when she slid in.

"Some ride," she said when he got in the driver's side.

"Thanks." He used the jammer again, and drove out of the lot. Glancing at her, he tried for mildly embarrassed. "It's family money. I'm trying to prove myself outside the businesses. Art is, well, it's everything for me."

"Uh-huh. I'm going to need the rest of the money when we get to your studio."

"No problem. I just can't believe my luck."

"So is this a naked deal?"

"Oh, no. It's a portrait. Your face, some shoulder. It's a classic-style portrait. I have what you'll wear for it. It's all about your face, and especially your eyes."

Which wore far too much makeup. But he'd take care of that.

She gaped when he turned toward the building and the attached garage.

"You've got a studio in here?"

"Yeah." He pulled into the garage and felt that click again. "Actually, it's my place. The building. It used to be a warehouse."

"The whole fucking building?"

He hunched his shoulders as if embarrassed again. "Family money."

She got out, looked at the all-terrain. "I should've asked for more of that family money."

"Well, if this works out, I'd love to use you again. And I could recommend you as a model."

As she got in the elevator, she studied him. "This is no bullshit?"

"It's not. We'll go straight up to my studio. You know, sorry, I never asked your name."

"Leesa, no *i,* two *e*'s."

"Leesa. I'm Jonathan."

The elevator opened at his studio with its wide windows, its domed skylight. And the paintings.

"Wow, guess you're not starving in a garret — whatever that is. All of these are yours?"

"Yes."

"I don't know anything about art, but these are really nice. I figured you might be stringing me along, and they'd probably suck, but they're really nice."

Considering the source, he deemed that high praise.

"I have to ask you for something."

She rolled the eyes that had doomed her.

"And here it comes."

"No, no." As he spoke, he peeled off the rest of the money. "It's just, I need you to take off your makeup."

"Why?"

"The vision I have. A young woman, her pure beauty. There's a bathroom right there. Makeup remover, whatever you need. And the wardrobe's in there, too. I'll arrange the headpiece when you're done with the rest. The scarves."

He walked over, picked them up.

"To cover your hair."

"What's wrong with my hair?"

"Nothing." If you liked spiky, streaky brass and pink. "But for this study, again, it's the face. The scarf will highlight your face."

"Whatever. It's your money."

He just smiled. "I already know it's well spent. Do you want a drink? Maybe a glass of wine? Since you're new to modeling, it could help relax you?"

"Sure, pour away, Johnny."

He bristled at the "Johnny" as she walked into the bathroom. But he opened a bottle of Pouilly-Fuissé as she called out from behind the door.

"You want me to wear all this? It sure won't show off my talents. Really pretty color though. Classy."

He sipped some wine. He rarely drank when working, but he had to admit to nerves. This marked the beginning of a new era for him, and one he absolutely believed would bring him the notoriety he deserved.

When she stepped out, those nerves evaporated.

"I knew it. I knew you were perfect. Here, have some wine while I arrange the scarves. I want this deep, rich blue next to your face, a wide band of color with a sharp demarcation to the old gold of the rest, and the lighter blue in the ends a touch against the gold of the jacket."

"You know what you want. This wine's really good. I never had anything like it."

"You can have another glass a little later. Yes, the blue low on the forehead and over the top of the ears, the gold — almost like a turban with the ends trailing."

"Where'd you get the idea for all this?"

"Who knows where ideas come from? I need you to take off your earrings, and put these on."

She frowned at what he offered. "Those are like old lady deals."

"Trust me, they're just right."

"You're the boss."

He took a long look at her, nodded. "Wonderful. Amazing."

He led her to a stool. "I'm going to turn your body so your shoulder's facing me. Then your head turned toward me. Like three-quarter profile. Tip your chin a little — yeah, that's it. Just hold that, okay?"

He stepped back, picked up a camera.

"Why do you need that?"

"It'll help me work when you're not here. Now, without moving your head or your body, turn your eyes toward me. Just your eyes. Fabulous eyes. And part your lips. Not a smile, no, don't smile. It's like, like you're taking a breath. Better, good, a little less."

He took three photos, then set the camera down. "You can relax while I mix some paints. Then I need you to get into the pose and hold it."

"This sure isn't what I figured to be doing tonight."

He didn't want to talk to her — she was only an image — but he needed her to stay. Needed her relaxed.

"Do you like sex work?"

"It's a living. I'm going to work my way up to top level. Do you really think I could maybe make a living doing this?"

He smiled at her, and the hunger he heard in her voice. "I bet you could. Let's get you back in pose."

He helped her find it, then walked to the canvas. "Eyes on me, just your eyes."

Her eyes weren't as compelling as the original, and her nose not as elegant. But this would be his.

He worked an hour and a half, then let her break the pose, let her walk around the studio before he set her again.

"This is kind of interesting and boring at the same time. You've got some of the naked women paintings. I could do that. I look good naked."

"No doubt about it."

He worked on the blue now, the light and the shadows, the subtle folds, and found himself pleased with the contrast to her skin.

He worked another hour, a little more, and had to stop himself from snapping at her when she shifted.

So he stepped back. "It's tiring just to sit, isn't it?"

"Yeah. I'm getting kind of stiff."

"I've got a really good start. More than. You've been terrific. We'll take a break. You can have another glass of wine."

"I could use it."

"Get up, walk around a little. Loosen up."

He poured the wine, added the powder he'd made to hers.

"You sure got a view here. It must be nice, being rich and all."

"Here you go. Have some wine, then maybe we can do another half hour. After that, I'll take you wherever you need to go."

"You'll take me?"

"Sure."

"You're really nice." Holding the wine in one hand, she skimmed the index finger of her other down his shirt. "I could do this for you again tomorrow. And maybe a little extra."

She pressed her body to his, ran her hand down, stroked him.

Though he felt nothing, he brushed his lips to hers.

"The extra's tempting. But art first. It has to be for me. Maybe you want to see what I've done."

"Okay, sure."

Sipping her wine, she walked around the easel. Then she smiled, let out a quick, surprised laugh.

"I look good. Mysterious. Kind of plain, but pretty, too, and mysterious."

"That's the idea. Why don't you finish your wine, and we'll try for that half an hour more?"

"Sure. Can I see the rest of this place after? I bet it's really frosty."

"We can take the stairs down." He guided her back to the stool. "Drink up." The hunger gnawing inside him slid into his eyes as he tipped the glass to her mouth. "Then just a few minutes more."

"I feel sort of . . ."

He caught her when she slid off the stool.

"That's okay, sleep now. Why don't you

sleep now? I've got all I need to finish."

He'd considered poisoning her, or giving her enough of the drug to kill her. But those were passive ways, and for it all to matter, really matter, it had to be active.

Death had to come from him to bring the life.

He put his hands around her throat. Squeezed, squeezed. Her eyelids fluttered; her body convulsed. He hadn't known that would happen, and found it thrilling.

He felt, oh God, he felt it. Her life slipping from her and into his hands. The power of life, hers into him.

He'd use that life and power and pour it into the painting.

When it was done, he used thin wire, dabs of glue to adjust her head back into the pose. It took time, precision, but masterful art couldn't be rushed.

Satisfied, he picked her up. He carried her to the elevator and down to the all-terrain.

He knew just where she needed to go.

When Lieutenant Eve Dallas woke before the sun, the first thought on her mind was: Fucking paperwork.

She lay a moment, the tubby cat curled against her back. She imagined Roarke, always up before the sun, dressed in one of his king-of-all-he-surveyed suits, sitting at his desk wheeling and dealing.

And that's how the Dublin street rat became a gazillionaire. Not counting his years as a master in the art of thievery.

As a cop married to that past master, she tried to overlook it.

And she had to admit, lying here thinking about it didn't address the fucking paperwork.

She'd dumped all she could on Jenkinson. The price he paid for making detective sergeant. She'd pushed a little onto her partner, and that was the price Peabody paid just because.

But as lieutenant, the bulk of it fell to her. She'd promised herself she'd get up early, go in early, and get it the hell done.

But . . . did it really count if you broke a promise to yourself?

She spent about thirty seconds debating that, then gave up and rolled out of bed.

"Lights on full." She cursed when the bedroom lights assaulted her eyes. In bed, Galahad muttered what sounded like a curse and rolled over.

She hit the AutoChef for coffee, black and strong, and gulped it down like medicine.

Her brain cleared, and she decided to fill it with the positive.

She was drinking real coffee, wasn't she? And Roarke's blend was as good as you could get. She had a loyal cat currently winding his pudgy body around her legs.

She ordered him breakfast, and when she set it down for him, he pounced as if he hadn't eaten in weeks.

After downing some more coffee, she headed to the shower.

More positive. She had a big-ass shower with a dozen jets pummeling her awake from every direction with water as hot as she wanted.

More hot in the drying tube with air swirling all around her.

A robe waited. Since Roarke seemed to delight in buying her robes, she couldn't be sure if she'd worn this one before. She just wrapped on the silky and rich purple, then went out to explore her closet.

The positive wobbled, nearly dropped with a thud when she faced the dense forest of The Closet.

She could swear the clothes had multiplied overnight, and didn't put that mystery out of Roarke's reach.

Then positive occurred to her. If she actually spent some time choosing, matching or whatever, it put off the paperwork a little longer. Procrastination, sure. But positive procrastination.

Somehow.

And she wouldn't take the easy way with black. Bracing herself, she turned a circle; she faced the line of gray pants that ranged from the palest pearl to the deepest charcoal. Since charcoal came close to her default of black, she grabbed a pair in that shade.

Handily, they had some leather piping in navy, and navy belt loops. So she turned to the line of navy jackets, let out an *Aha!* when she spotted one in leather.

Shirts. Could she go with white? Was that right? How was she supposed to know? How did people just know this shit? And why did white have so many variations anyway?

Since summer kept its sweaty grip on September, she pulled out a sleeveless white shirt, started to turn toward the dizzying wall of boots.

She didn't yelp, but came damn close when she saw Roarke leaning against the closet door.

"Jesus! Why can't you make some noise?"

"Habit. You did get up early."

"I said I would. If I grab an hour before shift, I can knock out the damn paperwork." Then she let out a long breath. "Paperwork's necessary. It's part of the job. It keeps things organized and efficient. I'm approaching it with a positive attitude."

"Well now, that's interesting."

Ireland whispered through his voice like a warm breeze.

Eve studied him a moment, that glorious face, the impossibly blue eyes, the perfectly carved mouth, the black silk of his hair.

A definite positive.

And he smiled at her in a way that still brought a quick flutter to her heart.

He'd also chosen gray, more slate than charcoal, in his perfect and elegant suit, and paired it with a shirt in that pearly gray, a tie in what she thought was, maybe, maroon with subtle gray diagonal stripes.

"How did you pick that outfit?" She gestured at him. "I mean, do you wake up in the morning — or basically in the middle of the night for you — and think: Ah well, today's the day for the slate-gray suit, I'm thinking, and won't it look grand with the pearl-gray shirt and the maroon tie then."

"Your Irish accent needs some work, darling, but thanks for trying."

He moved into the closet, kissed her.

Another positive.

"The clothes are image, and image is part of the job. You've gone classic, with a bit of an edge with the leather. Finish it out with the navy leather boots there and the same with the belt."

"Which navy leather boots?" Frustration smothered the positive. When she reached for a pair, he just shook his head.

"Not those, no. They're too heavy for the outfit." He chose a pair himself. "These. More streamlined, as you are, darling Eve."

"Ha. Fine. And that's enough positive procrastination."

"Then I'll see to our early breakfast."

She took another breath, said, "Thanks."

"Just how long do you think your positive attitude will last?"

"I'm figuring until I get to Central and start on the paperwork. I already fed the cat. Don't let him tell you otherwise."

She dressed, a tall — and yes, streamlined — woman with a choppy cap of brown hair that held shades as varied as the line of brown pants in her closet.

She had long, whiskey-colored eyes in a face of sharp angles. Those eyes scanned the selection of belts before she grabbed one.

She stepped out, set the jacket aside as she walked over to pick up her weapon harness. As she hooked it on, Roarke poured her another cup of coffee.

He sat, PPC in hand, while the wall screen scrolled the early stock reports, and the cat sprawled on his belly on the floor. Hoping, Eve knew, the humans would be distracted enough, at some point, to let him at whatever was under the domes on the table.

"I thought to meet you at Central."

"Why? When?"

"Eve." He shook his head as he removed the dome on — yay! — pancakes. "It's the official move-in. The Great House Project is finished. We're to have dinner there tonight."

"I didn't forget. It's just . . ." She waved a hand at the back of her head. "Compartmentalized. Anyway, they all moved in over the weekend."

"A project of its own, no doubt. Now they're fairly settled, and dinner with us tonight makes it official for them."

"Everything got there, right? You said the stuff we picked out for them got there, so we don't have to take anything else."

"We're taking champagne."

"Okay, good. That's good. We said we'd give them a hand with it over the weekend, but they nixed that."

"They wanted, in their way, to present the house to us. Obviously we've seen it in progress."

"But this is different. I get it."

She started to walk over to pancakes, and her communicator signaled.

She picked it up. "Dallas."

Dispatch, Dallas, Lieutenant Eve. Report to 17 King Street. Possible homicide, female victim. Officers on scene.

"Copy that. Contact Peabody, Detective Delia. I'm on my way."

She shoved the communicator in her pocket.

"Now you're stuck, aren't you then? Between regret at a death, the pancakes you won't eat, and the relief at the further, and necessary, procrastination of your paper-work."

Though she couldn't drown it in butter and syrup, she plucked up a pancake, folded it, ate it. "One less regret." She grabbed her jacket, swung it on, then loaded pockets with her 'link, her badge, and everything else.

"And positive? I'm already up and dressed. I'll see you at Central later, unless."

"Understood." He gave the cat a hard, warning look, then stood, crossed to Eve. "Take care of my well-dressed cop."

"That's the plan." She stroked her knuckles over Roarke's cheek.

"He's making his move," she said.

At their unified stares, Galahad stopped his belly crawl toward the table and rolled over as if to study the ceiling.

She gave Roarke another quick kiss, and as she headed out, heard him speak to the cat.

"And don't think because she's called to duty you'll get her share."

Chapter Two

She drove downtown in that strange hour when night and day met, and neither dominated. The early hour offered light traffic, maxi-buses carting commuters home after the night shift or to work for the early shift, a few cabs — night revelers finally calling it, travelers heading out for an early flight.

Shops and restaurants remained closed but for the occasional twenty-four/seven or round-the-clock café. Pedestrian traffic consisted of a couple of street-level LCs hoping for one more score before breakfast, and a couple of guys, obviously drunk, weaving their way toward one of the cafés.

Lights flickered in the occasional window in darkened buildings, but for the most part, the city slept. Not all of it, Eve knew. There were sectors where the party never quit, where the music would bang and boom in clubs and joints and dives until well after dawn broke.

However, along her route, her city held quiet. But like a breath caught, when it exhaled, life began another day.

Unfortunately, as a murder cop she knew, too well, the dawn didn't break for everyone.

King Street, she mused. Kind of arty on its edge between SoHo and Greenwich Village. Some buildings thrown up after the Urbans, but more old ones, condos, single-family (if you had the scratch for it), lofts, cafés, art shops, boutiques.

She rated the general neighborhood as solid, established, and the sort of place frequented by people who liked to discuss art or other intellectual themes as they downed shit coffee or organic teas while someone recited poetry or played an acoustic guitar.

But then, people killed people everywhere from the hell of the underground to the loftiest penthouse.

It was her job to find out who, how, and why, and she felt it her duty to build a case that brought justice to the victims and those who mourned them.

She spotted the pair of police cruisers, pulled in behind them. She took out her badge as she approached the yellow tape blocking off a pre-Urban, three-story brownstone currently lit up like Christmas.

"Lieutenant." The female uniform gave her a nod. "Officer Cyril."

"What've you got, Officer Cyril?"

"My partner — Officer Stowe — and I responded to a nine-one-one at approximately oh-five-fifty. The wit resides here. Seventeen, snuck out last night, and was sneaking back in when she saw the body."

As Eve ducked under the tape, Cyril gestured. "The wit — Fiona Whittier — has the basement apartment. The body's at the bottom of the stairs in front of the secured door."

"So I see. I also see a door cam."

"Sir, the witness admitted to deactivating that camera at about midnight. Intending to reactivate when she got back inside."

"Great."

"We have two officers inside with the family. Ah, we asked for the backup, as the wit and her family — mother, father, younger brother — were argumentative, mostly with each other — and hell, sir, damn near hysterical."

"Got it. Detective Peabody will be here shortly. She's good at dealing with civilian hysteria, if necessary. I'll take the body. Stand by."

Eve took Seal-It out of her field kit, coated her shoes, her hands, then turned on her recorder.

She walked down the concrete steps to the small, flagstoned area in front of the door.

"The victim's female, Caucasian, early twenties. She's been placed — posed — with her right side and shoulder against the door of the basement apartment of the residence. Her head's turned as if looking over her left shoulder. There's some wire here."

She pulled out her microgoggles.

"There's wire holding her head in this position. The vic's wearing what appears to be a costume, with a head scarf — no, looks like two scarves wound together — covering her hair, a long tunic and skirt, both gold, a white shirt — no, like a collar or scarf — under the tunic. Big pearl earrings."

She took the left hand lying over the right in the victim's lap, and pressed a finger to her Identi-pad.

"Victim is identified as Leesa Culver, age twenty-two. Licensed companion, street level. Resides 215 Tenth Avenue, apartment 403."

Eve eased closer, angled her head. "Bruising on neck consistent with strangulation, as are the broken vessels in the eyes. ME to determine.

"Something about the eyes . . ." Carefully, Eve touched a fingertip to an eyelid. "The victim's eyes are held open, likely with some sort of adhesive. Glue, tape."

She sat back on her heels. "The killer wanted her eyes open. Wanted her head at this angle. Wanted it enough to use wire and adhesive to leave her in this pose."

Pulling out her gauges she established time of death.

"TOD, oh-two-fifty-three. Was she already wearing the outfit? I'm going to say most probable given the need to wire and glue her up, the need to transport to this location, then wire her to the door. But . . . three hours between TOD and the nine-one-one, so enough to dress her up."

Unlike Roarke, Peabody made noise. Eve heard the distinctive clomp.

"You're already on the body?" Peabody started down the steps. "You got here fast."

"I was already up and dressed. Paperwork."

"Oh, right. Those are beautiful scarves, and she's wearing earrings so it doesn't look like a mugging. I . . . wait. Can you move over so I can get a better look?"

"Do you know her?"

"No, no." Peabody, black, red-streaked hair in a jaunty tail, khaki jacket and pants offset with a shirt in bold pink-and-white stripes, studied the body. "The outfit. It's something. It's like I recognize the outfit, and how she's sitting. Like she's posing."

She shook her head, rapped her fingers against her temple as if to knock something loose. "It's . . . I think it's like a painting, but I can't place it exactly."

"A painting? If it is, I know who can."

Eve pulled out her 'link, tagged Roarke.

He gave her a puzzled smile when his face filled the screen. "Lieutenant."

"I'm going to show you the vic. Tell me if what she's wearing, how she looks reminds you of anything."

"All right then."

She turned so the body came on his screen. It took him under two seconds.

"*Girl with a Pearl Earring,* Johannes Vermeer. The original's in The Hague."

"Yes," Peabody said, and rapped her

temple again. “That’s the one.”

“You got that in about one second.”

“It’s a very famous painting, arguably Vermeer’s most well-known. Your victim’s face isn’t quite right — the features — but the eyes are close in shape.”

“Who was she, the model for the painting? Was she a prostitute?”

“Unknown, but unlikely. She’s what the Dutch — he was Dutch — call a tronie. A character type,” he explained. “Vermeer, by and large, painted people at their work, their daily routine or chores. She’s not meant to represent a specific person, but simply a young woman in rather exotic dress. It’s a study of her face, her expression, of light.”

“Okay. That’s helpful.”

“She’s very young, isn’t she? Wasn’t she?” Roarke corrected.

“Yeah.”

“How did the killer hold her in that specific pose after death?”

“Wire and adhesive.”

“Ah,” he said.

“Yeah, it earns an ‘ah.’ Thanks for the help. I need to get back to it.”

“Good hunting.”

Eve slipped the ’link back in her pocket. “So he poses her, very specific, dresses her, very specific — to mimic a painting."

"It's a really beautiful painting." Peabody held out her PPC, where she'd brought the image up.

"Roarke's right, the face isn't there, but the eyes are close. So they were important enough. Hold on."

She crouched down again, used her penlight to shine in the victim's mouth. "He's glued inside her mouth to hold her lips like the painting — really fucking specific."

"Maybe an art student, art historian, struggling or failed artist. She might have modeled for him."

"She was an LC, street level. But yeah, he had to see her to kill her, had to see her as this — what did Roarke call it? — tronie to go through all this to replicate. The outfit, the earring, the angle of the body. He wired her to the doorknob. He had to do that here, onsite, take that time."

"So it was important. It's part of the kill. COD?"

"She was strangled. Morris will confirm, but it looks like manual strangulation from my visual. Let's call in the morgue team, the sweepers."

She straightened. "Teenage daughter sneaking back into the house after a night of partying — I assume — found her. Officer on scene states she and her family got into it, lot of arguing and hysteria. If that's not cooled by now, you'll need to smooth it out. Or I'll cut it off. Whichever works."

"I'll try the smooth first."

Eve walked back up the stairs to talk to the uniforms. "Stay on the body. My partner's calling in the dead wagon and the sweepers. We'll go talk to the wit and her family."

Day had begun to push back the night so the air was a soft, filmy gray when Eve walked up the steps to the front door of the brownstone.

She noted good security.

So did Peabody. "We should get something from the security feed on the basement door cam."

"Deactivated by the kid when she slipped out."

"Well, yeah, of course."

Eve hit the buzzer. A uniform answered, and one Eve recognized.

"Hey, LT, Detective."

"LaValle, what's the status in here?"

"Détente. Things were pretty, let's say fraught, but my trainee — he's only been on six weeks — got them smooth. He's got a way, I gotta give it to him. Plus, he's damn good-looking, and that helps. Officer Freemont, Jerry Freemont's boy."

"Sure, I know Sergeant Freemont. Peabody and I will take it from here. Appreciate your assist."

"No worries. Some place, huh?"

The foyer impressed with what looked like marble floors as white as the Alps, walls of the pearl gray of Roarke's shirt, and a three-tier chandelier of silver rings.

Art, too, that looked important.

"The rook talked them into going back to the kitchen, having coffee. Once he sat down back there with them, it toned the decibels down a lot. I'll show you. You've got the mother — mid-forties and I'll say starchy. The father, late forties, more wilted at this point. Younger brother, smart-mouthed. And the witness, defiant, teary. Can't decide, you ask me, whether to bitch at her parents or crawl into their laps."

As he spoke, Eve took in the house. Shiny, clean, contemporary style, and one that said money was plentiful. Spacious living area, a pair of home offices, a kind of den.

Art everywhere: paintings, sculptures, photographs, etchings.

It all opened up to a large white-on-white-

and-silver kitchen where the family and the rookie sat at a generous breakfast area.

The rookie rose, and he was very good-looking, with creamy brown skin, large dark eyes, a pair of perfect dimples that winked on as he smiled.

"Whittier family — Opal, Roger, Fiona, and Trent," Officer LaValle announced, "Lieutenant Dallas and Detective Peabody. Officer Freemont, we'll be on our way."

The girl groped for Freemont's hand. "Oh, but . . . Do you have to go?"

"I do. Everything's going to be fine, Fiona. You just tell the lieutenant and the detective what happened. They're here to help."

"The Clone Cops." The boy, his gold-streaked brown hair tousled from sleep, his grin wide, and his cat-green eyes avid, rubbed his hands together. "Now, this is XL to the frosty."

"Cram it, Trent." On a tear-soaked snarl, Fiona sent him a vicious look only a sibling could manage. "There's a dead woman outside my rooms, okay? How am I ever going to sleep there again?"

"You can swap rooms with me anytime." He added a cat smile to the cat's eyes. "You're grounded for the rest of your life anyhow."

"Why don't you fuck off and die?"

While the brother went *Oooooh* at that, both parents got into the mix. LaValle would've said the decibels rose again.

And lifting both hands for peace, Peabody stepped forward. "Everyone, please stop. This isn't helping. Why don't we all take a minute, take a breath?"

They rolled right over her, so Eve stepped forward.

"Quiet!" Her voice whip-snapped through the melee. "All of you, shut up, and now. Otherwise, we'll take Fiona down to Central and interview her there."

"Mom! I don't want to go to —"

"Then be quiet," Eve suggested.

Fiona snapped her mouth shut as her brother snickered.

"That goes for you, too. You want to stay, knock it off. Otherwise we can give Child Services a tag and take you down for interfering with a police investigation."

He rolled his eyes at her, but subsided.

"I don't appreciate you speaking to our children in that manner," Opal Whittier began.

"Maybe weigh what you appreciate less: me keeping your kids under control or the dead woman outside your house. The sooner we get to the second of those choices, the sooner you can go back to the family drama."

"This is a very difficult time." Roger Whittier rubbed his tired eyes. "It's all shocking, and it's very stressful for all of us."

"I'm sure it is." Peabody went back to smoothing and soothing. "We need to ask questions, and when we're done, we'll leave you alone. I'm sure all of you want some time to regroup after this shock."

"You're right, of course, you're right. Opal." Roger reached for his wife's hand.

"Yes, yes." Most of the angry color drained out of her cheeks. "My head's still reeling. What if that murderer had still been there when Fiona got home? What if he'd broken in while she was alone in bed, or —"

"None of that happened," Eve said. "Let's deal with what did."

"Yes, let's please do that."

The family shifted to sit on the back of the banquette. Peabody and Eve sat on the ends.

"I'm going to show you a photo, and ask if you recognize this person."

Eve pulled up the victim's ID shot, and had the family pass her 'link around starting with Roger.

"No. Opal?"

She shook her head.

Trent took a long look. "Nope, but she's pretty steamy."

"I think, maybe, it's the woman." Fiona's chin wobbled. "The dead woman, but she looks different."

"Have you seen her before tonight?"

"No. I swear." Tears began to leak. "At first I thought she was a sidewalk sleeper with weird clothes on. Or maybe somebody who got drunk at like a costume party or something and just passed out there. I even yelled at her to get up, and she didn't move at all. But then I got closer, and I could see she . . . The way she was staring, and how she didn't move. She didn't move."

"What time was that?"

"It was around five-thirty, I guess. Maybe a little later. A little later, I guess. There was a rave, and I really wanted to go. I'm almost eighteen!"

"Not for another eleven months," Opal said, sharp as a blade. "We trusted you, Fiona."

More tears leaked. "Pats and Haven and Rush and Zoe all went."

"And we'll see if their parents knew about that."

"You can't narc on them!"

"Oh." This time her father spoke up. "Watch us."

"Let's get into that later." Eve held up a hand before the situation devolved again. "Did you see anyone, hear anything when you got home? Someone on the street, near the house."

"I didn't, and I was really careful. Until I found her. I think I screamed when I realized . . . When I realized she was dead, I think I screamed. And I just ran back up the steps, then to the front door. I just started banging and yelling for Mom and Dad. I didn't even think at first that I had my swipe, the passcode. I was just scared."

"We couldn't understand her at first." Opal spoke, calmer now. "She wasn't making sense, and of course, she was fully dressed. We realized she'd been out, and we were angry. Then she's shouting about a dead woman, and we were terrified she'd been in an accident."

"She was totally whacked," Trent put in, then shrugged at his sister's hard look. "I'd probably be totally whacked if I found a dead body. I was going to go out and see what the what, but Dad wouldn't let me."

"I went out myself. I was sure I'd find

someone had tossed some old clothes or garbage down there, but . . ." Roger closed his eyes. "I saw her."

"Did you touch anything? Either of you."

"I — I started to shake her shoulder, but then I realized." Fiona sucked in a sob. "Her eyes. They were open and staring. I yelled at her, like I said, when I first saw her, and she didn't move."

"I didn't go all the way down," Roger continued. "I took a flashlight, and as I started down — thinking, like Fiona at first, she was sleeping or passed out — I could see."

"He came back in, and we called the police," Opal finished.

"You have a lot of art," Eve commented.

"Opal's an artist," Roger told her, with pride.

Opal waved that away. "I like to think so, but I'm more a patron. Roger and I own the Charles Street Gallery in the Village, and an attached art supply store with a studio space above."

"Studio."

"Yes. We bring in an artist whose work we're featuring to teach and guide students. Once a week for a month, then another artist, perhaps another medium."

"Peabody, the painting."

Peabody took out her PPC, pulled it up. "Do you recognize this."

Opal glanced at the screen. "Of course. *Girl with a Pearl Earring.*"

"Wait." Fiona snatched at the PPC. "That's what she's wearing! That's how she looks!"

"What are you talking about?"

"She's right." Eve drew Opal's attention back to her. "The victim was dressed and posed to replicate this painting. Does it have any specific meaning for you?"

"What? No. I mean, of course it's a magnificent portrait, but I don't understand. Why would anyone . . . It's just sick, and horrible. Why would anyone do that, and leave her here, on our doorstep?"

"Maybe you pissed somebody off."

"Trent!"

"Did you?" Eve countered. "An employee, an artist, a neighbor?"

"Certainly not! Not in any way that would drive someone to do this."

"Do you teach this kind of art? What would it be, classical?"

"The featured artist selects the style and medium. I myself teach once or twice a year, depending. But I focus on still lifes and watercolor. The Vermeer's an oil painting. I'm a watercolorist."

"We'd like the names and contacts of those featured artists for the last year, and the same from employees. What about artists you turn down?"

"I —" Opal looked helplessly at her husband.

"Opal and I co-manage the gallery and the shop. I'm going to say for every artist whose work we accept, there are easily half a dozen we feel don't meet our standards or needs."

"Everybody thinks they're the next Matisse or whoever," Trent commented. "But mostly?" Face mockingly stern, he did an exaggerated thumbs-down.

For the first time Opal smiled. "Rude, but not wrong. Why would anyone murder that poor young woman because I made them angry?"

"It could be they chose your location because it just worked. The quiet street, the below-street-level area. But we'll look at every possibility."

"Clone Cops. It was a pretty mag vid" was Trent's opinion. "I heard they're going to make another one about when people started going crazy and slicing and dicing each other."

He slid a glance toward his parents. "Mom and Dad freaked, so Fi and I were on house arrest for like a week because of all that. But like I told them, I don't need some weird-ass virus or whatever to want to slice and dice Fiona."

His sister sneered, but this time with a touch of amusement in her eyes. "Yeah? Smothering you in your sleep's my lifelong dream."

Before the parents could speak, Eve rose.

"Well, if you end up sliced and diced, or you end up smothered in your sleep, we'll know who to arrest. That cuts down on legwork."

That brought a delighted cackle from the boy, and a half smile from his sister.

"If you could get us those names and contacts — add any of the students — we'd appreciate it. And if you think of anything at all?" Eve put one of her cards on the table. "Reach out. We appreciate your time and cooperation."

"The woman," Opal began. "The, ah, body."

"Will be transported to the morgue. The Crime Scene Unit will need some time to process the area. Fiona, you should use the entrance inside until they're done."

"What a night." On a sigh, Roger got to his feet. "I'll walk you out."

Eve waited until they were out of earshot. "Mr. Whittier, I'm going to ask this to open or to eliminate a connection. You obviously care deeply about your family, so I'm asking you to be honest. You didn't recognize Leesa Culver?"

"Who? Oh, was that her name? No, I've never seen her before. At least that I remember."

"Do you or have you previously engaged licensed companions?"

He stopped, gaped. "I — What a question."

"The victim was an LC."

"Oh. Oh, I see. I don't. I haven't, not ever. Opal and I . . . we're in tune in that area. In most areas, actually. Lieutenant, I'm a family man, and this has terrified my family. I can only swear to you if anything I've done had even the most remote application to what happened tonight, I'd tell you."

When they reached the door, he paused. "We're a loud, often unruly family, but we love each other. My wife and kids are the most important things in the world to me.

"Please find who did this, who killed that poor woman, who brought my family into this horror. I doubt any of us will sleep easy until you do."

When they stepped outside into bright daylight, Peabody circled her neck. "I believe him on that last bit. They're pissed off at the daughter, and she's pissed off at them. She has to be to justify being stupid. But they're a unit. You could see how they sat together."

"That sums that up. But it doesn't tell us why here. It could have been for the relative convenience. But the rest? The pose, the costume. All that's so deliberate and specific. Why wouldn't the dump spot be deliberate and specific?"

They started toward the car. New York had wakened fully. Cars buzzed along the streets; pedestrians clipped along the sidewalks.

A group of kids in navy pants and blazers, crisp white shirts, trudged their way to their private school. Across the street another pair in baggies and tees rode airboards to their less tony education facility.

"We'll check the vic's apartment. I'll do the notification after that, and see what

Morris can tell us. She's got a mother in Vegas — a dealer at a casino. A father based in Maine. He runs a whale-watching gig."

She got behind the wheel. "What if the whale objects to being watched? He's going to be bigger than the boat, because whale. So, if he's feeling pissy, he could be: 'Watch this, assholes.' Then he rams the boat and people are splashing around in the water. Screams fill the air. Then glug-glug, all because they're going out there on some boat playing Peeping Tom on a whale."

Peabody sat quietly for a moment. "You know, up until now I've always wanted to go whale watching. There's another dream crushed."

"You're better off."

Eve slid into traffic.

"Coffee, please?"

Eve held up two fingers as she navigated out of the more subdued neighborhood into the crowds, the glide-carts selling crap coffee and egg pockets filled with a substance barely resembling anything laid by a chicken.

She took the coffee Peabody passed her and thought of her single undressed pancake breakfast.

She, too, was better off.

"We're all so excited you and Roarke are coming over tonight. And I just have to say, the lamp. I never expected — it's so perfect. Just when I think you're tuning me out, you're not. You remembered how much I loved that metalwork."

"I could be tuning you out now."

"But you're not, so I'm going to gush for a minute. I thought I'd put it in my craft room, then our home office, and it looked so good in both. But then I realized, no, it belongs in the living room, and I found just the right place. It's wonderful."

"You're welcome, sincerely. Move on."

"I'm moving on to the birdbath with the little fountain you and Roarke gave Mavis and Leonardo. It's so them. Birds and fairies. Fanciful, unique. Bella's crazy about it, so bonus. Then the chair for Number Two's nursery? Mavis cried over it, that's how much it meant to her you'd think of it."

"I didn't really."

"You made it happen, you and Roarke. And the sculpture my parents sent? Jeez, I think we all shed a few over that. And God, the blown-glass light my mother made. It's . . ."

Peabody just pressed a hand to her heart. "Wait until you see it. Wait until my mom and dad see it, hanging over the table my dad made the year I was born! He doesn't even know I found it in that secondhand shop.

"It's all . . . The moving in, spending our first weekend there. Knowing that's home, that's really our home now. It's not just having our things there, even seeing it finished. It's having things people who matter to us gave us for our home."

She let out another sigh.

"Anyway, we're all stupid happy."

Eve pulled into a street slot on Tenth, then sat a moment.

"It took me a year, maybe more before I started to think about Roarke's house as mine, as ours. As home, for me. It took longer before I really felt it. So I know what it means, I know how much it matters to have home."

Eve got out of the car, waited for Peabody on the sidewalk.

"Now, save anything else on all that for tonight, and get your head into the job."

"Done. Thanks for letting me spill."

"Spill what? I tuned you out." On Peabody's laugh, Eve pointed. "The vic's building's there, across the street."

Together they walked to the corner to cross.

Chapter Three

Unlike the Whittier's elegant, prewar brownstone, the building that housed Leesa Culver's apartment was a postwar concrete block with crap security.

Eve considered the graffiti adorning it reasonably artistic and remarkably lacking in obscenities.

On street level, it stood beside a diner, called just that. A Diner advertised twenty-four-hour service. Something she imagined a woman in the victim's line of work appreciated. On the other side, another post-Urbans building someone had faced with fake brick offered a street-level pair of retail spaces. One had a sign announcing FOR RENT, and the other housed something called the Witchery that had a lot of crystals hanging in the window.

Eve caught Peabody eyeing it.

"Don't even think about it."

"Too late, I already did."

But with Eve, she walked to the doors of Leesa's building, and waited for Eve to master in.

The lobby with its dingy walls and grimy floors offered a single elevator painted battleship gray. Eve barely glanced at it before pushing open the door to the stairwell.

She said, "Apartment 403."

"Looser pants. Looser pants. Yours are really nice, by the way, but the jacket? That hits ult. I'm thinking about making myself one."

The stairwell echoed with sounds of a crying baby, someone's too-loud music, voices raised in a fight about making the month's rent.

And it smelled like spoiled cabbage soaked in urine.

"Making a jacket?"

"A leather jacket. In my abso-mag-to-the-ult craft room. I just have to decide on the color."

"If you make yourself a pink leather jacket, you'll leave me no choice. I'll have to kill you, but I can make sure you're buried in it."

"Good thing I'm thinking more classic

and go-with-everything color. Not black, but maybe a gray with some blue undertones, or a deep brown or maybe a more coppery brown or —"

"This is your mind on the job?"

"It distracts me from four flights of stairs. But job-wise, maybe he — and it feels like a he — hired Culver before. Maybe she knew him from her work."

"She wasn't registered for female clients, so that reads male. Unless her killer didn't like her spouse, lover, father, brother screwing an LC."

"That also plays."

"No 'link, no ID, no other jewelry on the body, and no money. LCs have to carry their registration and ID when they're working."

"Those would have been anachronistic with the pose, the painting."

"That, and without a 'link we can't know if she had any previous contact with the killer."

She pushed open the door on four to a skinny hallway lined with doors of the same battleship gray as the elevator.

Up here, the lack of soundproofing allowed Eve to hear a woman in 404 shout: "Get up and get out, you lazy son of a bitch.

I'm done! Do you hear me? Done!"

"Record on. Dallas and Peabody entering the apartment of Leesa Culver."

She mastered into chaos.

The tiny space held a sagging two-cushion sofa wrapped in an ill-fitting red-and-gold cover and buried under clothes. Someone — she assumed Leesa — had tossed a couple of wigs, one black, one as red as the sofa, on the single chair.

Upside-down plastic crates made a kind of coffee table where several dishes piled. A tiny screen adorned the beige walls along with a couple of unframed posters. One of the Eiffel Tower, one of Big Ben.

A table barely bigger than a dinner plate and also piled with dishes, take-out containers, and a long-dead rose in a black vase had one chair. Currently serving as another depository for clothes.

Separated by a half wall, the kitchen consisted of a mini-AutoChef, a small friggie, a couple of cabinets, and a sink that would have accommodated a single goldfish.

Peabody handed Eve the Seal-It so they could both reseal.

"It's not much," Peabody said, "but with a little care, it could be cute and cozy."

"Obviously she didn't care about the cute

and cozy."

She moved toward the open gold shower curtain that separated the bedroom.

The room was, basically, unmade bed. What floor space there was provided a home for more clothes, shoes, an empty bottle of wine.

The closet held a few pieces she'd actually hung up, a few more shoes, a pair of over-the-knee boots in fake black leather that shined like a mirror.

Between the side of the bed and the single window jammed a table smothered with various facial enhancements along with a stand-up magnifying mirror.

On the wall facing the bed a tall, skinny cabinet wedged in.

She turned, looked into the bathroom.

A wall sink with rust spots. A stick-thin shower, a toilet. And barely enough floor space to maneuver from one to the other. Particularly considering the pile of towels heaped there.

"She took sloppy to a very high level."

"I don't know how anybody lives like this," Peabody said. "Honestly, how did she find anything?"

"That's our job now. I'll take the bedroom and the bath, you take the kitchen and eating area. We'll tackle the rest together. Check any drawers — she had to keep records somewhere, somehow."

"I'll get to it."

Since the makeup table had a drawer above bed height, Eve sat on the side of the bed, angling her long legs through the space.

She found more makeup, a jumbo pack of condoms, and a tablet.

It didn't surprise her to find the tablet sprang to life with a tap of the finger.

Leesa Culver hadn't bothered with passcodes or security.

She found the victim's financial records considerably more organized than the rest of her life.

Eve found every night's income for the nineteen months Leesa had been licensed tallied.

She'd also listed the standard rates and each act performed — the occasional tip. She'd carefully deducted her fees and taxes, kept a calendar for her mandated medical exams, screenings, and clearance.

No customer names, of course. Street levels didn't deal with names.

But she had the address for the flop she used when the client wanted more privacy than a doorway or alley, or his own vehicle.

Eve bagged and sealed the tablet, set it aside, then rose to try the cabinet.

Cheap jewelry, cheap, sexy underwear, crop tops, tiny shorts, a selection of purses just big enough for a 'link, an ID, her key — she had a spare one in one of the bags. In a pair of sweats that actually looked comfortable, Eve found two-fifty in cash.

She bagged, labeled, and sealed it.

She found another fifty in the toe of a shiny white bootie, then another twenty in the pocket of a skirt the size of a dinner napkin.

She looked under the mattress, dumped pillows out of their cases. Then had to curve her body to get down and look under the bed.

It occurred to her she hadn't been the best at housekeeping during her apartment days, but even she hadn't grown dust bunnies the size of a Saint Bernard.

Peabody stepped in.

"Why dust bunnies? They're just dust. Why are they bunnies?"

Peabody considered. "Maybe because when you're not watching, they hop around?"

"Do they? Do they really?"

"I don't know. I never let them grow into bunnies. Even if I didn't care, and I do, my mom's disapproval would reach across the miles and shame me. I found a hundred cash in the kitchen, inside a cereal box."

"Three-twenty in here. Sweatpants and shoe."

"Otherwise, she had another bottle of wine like that one, but half-full, an empty AC, some snack food — chips, cookies. Crap coffee, and a bunch of little creamers she palmed from the diner next door. Fake sugar packs, same thing. Salt and pepper packs she probably hoarded from fast food joints or takeout. No cookware — I mean zero. Other than what's dirty and scattered around, a couple of forks and a single spoon, one plate, two mugs, two wine-glasses, and one regular glass.

"You know what I don't find anywhere?"

Eve glanced over. "Not a single photograph, nothing that strikes as a family or childhood memento."

"Exactly. I'll start on the living room."

"I'll hit the bathroom, then join you."

Eve found the medicine cabinet stuffed with skin care products and over-the-counter meds. A thorough check revealed no illegals.

She found another twenty in an empty face cream jar.

Shampoos and soaps littered the lip of the tub, and a full-length mirror hung on the back of the door.

She went out to join Peabody.

"Another twenty in an empty face gunk jar. Plenty more face gunk, hair gunk."

"I got fifty so far. The inside of that lamp's hollow, and she rolled a fifty in there. How the hell did she keep track of where she hid cash?"

"Bigger question. Why did she bother to spread it all over this place? A couple hidey-holes, okay, fine. All this? Pathological."

"A guess?" Peabody continued to work as Eve pulled off the couch cover. "She figures when someone breaks in — though a place like this isn't going to rank high for a B and E — and they find a stash, they'll figure that's it. Which isn't pathological as much as stupid.

"Did you ever hide cash?"

"No." Eve started on the couch cushions. "I figured if someone broke in while I was there, they'd have to get through me. I favored my odds. If they broke in when I wasn't there, why should I add my hard-earned cash to their haul? Such as."

She held up more.

"This hundred and fifty zipped inside this disgusting couch cushion."

Peabody pulled two wrinkled twenties from behind the wall screen. "Add forty more, and I'm now giving you the pathological."

"She kept her financial records on a tablet, and they're precise and detailed. Then she hides — what is it?"

"Ah." Peabody closed her eyes, did the math. "Six-sixty. No! Six-eighty. Pretty sure."

"Hides six-eighty in more than a half dozen places in this sloppy dump. The woman had issues, but she also had a bank. She had somewhere she kept the bulk of her income."

"She spent a lot on clothes. They're cheap — style and value — but she had a ton of them."

"Add the face gunk, etc. She invested in herself, but it doesn't come close to what she pulled in. Even adding in rent, food. It probably doesn't apply, but it's curious."

They finished the search, found another twenty inside the vase with the dead rose.

"Let's talk to the neighbor across the hall."

Eve judged the woman who answered as early thirties, a mixed-race female in black sweatpants, a gray T-shirt over a thin body. She had blond hair that needed a root job pulled back in a tail. Her eyes, a hazel that pulled toward the green, were red and swollen from weeping.

"Ma'am, Lieutenant Dallas, Detective Peabody, NYPSD."

The woman looked at the badge, looked at Eve as another tear spilled. "Whatever he's done, I kicked him out. He doesn't live here anymore."

"We'd like to speak to you about your neighbor, Leesa Culver."

"Oh." Now she glanced across the hall and anger dissolved any more tears. "It wouldn't surprise me if he slipped her a fifty — of my money, too — for a BJ when I was out working for a living. I work nights, cleaning office buildings, and what happens? I come home, again, and he's lying in bed. Says he quit his job. Again. Which is bullshit. I bet you twice that fifty he got fired again. I'm finished."

So we heard, Eve thought.

"Could we come in and speak to you for a few minutes?"

"Hell, I guess I could use the distraction."

The apartment seemed to be the same footprint as Culver's, but a world apart. The neighbor obviously used her cleaning skills at home.

She, too, had a two-cushioned sofa, but in a cream color that was spotless. She'd paired it with a chair that had tiny cream-and-blue checks, a small blue rug. The wall screen was double the size of Culver's and was joined with a few framed prints.

The small white table in the eating area had four blue stools. The kitchen shined.

She'd hit Peabody's cute and cozy, Eve thought.

"You might as well sit. Do you want coffee? I was late getting home this morning because I stopped to get coffee — since he forgot to pick any up yesterday — and I got pastries because he likes them.

"I'm an idiot." She pressed her fingers to her swollen eyes. "Two years, two years wasted on that lying, lazy son of a bitch, and I buy him pastries. Do you want some?"

"Thanks, but we're fine. We don't want to take up too much of your time, Ms. . . ."

"Boxer, Stasha Boxer." She walked over to take the chair, gestured to the sofa. "So what did Leesa do?"

"Ms. Culver was murdered last night."

"What! Oh God." Stasha pressed her hands to her face. "Murdered. Now I'm going to hell for thinking bad thoughts about a dead person. I didn't like her very much, but . . . She was hardly more than a kid."

"Could you tell us the last time you saw her, spoke to her?"

"A couple of nights ago, I guess. I think. I'm not really sure. Once in a while we leave for work about the same time. Mostly not, but sometimes. I think we did a few nights ago. How did it happen?"

"We're investigating that. Can you tell us anything about her personal relationships? Romantic relationships, friendships, family?"

"I don't think she had any. I sleep during the day, try to get a solid six, maybe seven hours in. That's the workweek. Weekends I clean around here, do laundry, get the shopping and whatever errands done."

She paused, closed her eyes. "Listen to that. Not once in there did I say he did any of it. Because he didn't, and I kept letting that go."

She drew a breath. "Done. I'd see her now and then on my days off. We've got a laundry in the basement, and she came in once or twice while I was doing mine. She didn't know what the hell she was doing there, just dumping everything in together."

Stasha shrugged. "She was young, you know, so I said how she should separate things, and showed her. Anyway, I don't remember ever hearing — and you can hear everything in this place, which is why I wear earplugs to sleep — or seeing anybody go to her door, or hear or see her come home with anybody."

Stasha lifted a hand. "I remember now. Showing her how to do something as basic as laundry, I asked why a pretty girl like her didn't have a boyfriend. And she said she didn't have time for that. She was working her way up, saving her money. She was going to be a top-level LC inside three years, and rich guys would take her places, buy her things. She wanted to travel to Europe — oh, and pay somebody to do the stupid laundry.

"Did she have family?" Stasha wondered. "She never mentioned family. I guess we didn't talk more than a handful of times over hi, how's it going."

Stasha shook her head. "God, she was so young, and pretty, too. But I don't know if she had anybody who cared about her. I really didn't know her."

"Did she have any interest in art?"

"Art who? Oh, oh, you mean like paintings and that kind of thing? I don't know, but I don't think so. The best I can tell you is she was ambitious, and I think she liked her work. Around here? She absolutely kept to herself as far as I know. I'm friendly enough, with a lot of other people in the building. I don't remember anyone ever bringing her up in conversation."

Stasha lifted her hands, let them fall. "I can wish I'd made more of an effort, I guess, to get to know her. But we just didn't have much — anything, really — in common."

"We appreciate your time."

"I'm so sorry for what happened to her," Stasha said as Eve and Peabody rose. "I hope you find whoever killed her."

As they left, Peabody glanced back at Culver's apartment. "Do you want to knock on more doors?"

"I think we hit our best source. We'll put a couple of uniforms on that, but it fits the space she lived in. She lived for herself."

"Ms. Boxer took the time to show her how to sort laundry. If she'd wanted a friend," Peabody said, "she could have had one across the hall."

"Friends take time and effort. I lived like that for a while. I was focused on getting out, getting here. One goal — well, two. New York and the badge. Hers? Making top level and living high. So I get her, to a point."

"Why New York? For you, I mean. Why here especially?"

"Because you can be anybody here. You can disappear if you want. Nobody knows you, and nobody cares where you came from. It's the whole fucking world in one place."

"That? That last bit? For me, too. The excitement, the so much of it. I wanted the badge, also, but I wanted it here. I wanted some of that so much. It scared me a little, at first, and even that was exciting."

As they got in the car, Peabody belted up. "Did it scare you at first?"

"No, it was the answer." Eve thought of herself sitting at the counter window, eating her first slice of New York pizza.

Freedom, at last.

"It was all the answers. I thought I could shake off everything that happened before, shut it away. That the city would just burn it off. I was wrong about that, because you never shake it all off."

She considered a moment. "Maybe you shouldn't."

She pulled into traffic. "But it was still all the answers. We'll hit the morgue."

"You made friends in New York."

"Mavis didn't give me a choice."

"She's pretty irresistible. You had Feeney, too. And connections with other cops, and in your apartment building, that used to be my apartment building until this weekend. I made friends, and I had connections on the job when I made it, in my first apartment building, and in the second. If you don't have those connections, you end up like Culver — in a sloppy chaotic mess, because fuck everything but me. Or in a lifeless sterile space for the same reason."

"We'll need to talk to some of her coworkers, LCs that worked that same block. But how it reads right now? She went with someone. And if she went off with someone to a place he could kill her, dress her in that outfit, which meant a private place, not whatever flop she used, he offered enough money to make it worth the time. And she'd have wanted half up front. She'd been working for over a year and a half, she wouldn't have left her block without a solid deposit in hand."

"Do you think she had friends on the street?"

"No. She had competitors."

"That's sad. But sounds true."

"We'll check it out anyway. One of them might have seen whoever hired her. We could get a description. If he used a vehicle, we could get a description of that. Meanwhile, maybe Morris can tell us something more."

She drummed her fingers on the wheel when she stopped for a light. "Find out what cops work that sector. Most street levels work close to home. We'll run this by them. Probably beat droids. As annoying as droids can be, we'll get straight facts."

"Straight facts are great, but they leave out impressions and instincts."

"Yeah, one of the annoying things about droids."

When they walked down the white tunnel of the morgue, Peabody glanced up from her PPC. "Droids. Officers Campbell and Winters. Both female replicas."

"We'll call them into Central after we're finished here."

Eve pushed through the double doors of Morris's theater.

She'd have called the music he had playing peppy. Something with a bouncy beat and a couple of girl voices playing with harmony.

Leesa Culver lay on the slab, and Morris stood beside it.

He wore a kind of rusty red suit today, one with a faint metallic sheen. His shirt had tiny stripes of the same color against white. He'd added a tie of deep sapphire blue with cords of that blue winding through a complicated braid he'd looped in a circle at the back of his head.

As he reached into the Y-cut to lift out Leesa's heart and weigh it, Peabody looked carefully away.

"Lower music volume by half," Morris ordered. "I thought she'd enjoy something young and energetic. She had a very short life."

"Somebody ended it after dressing her up like a girl in a painting."

"So I'm told. The slight injuries from the wiring, the glue, all postmortem. Your call of manual strangulation is correct. You're looking for someone with wide-palmed, long-fingered hands. Strong ones. Her larynx was crushed. I'll give you measurements on the hands — and they'll be close

— in my report."

"A chance for prints?"

"No, He was careful enough to seal them before he killed her. No other injuries on the body. Internally, she'd consumed a very nice Pouilly-Fuissé, about eight ounces, approximately three hours prior to her death, and another six within minutes of death. In that six ounces? Enough barbiturates — powder form, I believe — to knock out someone double her weight."

"He drugged her, then he killed her." Considering, Eve walked around the slab. "Didn't want her to fight back. He gave her something to put her out so he could strangle her, and with his hands. Personal, intimate. He doesn't just bash her over the head, stab her in the heart. Can't do that and have her intact for the final pose."

She looked down at the body.

"So that's important, that final pose. And he's a coward who needed her unconscious before he killed her. He doesn't need the rush of the struggle."

"Um." Eyes still averted, Peabody added, "A struggle could mess up the costume, or maybe end up putting a bruise on her face."

"That's right. But he could've given her a heavier dose, or injected her with a lethal dose. She'd die nice and neat that way. But he wanted the intimacy, his hands around her throat. It takes effort to squeeze the life out of somebody using your own hands."

Morris walked over to wash up. "She'd have felt nothing, which is a blessing for her if there can be one. Her body would have fought for air, but she wouldn't have been aware of it, wouldn't have felt the panic and pain over the three or four minutes it took him to kill her."

He pulled a tube of Pepsi, and Peabody's choice of Diet, out of his friggie.

"Thanks. Illegals or alcohol abuse?"

"No. Her last meal, about six hours before death, a soy dog and fries, a Coke. While a healthy weight, she was borderline on malnutrition. She needed more iron, fiber, and green vegetables in her diet.

"She used a six-month injection for birth control, was naturally a brunette who'd recently refreshed the blond and added the streaks. Harvo has a sample and, being the Queen of Hair and Fiber, will tell you what she used there — home or salon grade. Harvo also has the clothes."

Eve nodded. "He had to get them from somewhere. They're not exactly today. What about the wire, the glue?"

"I can tell you the wire's one and a half millimeters, and strong. Metal with a protective jacket. The lab will take it from there. And the glue, also very strong. I needed acetone to remove it."

Morris laid a hand on Leesa's head. "Her eyelids already had a slight rash by the time she got to me, as had the other areas where he'd used glue to secure the wire, to keep her head in that exact position."

Morris looked down, then eased the body's head over to show Eve the spotty redness. "It's a different kind of cruelty, but cruelty nonetheless."

"She was nothing more than a droid to him by that point — maybe all along. Less, really. Like some doll he could dress up, use, destroy. Sex?"

"She'd had intercourse, yes, but hours before her death. At least four, closer, I think, to five hours before. And she followed the regulations, douched thoroughly."

"Why would he give her time for that? He'd've used a sperm killer. It probably wasn't him. If it wasn't, he didn't care about sex. Or we're wrong, and it's a woman."

Pacing, she cracked the tube. "No, not a woman. She's not registered for females, and she wanted to work up to top level. That means following regulations."

She took a drink from the tube, nodded. "Okay. We know what we know now. Thanks, Morris. You added to it."

"Family?"

"I'm going to make the notification when I get to Central. She didn't have a sign of either parent in her apartment, and neither live in or around New York. But I'll let you know if they, or anyone, wants to come see her or make arrangements for her."

"They brought her into this world. I hope they care enough to see her out of it."

"I'll let you know."

"Morris?" Peabody paused at the door. "Can I ask why you decided to be an ME?"

He sent her a surprised look, then an easy smile.

"It's simple, really. There are those who tend to the living and those who tend to the dead. Those, like me, work to find answers to give those like you. Those who stand for the ones who had their lives taken."

He laid a hand on Leesa's head again. "The dead also need tending."

"Thanks."

"Let me add congratulations on your new home."

"Double thanks. We're going to throw a

hell of a party soon."

"I look forward to it."

As the doors closed, they heard him say, "Music at previous volume."

Chapter Four

Since they wouldn't get anything substantial from the lab yet, Eve headed straight to Central.

After she made the notification, she would set up her board and book. Then take time to reevaluate, to think.

And contact Mira, she decided. She had no doubt this one would need the valued analysis of the department's best profiler.

"A human replication of an old, important painting," she said aloud. "Left on the doorstep of people who own an art gallery. The arrow's pointing, and with bright, flashing lights, to an artist. If not a painter type, a want-to-be-a-painter type, certainly someone connected to the art world."

"Another gallery owner," Peabody speculated. "An employee with a grudge. An art collector, or somebody who lost their art collection somehow."

"And some of the pieces reverted to that particular gallery. That's not bad. What it doesn't feel like? Victim specific. Culver's dead because, first, street-level LC who can be hired on the spot, and she fit the costume, had, basically, the right look. Close enough for replication."

"Did he kill her because she wasn't close enough? Maybe he started painting her, and she couldn't hold the pose, or he saw the flaws? Or his work just sucks, he can't bring his vision to life, but it has to be her fault?"

"The painting lacks life, so now so does she?" Eve folded that one into the mix. "He always planned to kill her. All of the above may be true, but he always planned to kill her. Maybe it's as simple as, well, the original model's dead, so this one has to die, too."

"Or, if it's to smack at the Whittiers, it's: 'See what you made me do?' "

"Also not bad."

"I'm getting the hang of this detective thing."

Eve had to smile as she pulled into Central's garage. "You're coming along."

"Yay me. If he just wanted to replicate the painting, maybe on canvas, too, he didn't have to kill her. He just pays her, and bye.

But you're right, he always planned to kill her."

"And always planned to dump her, in costume, in pose, where he dumped her."

"Yeah." Peabody whooshed out a breath. "It's too weird and time-consuming, and risky, for otherwise. Add people might have wire and glue handy, but most don't have sealant hanging around. Plus, to copy the painting, he could hire plenty of others who had a similar look. He could've hired a professional artist's model."

"And," Eve said as they walked to the elevator, "if he's an artist or a wannabe, maybe he's hired one in the past. Or he just goes for LCs. Those are angles. Give like crimes a shot. Victims dressed as famous paintings, or icons."

They stepped onto the elevator.

"You sometimes see art students sitting in museums, sketching famous works of art."

Eve supposed she had. But. "Why?"

"It's practice, it's homage. It's learning how that artist accomplished it. I'd say anyway. And some schools have students try their version of a well-known painting."

"So art students." Eve stuck her hands in her pockets. "Maybe art historians, considering the age of the original. Add art forgers, and those people who restore art. The victim can't tell us much more, but we've got plenty of lines to tug. Start tugging."

The doors opened. DS Jenkinson and his tie walked on.

"LT, Peabody."

"Why, God, why!" Too late, Eve slapped a hand over her eyes. "In this closed space, it's burning my corneas."

"Aw, Loo." With a kind of affection, Jenkinson ran his hand down a tie with a field that spread like a nasty, purpling bruise. Over it, flowers the color of a concerning urine sample bloomed. "It's real subtle."

"Yeah, subtle like a pipe wrench slammed repeatedly on the back of the skull. What are you doing here?"

"Had to run down, talk to a guy. Carmichael and Santiago caught one about an hour ago. He's wearing the hat."

"Are you kidding me?"

"Looks like he bet Carmichael the Cubs would beat the Mets in Saturday's game."

Eve narrowed her burning eyes. There were lines, hard, deep lines, not to be crossed.

"One of my detectives bet against the Mets?"

"Well, Santiago's from Chicago, and it

turns out he's got a pal from his high school days who's a relief pitcher on the Cubs' roster. Plus, he's paying, boss. He has to wear the hat all week."

Jenkinson shrugged. "No money on it, and the Mets took them down four to two. And he's in for the Mets unless they're playing the Cubs. You can't hold it against him for rooting for a pal."

"Can't I?"

"Come on."

The conversation held her on the elevator as it stopped and started, as cops shuffled in, squeezed out.

"You see the game?" Jenkinson asked.

"I caught the last couple innings."

"Then you saw Santiago's pal. They brought him in, in the seventh. He's got an arm on him. Held us to the four."

Eve played it back in her mind. "Yeah, he's got a wicked fastball. Franx almost dinged him good in the eighth, two out."

"Curved foul last minute or that baby was gone. Still, we won."

"Yeah, there's that."

"Anyway." All three squeezed off at Homicide. "Baxter and Trueheart are in-house, working the 'links right now on one they caught Saturday night. They were on the roll."

"Right."

One of the reasons she'd nudged Jenkinson to take the Detective Sergeant's exam was just this. He knew everything, sometimes before it happened.

"Me and Reineke are clear right now, if you need some help."

"Did you finish the paperwork?"

Hunching his shoulders, he looked like a man who'd just swallowed something nasty. "I'm working on it."

"Do that. I can't get to my pile yet."

"The woman dressed up like the painting. Street LC, manual strangulation."

Yeah, she thought, that was one of the reasons.

"Finish the paperwork, and if you're still clear, I'll tap you in. Peabody, you can tap Reineke in. Start him looking for artists' models."

"Where's the justice? He gets models, I get paperwork." Jenkinson shook his head.

"With rank," Eve said, "comes bullshit."

"You're telling me," Jenkinson said as she strode to her office.

She went for coffee first, and with it sat at her desk to do the notifications. In general, notifying a parent their daughter was dead brought shock, disbelief, and a flood of grief.

With Mitzi Lee Starr, the leading reaction was annoyance.

Sure, Eve thought, due to the stupid planet's dumbass rotation around the sun, it was earlier in Las Vegas, and who wants to get pulled out of sleep with bad news?

But.

"She probably asked for it." Mitzi Lee, her gilded hair tipped in scarlet, sat up in a bed with a fluffy pink headboard shaped like a heart. The sheets she tugged up covered a small portion of her impressive, manmade boobs.

"Excuse me?"

"Girl always does what she wants, when she wants." As the other woman shrugged, Eve got the full, and unwanted, view of said boobs. "Always thinking she's better than anyone. Probably her bad attitude and big mouth got her killed."

Yawning, she leaned back against the fluffy pink heart. "What do you want me to do about it?"

"I can arrange for you to see your daughter."

"What for? Dead, isn't she?"

"Yes, she is. In order for you to make arrangements for her body —"

"What? Like for a funeral? Forget it. She's a grown-ass adult. Walked out when she was seventeen, and good riddance. Helped herself to a couple hundred I had stashed, too. I'm not spending my hard-earned money on funerals. Dead's dead. You got her, you deal with it."

Eve kept her tone neutral. "There are also personal effects and possessions."

"What do I want with her junk?"

With that, Mitzi Lee broke the connection.

"Okay then."

Eve took a moment, drank coffee, then tried the father.

He registered some shock if not grief. Though he wasn't as abrupt as the woman he'd created a daughter with, the upshot came to the same.

Nobody was coming for Leesa.

She sent Morris a memo.

Leesa Culver's next of kin will not view or claim her body. Please hold the body for forty-eight hours after you complete your report. During that period we will attempt to locate any other family members. Failing that, file for standard cremation and disposal for unclaimed remains.

She went into the bullpen, scanned, and spotted Officer Shelby in her cube.

"Officer Shelby."

"Sir."

"I'm going to send you the data on a homicide victim. I need you to search for family members beyond her parents. Whatever you find, send to me and copy Peabody."

"Yes, sir, Lieutenant. How far out do you want me to go?"

"Up the generational train, and out as far as first cousins. No minors necessary."

"I'll get right on it."

On the way back, Eve stopped at Peabody's desk. "Culver's parents aren't interested. I have Shelby searching for other family. When she has any, she'll send to you and me."

"Her parents don't want to claim her body?"

"No, they don't. Since neither of them asked how she died, I'd say she was already dead to them."

"Harsh."

"It's all of that."

She went back to her office, sent the data to Shelby, then began to set up her board.

She put Leesa's ID shot up first.

"You and the woman who gave birth to you have the same eyes. That may be the only connection between you."

She added the crime scene shots, including a close-up of the neck bruising. And a photo of the original painting beside one of the victim in the same pose.

When she finished her board, she sat to open her murder book.

Before she'd finished, she heard Peabody coming.

"Beat droids are here."

"Bring them on back."

Eve closed the book, turned in her chair as they came in.

"Officer Campbell, Officer Winters," Peabody said.

Campbell replicated an attractive Black female of about thirty, with a slim build. They'd built Winters as a fortyish white woman with a tougher face and body.

Both stood at attention.

"Relax." Though droids didn't, really. She gestured to the board. "Leesa Culver."

"Leesa Culver," Campbell began. "Age twenty-two, Caucasian female —"

"We've got all that. Who works her block, what other LCs?"

"Dana aka Starlight Chumbly." Winters took over.

As it recited the data, the eyes flickered. An indication it accessed memory banks.

"Age twenty-six. Mixed-race female, licensed for males. Monique Varr, age twenty-eight, Caucasian female, licensed for male and female and nonbinary."

"On the east side of the block," Campbell continued, "Zola Messner, age twenty-three, Black female, licensed for all genders. Diego Quint, age twenty-two, Hispanic male, licensed for all genders."

"That's it?" Eve said after a pause.

Campbell nodded. "Affirmative, Lieutenant. These five street-level licensed companions, excluding the deceased, routinely work that block."

"Have you observed any relationship, including animosity toward the deceased, from any of these individuals?"

"In my observation, individuals Chumbly and Varr engaged in conversation with each other, while the deceased did not."

"Quint and Messner also engaged in conversations with each other, and on occasion with Chumbly and Varr, while the deceased appeared to distance herself."

"We observed no particular animosity," Campbell concluded, "and no sense of solidarity."

"Okay, thanks for coming in. Dismissed."

Peabody lingered when the droids left. "Should I do a run on those names?"

"I'll do a quick one once I finish the book."

"I saw we got the lists of employees, artists, and art students from Whittier. It might be more productive if I started on that."

"Do that."

Eve finished the book, started the runs.

She'd just finished when Shelby's list came through.

Shelby had found a handful of relatives with contacts. A few more who'd gone off the grid, or were deceased.

Eve started at the top with great-grandparents.

By the time she got down to an aunt, she wondered how anyone could claim that blood ran thicker than water.

Carmen Young, Mitzi Lee Starr's sister, answered fast, and looked terrified. "New York police? What happened to Ethan? Is he hurt? Is he —"

"Ms. Young, I'm not contacting you about

Ethan." Her son, Eve noted from Shelby's list — age sixteen. "I'm contacting you about your niece."

"Niece? I don't understand, neither Alice nor Chloe are in New York. They're in school right here in Richmond! Ethan's in New York on a school trip. If something happened —"

"I hope he's enjoying the city, and this has nothing to do with him. Again, I'm contacting you about your niece Leesa Culver. Your sister's daughter."

"My . . ." The fear died, and lapsed into resignation. "I'm sorry, I didn't know Mitzi had a daughter. She, Mitzi, ran away at sixteen. I was a couple years older, had already moved out. She hasn't contacted me since. Is her daughter in trouble in New York?"

"I regret to inform you Leesa Culver was murdered last night."

"Oh God, oh my God." She covered her mouth with her hand, and her eyes went wide with horror. "Murdered? Oh God. Give me a minute, please. I was just about to go into a meeting. Let me postpone that. Just one minute."

The 'link went to holding blue, thankfully without music.

As she waited, Eve took another quick look at Shelby's notes.

Carmen Young, age forty-six, married to Liam Young for twenty-two years. Three offspring, with the visiting Ethan the middle child. She worked as an office manager in Richmond, Virginia.

When Carmen came back on, she appeared to have steadied. She wore her brown hair in a long bob around an attractive face with dominant bright blue eyes.

At the moment, they held a sheen of tears.

"Can you tell me what happened to her?"

"She was strangled."

"Good God. Do you know who? Do you know why?"

"We're investigating. Ms. Young —"

"How old was she?"

"Twenty-two."

"Does Mitzi know? Have you reached her mother?"

"Yes, I informed her mother."

"Could you give me Mitzi's contact? Or you could give her mine. I can't imagine what she's going through. Losing a child. Having a child killed this way. If there's anything we can do to help . . ."

"Ms. Young, Ms. Starr —"

"Who?"

"Your sister changed her surname from Lauder to Starr."

The bright blue eyes went blank as she nodded. "I see."

"Your sister has declined to view or to claim her daughter's body. She's declined making any arrangements for her daughter's burial or cremation."

On that blank stare, Carmen shut her eyes. "Some things don't change, do they?" she murmured. "Some people just never change."

"I've notified your mother, and your father, your grandfather. We're unable to find a location or contact for your grandmother."

"Join the club," Carmen said flatly, then shook her head. "It doesn't matter. It really can't matter. I assume none of them have changed either. I'm sorry, this is all so upsetting. What is your name?"

"Lieutenant Dallas."

"Lieutenant, we'll, of course, make arrangements for . . . Oh my Jesus." Her eyes filled again. "I've already forgotten her name."

"It's Leesa. L-e-e-s-a. Leesa Culver. Listen, don't beat yourself up. You've been blindsided."

"You're right about that."

"Leesa's father has also expressed no interest in making arrangements. Nor have the few family members on her paternal side we were able to contact."

"All right." Again, she covered her mouth with her hand. This time she took three slow breaths, then dropped it. "All right," she repeated. "Can you tell me what I need to do? How we go about . . . Give me a second to get my thoughts in order."

"Take the time you need."

"I don't think we should bring her here. No one knows her, and that's so sad. No formal funeral or memorial. It doesn't make sense, does it? And that's even more sad. How do I arrange for cremation, and maybe, ah . . ." She pressed a hand over her eyes a moment. "Okay, yes, is there a way to have a tree planted for her? Is there a way to arrange that?"

"Yes, I can put you in touch with someone to help you with that."

"We'll plant one here, too. In the yard, I think. I think that's the right thing to do. I don't know what else we could do for her. For Leesa. All right, tell me how we go about it all, and we'll take care of it."

Eve gave her Morris's information, then, as she and Roarke had once planted a tree for a friend's murdered sister, passed on that process.

"All right, thank you so much for the help. We'll take care of this. Is my sister in New York?"

"No."

"Just as well."

"Ms. Young? Thank you." When Carmen shook her head, Eve pressed on. "You were the last on my list, and the only one who's shown compassion, who's willing to make the effort. Leesa's my responsibility now. It's my job to find out who took her life, to bring her justice. It's my duty to stand for her. You didn't know her, but you're willing to stand for her, too."

"I have a family, a wonderful, frustrating, loving family. Considering what came before, I think I'm the luckiest woman in the world. I wish I'd known Leesa and had a chance to bring her into my family. I didn't, so now this is all I can do for her.

"Lieutenant, will you let me know when you find who did this?"

"Yes, I will."

Afterward, she got more coffee, and stood for a moment drinking it by her skinny window.

There were some, she thought, no matter what they came from, who worked to make themselves better.

She glanced back at the board and Leesa.

"Maybe you'd have had a better chance with her. Or maybe that wouldn't have changed your direction at all. Either way, you've got someone with enough heart who'll plant a tree for you."

She went back to her desk to send a memo to Mira, with the case file attached. And asked for a consult at Mira's convenience.

Then she walked out to Peabody in the bullpen.

"I've carved it down some," Peabody told her. "I separated the females, and I've eliminated some who either relocated or are currently out of New York, even the country. Like one of the students — he was a regular — he's doing a year in Florence at an art school, and one of the featured artists — multiple times — moved to Paris six months ago."

"Any with dings?"

"A few. Top of the list, Simon Standish, twenty-eight, in SoHo. Day job, barista. He's on his third café. Arrested last year when he became verbally abusive at an art show, escalated that when he punched the featured artist in the face. He did sixty days in, mandatory anger management, and three months of community service.

"And it happens to be Glenda Frost's gallery where he went off, so it was easy to get some impressions of him from her. She's doing that show for Erin Albright's work next month. Did you buy that painting?" Peabody wondered. "The one of the pizza place?"

"Yeah. Frost asked me if she could keep it for the show."

Erin Albright would never marry the love of her life, or take her to Hawaii on their honeymoon.

But her art would live on.

"Standish."

"Frost said he's a high-strung, angry young man whose work shows promise, but isn't ready yet. Which he doesn't like to hear. She also doesn't think he could or will kill, and certainly not this way. Or mimic an old master, as he does abstracts."

"We'll have a chat anyway."

"I figured. I've got a couple more."

"Tell me on the way. Hold on. Reineke, anything look good?"

Reineke shifted, and when he crossed his

leg over his other knee, she got a peek at the urine-colored flower adorning his sock.

"I got a lot of stories about eccentric artists, nutty artists, lousy ones, and a couple with tempers. Sexy's in there, too. Temper? I got a Kyle Drew the model — goes by Adora — claims screamed at her when she didn't hold the pose, put a few bruises on her when he yanked her back into it. Then ended up throwing a table at her — just missed. That's when she grabbed her clothes and walked out.

"Got another, Martin J. Martin — no shit on that. This model says he slapped her, twice, when he didn't get what he wanted. And when she started to cry, yelled out that was perfect, told her to sit her ass down, and so on. Which she did because she said she hadn't been paid yet."

"Send those locations. We're in the field. Jenkinson? Paperwork."

"I'm almost the fuck finished."

Because she sympathized, Eve recalculated. "Take a break. You and Reineke take your break. Reineke, Peabody's going to send you a list — current and former employees of the Whittiers. Check them out after your break."

She glanced around. "Baxter, Trueheart?"

"Working the 'links shook something loose. They're out tugging the line. Carmichael, Santiago and the hat got one in Interview."

"Well then . . ."

"We can break right here, boss, unless one of them comes back in."

"That'd be best. If either of you comes up with anything that has a good scent to it, send it. If you catch one, leave all this."

"Got it covered." Jenkinson looked at Reineke. "Well, partner, ready to hit Vending?"

"It could be worse. I'm thinking how, but I know it could be worse."

"We could hit a cart," Peabody said as they started out.

"Let's take the first one, see how that plays. Then a cart's fine."

"Good deal."

"Culver had an aunt."

"Yeah, I saw that."

"I had to work through the rest—none of them gave a rat's ass. Then I talked to her. Hasn't seen or heard from her sister in over twenty years, didn't know she had a daughter. But she's making arrangements anyway."

"That matters. It matters."

"Yeah, it does. Which one of yours is closest?"

"Actually, one I didn't give you yet. Allyn — with a *y* — Orion. He lives and works just a few blocks from here."

"Then he's first." Knowing what the elevators would be like at this time of day, Eve turned to the glides. "Why does he pop?"

"First? A fake suicide attempt."

"Fake how?"

"He took a few pills — not close to enough — then called his ex-boyfriend and claimed he was saying the long goodbye. The ex called it in, and they found Orion sort of woozy. Not even close to dead, just a little drugged up. So he grabbed a pair of scissors and threatened to cut off his ear. Like Van Gogh? But he didn't.

"But he did," Peabody continued, "about six months later, attack another more recent ex's current boyfriend. High on a combo of cheap wine and Ups, he went at him when the guy and the ex came out of a club, and managed to shove the boyfriend into the street. The oncoming car stopped, but it still gave the guy a good bump."

"Some time in, psych eval, alcohol and drug rehab," Eve concluded.

"You got it. He's been out for about a year."

"He sounds fun. Let's go have a conversation with Allyn with a *y*."

"Then a cart, right? Maybe even a deli or diner. I could go for a chef's salad."

"If it comes from a restaurant of any nature, shouldn't it always be a chef's salad?"

"Sometimes they just have cooks."

"Okay, that's a point. But they're never called cook's salads. Anyway." They jogged down the metal steps to the garage. "We'll see how it plays out with Orion.

"Is that an actual name?"

"He had it changed legally from Pecker."

"Seriously?" With a laugh, Eve walked to her car. "Well, you can't blame him."

"He was born Waldo Pecker."

"He sounds like a lunatic, but it's hard not to feel sorry for him. Still, it's unlikely the killer had sex with Culver, and the former Pecker prefers men. So."

"We'll see how it plays out," Peabody finished.

Rain blew in as Eve drove the handful of blocks, then another two before she found parking.

Peabody opened the glove box, pulled out

a pair of compact umbrellas. She passed one to Eve.

"How did you know they were in there?"

"Factored in Roarke and Summerset, then played the odds. I won!"

As she climbed out, Peabody opened one.

Since it was right there, Eve did the same, then had to admit to a kind of smugness as she watched other pedestrians scramble for cover or hunch against the wet.

"Give me a quick rundown of the artist formerly known as Pecker."

"Thirty-three, mixed race, currently working nights serving drinks and bar food at Saucy, a sex club." Peabody paused, pointed. "That one."

Eve took a glance at the blacked-out window with the currently quiet neon in the shape of an impossibly endowed naked woman.

"It's a good thing she's got that pole to hold on to. Otherwise, being that front-loaded, she'd keep falling on her face."

"I can't figure how she'd swing on the pole. The boobies would keep smacking into it."

"Peabody, tits that size are not, in any way, 'boobies.' The term *boobies* should be reserved exclusively for what begins to pop out of a twelve-year-old girl."

"Yeah, you're right."

After they walked to the middle of the next block, Eve studied Orion's building. Another post-Urbans toss-up. Eight floors of dingy and poorly secured, with a scatter of tags.

Given the nature of the tags, she deduced those particular artists patronized Saucy — if they managed to get their hands on fake ID.

Street level held a tat and piercing parlor attached to a handy retail space that sold nipple rings, tongue studs, and other accessories she further deduced could be attached to more private parts.

Since the residential door had no lock, they walked right in.

Peabody let out a sigh. "He's on five. I'm going to have to upgrade my underwear because my pants are going to get so loose, they'll fall off my ass."

As expected, Eve ignored the elevator and pushed open the door to the stairwell.

Chapter Five

It smelled like someone's three-day-old sweet-and-sour shrimp with a side of fresh puke.

"What an odor," Peabody commented as they started the climb.

"And another one without any kind of decent soundproofing. Why do babies always sound like someone's carving off their fingers with a dull knife?"

"Ew, but anyway. That's not an I'm-hurt cry. It's an I'm-hungry cry."

Frowning, Eve looked at her partner. "How can you tell?"

"It just sounds hungry, not like there goes my pinkie. You know if Mom had boobies — sorry, tits — like Neon Girl, she could fill that tank for a couple days with one feeding."

As they climbed, the stairwell echoed with the sounds of an electric keyboard, the wild, celebratory shrieks of the Game Show Channel, the boom and blast of some action flick, and someone shouting for someone to shut the fuck up.

Eve mostly agreed with the last.

When they rounded to four, she heard the bass-heavy, hard-edged shout and stomp of thrash metal at top volume.

"If you weren't already in a pissed-off mood," she commented, "listening to that would get you there."

It got louder as they got to the fifth floor, then threatened the eardrums when she opened the fire door and stepped into the hallway.

"Anybody who plays whatever the hell that is at that volume in an apartment is an asshole. What do you bet it's 'I Really Am a Pecker'?"

"Pretty sure you're correct. He's right there, 501, and I think I can see the door shuddering. He's got three locks on it, but I can see it shaking."

Eve pounded on the door with the side of her fist. "Should've brought the battering ram," she muttered, and pounded again.

"Allyn Orion! This is the police! Turn off that damn music and open the door."

"Fuck the fucking police!"

"Open the door, or I will arrest you for disturbing the peace."

"Try it!" She heard a riot bar thump, locks click, then the rattle of a chain as Orion opened the door a crack. "I'm in my own apartment in the middle of the day!"

Eve held up her badge. "Turn it off, open the door. We can have this conversation here or we can have it at Central."

"Fucking police." But he muttered it as he dragged off the chain. "What the hell do you want? I'm working! I need the noise, the anger, the *rage* of the music to create."

"Turn it off."

A man of about five-eight with a slender build in black lounge pants and a black muscle shirt — both paint splattered — turned to stride away to a small entertainment box.

He had white-blond hair swirled with bright blue that rained past his shoulders. The black goatee served as contrast on a face of deep gold skin with tawny eyes lined heavily with black.

After slapping the music off, he turned to snarl at her. "Happy now? Is it my fault the pathetic peasants in this building can't respect art and the creator of it?"

"I'd say it's your fault for not respecting

your neighbors or the city's noise pollution codes."

"You could try headphones," Peabody suggested.

"No! I need it to *fill,* to burn the very air, to surround me. For *Fury.*"

He gestured, dramatically, toward a canvas about six feet long, four feet high. Some of the paint still glistened. Black paint, harsh red, angry yellow fought some sort of bitter war over the field. In the morass of thick strokes, hard angles, Eve thought she — maybe — saw a human face.

"It's one of my series on unbridled emotions. And we have *Grief*!"

He gestured, again a dramatic sweep of the arm, across the room to another canvas. Blacks, reds, dark blues, dead spiderweb grays, and yeah, as if smothered by those strokes of color, a human face — the artist's face — covered with tears.

"I will have *Agony, Desire, Fear.*"

She didn't like them, but had to admit to a weirdly compelling vision.

"Okay. You also have a couple choices. You can soundproof your apartment."

"Do you know what that costs? I'm reduced to working like a slave every night to support my art."

"Uh-huh. You can wear headphones and fry your own eardrums. Or keep the music at a reasonable volume."

He held out his hands, palms lifted. "You're asking me to slit my own wrists."

"No, I'm telling you to knock it off. You've already done time inside. Want more?"

Now he threw up his hands, circled the room. Other than a single dumpy couch, he used the entire space as a studio, with canvases stacked or hung, with paints and tools littering a table.

Eve figured he'd go a few rounds with the landlord at some point, as he didn't bother to tarp the floor.

"Art transcends man-made laws."

"Yeah? Is that why you killed Leesa Culver?"

"I don't know who that is." He said it absently as he continued to circle, to gesture. "I need stimulation to create art. Music, movement, sex. How can I bring *Fury* to life without the stimuli?"

"Headphones," Eve repeated. "Get some. Where were you last night between midnight and four A.M.?"

"Don't you understand . . ." He paused, frowned. "What?"

"Midnight to four last night. Your whereabouts?"

"Didn't I already say I'm forced to work like a slave? But still, there is stimulation, and there is on occasion inspiration. I was doing the menial work I'm forced to do until my art is recognized. Serving others their drinks and food at Saucy. In the next block."

"From midnight to four?"

"From nine to two. Then, exhausted, I returned home, too depleted for my art, too restless to sleep. I took a sleep aid and slept. One day the pain will be too much, and I won't wake again."

Eve pulled up Leesa's ID on her 'link, turned the screen toward him. "How do you know her?"

He frowned, shook his head, then tossed back his hair. "I don't. If she modeled for me, and I put her on canvas, she would always live in me."

He pressed a hand to his heart.

"If she complained about my need for stimulation —"

"She's dead."

He frowned again, then just shrugged. "Death comes to all of us."

"Death comes sooner than it should when

someone's murdered."

"Murdered." He looked more intrigued than shocked. "Well, I certainly didn't murder her."

"You shoved a man into the street in front of moving vehicles."

"That was a moment of madness, an accident, really. Blind passion. I've moved on. Now, I have only a few precious hours for my work. I need to go back to *Fury.*"

Eve put the Vermeer on the screen. "Do you know this painting?"

He looked, sneered. "Boring. Ordinary."

"Right. If you turn the music up to that volume, or close to it, again, you'll find a couple of cops at your door with an arrest warrant." Eve started for the door. "You won't get anywhere with *Fury* in lockup. Remember that."

When they went out, Eve waited. The music came back on, but not at door-shuddering volume.

"What a dick" was Peabody's opinion. "He really shouldn't have bothered changing his last name."

"He's a dick, and we'll check out his alibi, see how close we can pinpoint when Leesa left the stroll. But he didn't kill her."

"Way too busy swimming in self-pity and

self-indulgence to plan out a murder. Plus, none of his stuff is in the same universe as the portrait. He'd never have used something like that."

"What universe is his stuff in?" Eve asked as they started down.

"The Shit Universe. Some would go for it, sure, because it has a creepy kind of gut punch, and I absolutely believe all art has value. However, well, shit has value. But otherwise, it's abstract, conceptional, and reeks of that self-indulgence. He's just using it as an excuse to suffer, or claim he's suffering."

"I agree with all that. We'll check the timing anyway. Who's next?"

Peabody checked, noted Reineke's list came through. "Standish, and he should be at his day job. Café Urbane, and that's just a block past where we parked, across the street, and another block."

"We can walk it."

When they reached street level, the storm that had blown in had blown out again.

Once she'd hiked back to the car, Eve opened the trunk. "Toss it in."

She shut the trunk on a pair of wet umbrellas.

"The Martin Martin's in Tribeca, and

Kyle Drew's the East Village."

"Still walking this one, then that only leaves two to find parking."

"Café Urbane has salads and sandwiches, as well as pockets, muffins, and cookies."

"Fine."

"It also closes at ten on Sunday night. So, he wouldn't have been working during the timeline."

Eve spotted the trench coat coming in her direction, and the way he eyed the bag of a woman chatting on her 'link as she clipped along.

Then his gaze shifted to Eve. She met it, angled her head. Barely lifted her eyebrows.

The way he turned around, strolled in the opposite direction reminded her of Galahad when caught bellying toward bacon.

She almost thought it a shame. She could've used a quick run.

But when she crossed the street with the river of others, trench coat kept going.

"Okay, Simon Standish, age twenty-eight, white guy, father's from London. Single, no cohabs. Does the barista thing for his day job, and lasts from like six months to a year. Looks like he's had one show at a coffee shop–slash–art gallery, and he fills in as an art teacher — substitute art teacher, high school level."

Peabody put away her PPC. "He's the one who punched another artist at the other artist's show."

"I remember."

She gave a wide berth to two women who burst out of a shoe store loaded with bags and laughing like hyenas. What was it about footwear that drove some women mad?

Through the doors of Café Urbane the lights glowed bright and the air was filled with the smell of reasonably decent coffee and chatter.

"Get your salad."

"What do you want?"

"I don't know. Ah . . ." Eve scanned the menu board and tried to shift her brain to food. "Just a grilled cheese."

She pulled cash out of her pocket and realized, damn it, she'd need to stop at a machine and get more.

"What kind of bread, what kind of cheese?"

"Whatever. Pick something. Go with Pepsi. I'm going to give Standish a tap."

She handed Peabody the cash, then moved to the coffee station.

Since of the two baristas, only one was

male, she got in his line.

Snippets of conversation swirled around her.

How Bart really needed to turn a report in. How someone else had a date to go salsa dancing. Someone else complained her kid dyed his hair purple, another expressed frustration with her mother.

She took the time to check Standish's ID to make sure she had the right individual.

Though he'd cut his blond hair into sharp, diagonal lines on the sides, the same face popped on her screen.

Round features, pale green eyes, powder-white skin with a sprinkle of blond stubble.

He stood about six feet, had well-cut arms and shoulders under his snug black tee. She considered he wouldn't have trouble carrying a dead woman of Leesa's weight.

When she got to the counter, he beamed her a smile. "What can I get you, Slim?"

"Lieutenant Slim." She palmed her badge, and the smile dropped away.

"Okay. Same question."

"My partner and I would like to speak with you regarding an investigation."

"I'm working."

"I can speak with your supervisor."

"Come on, man. I don't want to lose this job."

"When's your break?"

"In about twenty."

She looked behind her and to where Peabody grabbed a two-top.

"See the brunette, red streaks? Come there on your break. We'll try to make it quick."

"I didn't do anything."

"Then it'll be even quicker."

She walked to the table.

"Got your Pepsi. I'm trying their lemonade." She tapped the order box. "Salad and san in about five minutes."

Eve sat so she could keep an eye on Standish. "He's got a break coming up in twenty. He makes a move toward the door or toward the back, we go after him."

"Hope he doesn't." Peabody picked up her lemonade, sampled. "Hey, it's pretty good. Mavis has us spoiled though, since she learned how to make it from lemons. We're grilling tonight. McNab and Leonardo are getting good at it."

"He's nervous," Eve observed. "Keeps glancing over here. Nervous, but I'm not reading guilt. It's more . . . dejection maybe. Oh crap, cops."

"A lot of people feel that way about cops."

The box signaled the order up. Peabody pulled the salad, then the sandwich out of the opening.

"I went with whole wheat and a combo of Munster and American."

"Sure, that works."

"Oh, change." Peabody handed Eve the change — which still meant a stop to replenish cash.

Eve stuffed it away, then pulled out her 'link when it signaled a text.

"Mira's read the file. She can give me a window around sixteen hundred. That works, too. We should be able to fit this one in, and the other two."

"Maybe one of them will be working on a portrait of Leesa as the Girl, and — case closed!"

"Yeah, that'll happen." Eve bit into the sandwich.

"But don't you think that's what he's doing? Or did?"

"I think that's the strongest probability, yeah. There's no glory in dressing up a woman as an iconic image, then not painting her, since that's what you do. Paint. Most probable."

"Unless we're following the wrong trail,

and he doesn't paint. Like: Why did these — that word Pecker used — peasants get the talent? I'd do so much more with it. I deserve it, but I can only sell art, or restore art, or buy art."

"Can't discount it."

Eve watched Standish take off his apron. He came around the counter and walked to the table.

"I can take a few minutes. Listen, I told my manager you were cops, and there was some trouble in my building. I really want to keep this job."

"Why don't you grab a chair?"

When he had, and sat, what Eve read coming off him in waves was misery.

"I really didn't do anything. I know I screwed up before, but if Harmann's had any more trouble, I swear it wasn't me. I was a little drunk, and a lot jealous. He rubbed my face in it some, and I just punched him. Then I happened to see him a couple weeks ago, and I wanted to apologize. Sincere, right? And he started screaming how he'd get a restraining order.

"I was with some people. They'll back me up. I just walked away. I didn't do anything."

"All right. This is about another matter. Do you know this woman?" Eve held out her 'link.

Standish looked — didn't skim, but looked. "No. She's pretty. Too heavy on the eyes with the makeup, but under it, she's got a nice face.

"I don't understand."

"She was murdered last night."

If powder-white skin could lose color, his did. "Jesus, I'm sorry, okay. But I really don't understand."

Eve swiped, offered the 'link again. "How about this?"

"Sure, *Girl with a Pearl Earring.* It's beautiful work. The way Vermeer captured light, used the contrast, the way she stands out against the dark background."

"She was dressed like this."

"Like . . . like an artist's model?" Now both puzzlement and interest mixed together. "Usually if you're going to try to use a previous image, to learn, you use the image itself. Her face isn't really right for it."

"Can you give us your whereabouts last night? Say midnight to four?"

"Oh God, oh my God." Now his hands shook, so he put them under the table. "Look, I punched a guy, and that was stupid, but I wouldn't kill anybody."

"Why don't you tell us where you were?" Peabody said gently.

"I was — God — I was working, in my apartment. I paint there, too. I was working, with a model. Caryn — ah, Jesus — Caryn Lloyd. We started about nine, and went to . . . I think about twelve-thirty or one. Then she got dressed — I'm working on a figure study — and we talked a little, then she left. I'm not sure, I didn't check the time, but it was after one because I know it was close to two when I called it a night. I didn't go anywhere. The building has door cams. You can check."

"All right. Why don't you give us the model's contact?"

"Sure, fine, but please don't freak her, okay? She's supposed to pose for me again tonight."

He pulled out his 'link, looked up the contact, and gave it to them.

"Do you know anyone who does this? Uses models to replicate?"

"I don't. I'm not saying nobody does, but I don't know anybody who does. I'm just trying to straighten up, okay? Keep my day job, work on my art, stay out of trouble. My parents have really backed me, but punching Harmann? I'm like on parole here."

He tried to smile.

"I'm working up my nerve to approach the gallery manager. It's taken me too long to get there — but I need to do that to, well, get things right. My problem, my attitude, my fucking around, so I need to go see her.

"I'm hoping to finish this particular work, take it in to her, and show her I'm serious about doing the work and not blaming other people if it's just not good enough. And it's going to be good enough. Eventually."

"All right. We appreciate your time."

"Sure. Thanks. Wow."

He replaced the chair, then headed back to work.

"No buzz," Peabody said.

"Not even a little. But we verify. And we check the victim's timeline. East Village, then Tribeca."

"Kyle Drew," Peabody said as they walked back to the car in air humid from the come-and-gone rain. "Age thirty-eight, mixed race, one marriage, one divorce, no offspring. He actually had some early success, kudos and sales, married one of his models. About three years ago, the marriage went down the tubes and so did his kudos and sales. Basically, he's riding the Has-Been

Wagon."

Eve spotted the same trench coat, and he spotted her. Even with half a block between them, Eve swore she heard his resigned sigh as he turned around and kept walking.

"It could be worse to have gotten there, then dropped." Eve watched trench coat join the flood of pedestrians at the crosswalk — and shoot a quick glance back at her. "It might piss you off enough to try a whole new technique, like murdering your model."

Though tempted to follow the street thief and give him a really bad day, she stopped at the car.

She'd just have to find her fun elsewhere.

"Unless we hit your perfect scenario with one of these two, start looking at artists who work in restorations. There you are, always fixing up somebody else's work. Isn't it time you created your own? You replicate to show how much better you are than the original."

It didn't take long to eliminate Kyle C. Drew, as he answered the door of his impressive loft space with his right hand in a skin cast.

A big man, he wore his ink-black hair in long dreads loosely tied back in a tail. He covered his impressive build in a sleeveless white tee and black baggies, and gave both Peabody and Eve a long look out of sizzling blue eyes.

"Cops?" He had a voice like warm cream poured into rich coffee. "Too bad, unless you want to moonlight as artist's models. Interesting faces."

"No thanks." Eve nodded at the cast. "How'd that happen?"

"I pissed myself off, and punched a hole in the wall. That'll teach me."

"When did you do that?"

He frowned a little. "Saturday afternoon. What's this about?"

"Do you want to talk about it out here?"

"What do I care? But fine."

He stepped back to let them into an impressive space of wide windows and color. He displayed art on the walls as a gallery might, with a style that drew the eye.

He had enough living space for a pair of sofas, both in coppery shades, and chairs done in turquoise.

The area opened into a dining area with a table that looked old and important, as did the half dozen chairs around it.

A curve of stairs, wood with a copper railing, led to the second level.

Eve pulled out her 'link. "Do you know this woman?"

He took the 'link, studied it. "No, but I just saw this photo on a media report. Somebody killed her last night. Not a lot of details on it, but they said she'd been strangled."

He handed Eve back the 'link, lifted his cast. "I'd say that leaves me out of the running, but it doesn't explain why you're asking me about her in the first place. They said she was an LC. Are you just checking anyone who's used one, for sex, or as a model?"

"You have?"

He smiled. "I don't pay for sex — got no problem with it, but I haven't needed to. But sure, I've hired a few now and then to pose. Not her. I'd remember."

"How about this?" Eve brought up the Vermeer.

"Of course I do. Who doesn't? What does that . . ." He stopped, then held out his good hand. "Let me see the dead girl again."

When Eve obliged, his brows knitted. "It's the eyes, isn't it? Bone structure's off, nose, that's wrong. Mouth's almost there, but the eyes . . ."

He looked up. "Somebody had her stand in for, what, a forgery of the most famous Vermeer, then killed her?"

"Can you tell us where you were Saturday between eleven P.M. and four A.M.?"

"Well, Christ." A flicker of temper fired in his eyes. "Here, brooding. How the hell am I supposed to strangle a woman I don't know with this?"

He shook his casted hand.

"When and where was it treated, and by whom?"

"Give me a second." He shut his eyes, breathed deep in and out, then muttered something she couldn't quite catch. "It just doesn't work."

"What doesn't work?"

"Mindful breathing and a mantra. I'm still pissed off. I don't know the time, exactly. Three, maybe four on Saturday. The urgent care on East Eighth. Dr. Salvari. I have to go back to her in a few days so, please God, she can take this bastard off. I can't paint, can't sketch. I can't even tie my own goddamn shoes."

"Okay. How about you show us your studio, then we'll get out of your hair?"

"You want to see my studio? What, in case I have a reproduction of a Vermeer in progress?" Gesturing with his good hand, he turned to the steps.

When they followed him up, Peabody caught her breath.

Another large space, it held canvases, a worktable, shelves holding paints and tools and palettes. It included a curvy green couch, numerous throws, a bed with rumpled white sheets, a rack of what Eve supposed he used to dress or drape models.

Peabody walked straight to the unfinished painting on an easel.

He'd used the bed, and the rumpled sheets swirled over and around the model, who reclined with golden red hair spiraling down over her left shoulder. She lay propped on her right elbow and wore a lazy, I've-just-been-laid smile.

"Oh, this is wonderful! The light, the moonlight, it's luminous, and the way it streams through the window and hits her hair. The movement, the way her body's curved. The wine bottle and two glasses on the table. The shadows in every crease of the sheets.

"And you can just feel they're still warm, and she's smiling at the one who warmed them with her. She's about to say: 'Come back to bed.' It's so sensual. It's breathtaking."

"Okay, this was worth a trip up the stairs. Are you an art collector?"

"I wish. You have some wonderful art in your living space, your work and others', but this?"

"I was working on the background on Saturday. Just couldn't hit the groove I'd been in. I needed the model back. When I tried to contact her, it went straight to her v-mail. Can't reach her, can't find that groove."

He shook his head, pointed at the wall and the jagged, fist-sized hole in it.

"That's how I handled that. I'm leaving it like that to remind me losing it cost me days, if not a week or more, on something that matters. And hell, the doctor said if I'd hit wrong, it could've cost me a lot more. It's the best I've done in a long time, and I nearly fucked it up."

He turned back to Eve. "I don't do forgeries. I've got enough left from before Pilar screwed up our marriage, and I screwed up everything else, to keep me in paints and brushes. And I'm fixing what I screwed up."

"We appreciate your time and cooperation."

"Cooperating sucks, but I'm working on it."

When they got back downstairs, Eve paused at the door. "When I try meditation, my mantra's *Fuck this.* Sometimes it works for maybe a minute."

"Yeah? I'll try it. That beats my fifteen seconds."

Peabody pulled out her 'link when they walked out to the car. "I'll check with the clinic and the doctor, but they're going to confirm."

"Yeah, but we cross it off. He's got strong hands, but the killer used both, and he sure as hell can't. Plus, he just doesn't fit. His temper, it flashes. The killer's, it's always there."

Chapter Six

In Tribeca, Eve had to settle for a lot, then a two-block hike.

Martin Martin lived in an old, weathered brick building that clung to its dignity. Since he lived on the floor above a women's boutique, Peabody felt it unworthy of her loose-pants chant.

When Eve knocked on 1-C, the door opened across the hall.

A woman in her mid-twenties dressed in black skin pants and a flowy, hip-swinging white shirt shifted the red bag on her shoulder.

"Asshole — I mean Martin-Squared's not there."

"Would you know where he is?"

"No, and I'd be thrilled if he stays there. He went out about this time on Friday, with a weekender rolly. As far as I know, he hasn't been back.

"If you're thinking of modeling for him," she added, "do yourselves a favor. Don't. Because asshole."

"You've modeled for him?"

"Once. It started out fine, then he's yelling at me, calling me a stupid bitch and more. I don't have to take that, so I got up. He grabs me, shoves me back. I had bruises with his fingerprints on them for a week. He had worse, since I kneed him in the balls. I told him if he ever put his hands on me again, I'd slice them off."

She shifted the bag on her shoulder. "Anyway, I've got to get to rehearsal, but I'm saying the modeling fee's not worth it."

When the woman left, Eve nodded. "Okay, he's been physically abusive to models more than once. Maybe a pattern of it. Left here with a suitcase, so maybe he has another place. More private."

"I'll see if I can contact him."

"Yeah, do that. We'll head back. Try the contact from Central. We want him to come in. Say there's been a complaint about physical assault."

"Well, the neighbor did complain."

"Yeah, and I've got a feeling he doesn't meditate."

■ ■ ■ ■

Back at Central, Eve had time to update her board and book. Then took more time to do a deeper dive on Martin-Squared.

The only child of an upper middle-class family. He got his art degree from Pratt, did a year touring Europe, another year living in Paris before settling in New York.

He'd had a couple of shows, and Eve thought the word for the reviews she read would be *tepid.*

At twenty-nine, no day job for him. Ever. He had a small but adequate trust fund to live on while he pursued his art. And sold the occasional piece.

After checking the time, she left her office for Mira's.

Peabody signaled. "Martin's in Philadelphia. He was one of the artists featured in an exhibition that opened yesterday. He's heading back tonight, and with a lot of whining will come in tomorrow if we need him to deal with — I quote — 'some hysterical woman's overreaction.' "

"New York to Philadelphia and back. An easy trip. Go there, check in, come back, hire the victim, dress her, kill her, dump her, then go back in plenty of time for the exhibition."

"He rented a car, so he's got private transpo."

"Even better. I'm with Mira."

Eve took the glides to Mira, and because she'd timed it, arrived two minutes early. Only to find, in her admirable promptness, the dragon not at Mira's gates, and the gates open.

Eve stepped to the door, rapped knuckles against the jamb as Mira sat at her desk working with a keyboard.

She glanced up, smiled. "Come in, sit. Just give me another minute."

Rather than sit, Eve stood, looked around.

Mira had a couple of thriving plants — one bursting with purple blooms — some family photos, a few well-chosen dust catchers.

Disc files, of course, tidy paperwork, everything calm and organized.

As was the woman.

Today she'd chosen a pale blue dress paired with a deeper blue jacket. She wore neck chains with little stones of both blues interspersed with stones of pale and deep pink.

Eve took a personal bet that Mira wore

skyscraper heels that somehow picked up all four colors.

"There!" Mira sat back in her chair. "There's no real end to the reports and paperwork in our world, is there?"

"No, there is not. I was coming in early today to deal with paperwork. Then."

"Yes, I read the file. Very odd and disturbing."

Mira rose to walk to the AC, and Eve congratulated herself on winning the bet.

Long, fluid swirls of all four colors covered Mira's tall, skinny heels. Eve caught the floral scent of the tea before Mira took out the pair of delicate cups.

She passed one to Eve, then sat in one of her blue scoop chairs. And crossed her excellent legs.

"You have an organized killer, one who prepared by obtaining the scarves, the jacket, and so on."

"I've got searches going for where those could be obtained. There are a couple of costume shops in New York that have that sort of thing, and in Chicago, in the East Washington area, and so on. When I get Harvo's input, I may be able to narrow that part down."

"From what I could see, both the costume

and the pose were very carefully replicated. He's precise. I agree with your notes. The dump spot was also carefully chosen. Art gallery owners. None of this was random or impulsive. He'd certainly seen the victim before last night. She fit the general parameters. Her coloring, her youth, her eyes, and her size."

Mira sipped some tea. "I believe his choice of an LC, street level, was also planned and precise."

"Hire a professional model, she's likely to have an appointment book, maybe tell someone. Hire some woman you spot otherwise — if you can talk her into coming to your studio — she's also likely to tell someone. A street-level LC? It's part of the job to go with a customer.

"He probably gave her half up front, maybe promised a bonus if she did a good job. He gave her wine, a vintage a street level doesn't get. And if he took any time to find out about her, he'd have known she lives alone, isn't especially friendly, has no close family. Perfect target."

"I've no doubt he'd have done some basic research on her. Precise," Mira repeated. "Organized. And certainly a risk taker, as he took the time to pose her in front of a residential door, the door of a well-secured home."

"He's going to have a connection to the Whittiers, to their gallery."

"Yes. The Vermeer? He greatly admires it, and deeply despises it. It's a bar of talent, achievement, and recognition he can't reach. I've no doubt he believes he has scaled the bar of talent, but the recognition eludes him. He may have contemplated suicide, even attempted it. But as the idea of death for his art rooted, it twisted into causing the death of another."

Eve held out her hands. "With his own hands. The intimacy of that."

"Exactly."

"You're profiling him as an artist, a painter."

"I am. Haven't you?"

"It's highest probability for me. But if it's a hit directly at the Whittiers, that opens up other possibilities."

"There will always be other possibilities, but. An artist creates what he sees. Whether with the eyes or the mind. The killer re-created, and with great care and precision, what he saw. Why bother with the costume, the pose? He used wire and glue on the victim because she wasn't a person to him.

She wasn't a human being but a kind of mannequin to be turned and adjusted to represent his image."

"We're looking into people who restore art."

"Yes." Lips pursed, Mira nodded. "Yes. He may earn his living through that skill — because he can't earn it with his own work. Restoring isn't creating on a blank canvas. He's duplicating, true, but that isn't a restoration."

"All right. I ask myself what he gains by doing this. I come up with two things. His own sick artistic satisfaction, and notoriety. We don't know his name, but —"

"We know his work. We're studying it, talking about it. He may have failed as an artist. When he paints now, it could be under the cover of a hobby as he works for the Whittiers in another capacity."

"And that would burn."

"Yes, it would. Art, his art, is his reason to live. His failure at receiving accolades for it, his greatest pain. But one he shares with many great artists who weren't recognized during their lifetimes. With this? He's created a masterpiece, and one he believes superior to the original."

"If an artist paints or creates that masterpiece, wouldn't he want to do it again?"

"Yes. And more than want, Eve, need."

She'd already gone there, so just nodded.

"But not the same one — why do the same reproduction again?"

Mira considered. "I could see that if, for whatever reason, he felt he hadn't achieved the level he wanted. If he felt the model had been the reason."

"If he plans to do another, he'd already have the painting selected. The costume or wardrobe, he'd need that. He'd have scouted for the model, or already targeted one."

"I believe he's done that, yes. He sees himself as a perfectionist. He's exacting. You'll find his living and working space very organized. He lives alone. He has no time to waste with others. Sex? Secondary to art. He'd hired an LC, a young, attractive woman. He could have had sex with her first, but apparently didn't."

"Because the art was the reason. And, she wasn't a person. She represented someone long dead," Eve said slowly. "Once he had what he needed from her, she had to die or the painting couldn't live."

In silent approval, Mira angled her head. "As I see it? Perfectly put. He may be gifted, but he wants more, much more than simple success. He wants immortality, and before immortality comes that notoriety. He may consider or attempt suicide to gain immortality, but not before he gains the notoriety. Not until he's created enough masterpieces, as many as he's planned."

"Okay. I appreciate it. He's not the sort who'd smash his hand through a wall?"

"Oh, no. He's too controlled for that, and it could interfere with his painting."

"Yeah, that was my take. He's got money. You don't waste a high-dollar bottle of wine on a street LC you're going to kill anyway. A private space for his work, and private transpo."

Eve pushed to her feet. "This all gives me more to work with."

"Before you go, how did the move-in go this weekend?"

"Move-in? Oh, oh, right, that. Great. It was really just the last push." And she remembered. "We're going over there for dinner tonight. To, you know, seal the deal."

"A lovely way to do just that. Peabody and McNab met Mavis and Leonardo through you. They found the house through Roarke. The two of you are very much a part of the home they're making.

"Enjoy the evening with friends."

"Thanks."

She made her way back to Homicide, and found McNab hanging out by Santiago's desk.

Jenkinson stopped her first. "Paperwork's christing done. I got a jump on the restoration types for your portrait killer."

"Great. Good. Peabody, take off."

"Take off what?" she asked, and made McNab snicker.

"Go home."

"Really? I've still got some —"

"Go," Eve repeated, "and take the e-geek with you. I've got some things to wrap up, and Roarke's meeting me here. We'll be there whenever we're supposed to be."

Which, as she went to her office, she hoped wasn't for at least another hour. Maybe two.

She wrote up notes on her consult with Mira, then made herself set it aside.

Nothing, really nothing more she could do on that except think.

And thinking needed to wait.

Boosting herself with coffee, she started on her lion's share of the paperwork.

■ ■ ■ ■

She never heard him coming, but that was no surprise. The surprise came from carving a good-sized path through the forest of paperwork before Roarke walked in the door.

"Still at it then?"

She looked up with eyes bleary from numbers and words.

"If there's a hell, it's being chained to a desk doing paperwork. And the more you do, the more there is. It's eternal torment."

"Do you want more time in torment?"

"No, but I need another ten, then I can come in early tomorrow and wipe the rest out. For a minute."

"Then I'll go entertain myself."

She took the ten. Maybe her brain hurt, but the rest of her felt righteous and more than ready to call it a day.

She went out to find Roarke at Peabody's desk.

"Jenkinson and Reineke caught one five minutes ago. A dispute at happy hour that ended unhappily."

Which meant, Eve thought, more paperwork, as it would involve overtime. She didn't want to think about it.

She looked over at Santiago and his hat. "Why are you still here?"

"We closed it, so we did a coin toss for writing it up." He ended with a shrug.

"First the Cubs, then the coin. Detective, you ought to buy a clue. Or at least rent one."

"She's on a streak, but streaks don't last forever."

Eve smiled. "Wanna bet? Glides," she said to Roarke. "The elevators will be jammed."

"I put the champagne in your car," he told her as they walked out. "And now I'll lay a wager of my own you could use some."

"That's a safe bet."

"I'd say an evening with friends in their new, happy home will brighten things up as well."

"Every time Peabody talks about it, she teeters between teary and delirium." As they walked, Eve waved her hands. "It's all teary delirium. Since Jenkinson and Reineke caught one, I can't use them for grunt work on this tomorrow. Maybe I can tap Santiago and Carmichael, or Baxter and Trueheart."

"They have a double date, Baxter and Trueheart."

"What?" Her aching brain tried to process

slick Baxter, earnest Trueheart, and date. "With women?"

"Since they're both straight men, I so conclude. Baxter has a friend who has a friend, so they're having dinner."

"Baxter's a hound dog, and Trueheart's a teddy bear. Though bears will tear you up if you piss them off. I don't know if I've ever seen Trueheart really pissed off. Anyway, I can't see how this can work."

"I suppose they'll find out. Oh, and before he left, Jenkinson suggested I have one of my subsidiaries design and produce novelty ties and socks, perhaps pocket squares as well. He believes I'd make a tidy profit."

Eve gave Roarke one long and very sincere stare. "Are you actively trying to fry the rest of my brain?"

As they started down the metal steps, he stroked a hand down her back. "I do enjoy your bullpen, Lieutenant. I enjoy it very much. It's never dull."

He waited until they'd reached her car to turn her to him, kiss her. Despite the security cameras, she lingered there for an extra moment.

"Can you put the day behind you for a few hours?"

"If I do that, it's breathing down my neck.

Better to stuff it in a box, lock it up for a while."

"Not easy for you, I know." He flicked a finger along the shallow dent in her chin. "But you'll tell me about it later, when you open the box again."

"Count on it. You know art, and unless Peabody and I, and Mira along with us, have it wrong, art's at the center of this. So I'll be tapping you on art."

"Delighted to assist there."

Knowing she could count on just that, Eve took a breath. "Now it's in the box until."

She glanced in the back as she got in the passenger's side. "Where's the champagne?"

"Tucked in the trunk with your field kit and umbrellas. Caught in the rain, were you?"

"For about five minutes. That was enough time for me to ruin a street thief's day."

"Well then, that's a bright spot for you. Chase him down, did you?"

"I didn't have to. I made him, he made me. Then he pulled a Galahad and sort of sauntered in the other direction. Twice. Yeah," she realized. "A bright spot. Did you have any?"

"A few actually. Work on your Off Duty club is moving very well, as are the additions and improvements on the resort in Australia, and Caro's daughter's expecting."

"Expecting what?"

"A child, darling. She's been seeing someone for nearly a year now, and they decided they wanted a child. And so."

"Considering her first husband was a son of a bitch, that's either crazy or brave."

"A bit of both. Caro's thrilled. She likes the expectant father quite a lot."

"Then he probably deserves it. Caro's nobody's fool."

The short drive from Central took them to the gates of what had been the Great House Project. And was now, Eve thought, just a great house.

Those gates opened to a lush lawn with young trees and shrubs adding welcome. The house itself sprawled with its long porch and many windows. More welcome with the colorful chairs and tables, the burst of blooms in pots.

Two long chains of crystals hung from the eaves of the porch roof and caught the early evening light in quick flashes. And pots of lush and thriving flowers added more warmth.

Before they'd parked, all the residents came out on the porch, another welcome.

The minute Eve stepped out of the car, Bella — bright as those flashing crystals — raced down.

"Das, Ork! Yay! Come home!"

She took a running leap at Eve, a pint-sized rocket with her blond hair and the ribbons in it flying. She wore little pink kicks scattered with white stars that matched the frilly dress her designer father had no doubt made for her.

Eve found her arms full of wild excitement that babbled like a rushing brook and laughed like a lunatic.

Eve said, "Yeah, sure," without any idea what she'd agreed to.

As Roarke took the champagne, tucked in ice sleeves, from the trunk, Bella squealed at him. "Ork!" She threw out her arms.

He traded champagne for the toddler.

"There's that beauty."

"Ork." She gave him a coy look from under fluttering lashes before wiggling down. "Run!" she commanded, and did so.

If Bella's joy hit the outer rings of Saturn, her mother's wasn't far behind. Heavy with Number Two, Mavis bounced in her own pink kicks while the flirty skirt of her baby-blue dress danced around her thighs.

She didn't take the leap and run, but

threw her arms around Eve. "We live here," she said, and bounced again.

"I heard that. How's it fit?"

"As perfect as one of my moonpie's creations. Made for me. For all of us."

When Mavis shifted to throw her arms around Roarke, Eve handed Leonardo the champagne. "So, welcome home."

His face glowed as he wrapped an arm around her and kissed her cheek. "Thank you."

His long shirt of green-and-pink stripes flowed as he turned to embrace Roarke. "Both of you."

Peabody moved in next. "You've got to deal with it," she said, and hugged Eve.

"It's a moment." McNab lifted his shoulders, grinned at Eve. And hugged her.

"Okay, that's the moment. And now why is everyone wearing ribbons in their hair?"

"Bella's rules." Mavis pulled two more, one blue, one red, out of her pocket.

"You can't be serious."

"Just go with it." Mavis handed the red one to Roarke, then, moving around Eve, tied a blue bow at the back of her head. Obviously going with it, Roarke pulled his hair back in what Eve thought of as his work mode, and secured it with the red ribbon.

Delighted, Bella clapped her hands. "Party!"

"I'm going to need a lot of champagne."

With a laugh, Mavis squeezed her hand. "Welcome to the first official We Live Here house tour."

And she opened the door with a flourish.

Eve had seen it along the way, from confusing wreck to construction zone to the inching toward a vision. She'd seen the colorful walls, the clever lights, and the old floors brought back to life.

But now, it held furniture, and the pieces of the family that lived there.

The sitting room on one side with its big let's-take-a-nap sofa, with a trio of New York street scenes in pencil sketches behind it. The big living area on the other side, sofas covered in a bright and bold meadow of flowers, chairs picking up the variety of color in deep peach or soft greens.

Candles on the mantel of the restored fireplace, photos and mementos on shelves, splashes of more color in paintings.

"God, it's you all over, all three of you."

"It's everything we wanted. We want one more picture," Mavis added. "One of all of us. We'll take it when we go out back. It's going on the mantel."

"Let's work our way to the kitchen," Leonardo suggested. "I'll open the champagne for the tour of the second floor. Sparkle juice for you, Bellamina."

" 'Parkle joo! Yay!"

"And for me and Number Two." Mavis patted her baby mound and led the way.

A home office not at all businesslike, which included a Bella-sized desk and chair, a first-floor playroom as happy as the girl who would rule it.

"It's a kind of library, or a do-nothing room," Mavis said at the next. "We've got Nadine's books, some storybooks. And see, there's a friggie and AC built into the cabinet right here. So you could sit and read — and have the sweetest little electric fireplace in the winter. Or just plop down and do nothing. What hits mag extreme more than a do-nothing room?"

They moved into the kitchen with its multicolored cabinets, its spacious lounge, and the wall of glass doors that opened it to the back — the patio, the garden, the play area.

When Leonardo popped the champagne and poured, Eve looked at Roarke. "You've got words. You always do."

"I do indeed. To all who dwell here, may

today's joy be a drop in a cup that runs full."

"I love you." Mavis swiped a tear away. "I can't say any more or I'll flood, but I love you mega extreme. Just so you know."

They went up to the second floor, the guest rooms, guest baths, another play area, another sitting area. Then, clearly unable to wait any longer, Bella gripped Eve's hand and tugged.

The room, pink, white, frilly, and girly, suited Bella from top to bottom.

"Mine," Bella said with obvious delight. "Bella's!"

"It's pretty great."

The canopy bed fit for a princess held fluffy pillows and a herd of the stuffed animals kids went for.

But Bella walked to the chair Eve had given Mavis as a shower gift, and stroked a hand over its rainbow arm. "Das, Ork for Bella." Then to the toy box Peabody had made, another rainbow with Bella's name in bright, candy pink. "Peadobby, Nab, for Bella."

She sighed, and looked so like Mavis for a minute, Eve blinked.

"Love. Mag. Love."

Then she took Eve's hand again. "Baby now."

So Bella led the way to the nursery and its fairy-tale forest theme.

Mavis, blue eyes damp, rubbed one hand on her belly, laid the other on her heart. "You know what it means to me, the chair. It grabs every feel I have and adds more. We rocked Bella in hers — still do — and we'll rock Number Two in this one. And the toy box? Peabody, you're the serious ult to think of it."

They toured the main bedroom where — on Mavis's gauge — she'd gone subtle, nearly restful. If you didn't count the enormous closet with the ceiling wallpapered with big, bold blooming flowers and the wild colors of the clothes and accessories that filled it.

She'd had the wall behind the big bed painted with jewel-toned flowers and birds in flight.

And it worked, Eve thought. She couldn't say how or why, but it worked.

From there, they went up to Leonardo's design studio, and among the workstations, the reams of fabric, Eve noted a section separated for Bella.

As there was down in Mavis's recording studio.

"I've already worked here a few times, and I still can't believe it's mine. I can come down here and record, I can practice, and — no chuckles — I'm starting to write songs."

"Why would I chuckle?"

With a shake of her head, Mavis slid an arm around Eve's waist. "A big, long way from the Blue Squirrel. An even longer way from scouting for marks on the street."

She gestured to where Bella demonstrated the toy piano in her play area.

"She'll never have to wonder where her next meal comes from, or if it's gonna. She won't have to worry the person supposed to take care of her will hurt her instead. Maybe, in some weird-ass way, because we did, we ended up right here. But she won't have to go through that. It's our job to teach her, to show her how to appreciate that and share that, and just be freaking kind."

"She already is kind. You're damn good parents, Mavis."

"In the whole universe, hell, the multiverse, that's what I want to be most."

"Mission accomplished."

Laughing, Mavis shook her head. "I'm

pretty sure it's never really done. And I'm okay with that."

She beamed out a smile. "Peabody, McNab. You're up!"

Chapter Seven

Mavis insisted they all go out the front, then around to the side for the Peabody–McNab tour. For the mag start, she claimed, to the ult finish.

"Here goes." McNab opened the door, one flanked with stone-looking urns holding red and purple flowers.

Peabody had gone for softer colors, more dreamy ones than Mavis. Eve thought they highlighted the dark, original millwork Peabody had loved at first sight.

The fireplace with its old brick cleaned and repointed was topped by a new, chunkier mantel that looked old.

In a good way.

They'd started collecting street art, and it worked against the quiet color of the walls, with the deeper tones of the furniture that brought in a cozy, lived-in look.

The coffee table Peabody had built —

because she could do that — looked like it had come from an antiques shop and still invited you to put your feet up.

Flowers, candles, and the throws made by Peabody's clever hands all added personality.

"And this is all the two of you."

"I love the lamp to the extreme," McNab said. "But even the extreme doesn't reach the Peabody level."

"It's true. It's my favorite thing in this room, and . . ." As if seeing it for the first time, Peabody turned a circle. "I love everything in this room."

They wound their way through, a pretty sitting room with a pair of chairs scored from a thrift shop, which McNab had refinished and Peabody had reupholstered in stripes of subtle blue and green. And into their shared office with its energetic paint-splattered walls.

"Fun!" Bella declared.

"It's all that, isn't it? But this." Roarke ran a hand over the partner's desk. "This is magnificent work. A statement piece."

"I knew it'd be wonderful. My father makes the wonderful. But . . ." Like Roarke, Peabody ran her hand over the smooth, silky wood. "It's way over wonderful. And look."

She opened the center drawer. On the bottom, in the right corner, he'd carved *Dee 2061.*

"Over here." McNab opened his side to show *Ian 2061.* "Frosty," he said. "And means big giant bunches."

They moved on to Peabody's craft room. Against the quiet of the walls stood an enormous display holding what seemed to Eve to be every possible color and tone and texture of yarn, along with rolls of fabric, spools of thread, ribbons, lacy stuff, other materials that were all, Eve could only suppose, organized in some crafty Peabody fashion.

One worktable held a sewing machine that looked as if you'd need a license to drive it; another held tools Eve couldn't identify, with a series of cubbies above holding more.

In the corner stood an actual spinning wheel, and the basket beside it held yet more yarn.

"This to the ult-squared is my happy place. Swear to God, in my wildest dreams, and they can get wild, I never expected to have a room like this."

She grinned at Bella. "Mine!"

And Bella laughed like a maniac.

Through to the kitchen, where the living

wall of plants and herbs thrived, and through the wide case opening stood the table Peabody's father had built half a continent away in the year of her birth, and she'd found (Chance? Fate?) in a secondhand shop in New York.

Above it hung the blown-glass chandelier her mother had made.

Eve stared at it. "All right, wow. Just . . . That's a major wow."

Transparent glass in Peabody's dreamy blues and greens formed fluid shapes and combined into a flower in full bloom.

"That's a masterpiece," Roarke said.

"A tough word to swallow today, but yeah, it is."

"Wait. Chandelier on," McNab ordered.

It brought light, but more, it seemed to glow beyond what it spread over the table so each petal shimmered.

"It's — like the desk — it's beyond. You really have to see it at night for the full effect."

Eve shook her head at Peabody. "No, you don't. It's freaking fantastic."

"Fweaking," Bella echoed.

They finished the main floor, and Eve found herself ridiculously touched to see they'd designated a space for Bella to play with a pint-sized table and chairs. A toy box here looked — again in a good way — as if Bella's great-great-grandmother might have used it.

They went through the second floor. Guest rooms, each very individual, and all murmuring welcome and comfort.

A quilt for a bed here made by McNab's grandmother, a throw there made by Peabody's.

Family, Eve thought. The house was full of family.

In the main, where Mavis had gone subtle, Peabody chose bolder in walls of deep green, one made to look like panels behind the four-poster bed.

"I always wanted one," Peabody confessed. "And with the little fireplace. It's like sleeping in a castle."

"Our castle." McNab put an arm around her.

"That's the end of the interior tour. We haven't finished the lower level yet. The work's all done," Peabody explained, "but we haven't finished furnishing or playing with it. We're still picking up pieces. We'll have it done, or close enough, by big party time."

"Let's go out back." Bouncing a little,

stroking the mound of Number Two, Mavis just beamed. "I wanted that last because it'll make me weepy. And you guys need more bubbly."

They trooped down, then out to where Peabody's water feature spilled and sang.

And Mavis got weepy.

"The birdbath fountain. Look how abso-mag it looks there. Like it was made for that spot. It's so perfect with the garden, the waterfall, and the sculpture."

She had to press her hand to her mouth. "Look at us. Leonardo, look at our family."

The Peabodys had made and shipped the sculpture of Mavis, Leonardo, Bella, and the baby in Mavis's arms. It glowed with a hint of bronze in the lowering light.

"It's like a dream. I look out here, and it's like a dream."

"Happy cry," Bella said, and teared up herself in solidarity. "Bella's." She pointed to the table and benches by her playhouse.

"And baby's," Mavis reminded her.

Bella rolled her teary eyes. "Baby, too."

Eve didn't think it sounded sincere, but kept that to herself.

"Here's what I think," she said instead. "I think you've turned a weird, neglected eyesore of a house and grounds into something special, and uniquely yours. Something that says, yeah, you live here."

She lifted her glass. "Damn nice job."

"Damn nice job," Bella repeated, and got a narrow look from Eve.

"How come you can swear with perfect pronunciation?"

Bella grinned, then hooted before she ran to climb up her slide.

They had more champagne, and bruschetta with herbed-up tomatoes and peppers straight from the garden. Leonardo — with an assist/kibitz from Roarke and McNab — grilled steaks to go with some of Peabody's fancy potatoes — also from their own garden. As was a mix of grilled vegetables. Peabody took over for those, and Eve had to admit, they weren't half bad.

As they ate, the sun slid away to an indigo sky, and the lights flickered on.

Mavis's fairyland, Eve thought, twinkling around the garden, sparkling in the trees, glowing along the paths, even, she noted, shimmering against the rocks in Peabody's waterfall.

"I thought maybe we went totally over the board," Mavis said to Peabody. "But we didn't. All the lights? I mean, check it. Way mag."

"The effect's charming," Roarke told her. "As for security."

"Got it covered," McNab said to Eve. "Got cams, got sensors, anti-jammer shields, lockdown switches. The same system you guys have, house, grounds, gate, and the system rocks it hard. I'll be running weekly checks."

McNab wasn't Roarke, but who was, so Eve relaxed.

And after an evening with friends, with murder locked in a box, she stayed that way as they drove off.

"I need to make a stop on the way home, talk to some street LCs."

"What an interesting evening."

"And I might get more out of them with you along."

She gave him the block location, settled back.

"It's going to work, the five, soon to be six, of them in that house. They've got their separate spaces, yeah, but they like the together. None of them would be as stupid happy as they are without the together."

"They fit well, don't they? Five distinct personalities, but with a great deal of common ground. And what you said there, about them making it special and uniquely theirs? As true as it gets."

"It was good to see it, and yeah, to feel it. Plus, now I won't have to hear about tile samples and paint colors every day." She shifted to him, spotted the red ribbon.

She pulled it out of his hair, then removed her own blue bow.

"Party's over. You did a hell of a job, pal."

"I was, for the most part, an observer."

"Bollocks to that. I know all parties involved, and I can hear you saying, 'Well, now, Mavis, there's an idea, isn't it?' That would be when she talked about something like putting a koi pond in the foyer or a chicken house in one of the play areas."

"Coop, a chicken house is a coop."

"Whatever. You'd give her the 'well now,' then wind it up with alternatives."

"There was little of that, actually. She had a vision, and one that reflected her family. There is talk of chickens, as it happens."

"What? Seriously?"

"That came from Peabody."

"Of course it did." Why was she surprised? "Once a Free-Ager."

"They wanted to get in, settled, live awhile, but they're wanting a little coop, a few laying hens, and there's room, of course. Fresh eggs, amusement for Bella — and a chore she can learn."

"And a lot of chicken shit."

"Which, Peabody points out, can be used in the garden."

"Chickens inside a thing? I can deal with that. But if they end up with a cow, I'm out."

He turned onto the block, and with the luck of the Irish — if that was really a thing — slid into a spot at the curb.

"And why are we talking to LCs on this fine September night?"

"The vic worked this block. My best take is the killer hired her. I want a timeline, and whatever else I can get out of her coworkers. Maybe, jackpot, description of the killer."

She'd scanned their IDs, so even with the red wig with blue spikes, she recognized Dana Chumbley, and Monique Varr in her crotch-skimming skirt and spiral-curl blond wig.

She spotted Zola Messner across the street, one hand on the hip of a dress that looked more like body paint. Since she didn't see Diego Quint, Eve figured he either hadn't clocked in yet or was already with a customer.

Chumbley and Varr gave each other some

space, but stood close enough to toss around some conversation, some comments.

Chumbley eye-fucked Roarke, and went: "Mmm-mmm! Baby doll, whatever you want, twenty percent off. Twenty-five if you lose No-Tits."

"That's Lieutenant No-Tits," Eve said as she pulled out her badge.

"Well, shit. What you want to roust me for? Got my license right here. I'm working, and cops scare the johns away."

"Also working. Leesa Culver?"

"Who?"

Eve took out her 'link, brought up the ID shot.

"Oh, Pissy-Ass. What about her?"

"She's dead."

"That shit happens."

"Was she working last night?"

Varr walked over on glossy black shoes with two-inch platforms and five-inch heels. "You said Pissy-Ass is dead? No shit? Did somebody get tired of her pissy-ass ways and bash her one?"

"No. Somebody strangled her. Was she on the stroll last night?"

"Yeah, yeah." That came from Chumbley with a shrug.

"My associate and I, we make it clear she stays that end of the block. Always trying to horn in on our customers, so we make that clear."

"Try to be friendly at first, right?" Chumbley added. "We're all just making a living here. She's talking how she's better than the street, better than us, and she's gonna make high-class in no time. Pissy-ass bitch."

"Did you see her pick up a customer? Leave the block with him?"

"Can't say I did. She took a couple into the flop right down there. We got a deal with the manager."

"What time did you see her?"

"How the hell do I know?"

"She took that fat guy in, remember, Starlight?" Varr pursed her full red lips. "It was like eleven because I was heading out when she was heading in."

"Sure, sure, Fatso. He's a once- or twice-a-week regular of hers. Man, she can have him. He's got a gut on him! You'd have to work ten minutes to get past it to give him a BJ. No way he'd strangle her. Besides, the manager would've let us know if he found a dead one in there."

"She came back to the street?"

Now Chumbley frowned. "Yeah, yeah. She

was back when I took one in later. Look, you're costing us money here."

Before Eve could stop him, Roarke pulled out two fifties.

"Now she's not, is she then?"

"Ooh, I'm a sucker for an accent. Baby doll, the offer still stands."

"It's appreciated. Maybe you noticed when she wasn't in her section."

As the fifty disappeared, Chumbley pursed lips dyed somewhere between red and purple.

"I guess maybe, now that you put it that way, I didn't see her later on, like after midnight or one. You said something, Monique."

"Yeah, I did, right. I said how Pissy-Ass must've caught a live one. I didn't see her leave, didn't see the hookup, but I saw how she wasn't down there, and wasn't for a while. Wasn't, now that I'm thinking, when we called it a night."

Varr added her own shrug. "Look, truth? We won't miss her, but none of us like hearing one of us got killed. We're just out here making a living."

"And someone may be targeting street levels. You're making a living, but you've got to be alive to do it. Think twice before you agree to go with someone who's willing to pay too much, who wants you to go somewhere other than your flop or when you get there wants you to wear a costume."

"Costumes is extra." Chumbley grinned with it. "But not for you, baby doll."

"She's yanking you," Varr said. "We work the street, we stay on the street or the flop. She went off that way, she's stupid. Pissy-ass and stupid."

"Don't be stupid," Eve advised.

With Roarke, she walked down the block, gave the flop a quick study. "It didn't happen there. Dead LCs are bad for business. Plus, he had the costume."

She crossed the street to try Zola Messner.

"Pissy-Ass? I block her out. She tried taking my stroll once." She smiled. "Didn't try it again. Gives me this bullshit how she could make double what I do over here, and how she'll be top level while I'm still scraping."

She smiled again, fiercely. "Didn't give me bullshit more than once."

Diego Quint, obviously fresh off a roll, wandered over in his tight black muscle shirt and skin pants. He tossed back his luxurious hair. He didn't eye-fuck Roarke so much as give him an I'll-be-dreaming-of-you stare.

And said, breathlessly, "Hi."

"Turn it off, sweets," Messner told him. "He's with the cop."

"Oh." A heavy sigh. "Heart shattered."

"Pissy-Ass got herself strangled. Did you see her leave the stroll with anybody?"

He had liquid eyes that went sad as a kid with nothing under the Christmas tree. "Oh, that's horrible. She was really kind of mean, but that's horrible. Actually, I think it was about midnight, maybe a little later, I did —"

Messner held up a hand to stop him.

"You pulled off a couple of bills for Starlight and Monique. We're all losing work time here. So?"

Roarke pulled off two more fifties.

"Thank you!" Quint looked at Messner, who nodded. "I did happen to see her walking down the block and across to the next."

"Alone?"

"Oh, no. I noticed because she was walking with a man with a really nice caboose."

"You kill me, Diego." Monique laughed, gave him a friendly elbow jab. " 'Caboose.' You kill me."

"Can you describe anything other than

his caboose?"

"Not really." His forehead creased as he thought it over. "Ah, sorry, not really. I think . . . yeah. He was wearing a hat. He was a little taller than her. She had on four-inchers, so . . ." He closed his eyes, calculated. "Maybe he was like five-eight or -nine? Maybe. Not six feet anyway.

"I really go for the tall ones," he added with another wistful glance at Roarke.

"Race? Skin color?"

"Ah, not like my Black Beauty here." He sent Messner a sweet smile. "White or mixed or maybe Latino. I just noticed the caboose, and the excellent threads."

"Such as?"

"Casual black pants and shirt. But casual like a man who can afford high-class casual. I didn't see much because they were walking away." He pointed. "Then a gentleman asked me for a date, so I gave him my attention."

"That's helpful." She took out a card. "If anything else occurs to you, contact me."

She gave them the same warning she'd given the others and noticed Quint seemed to take it more seriously than his associate.

"She went," Eve began as they walked

back to the car, "at the very least a block off her territory with him. Maybe he has a place close enough and private enough. But it's mostly flops, apartments, dives unless you walk another block or so."

She got in the car.

"Rich casual clothes — I bet Diego knows what he sees there. Rich guys don't live on these couple blocks. He had a car. On the street, in a lot."

"While this was all a fascinating interlude, I'd like to hear more."

"Yeah, I'll get to it. And now I have to add your two hundred on the expense account. More paperwork."

"Why do you have to do that?"

"Because paying for information comes under expenses. You're a civilian consultant, and it goes under expenses."

"So strict."

"Yeah, that's me. I'm going to write this up as you drive, save time."

She wrote it up, added the fifty times four, the reason for it. Made notes about the estimated height, the perception of expensive clothes.

As their own gates opened, Eve looked at the lights glowing, on the grounds, in the windows, and yes, some sparkling in trees.

It mellowed her mood again.

It wasn't just good, it was everything to have home.

She said exactly that to Roarke.

"It is, yes. We might think about adding to that and doing a small garden."

That jerked her out of her mellow mood. "Did you hit your head on something?"

"Again, there's room, and it's something Summerset might enjoy. He likes his fresh herbs and so on from the greenhouse. I might speak to him about finding the right spot for a few raised beds."

"If you start talking about chickens, I'm hauling your Irish ass to an ER. Maybe to the psych ward."

"Not chickens, no." When he parked in front of the house, he reached over to give the dent in her chin a finger tap. "A bridge well too far for the likes of us."

"Okay, just don't expect me to wear some silly hat and start planting kumquats."

"That would be a tree, darling."

"Whatever they are, that's a solid no."

"It's fortunate, isn't it now, that's a no we share."

As they walked to the door, she looked at him. "I have to unlock the box again now."

"Understood." He leaned down, kissed

her lightly. "Absolutely understood. I'd like to hear about the rest of the contents."

"More fortunate."

She hadn't expected to find Summerset looming in the foyer, but there he was, the living skeleton in black with the cat at his feet.

Too bad he hadn't taken Roarke up on extending his stay in Italy a couple of weeks more after his friend's memorial.

"I figured you'd be ready to slide into your coffin for the night."

"As it happens I've just returned from dinner with friends. And while it often amazes me you have friends yourself, how was yours?"

"It was lovely." Roarke inserted before the exchange could escalate. "I hope you can get by to see it completed, and lived-in."

"It happens I'm invited to dinner later this week. I look forward to it."

"I've got work." Eve headed for the stairs with the cat at her heels.

"I'll be a moment."

As she walked up, she heard Roarke.

"Would you enjoy it if we put in some raised garden beds next spring?"

"For vegetables? I see you've been inspired."

Eve kept walking.

In her office, she went straight for coffee while the cat went straight for her sleep chair.

And since the night held warm, she opened the doors of the Juliet balcony before she started on her board.

She glanced over when Roarke came in.

"Why are they beds? The plants aren't sleeping in them. I don't think they're having sex in them."

"I have no idea, unless it's that some of them sleep in there through the winter, or wake up there in the spring. And I am not going to visualize tomatoes having an orgy with the green peppers and the squash."

"Bet you did. Anyway, how many of those raised things are you doing?"

Because she'd won the bet, he shoved a hand through his hair.

"We'll select the right spot and decide on that. Or he will, as it's in his wheelhouse and far out of mine."

"Part of this idea is to give him a distraction, a positive one. He lost a friend, and he and his Urban Wars spy pals went through a lot. And a lot of that brought back memories of losing his wife. I get it."

"He's grieving still. It's quiet and it's

internal, but it's there. So dinner with the happy family, as they surely are, insults by you, which is a step into normality. And garden beds."

"Whatever our issues with each other, I understand loss. And how sudden, violent loss twists up those left behind."

"And he knows you do."

"Okay, now that all goes in a box."

Roarke studied her emerging board. "Did this girl with the pearl earring leave someone twisted up behind?"

"No. Pissy-Ass they called her, and that seems accurate from what I know. And she came by it natural enough. Neither parent had any interest in seeing her body, claiming it. I tracked down an aunt who didn't even know about her who had more compassion than anyone else in her family.

"Let me ask you this," she said as she continued to work. "Is there anything in the history or lore about this painting that's weird or any kind of trigger? I couldn't find anything that popped out."

"They never identified the model, but Vermeer often used people at their work for his paintings. This one's a bit unusual because she's not at work, but aware of the onlooker. Hardly a trigger for murder. He had a family, worked at his art, certainly didn't die wealthy or particularly famous."

"Family. Maybe the killer's a descendant, or thinks he is. Or sees himself as a reincarnated Vermeer guy. A replica," she murmured. "As he used a replica for the portrait."

She stopped and decided taking a few hours might have opened something.

"He did others — Vermeer? Other portraits?"

"He did, of course."

Low odds he'd repeat the same portrait, but not low he could choose another from the same artist.

"Can you get me those — names, images — while I update the book?"

"Easily enough."

"He left her body — and he used wire and glue to fix her in the pose — at the door of the basement level of a brownstone. Owned by people who own an art gallery."

"That earns an 'ah.' "

"Yeah. I'm looking for an artist, and I bet a pissy-ass one, who's — we theorize — decided he's underappreciated. Wants to make a splash anyway."

"With murder."

Eve rolled her shoulders. "You never know

what people will kill for or over. Maybe he has a grudge against the Whittiers — the gallery owners. We interviewed a few today, but nobody clicked right in.

"Now I'm adding he either has money or spends it like he does. Probably the first because he has to have a private enough space to do what he's done, most likely his own vehicle. Could have rented one, and that's already a dead end because we don't have a description of the vehicle."

She circled the board.

"He could've taken her anywhere, but he had to see her first, plan all this. So he either scouted that area or lives close enough to have spotted her."

She circled the board again. "He's organized, precise. He sealed up before he strangled her. Used his hands when a cord's easier, quicker."

"But not as intimate."

Eyes on the board, she pointed a finger at Roarke.

"That's just right. If he is an artist, he at least started the portrait. Maybe a photographer, but then why not replicate a famous photograph?"

"An artist, or one who aspires to be," Roarke agreed. "Someone who knows the

Vermeer, or studied it enough to duplicate the costume — down to the way the scarves are tied."

"Yeah, right down to that. I may catch a break tomorrow when Harvo does her magic with the fabrics. Until then, I've got this."

"I'll get you the other portraits."

"Thanks."

When he went into his office, Eve sat down at her command center.

"Open operations," she ordered, and got to work.

By the time she'd updated her book, added to her notes, Roarke came back.

"That was fast."

"It's a simple search. A considerable number of paintings, but a simple search. I sent you thumbnails. You can expand them individually."

"Great." After opening the file, she sat back. "Shit, that is considerable."

"You have a separate file on portraits of multiple people."

"We'll stick with this for now. Did he do anything besides paint? Like eat, sleep?"

"Says the woman at her command center long after the workday is done."

Since she didn't have a comeback for that

one, she ignored the comment.

"He's got old, young, male, female. A lot of detail. This one here? *Study of a Young Woman*? It's similar to the other. The way the head's turned, a head scarf thing. Different model. Younger. Jesus."

Now she scrubbed her hands over her face. "I don't want to think about him going after a kid."

As he felt the same, Roarke stepped behind her, rubbed at the tension in her shoulders.

"If he hits again before we find him, and if he sticks with this artist, I'll have the cheat sheet. I'll recognize the replication, for what that's worth."

She leaned back into his hands. "If he kills again, and sticks this way, there's a connection to this artist. Vermeer. Maybe he's delusional and thinks he's Vermeer reborn. Or just obsessively admires the portraits. And maybe . . . he teaches or studies this art and artist. I can work with that."

She looked over her shoulder. "Are any of these in New York?"

He reached over, hit expand on several. "These, at the Met, the Frick."

"I don't know what's weirder, that I knew you'd know that or that you know that. But

I can check there, see if anyone's shown them unusual interest, or claimed ownership, something like that."

Now she swiveled in the chair to face him. "Did you ever steal one of his?"

"Well, you could say I reacquired one."

"You've got one here?" Reaching up, she pulled at her hair. "One of these?"

"I don't, no. I might have, but at that time money trumped art collecting for me." Amused, he smoothed down her hair. "It was stolen before I was born, from a museum in Boston. I happened to, as I said, reacquire it from a private collection in Dublin."

"You stole it from the thief?"

"I reacquired it from a descendant of the thief, as this was roughly a half century after the original theft." Nudging her over a bit, he called up the painting in question.

"*The Concert.* Back in 1990, a group of thieves, disguised as coppers, bagged thirteen paintings from the museum in Boston — where the patron had acquired this particular work for only five thousand at a Paris auction."

"So it wasn't worth much."

"Darling Eve, by the time I reacquired it, *The Concert* was valued at nearly four hundred million, and considered one of the most valuable unrecovered works."

"For that?"

"It's fascinating — the light, shadows, details. The details in the two paintings on the wall in the scene, the landscape painted on the lid of the harpsichord."

He paused, and she imagined him imagining holding the painting in his hands, studying that light, those shadows, those details.

"In any case," he continued, "I arranged for its discovery and return, for a tidy finder's fee."

"What's tidy in your world?"

"As I recall, we negotiated and finalized at thirty-five million."

"That's pretty fucking tidy, Ace."

Bending down, he kissed the top of her head. "It helped build this house. So, in a serendipitous way, it's why we're both here."

"So we're both here because a bunch of guys pretending to be cops stole a bunch of paintings in Boston last century?"

"And see how well that worked out? And since it did, and we are . . ." He pulled her up out of the chair. "Save data, close operations."

"Hey!"

He cut off her protest with a long, hungry kiss even as he tugged off her jacket.

CHAPTER EIGHT

"Museums are closed," he pointed out, and flipped the release on her weapon harness. "You're circling the ifs at this point, aren't you?"

"Maybe."

"And as I recall," he said as he unhooked her belt, "you've plans to be up and out early, since you're a boss with paperwork to complete."

"You added to that tonight." While he nipped his way down her throat, she pushed at his suit jacket. "And shit, I never hit a machine."

He felt her sigh, recognized both pleasure and resignation.

"I'm going to need a cash loan, if you don't mind."

His lips curved in a grin just under her jaw. And there, he thought, the resignation.

"I don't mind at all. We'll do the transaction in the morning. But for now, I want my wife."

His mouth came back to hers, and that want heated as lips and tongues met.

He wanted to seduce her, to take, and be taken. He wanted to know she felt, she needed all that he did.

"I want her body, her mind, her heart."

He had them. She knew he always would. It was a daily miracle for her to know she had his.

And he could take her, in one thick heartbeat, into a world ruled by the senses, driven by needs both simple and complex, and warmed by a love that had no end.

She fought off his tie. "You're wearing all the clothes."

"We can fix that."

He boosted her up, set her on the command center, then pulled off her right boot.

Her eyes met his as she unbuttoned his shirt. "Here?"

He pulled off the left boot. "We've tested it before. It's more than sturdy enough. And what a picture you make, Lieutenant Dallas, half-dressed on your center of command. It's no wonder, is it, I can never get enough of you."

"It is to me."

When he shrugged out of his shirt, she reached for his belt, and using it, yanked him to her.

They sprawled over the counter as she struggled with the belt. As his hands, and the magic in them, turned her body into a furnace fired with needs.

When his mouth took hers again, all those needs poured into the kiss, all that fire burned through her blood. And every minute of the day before that moment blew away like feathers in the wind.

Only him, only now, only them.

He peeled her support tank away, cupped her breasts in his hands as his lips glided down to them.

So firm, so smooth, a glorious contrast to tough muscle, long, lean lines, fascinating angles. No, he could never get enough of her, so he let his hands, his mouth, touch and taste the strong and the subtle, the soft and the smooth while the beat of her heart quickened under his lips, while her body trembled under his hands.

He murmured in the language of his blood when she moaned. He felt his own heart spring to a gallop as her hips rocked, as her hands took.

"We'll need more room after all," he managed. He pulled her up, then down with him to the floor.

She rolled over him, pressed down to him, and her mouth went on a crazed journey over heated skin the light breeze from the open terrace doors couldn't cool.

Rolling again, yet again, he dragged at her pants as she dragged at his until there were no barriers between them.

When she rose over him, she wore nothing but the flash of the diamond he'd given her. She took him in, held there one glorious, torturous moment, held him there until the eyes locked on his went blind.

When she moved, they shared a kind of madness, rising and falling in a storm, all drenched in pleasure. It went deep, deeper still until she cried out from the shock of sensation.

When she shuddered, he pulled her down to him, rolled once more.

"Take." He covered her mouth in a desperate kiss. "Take again."

Helpless to deny him, herself, she leaped back into the storm and rode it with him.

Spent, sated, saturated, she lay under him. She thought she might regain the use of her extremities in a few hours. Possibly a couple days.

She found she didn't mind that considering he appeared to be in the same boat.

"We could sleep right here."

"Aye." He didn't move a muscle. "I'm thinking about that option right at the moment."

"You're the one who didn't want to go up to the bedroom."

"True enough. It might be all that talk of old masters and the thieving of them started it. It's always been a passion for me, after all. But no." He managed to turn his head and brush his lips against the side of her throat. "I think it was you all along."

He feathered on another kiss.

"Just give us another minute here."

"I can give you until oh-six hundred." Then she remembered. "No, damn it, oh-five-thirty. I'm going to get that christing paperwork done."

"Then you need a bed under you."

He rolled off her, shoved at his wonderfully tousled hair. "Come on then, Lieutenant." He reached down for her hand. "Let's get you up."

When he pulled her to her feet, she looked at the scatter of clothes.

"We need to get all this. I've said it before, and I'm saying it now. We don't leave evidence of sex all over the place."

"Evidence of sex. Always the cop." And delighted with her, he helped gather up clothes.

She hitched her weapon harness on one naked shoulder, and made him smile.

"Christ Jesus, how can you make me want you again when I'm barely breathing from the last?"

"I'm not picking all this up a second time."

He laughed and walked over to shut the balcony doors. "To bed. You need some sleep."

She glanced back as she walked to the elevator. "Looks like the cat beat us there."

"Then he'll need to make room."

Not long after Eve opened operations, Jonathan Harper Ebersole went on the hunt.

He'd painted for hours that day. The music soaring, and his heart with it, as every stroke of his brush brought him joy. He knew the portrait was his best work, magnificent work, and no wonder. He'd taken her life with his hands, and her death brought life to the art.

He understood that as he never had before.

It would take time to finish, to perfect the portrait. And it needed to wait, to allow him to begin another.

He'd prepared it all, and very carefully. He'd selected the model. Not from the same block, oh no, he thought as he walked. He'd spotted and studied this one hustling in Times Square.

The beauty there? Not only had he found an excellent representation for the work he'd do, but no one would notice a man picking up an LC in Times Square.

It was, to him, a charmless, classless blight on the city. But for this purpose? Perfection.

The lights, so brilliant, all flashing. The noise, huge, rolling like thunder. The crowd? Thick, stupidly energetic, and for the most part, gawking tourists.

And those who hustled and hyped, who picked pockets or pushed discounts for sex clubs into greedy hands.

He knew it was fate, was *right,* when he spotted his next model soliciting in front of the theater he used in lieu of a flop.

Careful to stay out of the view of street cams, even though he'd worn a hat, sunshades, Jonathan gestured.

Bobby Ren sauntered over. He wore a

cropped skin shirt that exposed tight abs, and skin pants cut to a *V,* front and back.

"Looking for some action?"

"I have a proposition," Jonathan began.

Because she'd requested it, Roarke buzzed Eve awake from his office at five-thirty.

"I've a meeting to finish, but I'll be up shortly."

"Great." She cast a sleepy, gimlet eye at his perfectly groomed hair, the dark blue suit jacket, pale blue shirt, and, of course, perfectly knotted and coordinated tie. "Later."

She signed off, rolled out of bed. Hit the coffee, hit the shower, all while keeping paperwork in the locked box so it didn't lower her already sour mood.

What she wanted? Another hour's sleep. A quick workout, a swim. Instead, she faced her closet.

"Why does this keep happening to me?"

Inside, she found an outfit, hung together, boots at its feet. And a memo cube.

Roarke's voice cruised out. "Just to save you a bit of time and frustration this morning."

When she hissed out a breath, part of her

wanted to reject the choices just to . . . to be a pissy-ass, she admitted. But the part of her that wanted to get it over with accepted the chocolate brown pants, the jacket she called tan that probably had a fancy name. It also had chocolate brown buttons. The white shirt — no, she corrected, he'd say cream — had a silkier flow to it than she'd have chosen.

But it was right there.

The boots, chocolate brown, had fake tan laces and a zip on the side. She'd never understand fake laces, and these, in the Roarke way, matched the chunky belt.

When she came out for her weapon, he stood at the AutoChef programming breakfast.

Before she could speak, her communicator signaled. She picked it up, said, "Fuck."

It said,

Dispatch, Dallas, Lieutenant Eve.

She listened, acknowledged. "Contact Peabody, Detective Delia. I'm on my way."

As she stuffed the communicator in her pocket, Roarke did the same with his 'link. Then handed her an omelet with a side of bacon. "Eat a bit, won't you? Your address on West Thirty-Seventh is Midtown Gallery."

"He moved fast. He's got everything prepped, everything planned, and he's moving fast." She shoveled in some eggs, then plucked up a slice of bacon before she set the plate down. "I can move fast, too."

She gulped down some of the coffee he gave her, then swung on her jacket, loaded her pockets.

He offered her a wad of cash.

"What — Oh, right. I don't need that much."

"You may be too pressed today to stop for a withdrawal, so this carries you through until." He tapped her chin. "Now, you're graciously accepting a loan, as I'll be equally gracious when you repay it."

Since they'd made exactly that deal, she stuffed the wad in her pocket. "Right," she said again, "thanks."

He kissed her. "While you're taking care of my cop today, feed her a bit more."

Eve grabbed another slice of bacon, bit in. "Done." She kissed him back, then rushed out.

"Not quite what I meant." Roarke rubbed at the gray button in his pocket. Then spotted the cat. "And stop where you are, mate.

Don't think you'll help yourself to her breakfast."

The cat looked at Roarke; Roarke looked at the cat. Then he shrugged. "Well then, I don't suppose there's any harm in a bite or two of an omelet."

As he caved and crumbled a slice of bacon over a portion of the eggs, Eve drove through the gates.

Not the gallery owners, this time, she thought, but a gallery. Midtown rather than downtown. That took location out of the mix, but left the art world at the center.

She'd hoped for another day, some data from the lab to work on before she stood over another body. But no cooling-off period for this one. She'd add impatient, likely driven, organized, precise, and in her opinion, batshit.

As she headed south, pockets of the city yawned itself awake. Light flicking on in windows, a handful of people taking the stairs down to the subway, the inevitable blat of a maxibus rolling to a stop for another handful to get off, yet another to drag themselves on.

She rounded the corner, noted the cruiser, saw the barricade already in place. Two uniforms stood with a man in red-and-black-checked pants, white T-shirt, and what looked like old house skids.

He had a fluffy, tail-swinging yellow dog on a leash.

She pulled in behind the cruiser, then held up her badge as she crossed to the police tape, then under.

And noted she wouldn't literally stand over the body, initially at least, as the body itself stood in the recessed doorway of the gallery.

The dog bounded to her, dragged the guy on the other end of the leash along. With eyes crazed with love, the dog planted his paws on her legs.

"Sorry! Sorry! Hand to God, he's harmless. Still a puppy, and real friendly. C'mon, Bouncer, get down!"

Bouncer got down, and immediately attacked the fake laces in Eve's boots.

"Aw, jeez." Instead of tugging, the man hauled the dog up in his arms, where it wiggled joyfully and lapped at his face. "Six months old, that's all. We got him for the kids, and you can see who's walking him before the damn sun comes up. I was walking him, and I see . . . I thought it was a display, you know? And Bouncer's headed over because he thinks it's a person, and he's never met a person he doesn't love."

"Did either you or the dog touch the body, Mister . . ."

"Franks, Glenn Franks. No. I managed to hold him back, and I started to . . . I thought it was a display, until. Jeez, what a way to start the day."

He paused a moment, shifted the puppy. "I called nine-one-one, and the officers, they got here real fast. I'm glad they got here fast. It's, sorry, but it's creepy. All dressed up like that, and standing there dead. It's really fucking — sorry — creepy."

"Did you see anyone else in the area, Mr. Franks?"

"I sure didn't. We live just up on the next block. This one woke me up like every morning. Like 'Man, I gotta go.' But does he?"

"Do you usually walk this way at this time?"

"Time's pretty regular. Sometimes we go the other way. Mix it up, you know? It can take a few blocks before he does what he got me out of bed to do. Usually don't see anybody else walking around."

Since Bouncer looked ready to leap out of the man's arms and into hers, Eve shifted back a little, pulled out a card. "If I could have your contact information? This is mine if you think of anything else."

"Sure, sure. I gave mine to the officers." He repeated it for Eve, took her card. "I'm going to walk him back now." He took another quick glance toward the doorway. "Man, you couldn't pay me enough to do your job."

"I'd add weird to creepy. Officer Cunningham, Lieutenant. Mr. Franks and Bouncer's nine-one-one relayed to us at zero-five-forty-two. Officer Su and I arrived on scene at zero-five-forty-six. We determined, visually, the individual who looks like he went to a costume party was dead. We secured the scene and took Mr. Franks's statement."

"Bouncer had plenty to say," Su added. "But we didn't have an interpreter. Nice pup. We had the alert about the body downtown, the weird outfit angle and all that, so informed Dispatch."

Since the sun had yet to rise, Cunningham shined his flashlight on the body. "You can see the wires and the plank of something holding him up there. Looks like a kid, and that adds ugly to creepy and weird."

"All right. Stand by."

She didn't recognize the pose or costume from her cheat sheet, but checked. Nowhere did she find a portrait of a boy or young man wearing a fancy blue jacket with a lacy white color, matching pants that stopped at the knee, white stockings, shoes with blue bows on them. He had a black hat with a white feather held down by his side in his right hand, and his left cocked on his hip.

He had curly brown hair past that lacy collar, with some swept over his forehead. He stared straight ahead, unsmiling.

To save time, Eve tagged Roarke.

"How can I help?"

"Tell me if there's a painting like this."

"The Blue Boy," he said immediately. "Gainsborough. Thomas Gainsborough. The original is, ah — let me think — in the Huntington, in California."

He paused a moment. "So it's not a connection to Vermeer after all."

"Were they pals, associates, competitors?"

"As the two paintings were done about a hundred years apart, that's not an angle for you."

"Okay. Thanks. I have to get to the body."

She pocketed her 'link, opened her field kit, and sealed up.

"The victim is a Caucasian male, dressed in a blue costume, with white lacy collar and cuffs, white stockings to the knee with blue ribbons holding them up, and a kind of blue cape over the jacket. There's some white detailing on the jacket from the armpit to about halfway to the elbow. He's holding a black hat with a white feather in his right hand."

She used her penlight. "The hat's glued to the hand. The left is set on the left hip with glue. The body is posed in a standing position, wired to a board propped in the doorway."

She lifted the material covering the left hand, managed to maneuver the pad to get a fingerprint.

"Victim is identified as Robert Ren, age twenty-three, residence 716 Seventh Avenue, number 4-D. Victim is a licensed companion, street level. Mother, Suzann Ren, Bronx; father deceased; one sibling, female, age twenty-one, Rachel Ren. Victim is single, no official cohabs."

Shifting, she used a fingertip to ease the chin up, hit resistance immediately.

"The head's glued in position. Visible indications of strangulation. Manual. Eyelids glued open, lips glued closed. It looks like some lip dye, some color added to the cheeks. Well, Christ, the hair on the forehead's glued in place. It's a wig, but glued in place."

"Sick bastard," Su commented from behind her.

Eve just grunted and got out her gauges. "Time of death, oh-three-ten."

Behind her, she heard Peabody's voice and Cunningham's response.

"Shit," Peabody said as she stepped closer. "It's *The Blue Boy.*"

"So Roarke tells me. Robert Ren, another street level. Carted here on this board, glued and wired. He wanted this one standing."

"It's a full-length portrait. The original, I mean."

"And it has to be exact, every detail exact."

"Let me pull up the original."

When she had, she held it out for Eve to see.

"The victim looks younger than twenty-three, but still a little older than the model in the portrait. But the build's close, and I'd say the height. And look, Dallas, the board's painted to replicate the background of the painting. See the colors — dark with some light around the shoulders, and right around the hat and the cocked elbow, some green that goes into brown.

"It doesn't have the same . . . flair, I guess,

for light, shadow," Peabody added, "but it's the same background."

"Yeah, I see it. Exact, precise. This takes time, and still he kills two in two days. Pulls them in, dresses them up. Takes — at least took a couple hours with Culver. Facts not in evidence, but I'm saying he starts painting them, or takes photos. He needed this one standing, so needed the board. Can't just have a board. It needs to represent the background in the original."

"He'd have had that ready."

"Yeah. Still took time. Have the officers seal up. Let's turn this board. We'll get the back on record. And I want measurements on the record."

When they'd turned it, Peabody measured.

"It's seventy inches high, twenty-two-and-a-half inches wide. And I can tell you this board is man-made. Lightweight composite."

"What's the painting? Measurements."

"Oh, good one." Peabody did the search. "Seventy inches tall, forty-four-point-one wide. So he went for the full height, but cut the width in half."

"Needed the height, not the full width. Harder to carry something that wide. And the background? Afterthought for him. It's the portrait, the person. Let's call for the morgue, tag for Morris, and get the sweepers."

While Peabody did that, Eve looked up the owner of the gallery.

She found a trust in the name of Harriet Beecham, enacted four years prior at her death — at a hundred and eighteen.

"On their way," Peabody told Eve.

"The gallery was the home of a Harriet Beecham, big patron of the arts. In her will, she decreed the town house be opened as a gallery. Her great-granddaughter operates the place, and she lives close enough. We'll go inform her, then take the victim's place.

"Officers, hold the scene."

"Two days running," Peabody said as they got into Eve's car. "We deserve coffee."

"The victim deserves wide-awake investigators, so coffee."

"One of these days when I'm on the roll, I'm going to wake up and have breakfast with McNab in our mag kitchen. Or maybe on our sweet patio. But for now."

She handed Eve coffee.

"You were probably up and dressed again."

"I was." And paperwork would, again,

have to wait. "Nine-one-one caller was walking his dog."

"Early for that. I'm guessing puppy or senior dog."

"He said puppy. It's the second time on this we got lucky with a witness and an early nine-one-one. Before oh-six hundred for both."

"Tell me," Peabody said, and yawned.

"But he got luckier placing the body earlier than that. Did you read the report from my interviews with Culver's coworkers?"

"I scanned it on the subway. This victim wasn't one of those."

"No. We'll find out what area he worked after we talk to the gallery operator. This widens the killer's territory. He's got his own transportation, and a vehicle big enough to carry a seventy-inch board."

She found Iona Beecham's address — half of a three-story duplex, a well-secured brownstone six spotless steps above street level. Flowerpots flanked the door painted in what Eve thought of now as Dreamy Peabody Blue.

Eve pressed the buzzer.

The computer-generated system answered promptly.

Barring emergency, the resident is currently unavailable to guests. Please leave your name, contact, and a brief summary of your business.

Eve held up her badge. "Lieutenant Dallas and Detective Peabody, NYPSD. Inform Ms. Beecham we need to speak with her."

One moment while your identification is scanned and verified.

. . . Please wait while the resident is informed.

"Nice place." Peabody glanced up. "A light just went on, second floor."

"Yeah, I saw it."

It took another couple minutes before the door opened.

"Who's hurt? My family —"

"We're not here about your family, Ms. Beecham. We're here about an incident at your gallery."

"Oh! Someone broke in!"

"No. I believe the building is secure. If we could come in and speak to you?"

"Oh, yeah, sure. Sorry. I was sound asleep."

For a woman who'd just been roused,

Iona Beecham managed to look stunning, with messy waves of black hair tumbled around a face with perfect skin that blended warm brown and rich cream. She had sleepy eyes of blue that edged toward lavender.

Slim and petite in a blue tee and white sleep baggies, she stepped back just as someone called down the stairs.

"Iona? Everything okay?"

She glanced back at the man who stood at the top of the steps wearing nothing but black pants, unfastened, over a build that dreams are made on.

"Yes. Just something about the gallery."

"Do you want me to bring you some coffee?"

"Oh . . . Yes, actually. Thanks."

"And your guests?"

"We're good."

Iona gestured to the living space.

"That's Mikhail. Big date last night." She eased out a breath. "Really big. Please sit down, tell me what happened."

Chapter Nine

The walls of the living area hit a color a few shades lighter than Iona's skin and held art. Like Peabody, she'd chosen with a variety of streetscapes here, all full of movement and color.

She'd gone quieter in the furniture, with a long white couch, another white two-seater, and a pair of chairs in the same blue as the door.

The fireplace held about a dozen white candles. The mantel above it held a sculpture of an elongated metal woman and a dark, deeply carved wooden box.

"Is there any damage?" she asked as she sat on the two-seater. "I should wake up my brother. He and his family have the other half of this building."

"There's no damage. A body was found in the gallery's doorway."

"A body? A — a person? A dead person!"

The color fluctuated in her cheeks as her eyes rounded in shock. "Someone died trying to break in?"

"No. There's no sign of an attempted break-in. Someone placed the body there early this morning."

"Oh God, this is horrible." Now she clutched at her throat as if to push the words out. "Is it someone I know?"

Eve pulled up Ren's ID photo, offered it.

"No. I shouldn't be relieved, but I am. I don't know him. What happened? Oh, Mikha, thanks. Someone died in front of the gallery."

"I'm so sorry. Can I sit with her, or . . ."

"No problem," Eve told him.

When he did, he took Iona's free hand.

"Ms. Beecham, do you know this painting?"

Eve brought up *The Blue Boy.*

"Of course. Gainsborough. I cut my teeth on art, sometimes literally. My great-grandmother founded the trust that supports the gallery. My grandfather and father are both artists. So's my sister. She's living in Italy right now. I don't understand."

"Yesterday," Mikhail murmured, "there was a woman killed and posed like Vermeer's *Girl with a Pearl Earring.*"

"I'd forgotten. I need this coffee. My mind is . . . Is this like that?"

"We believe so. Do you know the Whittiers?"

"Not personally, no. Grandy — my great-grandmother — knew everyone in the New York art world. And beyond. My father may. I know art, I value art, but Grandy asked me to run the gallery because while I didn't inherit my father's talent, I did my mother's. And that's for business."

"This isn't art. I'm sorry," Mikhail said quickly. "It's not for me to say."

"Why isn't it art?"

He shifted toward Eve. "This? Beyond the meanness of murder? A cheap gimmick, a cheap fake, and an excuse to hurt others. Whoever is doing this uses the genius of others, their talent, their history, and bastardizes their art."

He lifted those broad, naked shoulders in a kind of apologetic shrug. "I feel strongly."

"Mikhail's an artist."

"Not Gainsborough or Vermeer, but Barvynov. Myself. This person, this killer, he's not an artist. He's a pretender."

"Because he copies to kill. Or," Eve considers, "kills because he can only copy?"

"Either way, he's a fake. That's how I see

it, and I should be quiet."

"Let's get this out of the way. The two of you were together last night?"

"We went to dinner," Iona said. "About eight? Then a club. Then . . ." The faintest flush rose to that beautiful face, but Eve didn't see it as embarrassment. More as fondly remembered pleasure.

"Then here. I guess we got back here about one?"

Mikhail just smiled at her. "I didn't notice the time. It had already stopped." Then he looked at Eve. "Iona has security. You can check and see that once we got here, we haven't been out again."

"If we could, it would tie that off."

"Of course." Iona rose. "I'll show you."

"Peabody."

"We appreciate it, Ms. Beecham." Peabody got to her feet. "I admire your collection of art," she continued as she walked out with Iona.

"You have an interesting perspective on the killer."

Mikhail lifted his shoulders again. "It's how it strikes me, and I'm upset, angry that Iona's gallery was used. But what do I know?"

"You're an artist. You have that perspective. He must see himself as an artist, and obviously he has his."

"Seeing himself as one doesn't make him one. An artist, whether successful or struggling, has to own their art first. In here."

He thumped a fist on that bare and muscular chest. "Whether you're a hobbyist, a professional, whether you create to live or live to create, what you create has to be yours, you see. Or you're nothing. You have to own it, or you create nothing."

He edged forward. "Two people look at a work of art. One thinks: I don't get it, or that's crap. The other sees something that lifts them, that inspires or engages or simply speaks to them. Both are true, and the artist owns both."

"How do you feel when someone looks at your work and thinks it's crap?"

"Pain, anger, sorrow. Then I use all of that in the next work. You can't create for either of the two people who see two different things, but only for yourself. So you own your art."

"What if I said the killer's art *is* the kill?"

He blinked at her. "Oh, I see. I'd say I hope you find him quickly because . . . wouldn't he need to create another work?"

"All clear, Lieutenant." Peabody came back with Iona. "The security feed shows both of them coming in just after one A.M. No one in or out after until our arrival."

"All right. Ms. Beecham, if we could ask you for a list of featured artists, rejected artists, employees, former employees."

"Sure. We actually don't use the term *rejected.* Just *unsuitable for our needs at this time.*"

"I'm one of the featured artists. I'm happy to give you whatever information you need."

"Appreciate it. Peabody." Eve turned back to Iona. "Do any of the unsuitables stick in your mind? Someone who caused a scene, or threatened you or anyone else in any way?"

"Some are certainly disappointed, some are even angry if we feel unable to take on their work. We're fairly small, and we select with care. If I could think about it? I could discuss it with our manager and staff."

"That works." Eve handed her a card. "We're sorry to have disturbed you so early, and appreciate your time and cooperation."

"Whatever I can do to help. Art and artists are an essential part of my life, and always have been. And the gallery? A woman I loved and admired so much entrusted it to me. He can't get away with using that for his sickness."

As they walked back to the car, Peabody smiled. "They're either already crazy in love or heading there fast."

"Yeah, that's the important thing I got out of that conversation."

"It's a nice thing. Who can't use a nice thing when they start off the day with Dead Blue Boy? And holy shitfire, that guy was ripped. Cut. Built. An Adonis."

"And you know what else he was? Insightful. Let's go see how Dead Blue Boy lived."

He had a flop on the edge of Times Square above a shawarma joint and a game parlor. Eve parked in a loading zone, engaged her On Duty light. With Peabody, she wound her way through the endless party that swarmed the streets, the twenty-four-hour shops, the parade of LCs taking the early shift.

She smelled Zoner and cheap brew, whatever passed for meat on cart grills.

About half the party was drunk or stoned or on the prowl, the other half came to gawk, and half of those would end up having their pockets picked. Either by nimble fingers or laying out cash at a pop-up for a designer wrist unit on the cheap that would stop working before they got back to Milwaukee.

She felt the brush and bump, pivoted and grabbed the hand trying to lift her 'link out of her pocket.

"Are you serious?"

"Hey! Get off me, bitch!"

The woman, maybe twenty, with a rainbow fright wig and fake face tattoos, took a swing. Eve dodged it, and with a solid grip on the captured wrist, gave the woman a solid bump in the gut with her field kit.

That brought on a shriek that could have shattered glass.

"Help! Help!"

Eve countered with, "Cop, cop."

Peabody held up her badge, and more than one someone in the crowd started recording.

"I was just walking here."

"With your hand in my pocket? What else you got?"

Eve handed her field kit to Peabody, then gave the thief's trench coat a little shake. She heard rattles and clunks.

"Sounds like you had a pretty good night." Eve added a smile. "Up till now."

"Give me a break. I was just walking." She

turned to appeal to bystanders. "Police brutality!"

She stomped on Eve's foot, tried another swing, easily blocked with a forearm.

"That's called assaulting an officer. Peabody, pull in a couple of uniforms. You're under arrest."

The woman struggled, wiggled, bounced, elbow jabbed as Eve turned her to snap on restraints.

A couple of wallets, a wrist unit, and a 'link spilled out of the overfilled inner pockets of the trench.

"Anyone who tries to snag what just fell on the ground's going to end up like her," Eve warned.

Now the woman tried tears. "I was starving! I've got no place to sleep."

"Hey, I smell bullshit. But anyway, now you'll get three hots and a cot, problem solved."

Peabody juggled the field kits, got out an evidence bag for the loot on the sidewalk. She managed to seal and label as two uniforms jogged up.

Once they made the transfer, Eve took back her field kit.

"Nothing more to see here." Peabody put on her stern face, waved a hand. "Move along. I really wanted to say that," Peabody muttered to Eve as they continued down the street. "She actually tried to pick your pocket."

"Sloppy with it. She should've quit while she was ahead."

"How's your foot?"

"Fine. Good boots."

"Mag-looking, too. Love the laces."

"Of course you do."

Eve turned to the residential door of Ren's building. On its chipped red paint someone had painted an enormous penis at full alert.

Inside, the stairway loomed straight ahead. Eve didn't consider the single elevator. Even if she had, the OUT OF ORDER sign over-scored with a *Fuck You Simon* in red marker would have sealed the deal.

"Fourth floor," Peabody said. "Now I earn the schmear on the bagel I inhaled this morning. McNab made it for me," she continued as they started the climb.

"He was so sweet, getting up because I had to. He said, 'She-body, you need some chow,' and made me coffee and a bagel. He even offered to come with, but he's deep in a cyber scam case, and he thinks they'll break it today."

Rounding the second floor, Eve noted that

the single slit of a window had been broken and boarded over. She recognized the same artist's style in the multiple penises inside what looked like a take-out sack. It held the caption:

Eat a bag of dicks Simon.

"I suspect Simon is the building super."

"I agree with your deduction," Peabody said. "These stairs have about five years' worth of grime on them. I don't think Simon earns his pay."

On the third floor, the scent of Zoner and despair leaked out of an apartment doorway. Eve watched a mouse streak across the hall and under another door.

On four, someone played depression music just loud enough for misery to coat the air. She walked down to 4-D, keeping a wary eye out for rodents.

"Record on," she said, and sealed up. "Dallas and Peabody entering apartment of Robert Ren."

She mastered in to the surprise of a man about the same age as the street thief and buck naked. He stood beside the rumpled sheets over the lumpy mattress of a sagging pullout.

They caught him in full yawn and stretch — and with his wake-up hard-on still in place.

"What the fuck!"

He tossed his head to clear most of the blue hair that covered his face.

"NYPSD." Eve held up her badge.

"Okay, but what the fuck?" In a sudden swing to modesty, he crossed both hands over his crotch.

"Maybe you should put on your pants and we'll talk about what the fuck. Got a name?"

"Jed." He dragged on a pair of baggies way overdue for a wash. "Jed Jensson. Look, if Bobby got busted for something, I don't have the scratch to bail him. I'm tapped until payday."

"Do you live here, Jed?"

"Nah." Now he grabbed a T-shirt off the floor, pulled it over his head. "Bobby lets me flop here some nights. He works nights, I work days. I give him ten when I use the bunk. What'd he do?"

"Got killed."

Jed's next yawn ended on a gasp. "What? For real? Man, that's just down. All the way down."

"How long have you known him?"

"I dunno. Awhile, a few months. Like I

work the line at the all-day breakfast joint down the block, and he comes in most mornings after his stroll. I got booted from my place, and we made a deal about flopping some nights for ten.

"Are you sure he's dead, because man!"

"Yes. Where's his usual stroll?"

"He works the porn place — vids? On Seventh and, maybe Forty-Third? Around that. Bobby's got a deal with the manager, he says. Like the john coughs it up for two tickets. Bobby gives the manager, I think, five percent of the sex fee, and Bobby doesn't have to keep a separate flop for business, or pay the flop the going ten percent.

"Did one of the johns do him?"

"We're investigating. Do you know any of his friends, associates?"

He started to scratch his balls, then remembered himself.

"Sometimes he'd come in with a couple other LCs. Ah, a woman. Little — I mean short woman. Luce something. And a guy, big guy, Ansel. He said I could make a lot more working the streets, but I got a couple hits, and they look at all that."

"Yes, they do."

"Look, I really gotta piss, then I'm out of here. I got work, and I need the job. I'm sorry about Bobby and all, it's really down, but I just flop here some nights."

"Go ahead."

He hotfooted it to the bathroom, where Eve heard the stream through the paper-thin door, and had to admit. He'd really had to piss.

"Run him."

"Doing that. He's nineteen, got a juvie record. Illegals possession and intent, a car boost. Another illegals bust about three months ago. No fixed address. He is employed, the last seven months, at Breakfast Any Time."

When he came out, he tossed the hair out of his face again. "I'm just gonna grab my shoes and take off."

"We're going to need your key to the place, Jed."

Everything sagged, face, body. "Man. It's not like he'll be using it."

"No, he won't, and we'll have to seal the flop up for the time being." Eve held out her hand.

"Well, fuck it." He dug into a pocket, handed it over. "I don't have to leave the money for the nights I stayed this week, do I?"

"I think you're clear there."

"I guess that's solid. Maybe I can talk to that asswipe Simon about subletting it or whatever."

"Do that. And when you do, mention that Lieutenant Dallas, NYPSD, told you that since she personally observed a broken elevator, a poorly secured broken window, acres of grime, and a rodent, he can expect a building inspection by next week. We will be informing the owners of this building of same."

"That'll just piss him off."

"Or," Peabody said, "you could say you wanted to warn him, give him a heads-up on it."

Jed brightened up. "Yeah, yeah, like a favor. Okay." He shoved his feet in a pair of ragged kicks. "Um, anyway. Bye."

Eve just shook her head when the door banged shut behind him. "How bad is your life when bagging a place like this is a step up?"

She glanced around. In addition to the pullout, he'd had a single chair, a folding table. In lieu of a closet, clothes hung on a rod or piled in a clear tub. In lieu of a kitchen, shelves held a mini-AC with two glasses, two plates, with a mini-friggie beneath.

The place wasn't particularly messy. There weren't enough possessions to create one. But domestic cleanliness hadn't been high on Bobby's list.

"Let's give a look. It shouldn't take long. Then we'll see if we can hunt up the porn vid manager."

They found a code-locked tablet, carefully hidden under clothes in the tub, a single brew, a single tube of Coke Plus!, a number of hygiene products that said Bobby cared more about his personal hygiene than that of his environment.

"Baseboard's wrong there."

Eve glanced over. "Everything in here's wrong."

"No, it's just a little . . ." Peabody crouched down on the floor behind the single chair, gave the baseboard a tug.

A section came away in her hands.

"I knew it."

"Good eye. What's he hiding?"

Peabody took out a small plastic container. "Something's been chewing on it, so eeww."

"But didn't get through to his cash stash."

"No." Gingerly Peabody pulled off the lid, counted out. "Two-fifty, and one joint.

Smells like Zoner, and looks pretty fresh."

"Probably smoked right after a standard exam. Well, those days are over. Bag it up. We'll get EDD to open the tablet. Anything else look wrong to you?"

"No."

"Then let's seal it up. We'll find the porn guy, wake him up. When that's done, I'll do the notification while we're in the field. We'll hit the lab, then the morgue."

They tracked down Alex Minor, a mixed-race male of thirty-six who lived in a decent apartment in a decent building.

The woman who answered the door looked pleasant and puzzled. Kids could be heard squabbling in the background.

"Ms. Minor. Lieutenant Dallas, Detective Peabody, NYPSD. We'd like to speak to your husband."

"Oh. He's sleeping. He works nights. Is it important?"

"Yes, ma'am, it is. We could arrange for Mr. Minor to be brought down to Central later."

"Oh, I'd hate for you to have to do that. Boys! Hush now and eat your breakfast. It's nearly time to leave for school." She turned back to Eve. "Come in. I'll go tell Alex you're here." She gestured to the living area.

"Have a seat."

Eve glanced around as the woman hurried toward a hallway, then turned right.

The living area didn't have everything in place, but damn close. The furnishings weren't new and shiny, but well-kept, and the double front windows sparkled clear.

Two kids, spookily identical with their sandy hair, blue eyes, round chins, sat over bowls at a table in the eating area and stared at the newcomers with expressions of suspicion and curiosity.

"Police wear uniforms," the one on the right said.

"Not all of them." Peabody smiled.

"Uh-huh. Officer Friendly came to our school. He wore a uniform. And at the parades they wear them."

"That's how you know," the one on the left stated firmly.

"This is also how you know." Peabody stepped over, held out her badge. "This says I'm Detective Peabody with the NYPSD."

"Then where's your uniform?" the first one demanded.

"Boys!" Mom came out. "Don't badger the police officers. Alex will be right out. Get your bags, we're going in two minutes."

She scooped up the bowls, took them into

the kitchen.

Instead of getting their bags, both twins walked up to Eve.

"Do you have one of those?"

"Badges? Yeah." Eve took hers out again.

"Loo . . . Looie . . . What does that word say?"

"Lieutenant."

The second one frowned. "What does it mean?"

"That I'm the boss."

That seemed to please them, as both nodded, spookily in unison. "We're going to be the boss one day."

"Of what?"

Now she got a double eye roll. "We don't know yet. We're only seven."

"Boys, bags! Oh, Alex. This is . . . sorry, school morning brain."

"Lieutenant Dallas, Detective Peabody."

Both kids ran over to their father, wrapped around his waist.

"Scram, you maniacs." But he leaned down to give them both a quick wrestle. "I'll see you this afternoon."

"Park and ice cream," they cried in stereo.

"Park and ice cream. Beat it."

"There's coffee." His wife gave him a

quick kiss. "Breakfast meeting. I'll tag you after." She shot an apologetic smile at Eve and Peabody, then herded the twins out the door.

"Can you tell me what this is about?"

"Robert Ren."

"Robert . . . oh, Bobby." He pressed his fingers to sleepy hazel eyes. "Shit. Let me get that coffee. I didn't get home until almost six. You want some?"

"No, we're fine."

"Sit down." He went into the kitchen, separated by a half wall from the rest. "I'm sorry Bobby's in trouble, but I really try not to get involved in that area."

"Bobby Ren's body was found early this morning."

"His what? His . . . *body*?" When he almost tipped the mug, Alex grabbed it with both hands. "He's dead? Jesus. How? When? I just saw him last night."

"When was that?"

"Hell." As he stepped out of the kitchen, Alex rubbed at his forehead. "It had to be around eleven-thirty. He'd had a customer."

"The theater's considered a public business, and isn't licensed for sex work."

Alex sat. "And the only way to stop that

would be to hire guards to toss people out. I don't own the place, and I can tell you, there's no policing sex in a porn theater."

"So you profit off it, personally."

He looked into his coffee, sighed, looked up again. "Since I took over management eighteen months ago, we haven't had a single health violation. Instead of having them sneak in, I've worked out an arrangement with the LCs who work that strip. Yeah, I make some on the side. I also make sure the LCs are safe. If any customer gets rough, we toss them. Same with anybody who starts hassling the staff or other customers.

"I've got a family, and we want to move, get a house with a yard. Maybe a dog. So I make some on the side, and I keep the place clean and as safe as possible. Bobby didn't die in the theater, I know that. Nobody hurt him either, inside it."

"How about giving us your whereabouts last night between midnight and four A.M."

"Jesus. At work. Last show ended at four-fifteen. Then it takes close to an hour, sometimes more, to shut everything down, clean everything up."

"Anyone who can verify that?"

"Sure. Assistant manager, vid operator,

two security staff, ticket seller, concession workers, maintenance. And then the cleaning crew. I don't leave until they're done, or it might not get done."

"How well did you know Bobby Ren?"

"We had a business arrangement. I don't know about his personal life. I'll say he was cocky." Catching himself, Alex shook his head. "No lousy pun intended. Sure of himself. He told me once he wanted to get into the business end. Run a stable, do it right. He looked like a kid. I remember I checked his license, verified it because he looked like a kid."

"Where was he going when you last saw him?"

"Back out, I guess. I don't know if he came back in. I don't remember seeing him. Sometimes they get a customer who wants a flop, or doesn't want to pay for the tickets. I didn't think any more about it. I didn't notice one way or the other.

"What happened to him?"

"Someone strangled him."

"God." He covered his face with his hands a moment, rubbed hard, then dropped them. "I don't know what to say except it didn't happen in the theater. I can take you through, open it up for you. But after we close, we wash it down. But I'll open it up for you."

"Not necessary at this time. He wasn't killed there."

"I can be grateful for that. I'm sorry this happened to him, but I'm damn glad of that. And I honestly don't know what more I can tell you."

"I think we've got it." She signaled Peabody to give him a card.

"If you think of anything," Peabody said.

"I'll talk to the staff. If anybody saw anything, I'll make sure you hear about it. Nobody had anything against him I know of. He was . . . no-pun cocky, but likable."

"Thanks for the time." Eve started out, stopped. "Did he have any regulars?"

"Maybe. I really tried not to pay much attention to that part of things."

"Sounds real," Peabody said when they walked down another flight of steps.

"He'd have had a hard time dressing an LC up and strangling them with a wife and two spooky kids."

"Twins are kind of spooky."

"Tell me. Most of the art in there, that apartment? Kid art, family photos. I don't see him as an art buff. And we can easily confirm he was at the theater at TOD."

When they made it back to the car, Eve gestured for Peabody to take the wheel. "Lab. I'll notify the mother on the way."

Chapter Ten

Bobby's mother cried. She looked and sounded resigned, then cried again.

"Bobby always had to go his own way. After his dad died, there was no stopping him from going his own way. He was a good son, and a good brother to Rachel. He came to see me most every Sunday. He took me out to a fancy dinner in the city for my last birthday, even though I said he shouldn't spend his money that way. But he'd never let me come see him where he lived. He said it wasn't fit for me, and it was only temporary. And he never hurt anybody in his life. I don't know why somebody would hurt him."

"We're going to do everything we can to find out."

"I need to see him. I need to tell his sister, and we need to come see him. I need to take care of things for him now."

"Yes, ma'am. You'll be notified as soon as that's possible. Will you need transportation?"

"No, I know my way around." She swiped at her eyes. "I can get to my boy. You find who took him away like this, and you tell them he had a mother who loved him. You tell them Bobby was a good son and a good brother."

When Eve finished, she just sat a moment.

"Nobody who hasn't had to do a notification knows what it's like to do one."

Eve shook her head. "No, I guess they don't. We need something from Harvo we can work with. You don't pick up costumes like that on the street corner, damn it."

"If anybody can pin it down, it's Harvo."

"Counting on it."

But when they got to the lab, Eve aimed for Dick Berenski first. The chief lab tech slid up and down his long counter on his rolling stool, egg-shaped head bent, spidery fingers tapping keys, swiping screens.

He looked up and fixed Eve with beady eyes. "Figured you'd be in here this morning to nag my ass."

"I'm not interested in your ass. What did he use to dose the victims?"

"I'm looking right now to see if we got

the same in the second one, aren't I? What he used on Culver? He did a cocktail of secobarbital and phenobarbital. The one's short acting — it's going to last about fifteen minutes — and the other's long acting — you can get twelve hours out of it."

"Why mix them?"

"Can't tell you. Either one'd do the job. Maybe he wanted the sec — kicks in faster — but he wanted to be sure he had enough time, so went with the cocktail."

Yes, she thought. That played.

"Okay, what else?"

"He used powder. What he did, he ground up pills. Maybe got a prescription because he used medical grade on both. He ground up the pills, mixed the powders, and dosed the wine."

Something beeped, and he swiveled, rolled. "Yeah, yeah. Same with today's guest. Same mix, not the exact mix, not the exact amount, but close. Both of them had some wine already. Add this? They're good and out. Pretty quick and for probably, given the dose, four, maybe five hours."

He swiveled again, swiped again. "Thing is, what Morris tells me, he didn't need that long. Dosed them five to ten minutes before TOD."

"He wanted to be sure. He needed them good and out before he killed them. He's a coward."

"They're dead either way."

"What else have you got?"

"Got your glue — running the second now, but we know it'll match. It's Grip All. That's the brand name. You can get it in any hardware venue, hobby shop, craft stores, name it. Same with the wire. Nothing you couldn't pick up in half a million places. Common use, hanging pictures, so art supply store, hobby store, craft store, like that. It's thin, coated, strong."

"How about the paint on the board, second vic?"

"We're working on it, Dallas. Jesus."

"Yeah? Us, too. I just got off the 'link with the second vic's mother."

"Oh, well." He made a puffing sound. "Shit."

"Yeah."

"We're working on it," he repeated. "We've got no prints, no DNA. No fibers on the skin or the outfits. Get us the guy, and between us and Morris, we'll match his hands to the bruises on the DBs."

Another ding, another slide down the counter. "Same glue on both, same wire.

That's what I got. And it ain't nothing."

"Okay. We're going to see Harvo."

He held up one of his spider fingers, wagged it. "Don't give her any grief."

"When have I given her any grief?"

He shrugged. "Just reminding you."

"And so he remains a dickhead," Eve muttered as they wound their way through the maze of the lab.

"Some are born dickheads."

"Profound, Peabody. Profound and true."

Harvo sat at her station in the glass-walled box that always reminded Eve of a rare animal habitat. Yet she'd found it also profound and true that some thrived in glass-walled boxes.

Harvo qualified.

Her weird machines hummed as she bent over one of her scopes. She'd gone with her invisible boots today, with her visible toes painted in a neon rainbow. She'd streaked her hair to match.

She wore white cropped baggies with wide rainbow cuffs and a white T-shirt covered with multicolored question marks.

While she'd have fit right in with EDD's fashion circus, when it came to hair and fiber, Harvo ruled the lab.

Eve rapped knuckles on the jamb of the

open door.

Harvo looked up, shot out a smile. "Hey, and welcome to my queendom. Domicile tripping, Peabody?"

"Mag beyond the ult."

"Party up?"

"Total. Watch this space."

"Check it."

"If we could now return to standard English?" Eve asked. "Can you tell us anything?"

"I can start off telling you you're hunting for somebody rolling in it."

"Rolling in what?"

Harvo rubbed her fingers together. "Mega mucho moolah. At least it took the mega and the mucho to score the first outfit. I don't need my loyal associates" — she gestured to her humming equipment — "to tell me the same for the second. But we're running the analysis."

"Why mega moolah?"

"Okay, we've got a silk-and-linen blend in the jacket and skirt. Finely woven to give it that, you know, luster. It's a lot of yardage — you'll get the whole caboodle in the report. And it's hand-dyed with organics, including saffron. That's moolah, Dallas, mucho and mega. And the stitching? Silk thread."

She swiveled, gestured to Peabody, then brought an image on-screen.

Eve saw the inside of part of the jacket.

Peabody saw art.

"Whoa, that's genius skill. Machine, yeah, but with a way skilled operator. Perfect, uniform, delicate."

Harvo nodded. "Right? You pay for all this. You pay mega mucho moolah. And the scarves? A lot of yardage there, too, to get the whole . . ."

She waved her hands over her rainbow hair.

"Silk. One hundred percent, brought to you by Italian silkworms."

"You can tell the worms are Italian?"

Harvo grinned at Eve. "I can tell the silk came from Italy, and my run says the scarves cost about eight large, each."

"Eight thousand for a scarf."

"Probably more, since it had to be custom, right? To match the painting. Even the collar deal, the fabric just above the jacket? Silk. My pal Joker took the earrings, but I can tell you, since we caught a brew last night, they're man-made pearls, but high quality."

She swiveled again to face them both.

"Add it up? The outfit cost an easy hundred K. You wouldn't see my shocked face at half that again. So he's rolling in it. He could've got it for like, say, five hundred at an upscale costume shop. Not this quality, right, but the basic look."

"He's too precise and detailed for that."

"I'll say. To get this? You maybe go to a designer — top level like Leonardo? And that probably runs more than the hundred thou. Or you hunt up one of the venues I found that'll reproduce authentic historical costumes. Like for other people rolling in it for big-ass fancy costume parties or whatever."

"I need that list."

"Coming. Hold that," she said as something buzzed.

Instead of rolling over, Harvo got up, walked to a machine, and stood, hands on her hips as its screen rolled out data.

"Yeah, yeah. We agree down the line, baby. Got your second outfit coming. Satin, organic hand-dyed for the blue. Even the ribbons — went for silk there, but the same dye mix. Lots of yardage. White silk for the accents. White — handmade — lace for the collar, the cuffs. French satin and silk, Irish lace."

Satisfaction on her face, Harvo turned. "I need some time to get you a moolah estimate, but survey says, easy a hundred-fifty large. I'm leaning toward one-seventy-five. Add another ten for the hat — it's an ostrich feather."

"A hell of a lot for a one-time use."

Harvo nodded at Peabody. "You got that. Oh, the wig on number two? Haven't run it yet, but I can tell you by visual and touch, human hair, handmade, and top quality. I'll get you the estimates and general sources in a couple hours."

Eve met satisfied look with satisfied look. "You earn your crown, Harvo."

"And nobody wears it better." She plopped down again. "It had to cost seriously over a quarter mil to get all this just to dress people up to kill them. This asshole has too much money, and is one sick bastard."

"You're not wrong."

"What if he made them himself?"

As Eve turned to Peabody, Harvo angled her head. "That's why you're the detective. I hadn't gone there. You're also the sewing girl. Could you do it?"

"Maybe. If I had the time and money. To get all the detail and that quality of workmanship, it would take me weeks. Months maybe. But someone like Leonardo . . ."

She turned to the close-up of stitching still on-screen. "Maybe the costumes, that quality and precision in the replications. Maybe that's his art."

Eve said, "Well, shit."

"It's probably not. It seems like if it were, he'd have left the bodies at a design house, in the fashion or fabrics districts. But . . ."

"We have to look at it."

"I like my job better than yours," Harvo decided. "My questions have answers. Yours have a lot more questions to the questions before there's an answer. You keep going until you find the answer though. You both deserve crowns. Kick-Ass Queens of Investigation."

"No crowns till we bag him. Get us that list, and whatever you can when you can. We appreciate the quick and solid work, Harvo."

"That's how I roll, and how I rule."

Eve agreed with a "Check it" before they wound their way back through the lab.

"Get a hold of Leonardo, see if he has time to consult."

"That's a mag idea. He'll know a lot more than me."

"You can speak the language. If he's in his studio place and can take some time, I'm going to dump you. Go home, ask the questions, get some answers. I'll take the morgue."

"Best deal of the day for me."

By the time they got to the car, Peabody put her 'link away.

"I'm officially dumped. I'll subway home, consult, meet you back at Central.

"I want his take on designers — or design houses — who'd take a commission like this."

"I got it, Dallas. Estimated cost, estimated time from order, approval of design, delivery. Venues that have the fabrics and all of it. I got it."

They split, and Eve made her way to the dead house for the second morning running.

Morris played the blues, and she supposed it apt enough on a couple of levels. But his suit today hit green notes, rich ones so the tie of deep rosy pink, the shirt with thin green-and-pink stripes played harmony.

He wore the clear protective cape over it with his hair coiled in a braided knot at the nape of his neck. Behind the microgoggles, his eyes magnified as they met Eve's.

"Another young life ended. A healthy one, though he shared careless eating habits with his predecessor."

"The contents of his friggie? A brew and a Coke Plus!"

"Ah, those were the days. Barbiturates again, ingested with wine — a Malbec this time, and an excellent one — shortly before death by manual strangulation. He'd had six ounces of the wine three to three and a half hours before death. And two more, dosed, roughly ten minutes before death.

"His last meal, about nine last night, a soy burger with cheese substitute, fries, and eight ounces of Coke Plus!"

Eve studied the body. "Sexual activity?"

"None that show. He did, however, thoroughly cleanse, all expected areas, with an antiseptic liquid, followed by a moisturizing lotion.

"He took care of his body," Morris continued. "Healthy weight, good muscle tone. And his face, his hair. The mark here?" Morris laid a gentle finger on the forehead. "From the glue used to hold the wig in place, and the solvent I used to remove it. More slight damage from the removal of the glue used to hold his lips and eyelids in place, his right palm and fingers, glue to hold the hat."

"Dickhead says it's Grip All glue."

"Strong — very strong, and not meant for skin. Easily accessible. I have some myself, and seal up or wear gloves before using it."

"If it runs like Culver, the killer had him three to four hours before he dosed and strangled him."

"If there was sexual penetration within that time frame, it would most probably be evident. It's not."

"No, it's not about sex. It's . . . ego," she decided. "Basically it's about ego. Ren was no more than a vase of flowers to him, or a doll to dress up. Peabody suggested it might be about the costumes, the making of them. They're all custom-made, high-quality materials, high-quality workmanship. Maybe the art angle isn't painting. Maybe it's design."

"Ah. And where is our Peabody?"

"Talking to Leonardo about just that."

"An excellent source."

He walked to the sink, washed his hands, then got them each a cold tube.

"Thanks." She cracked it, drank. "The guy who managed the porn theater he used said Ren wanted to move into the business end of sex work."

"He had an ambition."

"Yeah, and he has a mother who gives a shit. She's in the Bronx, and wants to see him, make arrangements. Probably with his sister."

"He'll be ready for them to visit by one this afternoon."

"I'll let her know."

She studied the body again. Even in death, Bobby Ren looked about sixteen.

"He moved fast. He had everything ready for both him and Culver. Knew when and where to scoop them up, had the transportation, the place, the drugs, the costume, all of it. The costumes have to take time, the scoping out who you'll put in them takes time. He's been planning this for a while. A good long while."

"And if he's taken that good long while for two, he very likely has a third painting, costume, and model selected."

Eve's eyes went hard, went flat.

"I know he does. I have more to work with now. It's all about who gets there first."

She tagged Peabody on the way out. She heard voices, saw swirls of color in the background.

"I'm heading to Central."

"Give me another fifteen, maybe twenty here. I'll walk in." She flashed a grin. "I live really close."

"Oral report before you write it up. Later."

New York wasn't just wide-awake now, but just bitchy enough to entertain her.

A delivery truck blocking a side street received a chorus of blasting horns and inventive, shouted curses. On the next corner pedestrians risked life and limb trying to beat the Walk sign by a few seconds.

A woman in boots up to her crotch, blond hair down to her ass, and a red dress barely covering either body part strode along the sidewalk. A man trying to one-eighty his head on his neck to keep her in view walked hard into a recycler.

Another woman leaned out a fifth-story window and heaved out piles of clothes while a man below shouted: "Come on, Doris, goddamn it! It was *one* time!"

An emergency vehicle screamed in the distance, and somewhere closer an airjack hammered stone and thundered the air.

God, she loved New York.

She pulled into the garage, and her slot.

She managed three floors in the elevator in peace before it opened.

Two uniforms escorted a woman in who

looked more impatient than worried.

"You're a woman."

Eve gave her a wary look. "I am."

"Wearing a ring, so you married?"

"Yeah."

"Well, lemme ask you. You're married to a guy for seventeen years, shove a couple kids out of your body along the way. Work your ass off for a couple other men while you're dealing with kids, now teenage kids who'll bring their own kind of hell, and on one more morning when you're shoving teenagers out the damn door for school, trying to get yourself cleaned up to go work, the man you married says: 'Damn it, Cath, where's my breakfast?' What do you do?"

"It's difficult to say, as I've never been in that specific situation."

"I'll tell you what you'd do, you'd do just like I did. I said: 'Here's your breakfast, Charlie,' and gave him a good smack with a frypan.

"Then what happens?"

Cath shifted with the uniforms to let more cops on, and maneuvered Eve into the corner.

"I'll tell you what happens. He's yelling I tried to kill him. If I wanted to kill him, I'd've kept smacking that pan over his stupid head instead of giving him one little tap. And he's carrying on like I stabbed him, not even bleeding, but carrying on like I stabbed him in the guts. Got the lump he deserved is all. And one of the nosy neighbors calls the cops on me! Now I'm arrested and late for work. Where's the justice?"

"Ma'am." One of the uniforms rolled his eyes at Eve. "We have to get off here."

"Breakfast, my ass," she said as they escorted her off. "You'd do the same!" she shouted back at Eve.

Eve thought, no. Why would she use a frypan when she had a perfectly good fist?

She got off at Homicide and walked into the bullpen.

And, Peabody excluded, a full complement of detectives.

"Has murder taken a day off?"

Baxter, feet on his desk, gestured at the board. "Closed."

Carmichael gestured with her coffee. "Closed."

Jenkinson jerked a thumb. "And closed."

Today's tie, God help her, featured the Empire State Building with the backdrop of a virulent red-and-gold sunrise. And King Kong, eyes laser red, beating his massive chest at the top.

"Before you say anything," Jenkinson began, "the squad unanimously approves this one."

"It's iconic," Santiago said.

"So's your hat."

Eve turned and went to her office.

She grabbed coffee, then updated her board. Then sat, updated her book.

When she brought up Harvo's list of possible venues for the costumes, she blew out a breath.

More than she'd figured, but Harvo had gone global. And that was the right call.

It seemed logical to start in New York, so she tried the first. And listened to the off-hours message.

"Okay, shit. What the hell time is it in France? Damn it, computer, what the hell time is it in Paris, France?

Working . . . The current time in Paris, France, is fifteen-twenty-three and six seconds.

"Great." She highlighted Costumes Historiques Authentiques, engaged the translator, and started there.

She bounced from reception to a low-level assistant, bounced from there to someone in public relations, and finally hit the assistant to the assistant of accounts.

The way the woman had her zebra-striped hair piled reminded Eve of Trina. Her back went immediately stiff.

"And how may I assist you this afternoon, Mademoiselle Dallas?"

"Lieutenant Dallas, New York Police and Security Department."

The smug smile hit Trina notes. Eve's ears began to buzz.

"Of course. How can I help you?"

"There have been two murders in New York —"

"Ah, that is very unfortunate."

"Right. The first victim was dressed to replicate Vermeer's *Girl with a Pearl Earring.*"

"How interesting."

"I have the breakdown of fabrics used and the organic dye."

"So very thorough."

Even translated, the words dripped sarcasm.

"The second victim was dressed to replicate Gainsborough's *The Blue Boy.* We also have the fabrics and dyes analyzed."

"Well done."

Suddenly, Eve wanted to use her perfectly

good fist to punch the condescending smile off the woman's face.

"I need to know if you have a client who placed orders for these two costumes, with these fabrics and dyes used to create them."

"I'm sorry to inform you, mademoiselle, I'm unable to assist you in this matter. Our client information is strictly private. You also have laws for privacy in New York, do you not?"

"The individual who had these costumes made has murdered two people, and I believe he'll kill again."

"Of course, this is tragic, yes, but I am unable to share any client information."

Eve took a breath, signaled Peabody to wait when her partner came to the door. "You could check, see if you do have a client who ordered these two costumes. Then you could tell me yes or no. You have such a client, or you don't."

There came that damn Trina smile again.

"I believe this is — how do you say — skirting a line? We at Costumes Historiques Authentiques take our responsibilities very seriously."

"So do I. I can get an international warrant for the information."

"Please feel free to do so. We will, of

course, consult our attorneys and cooperate fully if advised to do so. Please enjoy the rest of your day. I wish you goodbye."

"Son of a bitch!"

"She sounded like the bitch somebody's a son of."

"Tell me you had better luck with Leonardo."

"I had better luck. I'm not risking my marginally-smaller-than-it-used-to-be ass in that chair."

Instead, Peabody eased some of it on the corner of Eve's desk.

"First, no one approached him or his company for the costumes. He hasn't heard about another designer taking them on, but he's going to check around."

"Appreciated."

"He gave me a few places where, if he had gotten the order, he'd have sourced the fabrics. He also said that since historical accuracy was so important, he'd have consulted with an art expert. Without a specific model to fit, he'd have either taken the measurements given him by the client, or would've run a program to determine the measurements of the models in the paintings. Whichever the client wanted."

"Okay, you definitely got more."

"And a little more yet. Can I get coffee since I think I'm going to be spending a lot of time at my desk on the 'link after this?"

"Get it. Get me more. It's doubtful the killer knew the exact sizes of his victims when he ordered the costumes. But he'd know what he was looking for. For the Girl, it's the face. It didn't matter if the outfit was a little too big, which it was. The Boy, that had to be closer, so he had to look for somebody who'd fit. The face wasn't as important. Youth was, but not specific features."

"Can't argue that." Peabody handed Eve fresh coffee, eased her ass down again while she sampled her own. "Leonardo took a really good look at the painting details, at Harvo's analysis of fabrics, yardage, all of it. Then he did some sort of program — so it took a little longer than I expected. But he said if he'd done these orders, the Girl would've taken six to eight weeks, if the materials were available. It could take twice that if they had to be manufactured to order. And considering the fabrics, the need for exact replication, he'd charge one-seventy-five. That's thousand, which would include the consult fee for the art expert. For the Boy — double the time and the fee."

"That's even more than Harvo estimated."

"Yeah. He couldn't say absolutely, but he thought a company that specialized in historical costumes would probably come closer to Harvo's take on moolah and time."

"Like the French Trina's place."

"Her name was Trina?"

"No. She just reminded me of Trina. Okay, let's start with placing the order three months ago. No, go back six months. You start with the fabric venues. Looking for the specific fabrics, the yardage, ordered going back six months and up to three months. He could have used more than one costume place or designer, so factor that."

"What if I go back a year? It's so much detail work, Dallas. It'll take longer, but we'll cover more ground."

"Do that. I'm going to try this place in London. At least they speak English even if it's not American, and I won't need the translator."

She ran into the same wall in London, another in Milan, then an excruciatingly polite wall in Tokyo.

Frustrated, she got up and paced.

International warrants, she thought, would be a major pain in the ass for everyone involved. She might as well give a friend a pain in the ass first.

She contacted APA Cher Reo.

Chapter Eleven

"Reo. I'm in court, Dallas, but on recess."

"I'll make it quick. I need some international warrants."

"Some?" Reo's eyebrows lifted up under her fluff of blond hair. "International?"

"They're pertaining to the back-to-back murders, street LCs, dressed up like people in famous old paintings."

"Yes, I know about that, but —"

"Let me just get it out. Harvo's ID'd the fancy fabrics, the fancy dyes, even the yardage used on both costumes. I've got venues that make this sort of thing, high quality, high cost, and a lot of them are outside the U.S. I'm getting nowhere, due to client confidentiality."

"All right, I see the issue. But these are — here's the pun — really loose threads on international."

"He had to have them made somewhere.

Goddamn it, Reo, it's . . ." Eve caught herself, scrubbed at her face. "I'm not swiping at you. It's the snooty snot fuckers I've been trying to deal with."

"I get it. And I'm tucking away *snooty snot fuckers* for my own use at the appropriate time."

"The costumes, they're minutely detailed, accurate down to frigging shoe ribbons. Peabody says the work, like the stitching, is expert."

Lips pursed, Reo nodded. "She'd know."

"Leonardo concurs, and estimates, if he'd done them, he'd have charged about half a damn million."

"Are you serious?"

"As serious as the two dead bodies in the morgue. This guy has money to spend on his kills. He's organized, rich, precise. It's possible he's a sewing guy and made them himself. Even so, he'd need the fabrics. But that's down on my probability list, since he left the bodies — the first at the residence of an art gallery owner, the second at a gallery.

"He's two for two, Reo. He'll go for three."

"I hear you." Reo sighed, and like Eve,

paced as she talked. "Send me the data, and I'll push on it. But, Dallas, we're not talking hours to get something like this through, if we do. It's days."

"All I need to know is yes or no. Did they take the orders or not? We get that, we can push harder, or I can find a way to use it."

"Send me the data. I'll start the wheels turning."

"Thanks. And, ah, good luck in court."

"I don't need luck." Smile smug, Reo brushed at her hair. "I've got the evidence."

And I don't, Eve thought as she stuffed the 'link back in her pocket and continued to pace.

She tried the New York venue again, and got an actual human.

She worked her way up the company chain until she managed to snag the person actually in charge of custom costume orders.

"Lieutenant." One Rodney Triston had an ink-black bush of a mustache, an eyebrow ring, and a thin veneer of disdain. "I certainly understand your dilemma, but we're bound by client confidentiality. Our clients insist on and expect absolute secrecy when they commission a costume. The element of surprise when attending a fancy dress event is essential."

"I've got a couple bodies in the morgue that were pretty surprised. And on their behalf, I can get a warrant."

"Please do so." He waved a hand so loaded with rings they'd serve as brass knuckles. "But until you do, I'm unable to give you client information."

"Try this. Check your records for any orders for custom costumes of the two figures I gave you. If you have said orders, you say yes. If you don't, you say no. That's not client information. It's yes or no, which if I approached you for one of these costumes, asked if you'd created them before, you'd answer."

He took a deep inhale, let out a deep exhale that had the bush over his lip shivering. "Yes, I suppose I could have my assistant look into that. For what period of time?"

"How long would it take to make them, with the level of detail I described?"

"That would be a question for the head of design."

"Never mind that. Go back a year."

He gave her a long look that edged toward outright dislike. "It will take some time."

"Assuming your records are in order, not that much. I'll wait."

He slapped her into holding blue.

"You'll make it take longer than it needs to because you don't want to do it, you asshole."

Resigned to that, she programmed more coffee, drank some looking out her skinny window. New York rolled right along.

She wondered what the killer was doing now. Painting? Out scouting for another victim? He already had the third model selected, she was sure of it. Just as he had the third costume waiting.

How many in all? How many had he planned?

She sat, put her boots up, and studied her board as her desk 'link held blue and some sort of creepy fluty music drifted out of it.

What was it about these two portraits that pulled at him? Not the people in them, no, she didn't believe that. People were simply vehicles to him. And the two original models, dead for hundreds of years?

So the current models had to die, too, and by his hands — literally. Because . . . they couldn't outlive the art.

His art lived; they died.

That rang for her.

What the originals represented, long gone. But the art lived on. It had to be the same for his work because . . .

"He's a great artist, as yet undiscovered. Okay, okay."

She pushed up, paced again.

"That's who he is. They die, his art rises up and lives on. But why these two portraits?"

She stepped over to the board, studied them again.

"The light, the details. Details matter, and the light's part of it. The confidence of the Boy, the quiet seduction of the Girl. Girl and Boy, does that matter?"

Before she could think that through, the assistant came on the 'link.

"Lieutenant Dallas?"

"Yes."

Mid-twenties, Eve judged, a very pretty woman with ebony skin and quiet brown eyes. "I'm Mr. Triston's assistant, Riley. I checked our records. I'm permitted to tell you, yes, three *Blue Boy*s and one *Girl with a Pearl Earring* in the last year."

"Can you tell me when ordered, when delivered?"

She glanced to the side, then lowering her voice, leaned in. "My dad's a cop in Columbus. I can't give you names. I'd lose my job.

But I can tell you one of the *Blue Boy*s is a regular customer — along with his wife of a few decades. They ordered *Pinkie* and *Blue Boy* costumes nearly a year ago for their annual costume ball in June."

"Pinkie?"

"It's another full-length portrait. Not the same artist and decades apart. But a youth in blue, a girl in pink."

"Got it."

"And the second one was for an actual boy. About thirteen. And the last one was shipped to Chicago last spring, for an art show."

"Okay. How about the girl one?"

She glanced behind her again. "It didn't have the matching skirt. This one was brown, and the scarves were a silk blend, not pure silk. But I was supposed to say yes anyway. I hope this helps."

"It helps a lot. I appreciate it, Riley."

"You're welcome. Just don't —"

"Not a word to your boss. Thanks again."

Eve crossed the first New York venue off her list as she heard Peabody coming.

"Wanted to give you a quick update. That French place you talked to got orders of material on both portraits. More than the yardage for each. The person I talked to said that wasn't unusual. And since I also found orders on those fabrics to one of the venues in Italy, another in London, and more, I have to say, not unusual.

"They're beautiful fabrics, Dallas. Pricey extreme, but beautiful. And not just used in costumes."

"Keep hacking away. I've got one New York venue off the list. I'm going to see if I have luck with the others. Who's out there?"

"Bullpen? Baxter and Trueheart caught one. Jenkinson and Reineke figured they had good luck with the last cold one they pulled, so they pulled another. They're in the field chasing a lead."

"So brief Carmichael and Santiago. Once I push my way through these two, we'll try some galleries, and they can try hacking away."

She didn't find a helpful cop's kid at any other New York venue, and hit the same client privacy walls.

She stuck long enough to try one in Chicago, then another in Boston with the same results. So decided it was time to get the hell out of the office.

She went out to the bullpen to find Carmichael and Santiago both at their screens, and Peabody on the 'link rhapsodizing about fabrics.

Peabody held up a finger out of 'link range, circled it to signal winding up.

"We're both looking at cold ones," Carmichael told her. "Maybe we'll shake something out."

"Did you bet on it?"

Santiago only hunched his shoulders.

"My esteemed partner proposed one, but I nixed it. Bad bet. We'll take Peabody's list."

"Sending it now." Peabody pushed back from her desk. "No luck on that one. Not enough yardage on the blue satin, and none of the gold fabric in the last year."

"If you catch one," Eve said to her detectives, "tag me or Jenkinson. Let's go, Peabody."

"Here's a snag." Since Eve ignored the elevators, Peabody joined her on the glides. "The lace — handmade in Ireland. Not all the fabric venues on the list carry that. Some use French lace, for instance. And it's a specific pattern, too. One of the contacts said they commission tatters in Ireland if they have a specific order."

"Tatters?"

"Tatting. It's a weaving method to make lace. I brought up the painting and the replication, compared. They're exact, so either the client — our killer — the fabric venue, or whoever made the costume could've ordered the lace from a craftsman in Ireland."

"More digging, more contacts. But . . . that may not be a snag. It could be an answer. Handmade lace, specific pattern, specific size, shape, from one country. That's not calling all over hell and back. It's focusing in."

"Well . . . yeah, I guess it is. Change snag to possible break. On the other hand —"

"How many tatter-type people are there in Ireland? Who the hell knows, but this guy isn't going to want somebody who makes lace for the village shops. He wants someone with an important rep."

They clattered down the steps to Eve's parking level.

"Start looking for the twelve best lace makers in Ireland. Or, shit — who use the Irish method, threads, tools."

"Got it. Where are we going first?"

"We're going to start in Tribeca, work our way to SoHo. Both areas are loaded with art galleries. If we get through there, we hit the Village."

■ ■ ■ ■

To Eve's mind, no angle explored equaled a true waste of time. Though it could and did often feel like one.

If an exploration didn't harvest any solid answers, that was an answer. When you ended up with a basket of mixed, conflicting, and multiple answers, you had more to pick from.

Though Harlee Prince ranked high on the cooperative scale, her responses hit typical for most. As manager of House of Art in Tribeca, she proved knowledgeable about every artist represented in the gallery.

She stood about six feet in her towering heels with a crown of russet curls adding another inch or two. In her sleek black dress, she showed them through various rooms where others browsed.

"As you can see, we offer a variety of styles, methods, mediums."

"How do you select the art, the artists?"

"We work mostly through an agent, or a trusted patron."

"No walk-ins?"

"You mean unrepresented or unsolicited work? Yes." Smiling, she gestured Eve and

Peabody into another section, then to a painting of a dancer en pointe, the one beside it of another in mid-leap, and a third caught in a pirouette.

"These were brought in by what you might call a hopeful. Ankha Haversnell. As many artists don't have representation, we at the very least try to look, evaluate. For the most part, the work doesn't suit, but every now and again, you find something wonderful."

"They really are wonderful," Peabody said. "You see the grace, the movement, but you can see the effort and focus."

"Yes, exactly." Harlee beamed at Peabody. "Do you paint, Detective?"

"No, not really. I just admire."

"As do I. We've only had these on display for a few days, and already had considerable interest."

"What about the ones you turn down?" Eve pressed.

"Reactions vary. Rejection's painful. Our standard response to work we find unsuitable is we work through agents. Of course, not every represented artist is accepted."

"Either way, represented or not, does anyone stand out? A negative reaction that concerned you."

"Oh my goodness, Lieutenant, they run the gamut. Tears, despair, anger, insults, even threats."

"What kind of threats?"

"Self-harm, or threats to bring violence. For instance, I should have my eyes gouged out, as I'm already blind, or they'd see the gallery burned to the ground before they'd allow their art to be displayed here."

"Have you reported the threats?"

With a head shake that had the curls dancing, she smiled.

"Lieutenant, it's a momentary and passionate response. Most of them make a dramatic exit, and a good many of them come back again with new work. Or they make the rounds of other galleries. A few come back to tell me they've had their work accepted elsewhere. I wish them all the best."

"Let's go back to repeaters. Someone who comes back, is turned down again. A male, someone who strikes you as having enough money to indulge himself."

Harlee pursed her lips. "We do get hobbyists — as I think of them — who can afford to devote their time to their hobby."

"Who think they're the next big deal."

She smiled again. "Of course. We had a

woman who'd taken up watercolor in her eighties. And they were pleasant enough paintings. She was, obviously, very used to getting her way. She offered me five thousand dollars to accept her work, and became quite irate when I refused. The next visit, she offered ten thousand. And on the third, she threatened to buy the gallery and have me fired."

Harlee lifted her shoulders. "I'm still here. I did hear that another gallery accepted her work. I expect they were . . . compensated."

"Anyone else like that? A man who tried bribes, threats, or intimidation?"

Harlee pursed her lips again.

"Now that you mention it . . ."

And they got their first buzz.

"There was someone, very persistent. It's been some months since he's come in. As I recall, he said he could buy this excuse for an art gallery ten times over. I didn't take that seriously, of course, but if I remember correctly, he dressed very well."

"Do you have a name?"

"Oh, no, I'm sorry. His work . . . what was it?" Now she squeezed her eyes shut. "Oil on canvas — I'm reasonably sure. I do remember it was, at best, pedestrian. As I said, it's been some months. It might be close to a year since he's come in. I honestly hadn't given him a thought until you asked."

"Give him a thought now. What did he paint?"

"What did he paint?" Harlee repeated. "Portraits. Yes, I remember that, as he didn't have the talent for portraits. His paintings lacked life. And he had no real style of his own. Stagnant is the best way I can describe them. I think he came in three, possibly four times.

"I didn't like him," she added. "I don't suppose that applies."

"It does. Why didn't you like him?"

"He was rude, arrogant right from the start, as if doing us a favor by offering his art. You will have this, but . . . I honestly can't tell you exactly why, but if he'd said I should have my eyes gouged out, I would've reported it. I found him disturbing."

"Can you describe him?"

"Oh my goodness, it's been some time. I . . . I'd say he was in his late twenties, maybe early thirties. Very slim, very pale complexion. I remember his eyes were a very, very dark blue. I remember his eyes because I found them . . . I'll say disturbing again. It's what I remember most. I can't quite see his face, if you understand me. But I remember his eyes."

"Would you work with a police artist?"

"Oh, well . . ."

"It's very important."

"I do have a meeting in . . ." She checked her wrist unit. "Well, I'll be a bit late for that. And an event this evening I can't miss. I could make some time tomorrow, if you think it would help."

"I think it could. I'll have the police artist contact you, and you can work out the best time. Meanwhile, is there anything else you remember about him — or anyone like him?"

"I suppose he stands out or I wouldn't have remembered him at all. And I'd say, like the watercolorist I mentioned, he struck me as someone used to getting whatever he wanted. I promise you I'll think about it, try to jog my memory. But I really am going to be late."

"We very much appreciate your time, Ms. Prince. You've been very helpful."

"You want Yancy," Peabody said when they walked outside.

"Yeah, I do. This guy fits several slots, so

we push there."

"I'll contact him."

"If anyone can pull more descriptive details from her memory, Yancy can. We're going to hit a few more, see if anyone else remembers a well-dressed, very white male in the age range with dark blue eyes and a bad attitude."

"There's a glide-cart down there, and I'm empty. You may not feel it, but you've got to be empty, too."

"Crap. Fine."

When they got to the cart, Eve had to admit there was something about the smell of soy dogs, boiled up just right, that reminded the system food was a good thing.

And a cart dog on a warm afternoon was a very good thing.

"I'm going for the dog, too," Peabody decided. "Veggie hash just won't fill the hole."

Eve dug in her pocket. "Shit. I need a cash machine."

"Oh, I can cover it."

"I've got it, but I borrowed most of what I've got from Roarke. I have to pay him back."

"Oh. Okay."

Eve heard the edge of surprise.

"It's a thing we do. Avoids conflict."

As they started back, eating dogs on the way, Eve shrugged.

"His money can be annoying."

Obviously amused, Peabody licked some mustard off her finger. "I think I could live with it. Somehow."

"I do live with it. I just don't like him handing me cash when I'm tapped like it's nothing. And I don't want to ever get to the point where I feel like it's nothing."

On another bite of dog, Peabody nodded. "Okay. I get that. I can absolutely get that."

"You can?"

"Yeah, I can, and do. If you treated the money like it was nothing, it's like saying hell, he doesn't need a few hundred back from me. And sure, he doesn't. But paying it back is respect, for him and for yourself."

"Exactly." Pleased, even vindicated, she gave Peabody a light punch in the biceps. "Exactly. So I need a machine."

She found one before she finished the soy dog. Took out the cash and stuffed it in another pocket.

As they got back in the car, Peabody ordered them both cold drinks from the in-dash. "McNab and I split expenses. I mean we worked it out — the rent and all that.

When we go out, sometimes he treats, sometimes I do. It just depends. But the monthly expenses, we split."

"It's respect, and avoids conflict."

"It's love, too. You can respect somebody without loving them, but if you don't respect somebody you love, it's never going to hold up."

"I'm going to use that one if he gets pissy about the payback." Tucking it away, Eve headed for the next gallery.

Though the level of cooperation dipped considerably, and the details blurred, they got a hit at another gallery in SoHo.

They found another in the Village, and another nibble of information.

Though the manager had only come on three months before and had no recollection, one of the staff did.

"I didn't really deal with him myself."

Mark Egbe cruised into his sixties with a round, pleasant face. He wore a black three-piece suit with a poppy-red bow tie.

"Brendita — she retired a few months ago — said he told her he'd had a brilliantly successful showing upstate."

"You never saw or spoke to him yourself, Mr. Egbe?"

"Not to speak to, no. I imagine I saw him at some point. I believe he came in two or three times, but would only speak with Brendita — Ms. Klein — and if I remember correctly, they spoke in her office.

"I recall her comment on this, as she was very frustrated, enough to say to me the only way someone whose portraits were so lifelessly done would have a showing anywhere would be to pay for it."

"Did she mention where upstate he claimed he'd had one?"

"I don't believe so, or I don't clearly remember. I'm sorry."

"Would she have his name in your records?"

"I don't see why. Frankly, Lieutenant, she didn't like him. Not that she said so," he added quickly. "She would never! But I worked with Brendita for more than a decade before she retired, so I knew."

"Would you have her contact information?"

"I do, yes. She's traveling. She and her wife plan to travel for at least a year, if not more. I can't tell you where she might be at this time, but I have her 'link contact and her email."

Eve noted them down, then checked the

time as they left the gallery.

"We need to head in. We'll see if we can reach Brendita Klein, get any more details. Right now it's clear he made the rounds."

"And if it's our man, his work's just not good. Or good enough."

"And that pisses him off because it's, to him, masterful. If he did have an art show upstate, maybe he did pay for it. Or found someone who would."

"We've got a lot of threads. The fabrics, the designer or costume makers, the LCs, the galleries, and some potential witnesses. We just have to pull the right one. And there's another one."

"What other one?"

"Oil on canvas," Peabody said as they got back in the car. "Prince was pretty sure there, and we haven't gotten the lab work back on the board, but it looked like oil paint to me."

"Okay, so we focus on oil paints."

"Not just. Since he thinks his work's so brilliant, and we think he's got the money for it, wouldn't he go for the best supplies?"

"Yes, he would." Eve sat a moment before pulling into traffic. "If he's replicating the portraits, wouldn't he want to use the same paints the original artists used?"

Peabody's eyes widened. "Sure he would! It fits! The details of the costumes. It absotruly fits. And more on that? I think he'd probably, at least maybe, make his own paints — like mixing the pigment and oil himself the way they did. I think they did," Peabody qualified.

"It's another thread. And we tug it. We find out what the two artists he copied used, go from there. How the hell do you make pigment?"

"I actually sort of know."

Eve spared her a glance. "Oddly, I fail to be surprised by this."

"Well, I have a cousin who makes her own paint — from nature."

"Of course you do."

"Okay. She grinds up minerals, rocks, plants, flowers, bark, nuts, shells, whatever. Since she only uses nature, she uses egg yolk as a binder, and water for the consistency she wants. It's a lot. So it's not oil paint like we want, but it's making pigments. I can ask her."

"Do that. But can you buy the stuff already ground up?"

"Sure you can!" Peabody tapped her forehead. "I've seen it in craft stores and art supplies. I needed more art supplies for the toy boxes so I've been in a lot. But he'd use higher end than I did."

"We start higher end."

"Okay, I'm going to say it right out loud. This part'll be fun for me."

"It's all yours. Find out what pigments — if you can — the original artists used. Find what you need to make those. Specifically."

"And I'll talk to Phina — Seraphina, my cousin. She'll know other natural artists, and maybe some who work in oil. This is a good thread!"

"Start now," Eve said when they pulled into Central. "Odds are strong he'll hit again tonight."

"Three in three nights? He can't be painting that fast, Dallas, especially in oil."

"He's getting what he wants, and that's the kill. He's got all the time in the world to play with his paints. He's spent time finding the right models."

As they walked to the elevator, Eve rolled it as she saw it. "He had to take some time before that selecting the paintings he wanted to replicate. And, if this angle's right, accessing the right pigments. He needs the payoff."

"And that's the kill."

"The way I see it. He can take his time

finishing the paintings. He must take pictures of the victims in costume, in the pose. And if not, he's got the originals to work from. But he takes pictures."

She got on the elevator. "He can get a start when they're alive and posing, but he works in details, and details take time. He kills them only hours after he picks them up, not enough time for details."

"They come later. That's what makes sense," Peabody agreed. "How long do you figure he can keep this up?"

"Until we stop him."

After the fifth stop, and the entrance of an undercover cop who smelled like raw sewage, Eve switched to the glides. Peabody headed out right behind her.

"I'm going to try the manager of the gallery uptown, the body dump. See if what others remember jogs anything with her. I'll try to reach Klein, and then try a few others uptown by 'link."

"You're betting he's tried galleries all over the city, and I'm with you on that bet."

"But at some point, he said fuck that. None of these assholes know real art. I'm going to try to track down Klein now, see what she remembers. You're pigments and fabrics."

"I have to say: Yippee."

Chapter Twelve

She left v- and e-mail for the retired gallery manager, then contacted Iona from the Midtown Gallery.

"I'm really vague on this, and it had to be last winter. Maybe January or February. I'm only remembering a little because you said oil on canvas, portraits, pedestrian, lifeless — according to the other gallery managers."

"What do you remember?"

"An artist who brought in a portrait of a woman — and I'm not a hundred percent clear on that. I only remember him coming in once, and he didn't cause any sort of scene or get nasty, so I didn't think about him this morning. The painting, it just wasn't good. I can't even recall the details, but I remember he needed to work on adding light and life to his work. It's something I might say to any hopeful artist. I probably encouraged him to take some classes. I can't say that absolutely, but it's something I often suggest.

"I am sure he never came back in, not with another piece."

"Can you describe him at all?"

"I'm just not sure. White, and . . ." With a look of frustration, Iona pressed a hand to her head. "I wish I could be sure, but I'm just not sure. I think probably not over thirty. He didn't make an impression, Lieutenant, not personally or professionally."

"All right. If you remember any more, contact me. If you wouldn't mind, you might ask your staff if they remember him."

"I absolutely will. We're all pretty shaken."

Who wouldn't be? Eve thought, and turned to her board just before she heard Peabody's cowboy boot clump.

"Leonardo reports!"

"What?"

"None of the colleagues he contacted created those costumes. He has more to reach out to, but so far, none. He did try a few venues, but they locked him out mostly because he's a designer. The way he explains it is some in his business might try to poach clients this way, so they keep it zipped. But he does bump up three fabric venues. He's also reaching out on the Irish lace. He actually has a mother-daughter team who does lace for him when he wants it.

"Another thread? I left a message for my cousin. If she's working, she shuts off her 'link. But she's good at getting back to me."

"Good."

Eve filled her in on Iona.

"He left enough of an impression for her to remember he didn't leave much of one."

Eve leaned back, gave Peabody a nod. "That's exactly right. Given some time, she might remember something else. But. She's more sure she remembers telling him he needed more light and life in his work."

"You think the way he decided to do that was to take lives."

"I do."

The more she considered it, the clearer, the louder it rang for her.

"If you want to punish the galleries for not recognizing your genius, you go after the galleries or the people in them who turned you down. But that's not it. He's using death to give his work life. And there'll never be another portrait of that person again. Only his."

"But they're copies of others."

"Which is something none of the managers who remember him at all said. Not one's said he copied classic portraits. This is new for him. A new — what do they call it when an artist . . . it's not era."

"Period. This is his Death Period, I guess."

"And he'll show all of them how brilliant he is, how gifted. I'm going to finish up here, then give this damn paperwork an hour. I'll hit a few galleries on the way home. You keep working the pigments and fabrics."

"And yet another yippee."

Eve considered it a bonus when an hour of paperwork didn't make her eyes actually bleed. She checked the time, then calculated what she had left.

After casting her non-bleeding eyes to the ceiling, she got another cup of coffee. If she put in thirty more, she could finish. Be done. Have it over.

So she bore down, blocked everything else out, sucked it up, and attacked the last miserable, sticky bunch of it.

When she finished in twenty, she pressed her fingers to her eyes. Still no blood.

She'd emerged victorious. And she deserved a reward. Forget trophies, medals, cash prizes.

She wanted candy.

She got up, walked to her office door, listened. Yeah, still some activity in her bullpen. She eased the door shut, just in case.

After turning her desk chair over, she sat on the floor. With her penknife, she carefully unscrewed the wheeled base, lifted it.

Instead of the jumbo chocolate bar, she stared down at a jumbo smiley face sticker. A big yellow smiley face with googly eyes.

"Son of a bitch!"

Because it looked puffy, she pressed a finger on it.

As the googly eyes shook, it went: "Ha ha ha! Ha ha ha!"

"That's not funny."

Maybe a little funny, she admitted. But now the insidious Candy Thief mocked her. Stealing her candy stash wasn't enough for them now?

She sat a moment, plotting revenge. Coating the next bar with liquid laxative before stashing it came to mind, and felt very satisfying.

But, as lieutenant, she couldn't afford to have anyone in her bullpen suddenly shitting their pants while in the pursuit of justice.

And yet as she stared down at the smiley face, she seriously weighed serve and protect against vengeance.

She'd think about it.

She replaced the wheelbase, righted the chair. To comfort herself, she looked at her cleared desk and told herself good work required no reward.

When she went out to the bullpen, Peabody still manned her desk.

"I'm just waiting for McNab. They busted that major cyber case, so he's pumped. We're going to catch a brew with Callendar and some of the others. I've got what might be a line, I think, on some of the fabric, but it's after hours in Europe."

"Right. The wheelbase on my desk chair was loose."

"Oh? Do you want me to call Maintenance?"

Innocence, Eve wondered, or caginess? Hard to tell.

"No, I fixed it. Ha ha ha."

Peabody's brow creased. "You okay, Dallas?"

"I'm dandy. Like candy. And I'm out."

In more ways than one, she thought as

she walked to the glides.

Remembering the Marriage Rules, she texted Roarke that she had a few stops to make on the way home.

Maybe she should backtrack on her candy hiding places. Try labeling it under something like broccoli in her office AC. No, she realized, reverse strategy. Put it under something tasty.

No one ever filched from her AC when she wasn't there. Because, she understood, in her strange cop world, that would simply be wrong.

Tacos, she considered. Tacos were tasty.

She'd think about it.

As she jogged down the last level, Roarke texted her back.

Running a bit late myself. I've something to clear up before I leave. I'll see you at home.

Satisfied the Marriage Rules held strong, she drove into the early evening insanity of Manhattan traffic.

She programmed in five addresses on the East Side, and wondered why the hell New York had so many art galleries. On her start, stop, wait, walk journey, her choices started with the tiny, with its trio of narrow aisles covered with paintings of cats, dogs, turtles, fish in bowls or tanks, birds in cages or on perches, a snake that looked ready to swallow a whole human.

She learned the display was: A Celebration of Pets.

Her final stop hit the other end of the scale with a two-story space with art carefully spaced on its bright white walls or on sturdy white stands.

Even the floors and the open curve of stairs glittered white. She might have reached for her sunshades, but she'd left them in the car.

Somewhere.

Everyone spoke in hushed tones, as they might in a church. All the staff wore severe black, and if of any length, their hair was pulled tightly into a bun, twist, or knot at the back of their head.

The man in charge, about five-six, had a wide white streak through his ink-black hair. He took Eve's hand, and when she realized he meant to lift it, kiss it, she gave his a hard squeeze and pulled hers back.

He blinked his nut-brown eyes, but kept his smile in place.

"Ms. Dallas."

"Lieutenant Dallas."

"Yes, of course. I'm Hale Vanderling. It's a pleasure to meet you. We're well aware your husband is an esteemed collector of art. Are you perhaps in search of a gift?"

"No. This is police business."

"I see." He might have wiped the smile away with a wet cloth. "Then perhaps we should adjourn to my office."

Maybe she wanted to needle him, but Eve stood her ground. "This shouldn't take long. This is a murder investigation with connection to art."

"How unfortunate."

"Yeah, you could say. We're looking for a male, late twenties to early thirties. An artist, or one who hopes to be. Have you turned away a man in that age range bringing in paintings they hope you'll display, take on commission, buy outright?"

As he stared at her, she wondered how he could breathe with his nostrils that pinched. "We here at Fine Arts do not accept *art* brought in off the street. What we house is most carefully curated for the discerning collector. I believe our vision, and therefore our reputation, is unmatched, as we offer our clients art selected for their elevated tastes."

"So that would be a no. Has anyone attempted to bring in their art for consideration?"

"If such a thing were to be attempted, security would immediately block their entrance. Accepted art is never delivered, hung, or set during open hours so as not to diminish the ambiance for our clients."

"That would also be a no. Has anyone ever offered a large sum of money to get their paintings in the door?"

Somehow he breathed through the pinched nostrils in a long, audible and derisive sniff. "Our art is sacrosanct! Our reputation unblemished! We are not to be *bribed*! We —"

Eve cut him off with a raised hand. "I got the no. Thanks for your time."

The smile popped right back on his face. "If your official duties are complete, I would be delighted to show you through our current collection."

"No thanks. My tastes aren't especially elevated."

Enough of that, she decided as she walked out. Just enough of that for tonight.

She walked back to her car and headed west in vicious crosstown traffic she liked a lot better than Hale Vanderling.

When she finally reached the gates, and those gates opened, the magic happened. The weight of the day, and those to come, didn't drop away, but it lessened. She could take a breath now, be at home now. Be at home with someone who understood her, and that weight, and wanted her anyway.

So when she stopped the car in front of the house, she took that breath.

Summerset and the cat waited when she stepped inside, but she'd expected that. Galahad padded over to ribbon between her legs.

Then stopped, arched his back.

"Look, pal, the fuzzy dog belonged to a wit, and it was before dawn. Deal with it."

He dealt with it by turning his back and ignoring her.

"Late," Summerset observed, "but apparently undamaged."

She gave him a long look, not unlike what the cat had given her.

"I met a guy today who could out-snoot you. So be careful. He could yank your championship belt right off your skinny ass."

"Perhaps I should call the cops."

"Don't look at me." She headed for the

stairs. "I'm over my quota of snoot for one day."

And exhausted with it, he thought as the cat ran up the stairs at her heels. He trusted Roarke, and the cat, would tend to that.

When she turned into her office, Roarke stepped out of his.

"I see I beat you home after all."

"Yeah."

And looking at him, just looking at him, cut the remaining weight in half.

She walked over, wrapped her arms around him, and pressed her face to his shoulder.

"My darling Eve." He pulled her closer, brushed his lips over her hair. "What's all this now?"

"Nothing. Nothing really. I'm just glad to be home. I'm glad you're here, and we're home. Even though I have to go out again later."

"Do we?"

"I need to talk to some of the victim's associates once they hit the stroll. Somebody might have seen him with the suspect."

"Of course." He stroked a hand down her back. "Well, we've time before that." He drew her back to study her face. "Had a day of it, haven't you, Lieutenant?"

"It's like pushing a big-ass boulder up a really steep hill. You're making progress, but it's by inches, and you can't see the top yet."

"We'll take a walk then, out to the pond. A walk and some wine, and you'll tell me about it."

She looked over at her board. "I really need to —"

He used a finger to turn her face back to his. "Will it make a difference if you take a half hour?"

"No. No, it won't make any difference. Someone's going to die tonight, and nothing I do here can stop it."

Now he cupped her face in his hands, kissed her. "Don't carry that, Eve."

"I can't not. I can know, absolutely, it's on him, not me. But I just can't not. So yeah, a walk is good, and wine."

He chose a bottle, pulled the cork. Then handed Eve two glasses.

"Why were you late?" she asked him.

"Ah, some of this, some of that. A couple of boulders reached the top of the hill this afternoon. A company I acquired a few months ago is now successfully restructured. We've broken ground on some new construction on Olympus. And you'll be pleased we've expanded by several acres our coffee plantation in South America. I've my eye on a small enterprise in Costa Rica."

And that, Roarke thought as they walked outside through the atrium, should have given her time to get her thoughts back in order.

"How do you keep it all straight? Coffee here, off-planet stuff there, restructuring somewhere else. I mean, don't you ever get the plantation mixed up with the resort with the company with all the rest?"

"I'd best not. For whatever reason, I was born with a head for, and an instinct for, business — legitimate and otherwise. Just as you were born with a head and instinct for police work."

He lifted her hand, kissed her fingers.

"And so here we are, *a ghrá,* together, never having had to put your head and instincts up against mine."

"So we can walk through an orchard in New York."

"Summerset tells me he made jam from the last of the peaches."

"You make jam from peaches?"

"You can, yes. I believe it's called peach jam."

"I don't mean that, smart-ass. I mean how do you . . . No, I don't want to know how.

That can remain a mystery."

When they crossed over to the pond, sat on the bench, Roarke poured the wine.

"Now then, tell me where your head and instincts took you today."

"Well, there was the porn theater, then the naked guy in the vic's flop before the morgue and the lab, then a conversation with some snotty Frenchwoman about fancy costumes."

"And I thought my day was interesting."

"This is good." She sipped some wine, leaned against him a little. "This is good."

And wound back to the beginning to tell him.

"Clever to consult with Leonardo," Roarke said. "Who — well, other than Harvo — knows fabric better?"

"Peabody's having yippees out of working on that end. And pigment. I thought, if he's so detailed on the costumes, on reproducing them exactly like the ones in the paintings, maybe he's using the same kind of paints. And back when they made their own."

"Clever girl," he murmured. "Vermeer used lapis lazuli for his ultramarine, and quite liberally, though it was very expensive."

"Why the hell didn't I consult with you on this part?"

"I'm no expert on how it's all done. I just know some trivia. Such as finely ground cinnabar made vermillion. Plants and so forth, made different colors. When one's acquiring a painting, however one acquires it, it's helpful to know a bit about it."

"Peabody's got a cousin who paints — natural paints, like from rocks and grass and stuff."

"I'm not a bit surprised, and that should be helpful. I also, hearing all this, agree with your head and instincts. He has the financial resources, it seems, the obsession with details. Why wouldn't he want to replicate using the same paints used by the master? Using commercial products would mean he wasn't as good."

"And he needs to be better, not just as good. I got one more potential hit from a gallery on the Lower East Side. The manager only remembered because he called her a fucking plebeian before he stormed out. But she said it was probably last fall, and she doesn't really remember him well at all — except she thought, maybe, he had long brown hair. Past his shoulders. But, she admits, that could've been someone else."

"Frustrating for you."

"It is all that. The last stop was this asshole who hoped I'd come in to buy a painting for you."

Roarke sipped some wine. "Why would you?"

"Well, yeah. Anyway, that was a bust." She tipped her head to his shoulder. "A lot of it dropped off just getting home. Then more when you were right there. And this was good. But the fucking boulder, Roarke. It's just stuck.

"I know he's a white male. I know his approximate age. He's got dark blue eyes and maybe long brown hair. He's got plenty of time — to paint, to scope out his victims. He's got money, and doesn't likely work in the real world. He's got a vehicle, a place of his own. He's not going to be close to anyone. He doesn't care about people. He's a — what was the word — pedestrian painter who thinks he's a genius.

"And he has a connection upstate."

"You think that because he said he had a show, a successful one, there?"

"That could be bullshit. But why upstate? He could've said anywhere, but he said upstate, so that means something to him. He could've said Paris or East Washington or anywhere. He's got a connection in upstate New York. And maybe he, or someone, paid for him to show his art."

"Another avenue to pursue."

"Yeah, one more." She rose. "I need to get back to the avenues. They make up a damn city at this point."

He rose, walked with her.

"Fabrics, designers, costume places for rich people, galleries, pigments, LCs, and now wealthy areas — it's going to be — upstate."

"I might be able to help with the costume places for rich people."

"How?"

"Perhaps I'm contemplating holding a fancy dress ball, and I'm considering various venues for my own costume, and of course, my lovely wife's. Naturally, I want absolute authenticity. I want guarantees there, and I require recommendations from previous clients."

She stopped a moment, just stopped and stared at him.

"Jesus, that could work. It could work because it's you."

He gave an easy shrug. "It could be fun as well. I haven't had any fun on this one as yet. Not a single finance search for me."

"It could be fun for you to bullshit snotty Frenchwomen, and their ilk, by pretending you're going to have a costume party?"

"Or."

She shook her head. "Uh-uh, no. No way in hell I'm ever wearing some dopey costume."

"Darling, I would never want or expect you to wear the dopey. But."

"Come on." She gave him a light elbow jab. "Just lie. That can be fun for you."

"That's true. It'll have to be tomorrow, of course."

"Tomorrow's good."

She glanced over as they went back inside. "What costume are you going to lie about?"

"Hmm. I might be a dashing highwayman with sword and pistol. Stand and deliver! And you?"

"It'd have to be somebody who kicked ass, and I'm never doing it anyway."

"You'd make a brilliant Grace O'Malley."

She gave him the side-eye. "The Irish pirate?"

"Pirate queen and warrior. You'd wear a sword."

"A sword." It took her a couple of beats, then she shook her head. "No."

Laughing, he gave her hair a tug. "But I had you there for a moment, didn't I then? The warrior and the thief would suit us well enough. But . . ." He kissed her hand again. "We hardly need costumes for that."

"Just lie," Eve repeated as they walked back into her office.

"Let's call it prevaricate."

"Whatever works."

"Now you'll see to your updates. I'll see to a meal."

Once she updated her board, she sat at her command center to write up the interviews she'd conducted on the way home.

As she worked, Roarke set out domed plates. He opened the balcony doors to the evening air, then walked over to study her board.

"The costumes are certainly precise replications. There's considerable skill there, I'd think. And Harvo's list . . . those materials? Both costly and exclusive."

"They had to be. He needs exact."

"With the clothing, yes. But not the faces. Those he settled for a type."

She glanced over before she finished and shut down. "That's right."

"For the girl, it's the eyes, the youth, and

fair skin. For the boy, it's the size, the look of youth, and the confidence. But he needed them, needed live models for whatever reason. Otherwise, he could have simply copied from the paintings themselves."

"His paintings needed life." She crossed to stand beside him. "Their lives."

"So at the bottom, they're a sacrifice to his art. Here now, sit and eat. And you can handle another glass of wine with dinner."

He stepped over, removed the domes.

She saw spaghetti and meatballs. For the second time that evening, she went to him, wrapped around him.

"It's the little things. It's just noodles and balls of meat, but . . ."

"It's comfort."

"It's that." She remembered what Peabody had said. "And it's love. Which reminds me." She stepped back, took the cash out of her pocket. "Thanks for the loan."

He looked at it, at her, then put it in his own pocket. "No problem at all."

Now she laughed, then grabbed his face and kissed him. "Yes, it is. For both of us. But we did it. And now, I'm hungry. I wanted a damn candy bar after I finished the godforsaken paperwork, but I lost it."

"In a bet?"

She gave a: *Ha!* "I'm no Santiago. To the damn Candy Thief." She wound some pasta, stuffed it in. Yes, comfort and love, she thought. And really, really good.

"I hid it inside the wheelbase of my desk chair. It was a prime spot. I mean, who the hell is going to unscrew the wheelbase of a chair for a candy bar?"

"Obviously you."

"Yeah." She forked into a meatball, then studied him. "You're not sneaking into my office and stealing my candy just to keep your hand in, are you?"

"Darling Eve, I'd never deny you candy, now would I?"

"Probably not. And you're too slick to taunt me." She ate, gestured with her fork. "They put a big yellow smiley face in there, with those googly eyes. You know the shaky eyes? It laughed when you pressed it. 'Ha ha ha. Ha ha ha.' "

He laughed — not a mocking *ha ha ha,* but a warm, appreciative roll of it. "You can't deny, it's clever."

"I call it escalation. What do you think about coating the next bar with liquid laxative?"

Wincing, he picked up his wine. "That seems a bit extreme."

"Maybe. Yeah. Probably." She wound more pasta. "I'll think of something."

"No doubt." He passed her some garlic bread. "You could stop hiding candy in your office and just keep some in your pocket."

She just shook her head. "It's a matter of principle. Anyway. A street thief tried to pick my pocket today. How stupid is that?"

Roarke smiled at her. "I'm sure they're sitting on a cot behind bars asking themselves that very question."

"You ever lift from a cop?"

"Of course." He ate some pasta. "It was a matter of principle."

Chapter Thirteen

After dinner, Roarke changed from his ruler-of-a-business-empire suit into casual pants and shirt. When he came back, Eve eyed the black leather jacket he'd added.

"You're wearing the jacket because you're carrying."

"We're going to Times Square in the area of porn theaters and sex shops. So I'm carrying, yes."

She only shrugged as they started out. "Like you never trolled Times Square in the area of porn theaters and sex shops before tonight."

"By the time I came to New York, I didn't have a need to resort to picking pockets."

"It wouldn't have been for need."

Amused, he gave her a cheerful one-arm hug.

"Ah, well, she knows me. If I did so for fun, I'd choose an area where the take would be more profitable. Or at least more challenging."

He crossed to the door. "No doubt if I'd come across you in your uniform, I'd have had other things in mind than your pockets."

She repeated her side-eye. "You think I wouldn't have made you as a street thief, Ace?"

"We'll never know, will we now?"

She stepped out, frowned at the sexy two-seater in screaming red. "That's not my vehicle."

"Would you like it?" Taking her hand, he led her to it.

She just shook her head and got in.

"It's a new model," Roarke told her, and started the engine with its lion's roar. "One that will hit the global market next week."

"What's new?"

"Well now, there's this. Sky mode." He pointed up.

She looked, and saw the sky through the now-transparent roof.

"And this."

The car didn't just shift to vertical. It soared so they were down the drive and over the gates in seconds flat.

"Okay, I'm giving you this and this. Sky

mode's pretty damn frosty, and this car moves."

He landed on the street again as smooth as a man spreading butter on warm bread.

"The battery's the size of my hand, and will fully auto-charge in under seven minutes. We've been working on that for near to three years. She has all the safety features and anti-theft shields of your DLE. And full luxury options."

"In a smaller, sexier package."

"We have a more sedate sedan model, a coupe, and an all-terrain, as well as a mini. We'll introduce vans and trucks after the first of the year."

"That should cover it. How many of those are in the garage back home?"

"Just this and an AT."

"How about limos and those big party buses?"

He glanced over with a smile. "In design at the moment."

"It's a wonder you have time to talk to a couple of street LCs strolling Times Square."

Reaching over, he rubbed a hand over hers. "A man needs his entertainment."

"Work is your entertainment."

"True enough. Aren't I the fortunate one?"

"Stay fortunate and find a lot for this thing. It's going to attract every jacker or booster in a five-mile radius. With the anti-theft shields, I'm going to end up with a pile of dazed thieves on the street and sidewalk."

She took a breath. "Which serves them right, but sticks me with a mountain of paperwork."

"I can personally attest vehicles can be boosted from car parks. Parking lots," he corrected.

"Not as easily as on the street." She looked at him, and his smile. "At least for boosters who don't end up owning the car, and the company that made it."

"All right then."

When he turned into the underground parking of a hotel, and the barricade lifted, she gave him one more look.

"Your hotel."

"Which caters largely to tourists who, for whatever reason, enjoy the madness of Times Square."

Another barricade lifted when he turned toward a reserved slot.

When she got out, Eve noted the roof now

held screaming red, and the windows had gone dark and opaque.

"So no one can see personal items left inside." She nodded. "Pretty slick."

He took her hand. "You should have one. In cop blue."

"Where would I drive something like that?"

"Anywhere you like."

She had to admit, she favored a vehicle that moved. But practicalities ruled.

"The DLE suits me all the way. You knew that when you had it made."

"I did, and it does."

They walked out to what Roarke rightfully called the madness.

"While I didn't scope this area for marks, even for the entertainment, did you ever work the beat here back in your uniform days?"

"No, and thank God. Backed up a few calls, sure, but never worked Times Square on the regular beat."

"I don't think I've ever asked you. Where did you meet Mavis?"

"Downtown, just off Broadway. Pretty sure. And you know what? She was nothing like the one I busted today. That one screamed, whined, tried to clock me. When

I busted Mavis, she was like: 'Hey, got me. You're really good at this. How long have you been on the job? I like your hair.' I'm 'You're under arrest,' and reading her rights. You know, to remain silent. She really just didn't.

"There's nobody like her."

"There isn't, no. And she recognized you."

"Sure, she might've seen me in her territory." She started to shrug, then realized what he meant.

"You mean in an Irish woo-woo way."

"I do."

"Maybe."

Because she had to admit there'd been . . . just something there. On both sides.

"After she got sprung, she hunted me up, told me she had a gig singing at . . . Not the Blue Squirrel, not then. Ah, Artie's Den, Marty's Den — something. It's gone now anyway. It made the Blue Squirrel look like a ballroom. I just couldn't shake her off. I don't know why I finally went."

As they walked, he skimmed a hand over her hair. "You recognized her."

"Maybe. That's the porn place up on the right. I'm looking for Luce and Ansel. Naked guy only had first names, and there's no telling if those are their legal names anyhow."

She stopped by the first LC she spotted. The woman, with a long fall of curly hair as red as Roarke's new toy and a trailing vine of flowers down both bare arms, cocked a hip.

"Look, Handsome might be good for business, but cops aren't. I'm licensed, and I'm working."

"Me, too, so let's make it quick. Bobby Ren. Did you know him?"

"Everybody working the Square knows Bobby, and what happened to him. Why aren't you out catching who killed him instead of hassling me?"

"That's what I'm trying to do. Did you see Bobby last night?"

"Before work. He was wolfing down a burger up the block. Me, I eat light and at home before work. I had a good night. Not a lot of time for socializing. I liked Bobby. Don't know any who didn't."

"Do you know Luce and Ansel?"

"Yeah, yeah. Come on, you're costing me."

Roarke gave her a fifty.

"Okay then, handsome and classy buys some time. They stroll, like literally. This block, up the next, down the next. Cover three or four easy most nights."

"What do they look like?"

"Depends. Luce has a shit-ton of wigs . . ."

Frowning, she trailed off, then nodded.

"No, wait, I saw her before. She's got the short blond going, with the little petal dress. If she had wings, she'd be a fairy. Little white girl, looks like she wouldn't know a cock from an elbow."

"Ansel?"

"Haven't seen him yet. Black guy, smooth looks. Usually wears his hair in twists and does the tips to match whatever he's wearing."

Pausing, she shifted, cocked her other hip.

"Look, they're especially tight with Bobby. Like next thing to family. No way they'd do a thing to hurt him."

"Maybe they saw him leave with whoever did. Thanks."

When Eve turned her back, Roarke slipped the LC another fifty. "The streets can be hard."

She slid it with the first into a slit pocket. "Like I said, you got class, Mr. Gorgeous."

"I know you gave her more," Eve said.

"But you didn't see it, so no paperwork

necessary."

Eve questioned a couple more, got nothing new. Then spotted Luce.

She did look like a fairy in a short dress that looked to be made out of flower petals. With it she wore heeled booties in powder pink.

Eve cut her off, and palmed her badge.

"I'm twenty-one and ten months. I got my license."

"This is about Bobby Ren."

Instantly, baby-blue eyes flooded with tears.

"Here now." Roarke spoke gently, put a hand on her arm. "Why don't we move a bit out of the crowd?"

"Somebody killed him. They just killed him. He didn't hurt anyone. Not never, not ever. He's my friend, and they just killed him."

"I want to find out who killed him. Did you see him last night?"

"Sure I did. Sure. He had his spot. I do the roam, so I saw him a few times. We were going to have breakfast after work, but he didn't show. And I thought . . ."

The sobs came next, and so did a smooth-looking Black man in a gold vest and skin pants, with his dark twists tipped in gold.

"You better move along."

Eve held up her badge. He gave it one snarly look.

"She's not breaking any laws, so leave her alone."

"It's about Bobby." On a fresh sob, Luce threw herself into Ansel's arms.

"I'm primary on his murder investigation. You were friends."

"Best friends," Luce wailed into Ansel's bare chest.

"Here now," Roarke said again, and handed Luce a handkerchief. "There's a café just up there. Why don't we go in, talk a bit?"

"Bar right here," Ansel said, and jerked his head toward it.

"Fine." Eve decided it had to be better than the noise and the bodies on the street.

It wasn't.

Music banged out of the speakers. Asses filled the stools at a bar that looked like it hadn't been properly wiped down since Christmas.

But Roarke nudged them all to a booth. And as if hosting guests, asked politely, "What would you like?"

"I'll take a brew."

Luce sniffled. "A half Zombie. I wouldn't

do a whole one when I'm working."

"I'll see to it."

Eyes narrowed, Ansel watched him go. "What kind of cop's the slick guy?"

"Consultant. Civilian."

"Figures."

"When did you last see Bobby?"

Ansel shrugged, but Eve saw grief rush into his eyes. "I don't know the time. Just passed by him a couple times, I guess. It was a good night, and I figure he was as busy as me. I hit two women who both wanted full service. They paid for a room. I know I wasn't done there until after midnight. I only know that because I made enough to take a break, and Bobby wasn't out, so I figured he was working inside."

"Did you see him after that?"

"No. The customers were a block south, and the hotel another block. If I had to guess, we made the date about ten, ten-thirty. But I'm guessing."

Roarke brought back the drinks.

"How do you get to be a consultant?" Ansel asked him.

"Try to be useful."

"You said you saw Bobby." Eve shifted to Luce.

"Several times, yeah." She took a tentative

sip of her drink. "We were going to have breakfast." She looked at Ansel, gripped his hand. "But he didn't show. We tried tagging him, but it didn't go through. I mean at all."

"Figured his 'link died. Didn't think any more about it." The grief deepened on his face, in his voice. "I should've gone by his place."

"We didn't know." A tear slid down Luce's cheek. She took another small sip.

"It wouldn't have helped him."

Ansel stared at Eve. "We heard somebody painted him fucking blue before they killed him."

"That's not accurate. When did you see him last?" she asked Luce.

"Well, I don't know when exactly. You're going to work till about sunup, so what's the difference? I passed him on my stroll, then he wasn't there, then he was. Then I saw him walking up toward the breakfast place. I figured he wanted a break. I thought maybe I'd take one, since he was. But he wasn't in there, so I went back to work."

"You saw him walking north."

"Ah yeah, I guess."

"With someone?"

"I didn't think so, but maybe."

"Another man?"

"Maybe. There's always a lot of people. It's why we work here."

"If Bobby left his spot," Ansel put in, "and it wasn't for a quick break, it was with a customer. And they'd have to make it worth his while. He's got the prime spot on the block. And he could handle himself, okay? You have to be able to handle yourself."

Ansel stared hard into his brew, then took a long drink. "He'd've left some marks on whoever did him. He'd have made the bastard bleed first."

"Maybe he was with somebody," Luce murmured. "I didn't think of it, but maybe there was a guy with him."

"Do you remember anything about the person with him?"

"I think, yeah, Bobby looked over at him, like they were talking. He was taller than Bobby, but not by much, and Bobby's kind of short. Long hair, I think. Longer than yours," she said to Roarke.

"But there were a lot of people, and I'm quite short, so I didn't really keep track of Bobby. I just thought he was going to grab some coffee.

"But he wasn't."

She looked over at Eve with drenched

eyes. “What’s going to happen to Bobby now?”

“His mother’s making arrangements for him.”

“He loved his mom. We never met her, but he really loved her, and his sister, too. Are they doing like a funeral?”

“I can’t give you her contact, but if you give me yours, I’ll check with her. If she okays it, I’ll let you know the arrangements.”

Luce looked at Ansel, who nodded.

“You can have mine.” Luce gave Eve her ’link number. “It’s Lucille Mulligan and . . .” Ansel nodded again. “Ansel Porter. Can you tell Bobby’s mom we loved him, too? We really did. And we’re sorry?”

“Yes.” Eve slid one of her cards onto the table. “If you think of anything else, contact me.”

“They shouldn’t get away with it,” Luce said. “They shouldn’t get away with killing Bobby.”

“No, they shouldn’t. I’m going to do everything I can to make sure they don’t.”

Luce read the card, then, blue eyes wide, stared at Eve. “Eve Dallas? Like in the vid?”

“Eve Dallas, like with the NYPSD.”

She nudged Roarke. He slid out, then laid two hundred on the table in front of each of them.

Ansel looked at him. "Why?"

"I've lost friends."

When he stepped out with Eve, she said, "I'm not even going to bother."

"Good. They did love him. Clearly."

"We're going to work our way north. Maybe somebody saw more, saw them get into a vehicle."

She tried more LCs, street vendors, the annoying hawkers. And finally hit on one that thought, possibly, they'd seen Bobby turn at Forty-Fifth Street, maybe with some dude.

Since some dude turned out to be the best description, she turned on Forty-Fifth.

"Could've parked along here, or shit, somewhere on Eighth."

"I'm happy to walk as long as you like, but."

"Yeah, but. Party's over down this far out, and the odds of anyone taking note of a couple of guys walking this way or getting into a parked car are slim to none. I'll have uniforms canvass tomorrow. Let's head back."

"You can't feel this was a waste of time."

"It's never a waste. And no. He walked this way with his killer. Killer taller than him — she didn't say tall. Bobby was five-seven. The other LC said around five-eight or -nine. I'm going with about five-eight. Long hair, Luce said. So I'm going with long brown hair.

"And I'm hoping Yancy can get something more solid from the gallery manager. Get enough pieces, you get a picture."

As they headed back to the car, the noise level rose.

Eve saw a man in swim trunks, face mask, and snorkel mime swimming along Broadway for a crowd that found it absolutely hilarious.

"Do you have extreme soundproofing in that hotel of yours?"

"We do have excellent soundproofing. We also have windows that open a few inches. You'd be amazed at how many prefer the noise."

"That's because they probably live on some prairie somewhere and never hear anything but . . . whatever else lives on prairies somewhere."

"Gophers?"

"Okay. Do gophers make sounds?"

"I can't say I've ever actually heard one,

but mammals tend to."

"They're like big, fat squirrels, right? They probably make squirrel sounds, but bigger."

"Well, now I'm curious."

As they walked, he pulled out his PPC, did a search. And came up with a kind of squeaking.

"See, like a rat, and squirrels are furry rats, so gophers are big squirrels." She scrubbed her hands over her face.

"I'm punchy. I'm having my ears assaulted by crazy people everywhere and talking about gophers, so I'm punchy."

They turned into the hotel parking. "But I'm driving."

And while she did, Jonathan Harper Ebersole walked up First Avenue. He felt excited, vindicated, prepared.

He knew the two portraits he'd begun — and he considered the first nearly finished — were his best work. The blind-to-true-talent gallery managers, the ignorant art critics, the shortsighted art collectors would all eat their words.

Galleries would soon vie to show his work. They'd beg. They'd grovel. The critics would shower him with praise, and the collectors would pay — oh, they would pay —

for the privilege of owning a J. H. Ebersole.

He could see it. He could feel it. He could taste it.

Tonight, he would begin a third portrait. He'd thought to wait, to complete the first two before beginning another.

But he simply couldn't. Nothing, he understood now, could replace that energy, that flood of power when he squeezed the life out of the model and into his hands.

Then onto the canvas.

It was that energy that propelled him, that life that streamed into his art.

No, he couldn't wait to begin the next.

And because he couldn't wait, he'd come earlier in the evening than before. But he saw her, the one he'd chosen for a kind of immortality. The shape of her face worked for him, with its softly rounded chin and the slightly bowed mouth.

He could see her with her face cleaned of the layers of makeup, and the luxurious wig covering the ridiculous blue hair. While her skin tone was deeper than he wanted, he could overlook that because she had the long, slender neck he needed.

He caught her eye, and as he'd hoped, she strutted toward him, farther away from the others who worked her trade.

"Looking for some fun, sweet cheeks?"

He shifted so she blocked him from any of her coworkers' prying eyes.

"I'd like to hire you."

"That's what I'm here for, sweets. You pay, we play."

"I want to paint you."

She grinned, ticked her shoulders back and forth. "What color?"

"No, I want to paint your portrait. In my studio."

"If you want me to leave the stroll, it'll cost you."

"I'll give you a thousand now, and another thousand when it's done. It'll take a few hours, and I'll compensate you."

He knew he had her by the way her eyes widened. "Let's see the money."

He had it ready, folded in his pocket. "If you wouldn't mind not counting it here. You could check — discreetly — as we walk to my car."

She ignored that, annoying him, and flipped through the bills. "Where's the car?"

"It's not far. A couple of blocks."

They were standing in one spot too long, so he tried something else.

"If you don't want to do it, I understand.

I'll find another model."

"I didn't say no, did I?" She tucked the bills in a little black purse chained around her waist. And began to walk. "So you're an artist or something."

"I'm an artist." He kept the conversation going as they walked. "I'm working on a series of period pieces. The costume you'll wear is lovely. It's a re-creation of a *chemise en gaulle* from the eighteenth century."

She snorted a laugh. "Listen to you! You're hiring me to wear a costume? You're one strange dude. Not my strangest, but up there. But you're paying me two thousand, so be as strange as you want."

When they reached the lot and his car, she widened her eyes again. "Woo-wee! I guess you can afford the two grand. Guess it pays to paint people."

He relaxed when he had her in the car, and smiled.

"It can, but you have to paint for the love of it first and last. For the love, and the life. You'll help bring this portrait to life."

She settled back as he drove. "For two thousand, honey, I'll give it all the life you want."

Oh, yes, he thought. You'll give me all the life I want.

"I'm Chablis, by the way," she told him.

He had to bite back a laugh at that absurdity, and when a little bubbled out, he added a smile.

"As fate would have it, I have a very nice bottle of Chablis at home. You'll have a glass, if you like, to relax you. It can be tedious to hold a pose. If you hold it well, I'll add a five-hundred-dollar bonus.

"I'm Jonathan."

"Well, Johnny, for five hundred extra, I'll stand on my head."

He laughed as if amused. And could hardly wait to kill her.

She gave him the expected reaction to his home, his studio, and with it, he caught some calculation. No doubt she'd try to squeeze more cash out of him.

He could let her believe she'd succeeded there. After all, it cost him nothing.

She complained about removing her makeup, but complied. She had more cleavage than he wanted, but he'd deal with that, he thought as he adjusted the white silk tie of the frilly white collar.

She smiled at him. "Sure you don't want to have some fun, Johnny?"

"Art first."

"Yeah, you're a strange one all right."

He drew a long curl of the wig down her left shoulder, added the props, set the angle of her arms, her hands.

"Look straight at me," he told her as he began mixing the paint on the palette. "The slightest smile. No, a little less. There, that's fine."

To his pleasure, she held the pose very well. Better, in fact, than either of the others. When she whined for food, he buried his impatience and gave her cheese and flat-bread, a little more wine.

And with that got another full hour.

Though he could have worked on, he knew timing mattered. So a last glass of wine, an invitation to sit and relax.

When he squeezed life out of her unconscious body, he felt that thrill, that indescribable power pour into him.

He used it to put her back in the pose with wire and glue. He'd planned to put her on a board, like the second, but he'd discovered that method was cumbersome.

And since it wasn't a full-length, he dispensed with it.

He drove her back across town, then carried her inside the useless gate of a tiny courtyard of a dignified brownstone.

Working in silence, he propped her against a wall of the house, took time to fluff at the shawl, the white collar.

Then, still riding on the thrill, he drove home to paint.

Chapter Fourteen

When she finally slept, Eve slept deep.

As night slid slowly toward morning, she dreamed.

In the dream and alone, Eve walked into a gallery through air absolutely still, like a breath held. On the white, white walls, paintings hung in ornate gold frames. But they all blurred, their subjects indistinct, as if someone had wiped their hands over the canvases before the paint could dry.

She saw only vague shapes and smeared colors. She heard only the sound of her own bootsteps, echoing as she crossed the white floors.

Light flooded the spaces she walked. It seemed to soak the large rooms joined together by wide, open archways.

Like a museum empty of life.

She passed from one room to another, unsure what she was seeing or why.

She caught a glimpse of a window, wide and crystal clear. And through it, the lights and movement of New York at night streamed. On the sidewalk, LCs, almost like paintings themselves in their bold colors, strutted and strolled. The johns and janes who wanted them took their pick.

And still she heard no sound, not the street chatter, not the lives being raucously lived, not the traffic cruising by.

Only her own bootsteps echoing as she walked alone in the empty space, over pristine white floors inside pristine white walls. Then she turned toward a room as dark as the others were light.

When she stepped through, the lights sprang on, so sudden and bright, it shocked the eyes. She saw the portraits on the facing wall.

She knew them now, the Girl with the pearl, the headscarf, the Boy all in blue with ribbons on his shoes and a feathered hat in his hand. But unlike the paintings she'd studied on-screen, these had the faces of the victims.

Is this how he saw them? she wondered. Is this how he painted them?

As she watched, Leesa's lips twisted into something between a sneer and a pout.

"I had plans," she told Eve. "I was going to be a top level and live as large as it gets. Larger! Then he killed me, and now I'm stuck up here wearing this stupid outfit."

"It blows hard," Eve agreed. "Tell me something I don't know. Or I guess it's tell me something I haven't figured out I know."

"You're the damn cop. I was just trying to make some easy money. He picked me because I was better than the rest of them on the block."

"Oh, bullshit." Inside the elaborate frame, Bobby turned to her. "He picked you because you fit the outfit and your face was close enough to some other dead girl."

"What do you know about it?"

"Because he picked me for the same goddamn reasons. I fit the outfit, and my build is close enough to the dead guy who wore it. Nothing special about it. Just bad luck."

"I was plenty special."

"You were street level just like me, making rent, giving BJs and hand jobs. So what? I liked my life fine. I was having a good night."

He turned to Eve with that. "A pretty good night. I was supposed to have breakfast with friends. I had friends, which is more than she ever had."

"When you're the best, when you're looking down from a penthouse, you don't need friends. And that's where I was going, to the top!"

"Yeah, right. All I wanted was to get solid enough to move to the business of sex, right? And I'd've taken my friends in with me if they'd wanted. Now I'm dead, dressed up like some weird-ass doll. Maybe worse? I'm stuck up here with her, and all she does is whine and bitch, bitch and whine."

"Fuck you, Bobby."

"Being dead means I don't have to fuck you, whining bitch, even if you had enough to pay me."

"If I were alive, I wouldn't do you for triple rate. You're nothing special."

On a sigh, Bobby shook his head. "You dumbass. That's the whole damn point. We weren't special. We just fit the stupid outfit."

"Is this how you want to spend your time now?" Eve wondered. "Bitching at each other?"

Bobby shrugged. "Nothing much else to do. I'm hoping the next one isn't a whiner."

He looked over, as Eve did, to the empty frame beside him.

Then there were more, more empty frames filling the wall.

Waiting to be filled with the dead.

"I'm going to stop him."

"Yeah? Then you'd better wake the hell up and get going on that."

And with another shrug, Bobby shifted and held the pose.

In the dark, in the stillness, Eve woke. When she rolled to her back, the cat gave her a quick jolt by climbing onto her chest. Then sitting, staring.

"You've got weight, pal." She gave his ears a scratch. "Just a dream, more weird than bad. Display time."

5:36

"If Bobby and Leesa hadn't decided to invade my subconscious to bitch at each other, I could've caught another twenty."

Instead, she rolled the cat over, gave him one long head-to-tail stroke, then called for lights at fifty percent.

She got up, got coffee, wondered vaguely what sort of gazillion-level deal Roarke directed in his office with somebody probably somewhere on the other side of the globe.

Then she decided to take that twenty in

the pool doing laps.

Staring at the communicator on the table beside the bed, she wondered if she could will it to stay silent. Since she couldn't, she walked over, picked it up, and took it with her.

She rode the elevator down to the tropical wonder with its crystal-blue water. Then she stripped off her nightshirt.

And dived.

For one moment she let the water take her, let the cool silkiness surround her and smooth away the rough spots from the dream. Then she cut through it, a sharp blade bent on speed. At the wall, she rolled, pushed off, and struck out again.

After ten hard laps, she slowed and varied her strokes for another ten.

Then, breathless, muscles loose, she floated for two more precious minutes.

When she came back upstairs, the cat sprawled and slept, the lights remained at fifty.

Long meeting this morning, she thought, and topped off her swim with a hot, steamy shower. She came out to find the lights on full, breakfast already under warming domes, and the cat sprawled over Roarke's lap.

"There she is. You're officially displaced." He nudged Galahad to the floor. "And you look reasonably rested as well. Come sit, eat."

She sat, lifted a dome to a full Irish.

"That's a way to start the day."

"If you have another long one, you'll need the good start. You were up a bit early," he added as he poured her coffee.

"I had a dream that told me I'd better. Not a nightmare," she said quickly.

"You'll tell me about it."

As they ate, she told him.

"It's not really weird to have victims talking to me that way, but paintings? They were like talking paintings, not weird as much as straight-out creepy. But interesting. Like horror-vid creepy and interesting. I mean sometimes you'll look at a painting of somebody and imagine it talking. But you don't expect it."

He rubbed a hand on her thigh. "Disturbing."

"Yeah, put creepy and interesting together, you get disturbing. So was the way they bitched at each other."

"From what you know of them, it's unlikely they'd have been friendly in life."

"Highly unlikely," she agreed, and eyed

Galahad as he eyed her when she ate some bacon. "They were in the same line of work, but they approached it and life in completely different ways. He had friends and family, she didn't. And clearly, she didn't want them. For him, it was a business, and he made deals, made contacts. For her, it was a way to beat back the competition and end up in a penthouse.

"But . . ."

"But." He buttered a triangle of toast, passed it to her. "What did you learn from it you didn't think you knew?"

"They were both for hire, and that made them easy pickings. That's been clear. But first, they fit the costumes — or close enough. Since the costumes are custom, have to be, he needed them to fit. It couldn't be the other way around. I mean he didn't pick them, then have the costumes made. For all he knew, they'd have moved on by the time the outfits were finished, or they'd turn him down. Too many variables for it to work that way, and he plans too well for all those variables."

She bit into the toast, and wondered why it always tasted better when he buttered it up.

"Second? He took the money back. I

hadn't given that much thought before, and still don't know if it matters. It all matters," she corrected. "I can't see either of them leaving their spot without a down payment. A substantial one. They're not going to just say sure, and drive off with some john, then put a couple hours in wearing a costume unless they had the cash in hand."

Roarke pointed a warning at the casually approaching Galahad, who sat, turned his back, and began to wash.

"And neither had that cash — or any at all?"

"None. Which tells me he kept whatever they'd earned before he hired them, too. And it's not the money, Roarke. The costumes cost a hell of a lot more, but he left those."

"To prove he's — what would it be? — a master of details as well as a gifted artist."

"Exactly. Most likely they'd have kept the money on them. They weren't hired for sex, and they're not going to leave their take somewhere he might try to snatch it back. But he took the time to remove it, all of it."

"What does that tell you?"

"They get nothing from him because they are nothing to him. The money's his. Whatever they brought with them, it's his. I'm betting he's the type who, as a kid, when somebody else had a toy he wanted and he couldn't have, he busted it. Culver and Ren, just objects that suited his requirements.

"And yet."

"He killed them with his hands."

Since he poured her more coffee, she didn't mention that was cop thinking.

"And that matters. He dosed them first — that's cowardice, but it's also making sure. Then he used his hands to kill, and face-to-face. What he took from them — the life people told him his paintings lacked?"

"Transferred to the art," Roarke concluded.

"Okay, Jesus, I didn't say it the first time, but don't blame me if you think like a cop. A good one, too."

"I see it as a man who knows his cop," he corrected. "You dream of living paintings. You see the killer as taking lives to create them."

"I'll let you pass with that." She got up to face her closet. "He might even think it works, and add when this type kills, it brings a sense of power, sexual gratification, a thrill they crave to feel again. But whatever he thinks, killing doesn't make him — who's another one? — like a Rembrandt or whoever. His work's still going to be that word. *Pedestrian.*

"Why does that mean like average anyway? Pedestrians walk. The sidewalks are loaded with pedestrians, and some of them are either way over or way under average."

"Language is fascinating, isn't it?"

She turned because he stood in the doorway of her closet. "Did you forget the cat?"

"I didn't, no. I banished him. Since he refuses to behave in a civilized manner, I put him out of the room and shut the door."

"Yeah, that'll teach him."

She pulled on black trousers, but now with Roarke's judgment looming, went for a jacket in some sort of bluish green, or greenish blue.

"Lovely color," he said easily, and plucked out a shirt in the same color blend, but a couple of shades deeper. "To spare you the anxiety."

"I never had wardrobe anxiety before you."

He just smiled. "You never had real coffee either."

"Okay, that's definitely your point." Since she apparently had a belt the same color as the shirt, she put it on. But went for simple black boots. "Then there's the sex," she added. "It's pretty good."

With the jacket in one hand, she tugged on his tie that perfectly melded the pale blue of his shirt with the deep midnight of his suit.

"Maybe I'll pick out your wardrobe one morning."

"You're welcome to try."

"But that would mean I'd have to get up at zero-Christ-knows-thirty, so you're probably safe. What solar system did you buy before dawn?"

"Oh, only a minute speck on planet Earth. A rather intriguing castle in County Waterford."

She stopped as she reached for her badge. "You bought a castle?"

"One being run as a hotel and in dire need of a good infusion of cash for updates and repair. We should have a look next time we're in Ireland."

"He bought a castle," she muttered.

"And since that deal went smoothly, I was able to contact the costume company in Paris. None of the European venues open before noon — their time, darling. I'll try the others later today. But I can tell you to cross that one off your list."

"You're sure?"

"Very. They were cooperative. While they have created *The Blue Boy* costume twice in the last eighteen months, both were for clients living in Paris — one an actual boy of twelve. And for the Vermeer, they've done one this year, but the client chose a different fabric than what you've got for the jacket, and both different fabrics and colors for the skirt."

"Why couldn't they have just told me that? Never mind. Thanks."

As she hooked on her weapon harness, her communicator signaled.

"Well, fuck and fuck again." She pulled it out of her pocket. "Dallas."

> Dispatch, Dallas, Lieutenant Eve. Report to residence, 212 East Fifth Street. Possible Homicide. Officers on scene.

"Copy. Notify Peabody, Detective Delia. I'm on my way."

"I'll drive you."

"What?" Eve swung on her jacket. "Why?"

"Because I have the time, and will, most likely, be able to identify the painting and artist. I'll get myself to Midtown afterward. I have an early meeting in any case."

"Fine. Let's move."

As she opened the door, the cat sat outside it. As she'd learned before, cats could definitely scowl.

"Don't look at me. He did it."

And Roarke closed the door behind them. "And he did it again, so take your complaints down to Summerset."

"Don't think he won't. Unless he figures out how to open the door first."

"Bloody hell. I wouldn't put it beyond him."

"Another costume," she said as they jogged downstairs. "I'm thinking he may not, probably didn't, have them all made at the same place. They have to have or order the specific fabrics, then . . . Maybe I'm wrong on the costume first. How and why would he choose the size, even more or less, unless he had specific models already picked out?"

"If you don't accuse me of thinking like a cop, I'll tell you what occurs to me. As a consultant."

"Deal. What?"

"You've said he's meticulous, and details matter very much to him. He could calculate the size — height, weight — at least a close approximation of the original models. Using the paintings for his guide. There are programs that would calculate that approximation."

"I like that. I like that," Eve repeated as he drove through the open gates. "It sounds exactly like something he'd do. He can't use the original models, but he needs to get as close as possible. In the end, the people he uses, he kills, are just fillers for the costumes, the canvas.

"And that's how we'll get him. Through the costumes, the paints he uses — because they're going to be what the original artist used, or as close as possible."

"You may have his face later today, from Yancy."

"Yeah, and I'm hoping we do. I was looking for mistakes, and I couldn't really find any. But it was right there, all along. His need to make himself great, by copying the great. Down to shoe ribbons and pearl earrings. That's the mistake.

"We'll track it. We will. Three people are dead, and if we don't track it in time, there'll be another. But we're going to track it, and track him."

"At some point, the LCs on the street will start paying attention, will pass the word on what he's doing and how."

"Some will still fall for it because he

flashes enough money. It's not just LCs working for tricks. It's people who have to pay the rent. You wouldn't have fallen for it." She shifted to him. "Back in Dublin. You're too smart, too cagey to fall for it. But plenty would. We've already got three."

She leaned back. "And he might not stick with LCs. He could pick out a sidewalk sleeper, a street thief, a grifter."

"But you think he will, stick with LCs."

One is one, she thought. Two is a repeat. But three?

Three was a pattern.

"Most street levels have a territory, and stay inside it. They've got routines, basic hours. And you pay for the service. So yeah, they're the easiest to lure."

The day had dawned with a sky so blue, so clear, the buildings looked etched on it. A painting of its own, Eve thought, alive, too, with people walking dogs, or jogging their mile. The street LCs would've called it a night. Some would grab some breakfast, others would go home to sleep.

Some at that level worked by day, maybe taking a shift in Times Square, or haunting dive bars.

The one on East Fifth hadn't, she thought. They'd embraced the night as most did. The night paid better.

When he turned onto East Fifth, Eve saw the squad car.

And noted that the first on scene had had the time and the forethought to put a shield around the body in this nice, quiet neighborhood.

From the position of the shield, the body had been propped or placed inside a small courtyard, against the front wall of the house, on the right-hand side of a set of stairs.

A woman, mixed race, about forty, dark hair clipped up in a messy knot at the back of her head, sat on the steps. She wore blue yoga pants and a sports bra on a well-toned body, with an unzipped hoodie over it.

The two uniforms nodded as Eve held up her badge, and the woman looked up. Eve noted relief when she spotted the badge, then surprise and a gleam of tears when her gaze skipped over to Roarke.

"Roarke." She rose, rushed over and threw her arms around him. "Oh God."

"Natalie. Where are the kids?"

"Sleeping. They're still sleeping. I have to get them up for school, but . . . Carter's coming back from Chicago this afternoon, so I have to . . . God, God."

Pulling back, she swiped at her face. "I'm sorry. I'm sorry. You're Eve Dallas, and I'm so glad you're here. Both of you. There's a woman, and she's dead. She's right over there, just sitting over there."

And shuddering, Natalie looked away from the shield.

"I was going to do some yoga, sun salutations. It gives me a better outlook on the day. And I wanted to water the pots out here first because the sprinklers don't reach them. And when I came out, I saw her. I thought I don't know what."

She took one quick breath before more words tumbled out.

"I shouted because I was so surprised. I went down, and I saw. I saw she was dead. She had a little smile on her face, she's all dressed up in an old-fashioned pink dress, but she was dead.

"I ran back in to check on the kids. I don't know why, I just did. Then I called the police."

"Did you recognize her, Ms. . . ."

"Natalie Hornesby," Roarke provided. "She works for me. A top-flight mechanical engineer."

"Hello. It's good to meet you." Natalie brought a hand to her face. "Oh Jesus, that sounds so wrong. No, no, I don't know her. I don't know what to do. She has terrible bruises on her throat. I could see them."

Eve glanced back as she heard Peabody's hurried clump and, yes, McNab's quick prance along the sidewalk.

"Ms. Hornesby, I see you have security cameras."

"Yes, yes. We bought the house last year, and it came with them."

"Why don't you go inside with my partner, Detective Peabody? You can give her your statement. And show Detective McNab from EDD where you locate your security feed."

"The security feed." Natalie pressed a hand to her temple, rubbed as if at an ache. "Of course. God, of course. I didn't even think."

"Peabody. Take Ms. Hornesby inside, and get her statement. McNab, check the security feed."

"The kids. I don't want them to see . . ."

"Let me know when they have to leave for school. If we're not finished, we'll make sure the shield's in place."

"Thank you. Thanks."

"Ms. Hornesby, what's your connection to the art world?"

She sent Eve a puzzled look. "That's so strange you'd ask. I don't know much of anything about it, but my husband — well, his family — owns the Morganstern Gallery on Third Avenue. Carter, my husband, he's in Chicago now looking at an emerging artist.

"I need to contact him. He needs to know . . . He could get an earlier shuttle home."

"He acquires the art for the gallery?"

"Primarily, yes. I don't understand."

"Detective, if you'd take Ms. Hornesby inside for her statement, and explain what's relevant."

"Yes, sir."

While Peabody and McNab led Natalie inside, Eve walked over to the shield.

"You be the judge, Lieutenant," the first officer began. "We were to be on the lookout for something like this. She sure fits."

He lifted the shield.

She did fit.

"The victim," Eve said for the record as she sealed up, "is a mixed-race female of about thirty. She's been posed to sit with her back against the wall of the residence. Due to visible bruising around the neck, strangulation is apparent cause of death. As the victim's clothing is relevant, she is dressed in a pink gown belted at the waist by what appears to be a scarf that trails down her right hip. The low *V* of the bodice has a white frilled collar tied with a bow, and white cuffs at the wrists. There is a black — shit, what's it? — shawl draped just below the shoulders."

Eve slid a finger along the hairline. "A light brown wig is glued in place at the ears, and a straw-colored hat is glued to the wig. The hat has flowers around the crown and a large feather curved over the left side of the wide brim.

"The eyes are glued open, and the mouth glued into a subtle smile. A brown artist's palette with blobs of paint has been wired to the victim's left forearm, and . . ." She counted. "Seven artist's brushes are in her left hand, wired and glued to hold them in place. Her right hand is posed in a downward position with the fingers slightly curled."

Pausing, she looked up at Roarke. "Do you know what painting she's been mocked up to replicate?"

"I do, yes. It's Vigée Le Brun's *Self-Portrait in a Straw Hat.*"

"Who was he?"

"She. Élisabeth Louise Vigée Le Brun, eighteenth-century France. You'd appreciate that in a field dominated by men, she became the most successful portraitist of her era. From what I can see, the costume is exact, as are the props, down to the color of the daubs of paint on the palette. But, in the portrait, she stands against the backdrop of the sky."

"Not sitting like this?"

"No, the arms are correct, but though it's not a full-length portrait, she's clearly standing."

"He didn't want to bother with a board again. Hard to manage that, so he lowered his standards for convenience this time."

With a nod, she pulled her gauges out of her field kit.

"TOD, oh-three-oh-seven. Officer."

"Kingsly, and Owen, sir."

"Kingsly, do me a favor, go ask Ms. Hornesby what time her sprinklers run." Eve took the pad, started to press the victim's right thumb onto it. "Something under the nail of her index finger. Just something."

She got out microgoggles, angled herself, and carefully scraped under the nail, then studied the result in the clear tube.

"It's fabric. It's a trace, dark gray." Satisfaction ran dark and it ran deep. "Here's a mistake. Here's a fucking mistake. Just a couple threads caught under her nail. He missed that. Had to get there after he glued and wired."

Closing her eyes, she imagined it. "Against his clothes? Maybe, possibly, but . . . More likely scraped across a rug as he was moving her.

"That's it," she murmured, studying the threads as another might have a precious gem. "The way he's glued her fingers, the index is lower, and it catches on a rug — in the transpo. It's glued to the next finger at the first knuckle so it can't really bend. It scraped along the carpet just enough to pick up some trace."

"You're a wonder, Lieutenant."

She shook her head at Roarke.

"Just a cop. Flagged for the lab, flagged for Harvo. Top priority."

She set the sealed tube in her field kit, and once again picked up the Identi-pad.

"Victim is identified as Janette Whithers, age thirty-one, mixed race, street name Chablis. Licensed companion, street level. Avenue B address — most work close to where they live. No marriages, no official cohabs. Parents, married thirty-three years, in Wichita, Kansas. Two siblings, brother age twenty-nine, sister age twenty-six. Kansas residents."

Eve sat back on her heels. "So Chablis came to the big city — she's been here for seven years — and ends up just as dead as the woman who painted herself in this outfit a few centuries ago."

She turned back to Roarke. "How about the face? Is it close to the original?"

"The skin tone's deeper, but the features? It's fairly close, yes, particularly the mouth. Here."

Since he'd already brought up the image, he turned the screen of his PPC so she could see.

"Yeah, yeah, the shape of the face, the mouth. Nose is wrong, and the skin tone. He has to settle on some points."

"Sir? The sprinkler system's timed to run from three-thirty to four every morning."

"Okay, good. She's not wet, but the dress, where it's laying on the ground? It's damp, so the body was placed here after four." She eased a hand behind the body. "Dry on the back, and the ground's pretty dry now. What time was the nine-one-one?"

"We got the call at oh-six-forty-five,

Lieutenant."

"All right. Probably put her here before five. Between four-thirty and five. Quiet neighborhood's going to be quiet."

McNab pranced out in his red-and-blue-checked baggies, long tail of red-tipped blond hair swinging. "Security system went down at oh-four-thirty-six, Dallas. We've got a fifteen-minute jam. It's a decent system. Not one of yours," he said to Roarke.

"No, not one of mine."

"He needed a decent jammer to interrupt the feed for fifteen."

"He can afford decent. So it took him one hour and nineteen minutes after he strangled her to glue, wire, transport." She turned back to the body. "He wouldn't rush it. He's too precise. Still, she's dead, so how long would it take? Forty-five, maybe fifty minutes? Then he needs to load her into the car. Drive here, and you've got to take a few minutes, check for lights, movement, insomniacs before you park — double-park because there's cars on the curb — then jam the feed before you get her out, carry her through the little gate.

"He lives downtown. He could live more Midtown East Side, but . . . New York's loaded with art, but what areas do you associate with art first?"

"The Village," Roarke said, "SoHo, Tribeca."

"That's exactly right. If he doesn't live there, he has a studio there, in the heart of it. Private, no neighbors in the building, with a garage. McNab, you just closed one, right?"

He rubbed his hands together. "A big, fat, juicy one."

"Check with Feeney, and if he clears it, you could start running a search for a single-occupancy building with garage. Upscale, nothing low-rent."

"Got you."

"I don't see him sharing a building, but filter in a multiple occupancy with a unit with a private elevator to a garage. I don't want to miss him by keeping the search too narrow."

"Commercial buildings?"

"Not yet. If we crap out on this, we'll try that."

"I can run a parallel auto-search on commercial without pulling time from the primary."

"You're the e-geek, your call."

She turned to Peabody as her partner

came out. "She's got to get her kids up in about fifteen."

"Contact the morgue, give them the situation with minors on-site. Then tag the sweepers. I need a few more minutes with the body. We need to bag the left arm holding the board thing and the brushes."

She crouched down to work. "The paint's dry, and the brushes look new. We may be able to trace those. He'd need the paint dry enough so it wouldn't run or drip because of the angle of the board. The board, palette, whatever, looks new, too. No other signs of paint on it, no smears, no drops, no wear."

When she'd finished with the body, she stepped back, closed the shield.

"Morgue's on the way, sweepers're tagged."

"Good. She had a place on Avenue B. We'll go check it out. We have to run evidence to the lab. She had some trace fabric threads — under her nail."

"Well, hot shit!"

"I can take it to the lab, Dallas," McNab offered. "And straight to Harvo."

"I've got a car coming," Roarke added. "I can give you a lift there."

"Bonus round!"

"Appreciated, both counts." Eve looked out at the quiet street. "There's a crack now. I can feel it."

"I've got some direction from my cousin on pigments from way back when."

"Good. You can fill me in there after I fill you in on the victim. We've got maybe fifteen hours before he hits again. Let's not waste any of it."

She put the sealed tube in a small evidence bag, sealed and labeled that. "Talk to Dickhead first. He can get bitchy otherwise."

McNab grinned. "He likes me."

"I don't believe I've ever heard anyone say that before in reference to Dickhead. Let Harvo know we'll be in later this morning."

"Here's our ride," Roarke told him as a sleek limo pulled up.

"Oh doggies, fancy time." He did the finger-twiddle thing with Peabody. "I'm off styling."

"Thanks for the help." Eve gave Roarke a look that warned against any and all public displays of affection.

And made him smile. "I'm at your disposal, Lieutenant. I'll let you know if I have luck with the costumes. Good hunting to both of you."

Since she had the scent now, Eve counted on just that.

CHAPTER FIFTEEN

"The victim's Janette Whithers, age thirty-one. She went by Chablis. Street level. She's got family in Kansas. We'll notify later this morning."

"What's the painting?"

"It's one of the self-deals. *Self-Portrait in a Straw Hat,* which she was wearing. A French artist, eighteenth century. But sitting instead of standing like in the original."

"The second victim had to be a bitch to carry on that board."

"She had props glued and wired. Paint-brushes, a palette with blobs of dried paint on it. Lab needs to identify the kind of paint. The brushes looked new to me, and exactly the same as in the painting. I'm betting the palette's real wood, because that's what the artist would have used back then. We've got more to tie in."

"Plus, the fabric trace. I can feel the crack, too."

"Meanwhile Roarke's doing the Roarke thing with the costume vendors. He got enough out of one in Paris already to cross them off from the first two costumes."

"We got a French artist now, and since a self-portrait, a French model."

"That's why the Paris place is back on the list. We'll have this family gallery to hit, the husband to talk to. Someone there rejected this bastard."

"And Yancy's working with the other gallery manager. The crack could widen enough to get us a face. I've got the fabric vendors lined up to knock down. I actually eliminated one before Dispatch contacted."

Peabody added a smug smile. "While sitting on my side of our new partner's desk in my pajamas. It felt really good."

"You can pick that up again when we get to Central."

Seconds after a beater pulled out of it, Eve shoved into a street slot between a mini with four flats and a coupe with a broken windshield.

Peabody studied the graffiti-laced prefab and counted twelve floors.

"You know, I'm getting pretty regular workouts in, but if you tell me she's on the top floor, I might cry. I'll try to do it quietly, but tears will fall."

"She was on two."

"Really!"

Since the building probably hadn't had viable security since some contractor tossed it up, Eve didn't have to master in.

"Would we have walked up twelve flights if?"

Eve glanced toward the pair of elevators. Someone had drawn a damn good example of a skull and crossbones on the one to the right.

"What do you think?" she said as she shoved open the door to the stairwell.

"I think I'm glad she lived on two." Peabody wrinkled her nose. "What do you think that smell is?"

"The moldering corpses of people who took the elevators combined with the sweat and despair of tenants who live above, oh, the fifth floor."

"I hate to say it, but I think you could be right. But look! Aw, somebody painted a rainbow on the wall here."

"What's at the end of that rainbow, Peabody?"

Peabody took a closer look. "It's a big pile of shit. Well, if you ignore that, the rainbow's pretty."

"No one ignores a big pile of shit, Peabody. No one."

Eve shoved open the door on the second floor.

Though the smell wasn't much better, and the street noise reverberated, the hallway was almost preternaturally quiet.

No thumping music, no screaming babies, no blasting entertainment screens or shouted arguments.

"Night shift workers," Eve concluded. "Street LCs."

As they started down the hall, the elevator behind them opened with a grind and thump.

Two women stepped out, one with a pink cloud of hair, the other with a fall of blond with roots done in what Eve thought might be vermillion.

One risked various infections and parasites in her bare feet with a pair of six-inch, shiny black spikes held in one hand. The other wore hers, with the crisscrossing red straps that climbed to her crotch.

Eve held up her badge.

Pink Cloud shrugged. "So what?"

"Chablis. Either of you know her?"

Red Straps added her own shrug. "So what?"

"So, she's dead."

At that the two women looked at each other.

"What the fuck's wrong with people?" Pink Cloud demanded. "I mean what the serious fuck? She kept out of trouble. Did her job, kept clean. How the hell did she get dead?"

"Did you see her last night, on the stroll?"

"Sure, sure, we saw her. Hell, I walked out and down with her. Shit, shit, this is really upsetting, you know? I gotta sit down. My feet are screaming, and I've gotta pee."

"Do you mind if we come in, ask you some questions?"

"Yeah, yeah, come on. Jesus, Chablis! We liked her fine. Marty?"

"Yeah, we liked her fine. And yeah, I'll come with you. We look out for each other when we can," Red Straps told Eve.

They walked down to 205.

Inside, the efficiency apartment was cluttered but clean enough. Pink Cloud tossed the shoes in the general direction of a lumpy sofa and went straight through a door to the bathroom. Shut it.

"Might as well sit down."

"Could we have your name?"

"I don't see why not. Martine — and

that's real — Saxton. This is Traci's place. Traci Barker. Chablis . . . shit, we always called her that."

"We have her legal name." Eve sat, and ignored the three faceless white heads that held wigs. "Did you see Chablis last night?"

"I guess I did. Sure. Yeah, early, and she said something about how she was thinking about heading south when the weather turned, doing at least some of the winter down there. She's got like five years in, no violations. She can get a winter license maybe out of the city."

"How early?"

"I don't know. Not long after I went out. Hell, this blows. It just blows." She looked over as Traci came out.

"You okay?"

"Just not." She swiped at her eyes. "She was nice to me right off when I moved in a couple years ago. Gave me pointers, looked out for me some. You, too, Marty, you looked out for me."

"We look out for each other when we can."

"Ms. Barker, can I get you some water?"

Swiping at more tears, Traci shook her head. "I'm okay. I'll be okay. It's really hitting me, is all."

"What the hell happened to her?"

Eve looked at Marty. "She went with someone."

And Marty snorted. "That's what we do, Slim."

"She went off with the wrong someone."

"She was smart," Traci insisted. "A good judge. And she had a screamer. You know, the button like this." She pulled one out of her pocket. "If you press it twice it lets out a scream you could hear in Hoboken. She told me to get one, and I did. Never had to use it."

"He would have looked right," Eve explained. "Clean, well-dressed. And he'd have offered her cash to leave the stroll and go with him."

Marty shook her head. "Have to be a lot of cash to get her off the stroll. She's good. She can pull in four, maybe five hundred on a good night."

"It would've been enough. He'd have had a vehicle. Did either of you see her walk off the stroll with someone?"

"I only saw her, now that I'm thinking, right after I came on, like I said. We talked for a minute, then I got a customer. He's a regular. Shy Guy," she said to Traci.

"Oh yeah. He always goes for Marty."

"You didn't see her after that?" Eve pressed.

"I guess I didn't. I didn't notice. You kind of keep track for the new ones, but she's got a solid five years."

"She was thinking of applying for the next level," Traci added.

"That's right, I forgot."

"What time did you go out, speak to her?"

"I don't know exactly. She goes out earlier. Mostly I don't head down until later. Maybe, this time of year, close to ten? I don't know. It's not a time thing, it's a hit thing. How many customers you log in a night."

"Did you see or speak to her once you were on the stroll?" Peabody asked Traci.

"Not really. Not after the first little while. I mean, you have to work it, and if you all stick too close, it makes it harder to score a job. But I guess I did see her talking to a guy. You said clean, well-dressed? Like that."

"Can you describe him?"

"Not really except he looked, from the back, like that. Clean, nice clothes. That was when this carload of assholes cruised up, and one's hanging out the window, and he's yelling how I should give him a freebie because he's got such a big cock."

She rolled her teary eyes. "I yelled back how if it's so big I'd have to charge him extra, so instead of getting pissed off or nasty, he laughed. Oh, and that's after Shy Guy came up. I saw him before the car pulled up."

"You didn't see Chablis after that?"

"I didn't. I didn't think about it. Sometimes we take a break together, or walk back home together. Sometimes not. So I didn't think about it."

"So, somewhere around ten you saw her with someone?"

"Yeah, if Marty came on at about ten, I guess it wouldn't have been much after. Maybe like ten-thirty, but it wasn't that long after."

"Okay, thanks."

"Can you tell us what happened to her?"

"He offered her money to pose for him. For a painting. He'll say he's an artist, and he'll pay you to come with him to his studio so he can paint you. A lot of money. That's what we believe. If anyone approaches you like that, don't go. Get the word out on this."

"Be damn sure of that," Marty said.

"You've got a screen there," Eve said as she rose. "Do you ever listen to media reports?"

"Not really."

"Who has time?" Marty added.

"Make time."

"Um, just one thing," Traci said as Eve and Peabody walked to the door. "Chablis, see, she has family in Kansas."

"Yes. We'll notify them this morning."

"It's just that . . ." Traci exchanged a look with Marty. "They think she works in, um, retail. She said it was just easier that way. Maybe you don't have to tell them she didn't."

"We can't lie to them. If questions about how she earned a living don't come up, they don't come up. If they do, we have to stick to the facts."

"Did she have a good relationship with her family?" Peabody asked.

"She really did. She went back every year for Christmas. And she talked to them every couple weeks for sure."

"Then I think, if we have to tell them, it won't matter how she made her living. What will matter to them is she's gone."

"They'll want to bring her back out there." Marty shrugged, but Eve saw tears glaze her eyes. "Maybe you could let us know where to send flowers."

"Chablis liked flowers." Traci gripped Marty's hand. "Can you do that? Can you tell us?"

"Yeah, we can do that. We're sorry for your loss."

When they went out, Peabody glanced back. "Looks like Chablis had a kind of family here, too."

"Why the hell aren't they paying more attention to the media reports?"

"Work all night, sleep most of the day. But I get you. Word needs to spread."

"I'm doing a departmental memo. Sergeants to brief patrol officers to inform street levels on the situation. Some will listen," Eve said as she mastered into Chablis's apartment. "Some won't."

A mirror image of Traci's apartment space-wise. No cheerful clutter here, but a clean, ordered room with a pumpkin-colored sofa hugging a trio of flower-covered pillows. A chair covered in flowers hugging a pumpkin-colored pillow.

A series of candles ranged over a low table, and a floor lamp with tiny colored beads at the hem of the shade stood beside the chair.

Under a small wall screen she'd placed a

small dresser and arranged framed photos on it. Family, Eve noted. Biological and found.

"She made it nice." Peabody nodded at the vase of flowers on the table in the eating area. "Kept it nice."

Eve opened the door to the bathroom and doubted Summerset could have kept it cleaner. She'd wedged a narrow floor-to-ceiling stand against a wall and lined it with skin care, hair care, makeup, and all the rest.

In the closet in the short hallway, clothes hung in careful order. Above them, head forms held wigs. Shoes ran up the side walls on shelves. Eve's feet hurt just looking at them.

"Let's get started."

It didn't take long. Eve found a tablet where the victim kept her calendar — family birthdays clearly marked — as well as her required health checks and screening appointments. The financial records on it proved as organized as the dresser drawers.

"She made a decent living," Eve noted. "Built up some savings. She'd already booked an econ flight to Wichita for December twenty-third, return on Dec twenty-seventh."

"I've got two hundred cash from this

stand — she used it as another dresser. More conservative clothes and winter wear. Stuff I'd say she wore when she went home. Some jewelry, same deal, not like what she kept in the other dresser in the living area."

"Separate lives. We'll keep it that way for her if we can." She checked the time. "God-damn it, what time with the Earth's stupid rotation is it in Kansas?"

"Unless they live on a farm, it's probably too early yet."

"Then let's see if Harvo's worked her magic."

The lab hummed and buzzed. This time, Eve bypassed Berenski and made her way straight to Harvo.

The Queen of Hair and Fiber had gone with bibbed baggies today in a sunny yellow and high-top kicks as pink as Peabody's boots. She stuck with the rainbow hair and added a number of studs to both ears, all connected with thin chains.

Eve imagined having those chains ripping through earlobes during a street fight, and nearly shuddered.

"You guys are quick." Harvo took a long pull from a carry-around bottle filled with something green.

Eve suppressed another shudder.

"My beauties and I are, too."

"You identified the fiber?"

Harvo fluffed her rainbow hair. "Was there any doubt?"

"Not even a smidge," Peabody told her.

"*Smidge.* Good word. You brought me less than a smidge, but enough. You've got premium wool — hundred percent — Wilton Wool, dyed in #15-B, which is basically dark gray. Loomed this way, it's used primarily in carpets and floor mats for ultra-luxury vehicles. The vehicle make is going to have its own fancy name for the color."

"Can you give us the makes, the models?"

"You bet your fine, toned asses." She swiveled, tickled some keys. "Sent. Just to add, you can also — with the ultras — option it if it's not standard. FYI? Roarke uses this material in some of his ultra-luxury models."

"I fail to be surprised."

"It's going to be plush, baby, lush and plush. Soft, dense. Nothing you'd want to spring for in a family ride with little critters munching cookies in the back."

"What about vans?"

"Vans?"

"Or ATs with large cargo areas?"

"Don't see why not. You got the moolah, you get what you want.

"The chief took the paint dabs. He's a little backed up, but he'll get that going inside an hour."

Harvo paused, smiled. "Just a heads-up on that. Give him a little time and space, quicker and less bitchy results."

"Noted."

"I'm just starting on the costume, so also a little time and space, but I eyeballed it already. You've got silk — I'll be getting specifics, but the dress is silk, and really fine material. Human hair for the wig. Paintbrushes —"

"You took the paintbrushes?"

"Hair, Dallas. They're hog hair, and they're attached to the handle with quills — natural feather quills. Struck me all kinds of weird, so I did a little poking. They didn't use metal for the collar deal — ah, it's called a ferrule — until into the nineteenth century."

"He needed eighteenth. I bet you can't pop into your average art supply and pick up seven of those — and seven that precisely match the ones in the painting."

"No, you cannot." Harvo grinned. "Frosty, huh?"

"It ranks frosty. Somebody made them for him, made them custom. This is excellent data, Harvo. It's all ego, Peabody. We're going to wrap him up in his own ego. Appreciation galore," she said to Harvo. "Let's move."

"I can start on brush makers." Peabody jogged to keep up with Eve's long stride. "Or the vehicles."

"Take the brushes. You're more likely to speak that language. You've got brushes, pigments, fabrics. Pigments mean you tag Dickhead in another hour or so to see where he is on those."

"There goes my yippee."

"Cross-reference any purchases or shipments. If and when Roarke narrows or hits on the costumes, we have that. I'll take the carpet. Head back now. I'm going to make a quick stop at the morgue."

"Do you think Morris will have anything new?"

"It only takes one thing."

"The crack's getting wider and wider."

Wrap him in his own ego, Eve thought again. Because that was his big mistake. His egotistical certainty that he could do what those famed artists had done, but better.

Every freaking detail of their work, but better.

Morris stood over the dead with his protective cloak over a forest-green suit. The shirt reminded Eve of the gold jacket the first victim had died wearing. His tie carried minute checks of both colors, and cords of both wove through the braid rounded into a knot high on the top of his head.

The music, a woman singing in what Eve thought might be French, sounded both sad and defiant.

"The late, great Édith Piaf," Morris said. "She sings she regrets nothing. I hope our victim could say the same."

"I bet she regrets going with the son of a bitch who put her on your table."

"Up until then." He walked over to wash his hands, got them both a cold tube. "She was in good health, no signs of alcohol or illegals abuse. She broke her left arm, about the age of twelve. It healed well. I have her street name as Chablis."

"That's right."

"It may have been for his amusement to have served her Chablis. Six ounces at about eleven, another four at about two, along with some rosemary and sea salt flatbread crackers and Saint-Nectaire."

"What the hell is that last thing?"

"Cheese. A soft French cheese." He touched a hand to Chablis's shoulder. "I hope she enjoyed it."

"Is it common? The cheese? You know, like cheddar or mozzarella?"

"My computer tells me it's a washed-rind cheese from the Auvergne region in France. Ah . . ."

He turned, called it up again. "Here we are. An uncooked, pressed cheese produced from Salers cow's milk.

"I have no idea what sort of cow that might be," he added, "but apparently they graze on the volcanic pastures of that region, which gives the cheese its flavor."

"How many kinds of cows are there? Too many," she decided instantly. "Who decided in the first place to grab a cow by the tits and squeeze out milk? Then drink what they squeezed out of a cow's tits. Then hey, let's make cheese from what we squeezed out of a cow's tits. What kind of mind goes there?"

His smile filled with amused affection. "They do the same with goats."

"I don't want to think about it. I like cheese. How am I supposed to eat cheese if I think about it? Salers cows. French cows.

You probably can't pick up that kind of thing at your neighborhood twenty-four/seven."

"Doubtful. More likely a fromagerie or high-end market."

"Fromagerie," she muttered.

"A cheese shop."

"Yeah, yeah, I got it." French cheese, French wine, French painting. Yeah, they'd hit Paris again on the costume.

"When did he dose her?"

"Her last glass of wine he laced with the same barbiturate mix as your other two victims. It would have been around three this morning."

He studied Eve as she studied the body. "You don't need any of this at this point."

"No. Well, the cheese gives me something else to look for. It's a detail. It's specific. We're picking up solid details this morning."

"You came for those, yes. But first, Dallas, you came for respect."

Sighing, she rubbed at the back of her neck.

"We didn't have enough, Morris. I hope we do now, but didn't have enough to save her from this. She had friends. She had family."

Now, Eve shoved at her hair. "Her family doesn't know what she did for a living. She told them she worked in retail. I don't know if any of them will come — they live in Kansas — but they'll want to bring her home. She talked to them regularly. She went home every Christmas. There's a photo of her with her family in front of a big Christmas tree on her dresser."

"If they come, or simply contact me for arrangements, I won't mention her work. I have her now, Dallas. Go, do your work, and I'll see to her."

"Thanks." At the door, she paused. "I really hope we don't have this conversation over another tomorrow."

But when she walked back down the white tunnel, she saw Chablis on the slab under Morris's compassionate hands.

And she saw her dressed in rosy pink silk, with a straw hat, standing in an ornate frame against a white wall.

She knew, if she couldn't bring those details together, someone else would fill a fourth.

Chapter Sixteen

Eve caught the scent of chocolate before she turned into Homicide. And saw Nadine Furst, camera ready in a red dress with a short, matching jacket, perched on the corner of Jenkinson's desk.

She momentarily blocked Eve's view of the tie. But when Nadine shifted, rose, Eve saw cows.

It just had to be cows.

Dozens of cows standing unnaturally on their hind legs, their front hooves joined as they spiraled down the atomic green field.

"That's just sick. It's sick."

"Not sick cows, boss. Happy cows."

"Sick." She held up a hand before Nadine could speak. "Peabody, does your family make cheese?"

"Yeah, sure."

"Do you know anything about Salers cows?"

"No. Why?"

"Later. Nadine, since you're good at your job, you know I've got three bodies. Since I'm good at mine, I don't have time to talk to you."

"Then I'll start the conversation," she said, and followed Eve into her office. "Plus, I brought you a brownie."

"I don't have time for a brownie either."

"Then save it for later." Nadine reached into her elephant-sized bag, took out a small pink box that smelled like heaven wrapped in glory.

"I do know you've got three bodies. We've reported. I've hit it pretty hard. I want to hit it harder, and I will."

Now, very much at home, Nadine eased a hip on Eve's desk as she had on Jenkinson's.

"It might help get the word out to street levels. It's clear they're being targeted, and you've already considered using the media for that."

On her list, Eve thought, and she could adjust priority rank, since Nadine was currently sitting on her desk anyway.

"If you can give me any details," Nadine continued, "anything I can air that gets through." She lifted both hands. "We're both trying to save lives here, Dallas."

Eve looked at her board. She'd be putting another victim on it now.

She walked to her AutoChef, programmed coffee for both of them.

"A source from the NYPSD states we believe the suspect is a white male between twenty-five and thirty. We believe he approaches a street-level licensed companion with the offer to hire them for the purpose of posing as a model for a painting. We believe he offers them a substantial amount of cash in order to persuade them to leave with him."

Nadine sat, absorbed. "That's it? That's all you can give me?"

Eve considered. "We believe the suspect is a failed artist whose substandard work has been rejected by multiple galleries in the city."

Nadine angled her head; her sharp green eyes narrowed. "You want to insult him. I can get behind that."

"Yeah, I do. Pissed-off psychopaths make more mistakes."

"Has he made any yet? I can hold it. You know I'll hold it until you tell me otherwise."

And since she did, Eve said, "Hold it. His precision and obsessive attention to details are mistakes. They're adding up. He's got money. He's got a place — a home, a studio — that costs money. He's got what Harvo calls ultra transportation."

Nadine pursed her perfectly dyed red lips. "I'm seeing a spoiled rich kid who's recreating famous portraits, then killing the models because nobody recognizes his genius."

"Close enough."

"I have some contacts on the stroll."

"I'm sending out a memo for patrols to spread the warnings."

"Good, but some might listen to me before they listen to a cop. If it's a substantial amount of money, it's a tough turndown."

"Talk to them, that's fine. That's good. If you go out tonight, don't go alone. He's got a pattern, but that doesn't mean he won't change it and go after a well-known reporter, especially one who's reported his work's crappy."

"Jake'll tag along. He's trying out Mavis's studio right now. I haven't had time to go by and see it since they finished. How is it?"

"It's . . . flat-out amazing."

"I'll get there soon. And I'll get out of your way now. Eat your brownie," Nadine added as she walked out. "You look like you could use it."

She eyed the little pink box. Maybe she could use it, but not now. Instead, she added Janette Whithers/Chablis to her board.

She updated board and book and, still ignoring the brownie, got more coffee. Sitting, she wrote and sent out the memo.

Maybe, she thought, just maybe it would do some good.

She brought up Harvo's list of vehicles.

More makes and models than she'd hoped for, but she could eliminate sedans, two-seaters, compacts, sports cars. He probably had a sports car, Eve decided. Might even use that for the pickup. But for the body dump, he'd need a van or an all-terrain with enough cargo area.

So she rubbed her eyes, rolled her shoulders, and began.

For a city with solid public transportation, New Yorkers sure as hell liked their luxury vehicles, she discovered.

As someone who drove one — despite its dead-ordinary looks, her DLE had all the chimes — she couldn't bitch.

At least not out loud.

Add to that, she'd married a man who had

a garage full of them. And as she skimmed the long, long list of Harvo's ultras, cross-checked with ownership, she deliberately refused to count the number registered to Roarke personally or any of his businesses.

Then again, she doubted she knew the names of all of his businesses.

She eliminated what she did know, filtered out all but vans, minivans, all-terrains. And noted she still had her work cut out for her.

Roarke wasn't the only one, by far, who had vehicles registered to businesses. The killer might have the same. He had money, she considered. Someone, at some point, had to have earned it.

For individuals, she fined it down to registrations with addresses in the areas she'd deemed most likely. But for businesses, organizations, corporations, she accepted she had to spread it out. All boroughs, and into New Jersey and Connecticut.

"Hell," she muttered. "They could have their HQ any-fucking-where. Start here," she told herself.

She got up, got more coffee. Studied the board, walked to the window.

Roarke had a garage full, she thought again.

"Computer, with current data, run a search on individuals or businesses with multiple vehicles registered in New York State, New Jersey, and Connecticut."

Acknowledged. Working . . .

He wants to impress, she thought. He doesn't make an impression, but he wants to. Fancy cars. Something big enough to cart bodies around, sure, but doesn't he want some shiny toy?

Search complete.

As she walked back to her desk, her 'link signaled.

"Dallas."

"Lieutenant, it's Natalie Hornesby. Carter — my husband's flight's delayed. He booked an earlier one as soon as I told him what happened, and he wanted to speak with you, see if he could help. But there's a delay, and I told him I'd let you know. Storms in Chicago, so he might be stuck there another hour or two."

"Thanks for letting me know. If he could contact me as soon as he arrives. Is there anyone else I could talk to about rejected art?"

"Carter really is the one, and his assistant's with him. I understand as much about Carter's work as he does mine, which is not a lot. The gallery's open — or will be at eleven — and the staff on duty would absolutely cooperate. But they'd refer any artist who came in to Carter or his assistant."

She could try tugging at his memory over the 'link. But Yancy would be tugging on a verified witness's memory.

"Understood. Please have him contact me as soon as possible. If his flight's delayed again, I'd like to arrange to interview him via 'link."

"If his flight's delayed again, I think he might explode. He's upset about what happened, about not being here when it did. He'll get in touch as soon as he's back. I promise."

A few more hours for that, she thought as she sat again. A couple more, at least, for Yancy. She wanted a face. But she'd push on getting a name.

Her 'link signaled again, and read out as Brendita Klein.

"Lieutenant Dallas. Ms. Klein, thank you for getting back to me."

"No problem at all, since I'm sitting at a

sidewalk table in Barcelona having a lovely glass of wine."

The sturdy-looking woman with flyaway blond hair and huge sunshades lifted a glass of red. "But I don't know how I can help you."

"An artist you rejected," Eve began. "A white male, twenty-five to thirty."

Brendita tipped down the sunshades to reveal hazy green eyes full of humor. "My dear lieutenant, imagine in my decades at the gallery how long that list runs."

"Long brown hair, dark blue eyes. Sometime within the last year or two. Bad attitude."

"So many own that."

"About five-eight, probably well-dressed. He does portraits, not very well according to others I've interviewed, and claimed he had a successful show upstate."

"All right, all right." Lips pursed, Brendita nudged her sunshades back in place, sipped more wine. "I'm getting a glimmer."

"Ms. Klein, we believe this man has killed three people. Anything you remember could help us stop him."

"But no pressure," Brendita murmured, and pushed at her flyaway hair. "I know, Annie, but . . . My wife's reminding me I bitched to her about someone like this. But I just can't see him. Young, yes, and as unimpressive as his work."

"Did he give you his name, a card, a contact?"

"No, no, I'm nearly sure there. What I have are vague impressions at best."

"I'll take them."

"Family money, as he certainly hadn't earned it himself. Arrogance, ego — extreme. Anger, though he was careful not to let it fly too high. It was in there. The eyes — oddly, I couldn't swear to the color, but there was something missing in them. Again, like the paintings."

Pausing, she shook her head. "I'm sorry, it's true my brain's on extended vacation, but beyond that he didn't impress, and I think it was months ago when he last came in. If I'm even thinking of the right person. The glimmer's mostly from the bragging about the successful showing, and . . ."

"Something else."

"He said something else that struck me. What the hell was it. What?" she looked away from the screen again. "That's right, I did. My wife's reminding me during my bitching I called him a mama's boy."

"Why?"

"Digging back," she muttered, "it seems to me — and again, it was months ago, maybe longer, but it seems to me he said something like his mother could buy the gallery and everything in it before he made his dramatic exit."

Eve noted down *mama's boy,* highlighted it.

"I wish I could remember more, but I honestly can't call up his face, or the paintings he brought in."

Eve pushed a bit more, but Brendita spoke the truth. She simply didn't remember more.

After the conversation, Eve looked at her notes. And tapped a finger on *mama's boy.*

"That's one more thing," she murmured. "One more piece. And it'll fit somewhere."

But for now, she shifted focus and looked over the search results on vehicles.

"Jesus, people, take the subway, ride a bus, hail a cab."

She shook off annoyance and dug in.

Some businesses had a fleet, some a handful. She couldn't discount either. The individuals ranged from two to a dozen or more, but most hit the two to three range.

She got up, paced.

"He doesn't work, not a job. No workweek

for him. He's an artist, and I swear he's living high on someone else's money. Family money hits for me, too. Mama's money — and he's the spoiled son. So why would he want a van or a cargo AT? He's young, single — has to be single. He's fucking important in his own mind."

She actively yearned for fifteen minutes to put her feet up, close her eyes, and think. But time, and the empty frame of her dream, pushed her to keep pacing.

"Computer, filter results for cargo all-terrains, vans, minivans purchased within the last two years."

Acknowledged. Working . . .

"It's probably less," she muttered to herself. "But we can't go too narrow. He's thought about this for a while, planned it out, detail by detail. Had to do at least a little research on the wardrobes, the props. Had to."

She sat again, considered giving her unit a little punch. "Come on, come on, give me something."

Search complete.

Just as she leaned forward, she heard

footsteps. And recognizing the stride, got to her feet.

"Commander," she said when Whitney filled her doorway.

"Lieutenant. I didn't want you to take the time to come to me."

He stepped in, a big man, broad in the shoulders, dark skin, dark eyes, close-cropped dark hair sprinkled with gray. Like his suit, command fit him well.

"I haven't requested an oral report." He glanced toward her board. "But now there are three, and three's the magic number."

"Yes, sir. We could request federal assistance. I've discounted that, for now, as in a matter of hours, there could be a fourth. We're pursuing multiple viable angles. I don't want to take time away from those pursuits to spend some of these vital hours briefing the FBI."

"You're convinced he'll hit again tonight?"

"We can't know how many he's planned for. We can't risk he'd only planned for three."

"Agreed. And if those angles don't pay off in time, and he kills another?" Still watching her, he gestured toward her AutoChef.

"Sir."

While she programmed coffee for him, he

shifted to scan her screen. And saw the pink box.

"Is that a brownie?"

"Yes, sir. Would you like it?"

"More than I can say, but she'd know. She always does. Anna has a way."

He shook his head over his wife's *ways,* and settled for the coffee.

"No one wants another life taken," he continued. "God knows we don't want a serial loose in New York. The media's heating up. They're calling him The Artist."

Well, of course they were, Eve thought.

"He'll love that. He'll celebrate that."

She'd have paced if Whitney hadn't taken up half her pacing space.

"It's acknowledgment, adulation. But I believe the media can help. The more warned and informed, the less likely the next target is to go with him. I've covered all three victims' financials. And all three earned, as a rule, three to five hundred a night. All three could and did hit on bigger nights, but that's the general range. To get them to leave with him, it had to be more than their nightly take. So all three went. But they weren't warned and informed."

He could overrule her, and she'd accept that. She expected he'd temper that with a deadline. Though she knew he'd have read all her reports, she made her case.

"I know what he is, Commander. He's rich, he's spoiled, and he's a second-rate artist at best. I lean toward family money and an indulgent mother. He drives a luxury vehicle, he lives, in my opinion, in an area from Tribeca up to the Village — possibly Chelsea. A private home — and it's a luxury because he can't settle for less. It has to have a garage or a place for his transportation. That has to be on-site.

"He's single, around thirty, he's white. He wants to make an impression, but he doesn't. People don't remember him well, or remember his work. He sees himself as great, as not just a master, but better than those who earned that title over the centuries.

"He's taken time, a lot of time, trouble, expense to create the art he's killing for. The time, trouble, and expense to have the costumes replicated. Perfectly, every single detail. French and Italian silks and satins, handmade Irish lace — and all of that's being tracked. We will find who made the costumes, and find him.

"His mistake is that need for exacting details. Not the victims, they just have to fit, have to be close enough. They're nothing but a vehicle. He takes their lives because his work lacks it.

"But the rest?" she continued as Whitney drank his coffee and watched her. "It has to be just right, otherwise he can't prove he's better than the artist he copies. The wigs, the hats, the pigments used. The glue and wires to hold the pose exactly. The paintbrushes he —"

She turned on her heel, stared at the brushes on her copy of the original, on the crime scene shot.

"Son of a bitch! Wait!"

She ran out of the office and straight to Peabody's desk. "The paintbrushes. Where's an eighteenth-century French artist going to get the brushes?"

"I —"

"France! They have to be exact. Focus on people or companies who make custom brushes in France. Forget New York, forget the rest. France. The first one, the earring girl. Vermeer. Dutch, right? Where would she have gotten the outfit?"

She shoved at her hair. "The material — on the vic — French again. But people traveled back then. They traded. But somebody had to make it — the original."

"She might have made it herself."

"Maybe, but somebody had to make it." Pacing the bullpen, she yanked out her 'link and tagged Roarke. "Tell me if you don't have time and I'll put someone else on it."

"I'll make time. What am I making it for?"

"The Dutch painter, that one. Where the hell are Dutch people from?"

"The Netherlands, darling."

"Okay, there. Costumes, high-end from there for that one. The second guy, Brit, right? So —"

"I'm following you. It'll take some time. I'll get back to you."

She shoved the 'link back in her pocket. "That's how he does it. Exact, precise. Duplicate as close as possible to the original, and that spreads it out. No big multiple orders from one source.

"He's not going to have them shipped. He can't demand any adjustments, can't see and feel them at the source if they ship them. He goes there to vet them, approve them, bring them home. Private shuttle."

She turned. "Detective Carmichael, start checking for private shuttles from New York to the Netherlands, to England, to France, most likely one trip for all three. Start with all three. There may be other locations, but those three.

"Shit, Ireland. Add Ireland, he had the lace made there.

"Detective Hat, luxury hotels — shit, he may have a second home, but luxury hotels in those four locations. Impressions," she muttered. "If he'd had an accent, they'd remember that. You're looking for an American, from New York who stayed in all four locations, no more than a few nights in each, and all within . . ."

She hissed. "Damn it, can't afford to narrow it. The last two years. Can't find that, work it with three. Bonus round for two trips. Detective Trueheart, are you clear?"

"I can be, sir."

"Peabody's got a list of fabrics, yardage included. I want to know if an American man, late twenties, white, came in personally to select those fabrics. Same time period. Start with the three locations.

"Peabody."

"Working on it. He'd have picked up the brushes. Dallas, the pigments."

"He got them over there. In Europe. Baxter, New York, fancy cheese places. Same description. West Side up to Chelsea. Saint-Nectaire cheese."

"Feeling pretty left out over here, aren't

we, partner?"

"Sad and lonely," Reineke agreed.

"You're clear?"

"Clear enough. You bag this fucker or the feds are going to want a piece. I say you bag him first."

"I have a mighty list of luxury vehicles. I'm tossing you registrations in Connecticut and New Jersey. If registered to a company, locate the HQ and add that to the search."

She stuffed her hands in her pockets. "We cross-check it all. McNab's doing a search on potential residences, so add him into that. This fucker's in there, he's in all of this, and he's going to show up. We're going to bag him.

"Detective Yancy's working with a witness on his face," she added. "I've got another coming in who may help with that."

She pulled out a hand, checked the time. Let herself curse mentally.

"We've got maybe nine hours before he will likely pick up his next victim. I want his ass in the box first. Hunt him down."

She turned, saw Whitney, and realized she'd completely forgotten him. "Sir, I apologize."

"For doing your job? Unnecessary. Nine hours, you said. How many before the kill?"

"Fourteen, sir, maybe less."

"You've got twelve. You're cleared for overtime." He nodded at the bullpen. "Get it done," he said, and walked out.

"Be prepared for a briefing this afternoon on a takedown op. You heard the commander. Get it done."

He'd show up, she thought as she went back to her office. His ego would wrap him just as tight as she would.

She got more coffee, sat, then sent the data on the vehicles to Jenkinson and Reineke.

And eyed the pink box.

As Eve opened it, she heard someone coming again. Heels.

"What now?"

Reo walked in on those heels, ones of bold scarlet that conflicted with the all-business navy suit.

Eve supposed that was intentional.

"I've got your international warrants. It wasn't easy, and it wasn't pretty, but I got them."

Maybe not necessary now, Eve thought (but didn't say), and still handy. "I may need one for the Netherlands."

Reo just sighed. "I'd hit you, but you'd hit back harder."

"Yeah, I would."

Reo narrowed her eyes. "That's some brownie. Did I mention how much time and sweat getting those warrants took?"

Eve broke the brownie in half, offered one. "I'm going to need a search, seize, and arrest warrant, too."

"You got him? I heard he hit again this morning. Court recessed early."

"Not yet, but we will. Too many good, solid lines to tug not to. And I really have to get tugging."

"Let me get coffee in a go-cup and I'm gone."

"Fine."

Reo stepped over, programmed. "I'm walking over to see the new house."

"You're walking over there in those shoes?"

Reo hitched the strap of her briefcase more securely on her shoulder. Took the go-cup in one hand, tried a nibble of the half a brownie with the other.

"You've got your superpowers, I've got mine. Tag me when you've got a name and location."

Eve added, eliminated, cross-checked. Little by little, as time ticked by, the list whittled down.

When her desk 'link signaled, she saw Carter Morganstern on the display and snatched it up.

"Mr. Morganstern, this is Lieutenant Dallas, thanks for getting back to me."

"I just got in. Jesus Christ, somebody put a dead woman in my front yard with my wife and kids alone in the house!"

"Yes, sir. I need —"

"I wasn't here, then I couldn't get home. We have security. I don't know how this could happen."

"I'll have answers for you. Mr. Morganstern —"

"Nat says you're married to her boss."

"That's correct. I'm also the primary investigator in this incident."

"Why would somebody kill somebody and leave her at my house?"

"I believe you were targeted because of your gallery. Mr. Morganstern, please," she said as he started to interrupt again, "I understand this is very stressful."

"That doesn't begin to cover the day I've had so far. I'm sorry." She heard him take a breath. "I'm sorry," he repeated. "Our gallery? My God, did she work for us? I haven't checked all the —"

"No, sir. If you'd come into Central, I can

explain. We could use your help. We believe the person responsible hoped your gallery would take his art, and was refused."

"Well, Christ, that happens several times a week. I don't see how . . . I'm apologizing again. Yes, I'll come in."

"As soon as possible, please. Cop Central, Homicide level, Lieutenant Dallas. I'll arrange for a visitor's pass."

"I'll come in now. I need those answers."

"Thank you."

She heard Peabody coming.

"Carter Morganstern's coming in now. Get him a visitor's pass."

"Okay. Dallas, I think I've got something on the brushes. The owner — it's a shop in Paris — isn't in. He's at a party. He and his wife's fiftieth anniversary party. But the woman who answered the 'link — I caught her right before they closed — said she thinks she remembers Monsieur Cabot working on the brushes. She remembers he had a print of the painting in his workshop because it's one of her favorites."

"Did she see the guy who ordered, picked them up?"

"She thinks so, but she's vague. It was, she thinks, months ago. But an American artist. She checked the records for the last six months. It's as far as she could go back. The owner needs to access anything prior. She didn't find the order, or a payment. But!"

Peabody held up two fingers, one on each hand and shook them. "She's seen the vid! She's in France and she saw the vid! She got invested because of that, I think. She's going to contact the owner, tell him it's vitally important. She'll give him my contact.

"It's him, Dallas. It has to be."

"It's going to be. Good work. Get the visitor's pass. Help Trueheart tug on fabric until Morganstern gets here."

"Those companies are going to shut down soon, if they haven't already."

"Tug fast, and let me know when Morganstern gets here. We've got momentum. We're not going to lose it."

She checked the time. Got more coffee. Got back to work.

Chapter Seventeen

After sleeping the sleep of the proud, Jonathan Harper Ebersole enjoyed brunch on his rooftop garden. One of his three house droids tended it, kept it lush year-round. From first frost to spring, the retractable glass shielded the plants and dwarf trees from the cold.

But Jonathan liked it best when that protection was tucked away and nothing separated him from his lofty view of his part of the city.

He liked to imagine people looking up from the street, or out through their windows, envying him, wondering about him, admiring him.

Now and again he brought an easel up to paint *en plein air,* and basked in the knowledge he could be seen at his art, and envied all the more.

He would rather be envied than loved.

Love, from his view, demanded time, attention, reactions he didn't care to spend energy on.

Comfortable in the warm September sun, he sipped his cappuccino, boosted with a double shot of espresso, and the frittata prepared by the droid who dealt with such things.

With a sense of pride, with a quickening thrill, he scanned the media reports as he ate. He hadn't expected such notoriety! Not before he revealed his portrait series.

After all, the models he'd disposed of had been nobodies. Nobodies, he corrected, until he'd made them special. He'd given them immortality.

They called him The Artist. *The* Artist, and that sparkled through his blood like wine. Of course, of course, it wasn't about the models at all, but his creativity.

He'd simply needed to shock the world awake, and he had.

Bathed in the sun, he looked out over the city and could see, perfectly see, the crowds at his major show in New York. How they'd look on his work with awe, how they would vie to have just a word with him, and praise him.

How they would wonder at his gift.

He could despise them, all of them, for making him wait for that praise. But he'd soak in it nonetheless.

His work would hang in the great museums of the world. Donated by his generosity.

The law would deem it murder, but the law would never stand against the art — or the money his mother would pay to protect him.

He had to continue to be careful, to protect himself until the series was complete. But once it was?

He would be envied, not only for the wealth and luxury he deserved by birth, but for his unmatched talent, and with it the gift he'd given the world.

Jonathan Harper Ebersole. The Artist.

After the showing, he thought he might spend at least part of the winter in New Caledonia, where he could refresh himself, take time away from the obligations of fame. He could paint in peace while the art world speculated on what he would bring to them next.

He would have to ask his mother, of course, for use of the family home there for a month or two. But she wouldn't refuse.

She never refused him anything.

Or he might spend some time at the château in the French Alps, a complete change of pace. Snow-drenched mountains, the icy blue lake, a roaring fire.

Something to think about, he decided. But either way, he'd need some solitude, some time away from the demands of the adoring public. Time to focus on himself and his gift.

Inspired, energized, he rose. He took one last look at the city that would soon celebrate his name.

He went directly to his studio, as his work wasn't just his joy, his passion, but his duty.

He uncovered the three canvases, and with pleasure, studied the progress on each. Then he stepped over to study the long scarlet robe, the white shirt with its ruffled collar and cuffs, the embroidered slippers.

Tonight, he'd fill them with a model, one that had taken him several weeks to select. The face mattered, of course. The model's dark beard would require some filling in. But he had that ready, as well as the wig.

But for this, the hands. The hands had to be elegant. Narrow, long-fingered, sensual. It was a shame the full-length had proven so difficult to display, even with a droid's assistance.

Then again, the model display was only, in essence, an advertisement for the painting.

He turned back to the canvases.

He'd finish the first today. If that went well, and he knew it would, he'd work on the second. Most important to him to finish the first, to have that accomplishment before he brought the fourth model into his studio.

He chose his pigments, his oil, carefully mixed his paints. With his selections on his palette, brush in hand, he began. The painted eyes watched him as he worked. To his mind they looked on him with gratitude.

And in his mind, he heard her say: "I was nothing. I was no one. You've made me beautiful. You've made me worthy. You've made me immortal."

"Yes," he murmured as he carefully added a glimmer of white to the girl's lips. "Yes, I have." With the same white, he dabbed an accent on the pearl earring.

Switching brushes, he gave his attention and skill to the blue of the turban to bring out the folds, the shadows.

Then the gold, lighter, a bit lighter there along the shoulder, there against the white collar.

He felt himself glowing with his own brilliance, energized by his own commitment.

When he finally stepped back, tears burned at the back of his eyes.

"You're magnificent. I created you. I gave you life, and a life that will never end."

After dabbing at his eyes with the back of his hand, he cleaned his brushes. He paused only long enough to call for the droid to bring him a double espresso he'd use to down what he thought of as his energy pill.

He wanted the jolt to carry him through his work on the next.

As he drank, his 'link chirped. When he glanced at the display, he saw his mother's name.

He could ignore it, but . . . Though he cast his eyes to the ceiling first, he answered. He could consider it a sign to decide between the island or the mountains for his winter retreat.

"Mommy! I was just thinking about you!"

He let her chat, laughed when he knew she expected it, inquired — also expected — about the rest of the family. And since he knew how to manipulate her, gradually wound the conversation around where he wanted.

"You timed this so well, Mommy. I was just taking a short break. My work is going beyond well. I'm working on a series of portraits, and there's a great deal of interest in them already, Mommy. I've planned for a series of eight, and expect to be finished for my showing here in New York."

"Darling! That's wonderful!" Phoebe Harper's eyes, deep and dark blue like her son's, lit with pride. "Where's your show? When? You know I wouldn't miss it for the world!"

"I'll give you the details when it's all set. You'll be my date, so Dad will just have to stand aside."

"Jonathan." She laughed. "I'm so proud of you. Haven't I always told you that you were meant for great things?"

He actually felt a little tug of sentiment. "You always did. You've always understood like no one else in the world."

"I know how much this means to you, and how much you deserve it. You've never given up on your dream. And I'm happy, my darling, to see and hear you so happy. You look a little tired though."

"The art, Mommy, it's consuming, and at the same time, so freeing."

"I hope you're getting enough sleep. And taking time out for a break, for some self-care. You know Mommy worries."

"When the series is finished, I'll take some time. In fact, I could use a break after the showing. Maybe I could use the house in New Caledonia for a month or so this winter. Recharge, get out of the city. Paint without pressure, soak up some tropical breezes."

"Of course you can. Whatever you want or need, you know that."

"I do."

"Your father and I were hoping the whole family could go down for a couple weeks after the first of the year. We'd have some time together, then you could stay on for a few weeks after. How does that sound?"

Horrible. And he'd find an excuse to avoid the family gathering, if possible.

His sisters weren't just annoying, but competition.

"It sounds perfect. You're the best. I miss you so much, I could talk to you all day! But I need to get back to it, Mommy. I'm actually bringing a model in later."

"I'm glad you're busy, Jonathan. I know you've had some disappointments, and I worried how that would hurt your tender heart. Now I can celebrate your success. Meanwhile, you take care of my baby boy. I love him to pieces."

"He loves you right back. Bye, Mommy."

After setting the 'link aside, he rolled his eyes again. Well, *that* was done.

He checked the time, annoyed the afternoon was getting away from him. Then he looked at the next canvas and the boy. His spirits soared again.

"I can give you another hour or so, then you'll have to wait. But don't worry," he added as he began to mix his paints. "You'll be magnificent when I'm done."

Peabody stepped into Eve's office.

"Carter Morganstern's here."

"Finally."

"He apologized. Crosstown traffic, caught behind a fender bender."

"Whatever. Give me a second. Go ahead and take him to the lounge. I'll be right there. What about the brush guy?"

"He's on his way to his shop. He'll check the records, but he does remember the order, and the — translator said — young man who picked them up. Paid cash. He's going to see if there's a name on the order or his copy of the receipt."

"If we can't get a name, get as good a

description as you can. Two minutes."

When Peabody left, Eve wound up what she was doing, sent it to Reineke and Jenkinson.

And checked the time.

Six hours if they were lucky, five if they weren't.

She went out to the bullpen.

"Jenkinson. I sent you and Reineke the most probable from my vehicle search. I've got it down to a handful. Three companies, two individuals. Add them to yours while I talk to the gallery guy."

"Will do."

"Dallas?" Santiago pushed at the brim of his hat. "I'm getting the runaround on the hotels. They don't want to give out guests' names."

"Same with the private shuttles," Carmichael put in. "I'm pushing it, but I'm using up my charm."

"Keep pushing." She glanced at Trueheart.

In mid-conversation on his 'link, he held up a hand, wagged it left and right.

Then Baxter.

"No hits yet, but I'm eliminating."

She left them to it and headed down to the lounge.

Carter Morganstern looked like a man who'd had it with the world. She could sympathize.

He had a lot of dark blond hair waving around a face with a solid twenty-four hours of stubble. His blue eyes had shadows under them, and his long mouth held in a frown.

"Mr. Morganstern." Eve walked to the table where he sat with Peabody, a vending cup of coffee in front of him. Peabody, wisely, went with water. "Lieutenant Dallas. Thanks for coming in."

"I should've taken the subway. Got stuck, kept thinking traffic would move. Damn near fell asleep in the cab, so one more apology."

"Not necessary." She sat. "The woman killed and left at your residence was, we believe, hired as a model. An artist's model sometime last night. She was a licensed companion."

"I don't get it."

"She's the third LC killed in this manner, then left at a residence — of a gallery owner — or at a gallery. In each case, the victim is dressed and posed to replicate a painting."

Eve brought up the image. "Do you recognize her?"

"God. No, not her, but that's *Self-Portrait*

in a Straw Hat. I mean to say, she's dressed and posed like that painting. Why would anyone do that?"

"We believe he's an unsuccessful artist who's been unable to place his work in a gallery. Your gallery for one. You'd be the one, correct, to decide yes or no?"

"Oh shit." He covered his face, rubbed, then picked up his coffee. "This coffee is terrible."

"It really is." Peabody smiled. "Can I get you something else?"

"No, sorry. It's fine."

"Detective? Get Mr. Morganstern some coffee from my office. It's a hell of a lot better," Eve added.

"Thanks." He let out a careful breath as Peabody left. "Yes, I'd make the final decision. We normally work through agents, or by recommendation, but if something comes in, makes the cut with my assistant, he'll bring it to me."

"Your assistant. Could I have his name?"

"Sure. Travis Barry."

"So Mr. Barry would be the first stop if an artist brought in a work on their own?"

"Usually, not always. I can and have been in the gallery and taken the first look."

"Let's start there. We're looking for a

white male, between twenty-five and thirty. Dark blue eyes, long brown hair. The other galleries we've spoken to who remembered someone with that description say his work wasn't good enough."

"Okay, let me think. Listen, why don't I tag Travis, put him on this?"

"That would be great."

As he made the call, Peabody brought in the coffee. Carter took a quick drink. Then closed his eyes.

"God bless you both. This is coffee. Hey, Travis, charge up your memory banks. Aspiring artist, white guy, late twenties, dark blue eyes, long brown hair. Turned him down."

"Well, Jesus, Carter. We might get a dozen like that a year. Maybe more."

"Yeah, but, it's important. My brain's muddled from all this."

"The art was likely portraits," Eve added. "He'd have been well-dressed. Rich guy casual wear. The eyes? Very dark blue, and maybe something off about them. Something that gave you a little buzz at the time."

"Portraits." Over the 'link, Carter's assistant frowned. "Maybe . . . It could be the man — yeah, late twenties most likely — hair was in a bun, the eyes. Yeah, I remember that. The painting — I can't remember at all — but I do remember trying to let him down easy. I probably gave him the line that we weren't accepting any new artists at that time."

"I've warned you about that one."

"Yeah, but I'm a softie. He came in again, which proves your point, Carter. We were both out there, so you took a look. I can't remember exactly what you said besides no. It was months ago. Maybe close to a year ago.

"But after, you said to me there was something spooky about him."

"That guy! Yeah, I've got it. He just gave me a bad feeling. That wouldn't have stopped me from taking a painting if it worked for me. But it didn't. I don't remember the work either."

"Yet you remember the artist?"

"Yes. Well, more or less. I wouldn't say I have a crystal clear picture, but I think I'd recognize him if you showed me one of him."

"We're working on it. Would you be willing to work with a police artist?"

"He left a dead woman practically at my front door. Whatever you want. I might be able to sketch him myself. I'm not sure, but maybe. If you've got something I can use, I'll try. Trav? Maybe you can hang with us here. You may remember something I don't."

"Sure I can."

"Let me get you something." Peabody pushed up, hurried out.

"I think he was a little shorter than me," Travis said. "I'm five-ten. He was shorter than you, Carter. I'm pretty sure."

"I'm six feet flat. Yeah, I think that's right. Does that help at all?"

"Everything helps."

Peabody brought in a sketch pad, a pencil. "Had one in my desk."

Carter flipped through, stopped at a sketch of Peabody's water feature. "This is pretty good." And another flip to what Eve saw was a sketch of the backyard garden. "So's this."

"Thanks. Don't worry, I won't bring them into your gallery."

"Nat would flip over a garden like this."

He turned to a blank page. "Okay. I'll start with what I think I know. Hair in a bun, right, Travis?"

"I know it was the first time, not sure about the second."

"I'm pretty sure. No hair around the face.

Shape of the face . . . I'm just going oval because I can't really see it. Clean-shaven, yeah. No beard, no facial hair. But the eyes. Not sure I remember the color, but I do the shape. There was, like you said, something off. Deep-set," he muttered as he worked. "Heavy lids. Smooth, no lines. Young. Pampered? Why do I want to say that? Don't know.

"Eyebrows . . . yeah, yeah, yeah. I can see them. Darker maybe than the hair. Arched like this, I think. Yeah, I think. Wrong about the lines. Got one here, between the eyebrows. That fuck-it line. Sorry."

He paused for a minute. "I think about it that way. The one you get when you frown or scowl a lot because — fuck it — I want it my way."

He turned the sketch. "Can you see it, Travis?"

"Yeah. I wish I remembered better, but I really think you've got the eyes."

"Lieutenant?"

She glanced over, saw Yancy. "Excuse me a minute. Keep going."

"Sorry to interrupt. The wit? She tried. I used every trick I've got, and she tried. What I got? I'm saying fifty-fifty at best."

He took out a sketch.

"The eyes."

"Yeah, she was more confident there. And about the hair. She contradicted, second-guessed herself on just about everything else. Except skin color, approximate age. Clean-shaven, and she thinks slender build."

"With me." Gesturing, Eve crossed back to the table.

"Mr. Morganstern."

"Carter. Your husband's my wife's boss. I'm not sure about the nose, but I think . . ."

"Carter, this is Detective Yancy. He's a police artist. The best we've got. The witness he worked with today didn't remember the suspect well. But he got this."

She handed Carter the sketch. "The eyes — hundred percent on the eyes. But there's a line between the eyebrows, and they're darker — I really think so — and more arched. And I don't think — Crap. I think, unless I'm wrong — his face is more oval — that was my first instinct, and I think it's right. More oval, a little thin, but oval, and soft in the chin."

After a glance at Eve, Yancy sat. "More like this?" he said, and corrected the sketch.

"Yeah, I think . . . a little leaner. I know how it sounds, but I'm going to say it anyway. He had a hungry look that had nothing to do with food. And his hair was up, bunned up, not down like that when I saw him. We saw him."

"Okay. Let's start fresh."

"I'm going to leave you to it. Thank you, Carter, this is very helpful. Thank you, Mr. Barry, for assisting."

"It's awful," Travis said. "But it's frosty, too."

"This is going to work," Eve told Peabody as they left. "Between what Yancy got from the other witness, and what they'll put together here, it'll work."

She quickened her stride. "It just has to work in time. Get us a conference room, Peabody. We're on the verge in a half dozen areas. Something's going to fall."

When she walked back into the bullpen, Trueheart raised his hand.

They'd washed most of the green off him, Eve thought, but Detective Troy Trueheart was just wired as polite and earnest.

"Speak."

"I lucked into a woman working late who answered the 'link. In France. Doing an inventory, and she said she gets through it better when everyone's gone."

"And?"

"She remembers him, Lieutenant. She doesn't have a name, and can't get to any of that paperwork, but she remembers him. I got a solid description. She didn't like him, said he was impolite. Spoiled and demanding. He ordered the fabric there for the costume the last victim wore. She remembers because she knows the painting, and commented. He said it was none of her business, and how he'd have her fired if she didn't keep to her place."

"He sounds nice," Eve muttered.

"So she remembers him. She's contacting her supervisor and asking him to access the records for the order. She said he came in the second week of March. She remembers because her friend got married that weekend. The one after he came in."

"This is good. If you don't hear back within the hour, call back. Nag."

"I got one." Rather than raising his hand, Baxter grinned. "The French cheese. Kept busting out, then hit on one in Tribeca. The clerk said he's a regular — the description matches. Pays cash, but he's almost sure he lives close enough to walk. He's next to — not all the way, but right next to — sure he's seen him in the neighborhood."

"Peabody, have McNab zero in on Tribeca. Jenkinson."

"Whittling it down."

"Carmichael, Santiago, push on March. Flights and rooms. Ordered the fabric then. Had to go back to pick it all up. How long, Peabody? Best guess."

"Jesus, *The Blue Boy* would take longer. But if he did spread out the orders . . . Three or four weeks. Maybe up to six."

"If it's three, he might just stay over there. He could pay for a rush job."

"It's probably more like four, but —" Peabody grabbed her 'link. "It's the paintbrush guy. Shit." She plopped at her desk, engaged the translator. "This is Detective Peabody. Thank you so much for getting back to me, Mr. Cabot."

He had a mane of snow-white hair that flowed to his shoulders and a luxurious mustache to match.

His blue eyes twinkled.

"My wife says this I must do. And since I want to make love to my wife on our anniversary, this I do. He pays in cash, both deposit and the final bill. He gives the deposit on the fourth of March of this year, yes?"

"Sir, do you have a name?"

"I think now this is not his true name. A joke, yes? He signs the receipt for the order — on this I insist — as J. H. Artiste. Artiste, you see. I think this is a joke, yes?"

"Possibly. When did he pick up the brushes?"

"Ah, I have this. The twenty-eighth of March. I charge more for so quick, but he agreed."

"Thank you very much."

"You're welcome. Now I will go home and make love with my bride."

"Happy anniversary."

"Hotels," Eve snapped. "In Paris, March four through March twenty-eight. Try the fake name. Private shuttles, New York to Paris, same. Peabody, have McNab run the Tribeca residences with the initials *J.H.* Jenkinson —"

"*J.H.,* boss. Got it."

"Baxter, what goes with fancy cheese?"

"Fancy wine. Wine shops, Tribeca. On that."

"I'll take my vehicle list back, run them in my office."

Time, she thought. They still had it.

"Computer," she said the minute she sat at her desk, "run search with current vehicle date for registrations containing the initials *J* and *H.*"

Acknowledged. Working . . .

"Work fast," she muttered.

He hadn't hit in Tribeca — not for victims or body dumps. Too close to home. He lived there, shopped there, likely haunted the galleries there.

Search complete. Result Justin Merrill Henry, age twenty-nine, 74 Grove Street, registered vehicle make Javlin, all-terrain Summit, 2059 model number 45193. No further matches.

"Display map, highlight Grove Street."

When it flashed up, she shook her head.

"Not Tribeca. Close, but not. Computer, display 74 Grove Street."

"No, damn it. Multiple residential, no garage. Still. Run data on Justin Merrill Henry of that address."

Acknowledged. Working . . .

"It's not him. Just not him, but gotta cover it anyway." She pushed up, paced.

Run complete. Justin Merrill Henry, Caucasian male, age twenty-nine. Occupation, actor. Currently starring in Up to You, a situational comedy set in —

"Forget it. Cancel run."

Acknowledged. Run canceled.

"Okay, all right, he could've made up initials, or they could mean something other than his name. Or the vehicles aren't registered to him. Not personally. Money, family money. Family business."

She sat again, tried vehicles registered to businesses with the initials.

Nothing.

"Long shot. Computer, try vehicles registered to businesses with a name beginning in *J* or *H*."

Acknowledged. Working . . .

"Spinning, just spinning." She shoved at her hair. "But something's going to pop out. Too much here, and something going to click."

Task complete. Two results. Hyperion Car

Service, twelve registered vehicles, two registered vehicles that meet search requirements. Make Rosari, 2058 model Luxe all-terrain.

"Is Hyperion an arm of another company or organization?"

Negative.

"Financial data on Hyperion. When established, current worth, owners."

She felt time bleeding away as the computer worked. Then scanned the result.

"No, you can't cruise around Europe on that. Next result."

The Harper Group. Private company, global with multiple subsidiaries, including Homestyle Food, Nature's Gift, Mrs. Harper's —

"Hold. That's it, that's fucking it. Private — odds are family or part family owned. Global. Mega mucho moolah. When established, current worth, owners. Send results to my PPC."

She strode into the bullpen. "The Harper Group, cross-reference with the Harper

Group."

As she spoke, Roarke walked in. As Roarke walked in, Trueheart shot up a hand. The other held the 'link he still spoke into.

"You've got something," she said to Roarke.

"As you do, it seems. The Harper Group. He used a company card for the costumes. While his signature was largely illegible, the initials —"

"J and *H."*

"J and *H,"* Roarke confirmed, "were legible."

"He placed the orders in March."

"Aren't you clever?"

"Lieutenant, sir. *J.H.* Harper Group card. They think the last name starts with an *E* or an *S,"* Trueheart added.

"Hit with Wine Flight." Baxter flipped off his 'link. "Tribeca. He's a regular. Harper Group company card."

"Peabody."

"McNab's on his way down. Feeney's with him. He hit on an address in Tribeca, single family residence, with garage. Harper Group owns it."

She turned to see Yancy come in, Carter beside him. "I think we've got him, Dallas."

"The more he worked, the more I remembered. I started to see him," Carter said. "I think this is him, I really do."

"Harper Group," Carmichael called out. She added a fist pump. "Company shuttle, New York to Paris, March three. Dallas, I've got it flying to Amsterdam. Tracking . . . Come on, come on. Yeah. Two days later, Amsterdam to London. And, oh yeah, here we go, three days later, London to Paris. A week there — no, eight days. Eight. Then Paris to Florence, back to Paris a couple days later."

Carmichael looked up. "Boom!" Another fist pump. "Dallas, I've got the shuttle hitting all those cities again before returning to New York on April one."

"April Fools," Santiago said. "I can't get through the privacy blocks on the hotels, LT, but I took a quick side trip. The Harper Group owns a home in Paris, a villa outside Florence. Nothing in Amsterdam, but they've got a place in London."

The crack hadn't just widened, Eve thought. It exploded.

"Yancy, grab a desk, run face rec."

"Take mine." Jenkinson got up. "Want a conference room, boss?"

"Peabody booked it."

"One."

"Want me to go set things up?"

"Do that. Peabody, with Jenkinson. Baxter, get me everything on the Harper Group. Find me J.H. — going to be a family member, younger son, New York resident."

"Actually," Roarke began.

"Never mind. Looks like our civilian's got that."

McNab pranced in a step ahead of Feeney. "Address in Tribeca, fits solid. Harper Group owned. The cap closed it up."

Feeney shrugged. "Wife's got a girl thing going tonight. Figured I'd hang and help the boy out."

"I want a name. I want a face. Roarke."

"Jonathan Harper —"

"Ebersole! Bam!" It was Yancy's turn to punch a fist in the air. "Nice work, Carter."

Looking a little dazed, Carter scanned the bullpen. "Does it always work like this?"

"Tonight it does," Eve told him. "Thank you very much for your help."

"Sure." He shook Eve's hand. "Can you let us know when you've arrested him? Man, I almost wish I could go with you and see it."

"Yes to the first, no to the second. Do you need transportation?"

“I’ll get you a car, Carter.”

He turned to Roarke. “Thanks. It’s been a hell of a day.”

Eve counted on it being a hell of a night.

Chapter Eighteen

When Roarke stepped out with Carter, Eve turned to Feeney. "I could use the van and McNab. We need to verify he's inside, and it may be necessary to shut down security and locks."

"You can have the boy. I'll take the wheel and tag along. Sheila's going to make a night of it."

"Fine with me. The rest of you are dismissed. Good work."

"Hey now," Baxter said. "We do good work and get tossed before the takedown? Come on, Dallas."

"He's one spoiled coward of an asshole. I don't need a squad to take him down."

"Seems like we're being punished," Carmichael put in. "Me and my hat-wearing partner dug pretty deep."

"Takedowns, they're the icing," Reineke added.

"I talked about silk and straw hats with a French lady." Trueheart added his earnest smile.

"You want to ride along? Ride along. Anyone else gets dead, the first up are out."

"She's a stern boss, but a fair one," Baxter concluded.

"Take ten, then conference room one."

She walked out, met Roarke in the corridor. "Tell me about Ebersole."

"Twenty-eight. Youngest child and only son of Phoebe Harper and Michael Ebersole. He has two older sisters. One, Laurin Ebersole, is the senator from New York. The other, Olivia Ebersole, heads their health supplement division. There's a seven-year gap between the younger sister and the son."

"The little brother, the baby boy. Does he do anything in the company?"

"He doesn't, no, not in a real sense. He has a substantial trust fund."

"What's substantial?"

"Fifty million a quarter."

"Two hundred million a year for doing nothing? That's above 'substantial.' "

"That doubles when he reaches the age of thirty. The Harper Group's in its fourth generation, successful, diverse. His parents steer the ship, primarily, though his grandparents — maternal — remain involved. The family enclave is in the Hudson Valley."

"Upstate, sure. Somebody — it'll be his mother — paid for him to show off his art up there. He doesn't have a job."

"He's listed as a consultant, and has another income stream as a voting member of their family foundation."

"He doesn't have a job," Eve repeated.

"Essentially, he doesn't, no. His data lists him as an artist, a portraitist, based in New York. He claims to have studied in Paris and in Florence. No marriages, cohabs, offspring."

"Criminal?" she asked as she paused at the conference room door. Because, she knew, he'd have looked.

"None that show."

"Financials beyond the trust fund and the bogus income streams you told me?"

"As a matter of fact."

Because he knew they'd be tense, he rubbed both hands lightly on her shoulders.

"He inherited around eighty million when his maternal great-grandmother died about three years ago. For his consultant and foundation work — using that term loosely — he adds another seven and a half million annually. He pays no rent or mortgage, no property taxes or insurance. No vehicles are registered in his name, and he has liberal use of the company card."

"So he's rolling in it, and his family picks up the majority of his expenses. Got it."

She checked the time again. "We're okay. I'm going to ask Mira if she'll holo in. If she can do that, can you set it up?"

"I can. I got the impression, which Jenkinson verified, no one's had time to eat. Pizza's on the way."

"You shouldn't . . . Oh, never mind. I need his place. Exterior, interior, the security system, locations of cameras. With this time frame, he could be out already. He won't kill his target, not this soon, but he could already be out."

"We'll set that up for you, won't we?" He put a hand on her shoulder again. "You've managed, with considerable obstacles, to identify him, compile a veritable international mountain of evidence against him in a matter of days. Your team's exceptional, Lieutenant, and exceptional begins with command."

"Three people are dead."

"And a fourth won't be. You'll carry the dead," he murmured, "but don't lose sight of the ones you'll save."

"I want him in a cage."

"And you'll put him there. He's pathetic, Eve, but that doesn't make him less vicious, and he's been shielded by a multibillion-dollar company that's not only allowed him to use their resources to kill but, I imagine Mira will conclude, indulged him to the point he feels he's entitled to whatever he wants, including murder."

"All of that." It churned in her belly. "Yeah, all of that. I need to update Whitney, then we'll get started."

She lingered in the hallway to contact her commander. "We have his name, his face, sir. And an address."

"And within your deadline. What do you need from me?"

"I have what I need, Commander. I'm about to contact Reo, then brief the team, then we'll bring him in."

"Let me know when he's in custody. Who is he?"

"Jonathan Harper Ebersole. His family's the Harper Group, multibillion global company."

"Yes, I know the Harper Group."

"He'll have the best team of lawyers that money can buy."

"You have the evidence?"

"Oh, yes, sir. I do. I could bring him in now, sir. But . . ."

"You intend to catch him in the act." He may ride a desk, but Jack Whitney was all cop. "Seal it up tight."

"It's a risk, Commander. I think it's one worth taking."

"Your call, Lieutenant. I'll contact Reo. Go brief your team."

Her call, she thought, and tucked her 'link away.

"McNab, find me any other properties owned by the Harper Group in the city. I want any that could be used as an art studio."

"We pulled them, Lieutenant. They've got what people like to call a pied-à-terre on the Upper East. A penthouse. The cap talked to the building manager. It's used when the family or a guest or exec, whatever, comes in."

"Not that. Anything else?"

"They've got offices downtown, Financial District, and own the building. No residential in it."

"No."

"They've got warehouses, one in Brooklyn, one over by Kennedy. No residential, used for housing product and shipping. That's it unless you want us to go wide."

"No, that's good." And it lowered the risk.

"He takes his targets home. Peabody, bring the suspect on-screen."

The eyes, she thought. The eyes weren't quite right. Other than that, he looked ordinary enough. Not unattractive, but not striking, not especially memorable. A narrow face, soft in the chin. Carter had that right. A high forehead with the brown hair pulled back and wound into a tight knot just behind the crown of the head.

"Jonathan Harper Ebersole," she began. "Age twenty-eight, five-eight, a hundred and thirty-five. Rich bastard who's done nothing to earn it. Mira?" she asked Roarke.

"She's ready when you want her."

"Please bring her in."

It always surprised her to see Mira in casual clothes. Instead of a suit, she wore pants cropped at the ankles with tennis shoes and a flowing shirt.

"Thank you for making the time, Dr. Mira."

"More than happy to."

"Ebersole, Jonathan Harper, the youngest child and only son of Phoebe Harper and Michael Ebersole, who own and operate the

Harper Group."

"Ah," Mira said. "A multigenerational family company. Highly successful. They make the chips Dennis is so fond of and the organic dish soap we use. As well as scores of other things found in most households. Their family foundation does good work."

"He doesn't. He lives on a two-hundred-mil-a-year trust fund, inherited money, and a bogus consultant fee, lives free in one of the company properties, drives — I'm damn sure — vehicles owned by the company. He has — what do you call it? — carte blanche with the company card, and has made considerable use of it in his plans to kill.

"He has two older sisters. One a U.S. senator, the other the head of one of Harper's many arms. He is seven years younger than his second sister."

Mira sat, crossed her legs.

"The subject is twenty-eight years old, lives without cost in a family residence, has no employment, is not pursuing further education. And while he has an annual trust fund in the millions, he also has full use of the company card? Correct?"

"Yes."

"It's unlikely the subject has ever paid a real price — not just monetarily, but in any way — for any behavior or decisions, however poor. The only son, two successful older sisters."

"Betting he was the prince in that house," Jenkinson commented.

"I agree," Mira said. "He has decided he's an artist, and even though he's had no success in that area, his family — or certain members of it — continue to indulge him. That indulgence is, at least partially, responsible for his lack of conscience, for his choice to take lives for the purpose of, somehow, bringing his art into the public eyes. Gaining the praise and adulation he believes he deserves as, I believe, he has always received praise and adulation from, most likely, his mother."

On hologram, Mira turned from the screen toward Eve. "He won't surrender easily. No one has the right to stop him, to accuse him, to punish him. He will certainly try to protect his art, and do whatever he can to finish what he began."

"I think we can handle that."

"No doubt. I'm sure you realize he'll have the best defense attorneys his family can find. And they have plenty of resources."

"Understood. It's why we're going to move in after he takes his next target. I don't care how many lawyers they pull in, they can't whine 'innocent' when he's got the next in there, in costume. When he'll have the barbiturates handy.

"Tell me: How big a risk to the target?"

"If he believes the target could somehow block his arrest, he may attempt to take them as a hostage. But harming the model? He can't finish the work, or what he's decided, as with the others, he needs before killing them."

"I'm betting on ten cops and a consultant against one spoiled rich kid killer."

Mira smiled. "I would, too."

"He'll have a male this time. Girl, boy, woman — the next is a male. For balance. He'd want balance. Male or female, once cops get there, if he tries to take a street LC by force? He's going to have a fight on his hands.

"Something goes wrong, it's on me. Let's make sure nothing goes wrong. Let's see the house."

She glanced around. "Where's Roarke?"

"He and Feeney stepped out. He got it programmed first. I've got it," McNab told her.

Eve studied the exterior first. "That's all one unit?"

"Three-story with accessible rooftop and attached garage," McNab told her. "Converted from multi-to single-family residence in 2054. Entrances, garage, front, rear, and west side. We've got the security system — it's one of Roarke's."

"Handy."

"Three-sixty cams, anti-jam shields, palm and retinal scanners, anti-hack digital locks with full lockdown mode and integrated alarm system. He's got the works, squared."

"And we've got the guy who designed the works."

As she spoke, Roarke and Feeney came in. She'd caught the scent, as had every cop in the room, from the stack of pizza boxes they both carried.

She should've known.

"McNab, put the interior up, then take five. Five, people! Grab your slice and keep the noise down."

On hologram, Mira watched the stampede in amusement.

"And now I want pizza."

Roarke smiled at her. "I spoke to Dennis, and he said you hadn't had dinner as yet. Yours should be arriving any minute. Only fair," he added as Eve's gaze tacked briefly to him from the screen. "Teamwork, after all."

"Thank you so much."

"Peabody, how long has Ebersole lived at this address?"

As she'd just taken her first bite of a veggie slice, Peabody held up a hand. Then juggled the slice and her PPC. "Since September of 2054."

"When's his DOB?"

"Ah . . . September 28, 2033."

"They converted it for him. Twenty-first birthday present."

"Highly probable," Mira agreed. "Which shows indulgence, but also strings. He lives there, but doesn't own it. I'll add, the level of the security system indicates they — and again, I lean toward the mother — will go to great lengths to protect him."

"He's closing in on thirty, but treated like a child. A spoiled one. I get it."

Roarke handed her a plate with a slice. So she ate pepperoni pizza while she studied the screen. And began to strategize the operation.

"How long will it take to get through his security?" she asked Roarke.

"Mmm. A bit of time. I'll need to make a few adjustments to Feeney's equipment, so

I'll want . . . twenty minutes for that before we load up. Then? Five or six on-site to clear for eyes and ears. About that again to shut down the alarms, then the cameras."

He paused, met her eyes. "This is assuming you want a stealth entry."

"I do."

"Well then, perhaps . . . mmm . . . five minutes to undermine the lockdown option, then two or three minutes at the outside to lift all locks."

"So, twenty here, twenty there."

She took the tube of Pepsi he'd already cracked for her and studied him as she drank. "Out of curiosity, how long if you hadn't designed the system?"

Considering, he sipped from a tube of his own.

"Ah, hypothetically, if I were a thief, and a clever one rather than a businessman and police consultant, I'd want to take several days, perhaps a week or two, to thoroughly study the system. Then I'd need to design the tools needed to get through the various layers. This might take another two weeks, even a month. After that? About the same time I gave you."

He ate some pizza. "But, unfortunately

for me, unless I were exceptionally clever, I would likely have missed at least one of the underlayers of the system, as they're designed for just that. So after that time, expense, and effort, I'd probably end up in the nick."

"What you're saying is he's got a system that's next to foolproof."

"Nothing's foolproof, but yes. It's a bloody good system. And they've added every security layer we offer, and at considerable expense." Nodding, she glanced around at cops eating pizza.

"It's different from when we went after Potter. I needed the whole squad there. He had a kid inside, and he had weapons. He was trained. This guy isn't trained, he's unlikely to be armed. He'll have a street LC who should know how to defend himself."

"But they worked it," Roarke concluded.

"Yeah, and because they did, we'll have him before he kills the next target. He'll feel safe inside," she added. "He'll never see us coming because he won't be looking. But he's got a bloody good security system around him personally, too. And shutting that down comes after we get him."

"The level of wealth the Harper Group can access is formidable, and it appears they'll use it for this . . . wayward son."

"You say wayward. I say shithouse rat crazy murdering fuck of a bastard."

"Your way does sum it up nicely."

"Who do you need to adjust the equipment?"

"Not to diminish McNab, but Feeney would be best for it."

"Take him, get started. I can brief you on the op on the way."

"Then we'll be taking some of this pizza with us. You'd best grab another slice yourself before there's nothing left but the memory."

Because she wanted one, she grabbed a second slice, and continued to study the screen.

She couldn't think of a word that topped *indulgence,* but if there was one, this hit that mark.

He had a three-vehicle garage that led into an anteroom, she assumed for coats or foul weather gear. Turn right, and you had a storage area, laundry area, the security hub, and an elevator. To the left, what was labeled an office with a full bath.

Straight ahead, the living area.

Come in the front, foyer — small sitting room on the left, large closet on the right.

Living area, half bath, game room.

Open stairs led to the second floor, and behind them, a lounge area, formal dining, kitchen with butler's pantry — and, she noted, droid storage.

So he likely had at least one droid in residence.

Second floor, four bedrooms including the main suite with its own bathroom, closet/dressing area, sitting area, outdoor terrace.

Third floor, studio. Full bath, dressing area, two storage areas, a bar area. Then the rooftop with retractable glass roof and sides, elevator access.

Windows, and they were generous and many, all one-way glass. He sees out, but no one sees in, she thought. Unless he's on the roof lounging, painting, observing.

She tagged Feeney.

"Working here."

"I want the elevators and interior locks shut down, too."

"What, am I stupid all of a sudden?"

"Since no, I need both of you to take a look at the third-floor interior/exterior, east. His studio takes up the third floor, and there's a large storage area. It looks off to me. He's got a big storage area on the main level. There's a basement for mechanicals and more storage down there. There's droid storage, security hub. Smaller storage area on the west side of the third floor. So why would he need a second storage room this big in his studio? And the walls aren't right on it. They're too thick compared to all the rest."

"You're thinking panic room, and they didn't permit for it."

"Another security layer," she said, "and keep it off the books so if anyone tries to hurt the baby boy, he has the safe room.

"I don't want him getting in there, Feeney. We'd get him out, sure, but why spend the time? Give him time to contact his family or lawyers before we have him in custody. Or worse, drag the target in there and use him for a hostage."

Feeney looked away from the screen. Eve spent the next couple of minutes listening to the foreign language of the e-geek.

"We'll need a few minutes to look into it. We'll block the locks if it's there, but we need time to figure it."

"Figure fast."

She stuck her 'link in her pocket.

"All right, you've had your pizza bonus. Now take a seat, cut the chatter. Here's how ten cops and one civilian consultant are going to take down one rich mama's boy murdering son of a bitch and keep his target — should he have one — safe.

"McNab, exterior again. Team one, Peabody, Roarke, myself, front entrance. Team two, Carmichael, Santiago, garage entrance. East side entrance, team three, Jenkinson, Reineke, McNab. Team four, Baxter, Trueheart, Feeney, rear entrance. No one moves into position until security is down and we have eyes and ears.

"The building has three-sixty cams," she continued. "It also, as you see, has a serious crapload of large windows. They're all one-way glass. We're not giving him any opportunity to spot cops, so we stay out of range until EDD clears it and I give the green."

Since she still had it, she drank more Pepsi.

"Interior, McNab. When we move, we move quick and quiet. He has at least one house droid. Storage area, as you see." She used her highlighter. "Feeney will shut it down. Alternately McNab or Roarke shuts it down if it's not in storage.

"Once team two is in the garage, EDD will disable the garage door. Team four clears the rear of the building. Team one moves directly via the stairs to the third floor. Team two clears the rest of the first level, team three second level. Elevators will be shut down before we enter. Rooftop, team two clears. All teams will clear their way to the third floor, or wherever the suspect is located."

"While he's unlikely to have a weapon," Mira put in, "it's not impossible, and he should be considered both desperate and dangerous."

"Everything's a weapon," Eve said. "As Dr. Mira said previously, he's unlikely to just throw up his hands and say: 'Hey, you got me.' There will almost certainly be a civilian present, one he may attempt to use as a shield.

"If team one doesn't have the suspect under control by the time the rest of the house is cleared, they — which includes me — deserve an ass-kicking. In that event, I trust the rest of you can handle him."

"Who delivers the ass-kicking?" Jenkinson wanted to know.

"In that eventuality, Detective Sergeant, you are the ranking officer in Homicide."

He gave her a sober nod, with his eyes twinkling. "I'll bear that responsibility, Loo."

"I have no doubt you'd perform that duty with enthusiasm and skill. Meanwhile, there's another area on the third floor. McNab?" She highlighted it. "Enhance this room. It's billed as storage, but —"

"Walls are too thick," Baxter said. "And check the ceiling. It's lower than the rest of the floor. I dated an architect." He added a wistful smile. "She was fine. Looks like they added girth to the walls, the floor, the ceiling. You sure don't need that for storage. Safe room."

"Did it without a permit," Carmichael said. "I dated a contractor. Some palms got greased along the way."

"I agree, both counts. Captain Feeney and Roarke are working to confirm it."

"Just did." Feeney strode into the room. His basset hound eyes showed pure satisfaction. "Turns out the suspect's father's brother-in-law has a company that designs and manufactures safes, lockboxes, vaults, and panic rooms. They call 'em secure rooms. We did a track back on the e's installed, the infrastructure. That area's loaded. Full house and exterior cams, data and communication, hardwired D and C, temp and air flow control separate from the rest of the house."

"Basically, it's a large vault." Roarke carried what looked like a small toolbox. "But with amenities."

"Can you shut it down?"

"Certainly. It would add a bit of time, but yes."

She glanced at the toolbox. "New toys?"

He only smiled. "Tools adjusted for the purpose."

"Peabody, check with Reo on the warrants. Feeney, looks like two vans."

"Already went there."

"You're team four, rear entrance. Droid or droids need to be shut down. Roarke, team one, in the front and straight up. When we're clear, we go Q and Q — quick and quiet. We clear, we secure the suspect, and we provide safety for any civilian who may be with him."

She turned to Roarke. "How much additional time to shut down the panic room?"

"I'll do better there once inside. It's on a separate system, of course. So the same twenty, we'd say, for eyes, ears, shutdown, and to gain entry. Then it would take one or two, possibly three, to shut down that accessibility."

"If he goes for it, manages to get in before you shut it down?"

"Same answer. With what I have now, one to three to shut it down, open the door. He won't be able to hide for long, Lieutenant."

She thought: Solid, then looked back at the screen.

"McNab, bring the suspect up, full screen. There he is. He doesn't look like much, but he's killed three people in three days. He spent months planning it, and he's not finished. We're going to make sure he's never going to finish.

"Any questions?"

There were a few. Good cops always had a few questions, she thought.

When she'd answered, she scanned the room.

Every one of them could've been kicked back watching the game, drinking a brew. And every one of them was exactly where they wanted to be.

"Warrants came through, Dallas."

"Okay then. Garage, level one. Jenkinson, drive the first van with McNab, Santiago, Carmichael, Reineke. Feeney at the whcel of the next with the rest of us. Everyone run checks on your earbuds. Once in the residence, we go silent. Hand signals or clicks only."

"Eve, I can come in to observe once you

bring him in if that's helpful."

"It may be," she said to Mira. "I'll keep you informed. Thank you for your input."

She turned to her cops. "Let's go get this asshole."

She started out, headed for the glides.

Chapter Nineteen

As they started down the glides, Roarke touched her arm.

"What worries you?"

"Plenty. That he has an escape route we can't see or anticipate. I don't see how, but I'm not going to eliminate it as impossible. If he gets out and runs, he's got access to the kind of money that can zip him off where we can't get him back. I worry that he'll find a way to use or harm the civilian, and if so, that's on me. I decided to wait, seal it up by catching him with his next target."

She hissed out a breath. "I know we've got him, got him cold on the evidence, but catching him with his next target puts a lid on it. It goes back to the goddamn money again. I know they'll bring in a team of lawyers who'll push hard, and with skill. They'll delay, pick apart every piece of evidence."

"You have a great deal of that evidence."

"Yeah, but. I need a confession, and it won't be straightforward. He doesn't take blame. I have to hit him over the art, and he'll have that team of lawyers shutting me down as much as possible.

"He could make bail. He shouldn't, but even with the lid on it, he could make bail unless they convince a judge he's a runner. And he fucking is. If they set bail, his family will pay it, whatever it is."

"And he'll run."

"He'll not only run, they'll help him."

It gnawed at her, and grated against every molecule of her sense of justice.

"They'll help him get out of the country and live his life in luxury somewhere he won't have to worry about extradition. And when they do, he'll kill again. He'll kill again," she repeated, "because he sure as hell has a taste for it now."

She shrugged it off her shoulders. "I have to put all that away. First, we take him down. Then I'll worry about the rest."

Step-by-step, she told herself.

"You go in the front with me and Peabody. We head straight for the studio. You get that safe room shut down."

"Don't worry there."

She briefed him on the rest as they worked their way to the garage and the vans.

She'd intended to make the arrest with a team of six. Now she had nearly double that and thought, considering the size of the building, the security features — including a panic room — she could use them all.

Better this way, she thought as she climbed in the van. And better, too, the show of force. Shake him up some, she decided. Let him see he had nowhere to run.

And after?

Step-by-step, she thought again.

"Out of cam range, Feeney."

"I got the memo, kid."

When Feeney pulled the van over, Eve shifted aside so he could climb into the back and work with Roarke.

She set the timer on her wrist unit to twenty minutes.

"Just across the street," McNab said in her ear. "I'm about to start coordinating with the cap and Roarke."

"Copy that."

She studied the building on-screen. Security lights on, lights glowing behind the windows, first and third floors.

Was he up there? Had he started his work?

"Another layer on the shield."

"That's the upgrade," Roarke said to Feeney. "I factored it. It's a bit of a worm crawl, then cloning the code. Miss that, the internals read intrusion, so that crawl under first. Nearly there."

Four minutes gone, she thought. Sixteen to go.

"There we are. Now . . ."

"Hold it open, nice and wide."

"I got that, Cap. I see it. I can hold it," McNab told him. "You slip through."

"Eyes and ears on your mark, Roarke."

"Hold it steady, Ian. That's the way. And mark."

"Motion detected, first floor. No heat source," Feeney added. "Droid, kitchen area. Ears aren't picking up any sound. No other movement — wait, rooftop. No heat source."

"He has two droids — minimum." Eve shifted closer. "I don't see any heat source."

"No heat sources throughout."

"He's not inside. Hold everything. Don't shut down the cams, the locks, nothing yet." She paused her countdown.

"We wait."

■ ■ ■ ■

It was his lucky night.

So Aaron Pine thought as he walked down the block. Some rich dude wanted to paint him? Hell, for two thousand — half of which already resided in the zip pocket of his skin pants — the weird guy could paint his ass, his works, his whole damn body.

Pick your colors.

He'd hit a rough patch, and the thousand in his pocket was more than he'd made all week. And another at the end of the night? He'd be cruising.

What he really wanted to do was act, but after three years of rejection, he'd realized he'd end up sleeping on the street if he didn't change his aim.

So he walked the streets instead.

And, to his mind, it was just another kind of theater.

Like right now, pretending interest in the rich dude's painting when he couldn't give the tiniest shit.

"Did you always want to be an artist?"

"It's what I was born for."

"I really admire artistic people. I wanted to be an actor, but I just couldn't get launched."

Aaron paused, and felt his spirits reach even higher when — Jonathan, he remembered — clicked the code on a sleek, black two-seater.

"Wow, this is some mag ride! Your art must really bring it in."

Jonathan's voice turned as cold as his eyes. "Art isn't about money."

"Yeah, I used to think that about acting." Absolutely delighted, Aaron slipped into the passenger seat. "But a man's got to eat. So tell me, Jonathan, what are you looking for from me? What mood? What emotion? I've never modeled before, but I think I could be good at it."

Jonathan flicked him a glance. "You're at your ease, at home. A sensual, elegant man. A man of confidence, an educated man. A nineteenth-century man."

"Nineteenth century? Historical."

Like snagging a plum part without the audition.

"Frosty."

"I want full-length. I have your costume. And we'll need to fill in your facial hair a bit more."

A thousand in the pocket, a thousand to come.

"Whatever you want." Aaron shifted, grinned. "So what am I wearing?"

"You'll see soon enough."

When Jonathan made the turn to the garage, Aaron's mouth dropped open.

"Wow! Your place? XL ult, man! I'm going to have to try my hand at painting."

"There he is. We wait," Eve said again. "Give him time to get to the studio. I don't want to rush it. He could check cameras before he gets started."

"Two heat sources in the garage," Feeney announced. "He's got a target with him. They're on the move."

Eve watched as they walked through the house. They didn't take the elevator, but continued through — a pause, one source circling.

"Target's taking it all in," she murmured. "Suspect's showing off. 'Yeah, this is all mine.' Up the stairs, second floor. We hold, we wait. Let him get set up. Third floor."

"More lights on up there now," McNab said in her ear.

"Yeah, I see it. One's wandering around — that's the target. Ebersole's crossing the room. What's he doing?"

"Opening a bottle of wine," Roarke said

after a moment. "Pouring it."

"He doesn't dose him yet. Just keeping it friendly. Relax, have some wine."

"Both sources moving toward the bathroom/dressing area," Feeney observed.

"Checking out the costume, that's what they're doing. Target's sitting down." Baffled, she watched the screen. "Suspect's fooling with target's face. What the hell's he doing?"

"Facial hair?" Peabody leaned closer. "Maybe adding facial hair, a beard? You said target would be a male, and he's taller than the target. He might need facial hair for the portrait."

"Yeah, yeah, that works. It has to be as close, as detailed as possible." Impatience gnawed at the base of her neck, and Eve mentally swatted it away.

"Taking his time," Roarke observed. "Getting it right."

"Yeah, he steps back, studies, moves in. Adding a wig? Yeah, see how his hands move? A wig, facial hair. There. That's got it. Target's getting up, patting at his face, now his head. Reaching up now. And suspect's moving back into the main room."

"Target's stripping down. Changing into the costume." Feeney nodded. "Yeah, that tracks. Suspect's . . ."

"Mixing paints. He's mixing paints," Peabody repeated.

"As soon as the target comes out, start taking security down. Wait for him to come out, wait until the suspect's focused on him.

"He thinks he's safe," Eve murmured. "Invulnerable in his glass palace. The rich prince who can do whatever he wants, to anyone he wants."

"Looks like the target's checking himself out in a mirror. He's coming out," McNab added. "Coming out now."

"Start the clock," Eve ordered. "Take it down."

They drank more wine — Eve could see it from the gestures. Chatting? Explaining what he wanted to the person he intended to kill in a matter of hours?

Setting the glasses down.

"Looks like the suspect's posing the target." Feeney glanced at Eve. "Target's standing up."

"Left hand on left hip? I can't tell on the right. Just looks like it's bent at the elbow. Not quite perfect, not quite. A little more this way, a little more that."

"External alarms deactivated," Roarke said.

"Mixing paints again. Peabody?"

"Yeah, that's how it looks to me. Now he's . . . I think he's started painting."

"Facing the target, turned to him — which puts his back to the studio door."

"Cameras down."

"All teams into positions. EDD members join after full shutdown. Into positions, and wait for the go. Peabody."

"I'm with you."

They climbed out, moved down the block.

A handful of people strolled along the sidewalks, taking in the clear September night. A few couples, hand in hand, a group of women laughing as they strolled by.

"If he looks out the window," Peabody commented, "looks down, he'd spot us."

"He won't. He's focused on the art now. But we'll edge closer to the building. Then we're just standing, out of the way of pedestrian traffic, having a conversation."

"Team two in position."

"Hold there."

"Team three moving into position."

"And hold there."

"You know, they gutted another building for that garage."

Peabody gave it a good study as they approached where Santiago and Carmichael waited for the go.

"Then what they did, took out the walls between the two buildings to expand the second and third floors. It's kind of mag to notice that kind of thing now that I've been all the way through a major rehab."

"Yeah? And it's sure fascinating to hear about the possible rehab of the murdering bastard's lair."

"Just having a conversation, right?"

"Team four, in position."

"Hold that position."

"Scanners off. Locks disengaged. And . . . security system offline," Roarke added with what came through clearly as satisfaction.

"EDD joining teams. You go, McNab," Feeney said. "Slick work, Roarke. Slick and smooth."

Though she'd learned to expect no less from him, Eve reminded herself not to take it for granted as she watched him move like a cat — slick and smooth — down the sidewalk.

"Team two, go. Secure garage, start clearing main level. Quick, quiet. Team three, go. Team four, you're go when you have Feeney. Team one's moving in."

She turned to Roarke. "Internal locks,

elevators?"

"When inside. It'll be quick, it'll be quiet."

"Then we're go."

They moved up the three steps from sidewalk level. Eve drew her weapon as Roarke put a hand on the doorknob. At her nod, he nudged the door open.

She went in low, Roarke and Peabody took high. They swept left, right, then moved in.

"Garage," Carmichael murmured in her ear. "Two vehicles, the two-seater and a cargo-style AT."

"Team four complete," Jenkinson said. "Moving in."

As they went up the stairs as a unit, Roarke gave Eve the all-clear signal. She gave her communicator two clicks to signal the same to the others.

At the second floor, she held up a fist for hold. She stopped, listened.

Not a sound, not from inside, not even the slightest hum from traffic outside. Once again, she signaled go.

Halfway up to the studio level, she heard voices.

"Hold the pose. Please. Your hands. Don't move your hands. I need them perfectly still."

"Doing my best, Jonathan. I have to tell

you, these shoes are killing my feet. So damn tight."

"I'll work on them next, then you can take them off. No, just . . ." She heard a heavy sigh. "Wait."

She didn't, but moved in fast.

The target, wearing a long red robe, stood facing the entrance while Jonathan's back was to her as he stepped toward his model.

The man in the robe said, "What the living fuck!"

Jonathan whirled around.

"Police! Jonathan Ebersole, put your hands up."

Instead, he spun behind his target, and held to the man's neck something that looked like a pie server.

For an instant, Eve just stared at him. "Really? You're just that stupid?"

"I'll slit his throat. Back off, get out of my house this *minute,* or I'll slit his throat."

"And then what? Next step, Jonathan? You try to cut him, when I'm standing here with a stunner and you're standing there with, what, a spatula? I win. Your house is surrounded. You're going nowhere. So — and it's my first time saying this — put down the spatula."

She saw his eyes cut to the safe room.

And saw him realize he'd have to go through her to get to it.

"I'm walking out of here, with him, or his blood's on your hands. I'm defending myself! I'm defending my home, and I'm defending my art!"

The man in the red robe said, "Just fuck this."

Eve watched as the LC delivered a damn good backfist. And when it struck Jonathan's nose, it turned out his blood was on the target's hands.

"Step away from him, please. No," Eve said quickly, "don't kick him. Tempting, I know, but just don't. Step away from him now."

"I knew it was too good to be true. Good shit's always too good to be true." Shoulders slumped, Aaron moved back.

"Jonathan Harper Ebersole, you're under arrest for —"

He charged her. She had an instant to think: Moron. Then as he lifted the thing in his hand, point toward her, she decided against stunning him.

Since her legs were longer than her arms, she kicked him in the balls, and he went down, gasping.

"Peabody, get the spatula."

"It's a palette knife, Dallas." But fighting a grin, Peabody stepped on it.

"Whatever. Roarke, see to the witness, would you? To repeat, Jonathan Harper Ebersole, you're under arrest for the murders of Leesa Culver, Robert Ren, Janette Whithers."

"M-m-murder?" Aaron sat down hard in the chair Roarke led him to.

"Further charges include dosing them with barbiturates without their knowledge or consent, and trespassing on private property to dispose of their bodies. As well as the attempted murder of — what's your name?"

"Aaron." His golden tan faded as he went pasty white. "I'm Aaron Pine."

"The attempted murder of Aaron Pine, and the attempted assault with intent on a police officer."

"Was he going to kill me?"

Eve cuffed the blubbering Jonathan, then looked at Aaron. "Don't you listen to media reports?"

"Why?" He lifted trembling hands. "Things are bad enough without hearing about more shit."

"Hard to argue. Suspect's in custody."

"We heard." Baxter strolled in. "This is

some excellent place."

"I guess I'm relieved of ass-kicking duties," Jenkinson added as he glanced around. "Who are you supposed to be?" he asked Aaron.

"I don't know. Some guy from history."

"Dr. Pozzi at Home," Roarke supplied. "John Singer Sargent. Dr. Pozzi was a nineteenth-century French gynecologist."

"Seriously?" was Jenkinson's response as Aaron just put his head in his hands and moaned.

"Also reputed to be quite the ladies' man — in nonprofessional ways. Can I get you something, Aaron?"

"Can I have the rest of my glass of wine? It's not dosed, is it? He drank some, too. I saw him pour both glasses from the bottle."

"Don't touch anything until you seal up," Eve told Roarke as she hauled Jonathan to his feet. "We need some field kits from the van."

"You broke into my home." Jonathan's voice wheezed a little but carried plenty of venom. "I'll have your job! You have no right to break into my home."

"Got a warrant." Curious, she looked at the portrait he'd begun. "Man, that's a lot of red. I know somebody with fingers like those. Spider fingers." She glanced back at Aaron. "Yours don't look like spiders."

"It's not finished! I'd barely started!"

"Maybe they'll let you finish it in prison. I really doubt it, but maybe. Who wants to take him in?"

"I don't get to kick ass, I might as well get some satisfaction. Me and Reineke have him, boss. We'll get him all nice and settled."

"I'm not going to prison. That's ridiculous! You have no idea who I am!"

"Well, you start with jail, but yeah, you are. And I know exactly who you are, you dumb fuck. I didn't finish reading the dumb fuck his rights, Detective Sergeant."

"We'll take care of that. Hey, dumb fuck, you have the right to remain silent."

"Get your filthy, disgusting hands off me!"

"I washed up. Anything you say can and will be used against you in a court of law —"

Jonathan looked back at Eve with those eyes — those eyes that weren't quite right.

"My family will ruin you. You have no idea who you're dealing with."

"I've got all the ideas."

He bared his teeth and said, "Lawyer."

"Yeah." Eve nodded as Jenkinson and Reineke hauled him out. "I knew that was coming. Step-by-step. Here's the next. Peabody, get Aaron's statement, then arrange for his transportation home or wherever he wants to go."

"Can I keep the money? He gave me a thousand, and . . . shit, why did I tell you that?" Aaron pressed his fingers to his eyes. "I think I'm in shock."

"It's helpful you did, and I'll see what I can do. Everybody else? Seal up. And let's take this place apart. Paintings, costumes, barbiturates, wire, glue, pigments. Bag 'em all. EDD, get into the e's, find travel, correspondence, anything that applies. We've got airtight, but let's put a big, shiny bow around it."

She took a field kit from McNab, sealed up.

She walked to a draped canvas, uncovered it.

She thought the colors were close to the portrait she'd studied, but without the light that sort of hit the senses. As far as the face of the girl, to her eye it didn't come near the same universe as the original, and not much closer to Leesa Culver.

"I'm no art expert, but I'm pretty sure I know crap when I see it."

After handing Aaron his glass of wine,

Roarke walked over, stood beside Eve to study.

"He killed to do this," Roarke murmured. "It's bollocks, absolute bollocks."

"Meaning, in this case, crap?"

"Complete and utter crap." Since his hands were sealed, he undraped another, and shook his head at Jonathan's version of *The Blue Boy.* "Quite obviously, his ego far exceeds his talent. He has no feel for human expression."

Eve dragged off the third drape. "He didn't get very far on this one, of Chablis."

"But Christ Jesus, what's done is poorly done. Look at the brushstrokes, the proportions, how clumsily he's painted her hands."

She didn't have to look at Roarke to see the anger, but she looked anyway. "It's pissing you off."

"Bloody well right it is."

Roarke's eyes had gone to ice-cold lasers with furious heat burning just behind.

"He killed three people, bastardized great works of art. He took their lives to feed his inflated sense of importance when he's less than an amateur. He had every advantage, every advantage in the world from the time he drew his first breath. And he chooses to do this?"

"Would it matter if he'd painted masterpieces here? Would that change the fact he killed to do it?"

She watched Roarke take a calming breath.

"Of course not. No. But it somehow grinds down to my soul he's not just a monster, and a spoiled git with it, but a talentless one who insists he's gifted. Who's murdered, and would have continued to, because he thinks that will bring him the accolades he deserves."

She was strict and careful on the job, but she gave Roarke's hand a quick squeeze. "That's how we're going to put him away. That, as much as rock-solid evidence, is why he's going to spend the rest of his life in a cage.

"And," she added with a glance back at where Peabody spoke with a visibly shaken Aaron, "you helped save a life tonight. His, and however many Ebersole planned for after him. Also? He won't be finishing these crappy bollocks paintings."

"I suppose that's something."

"Feeney and McNab can handle the e's, for now anyway. Maybe you can hunt up any other costumes. You'd recognize the paintings he cribbed from quicker than any of us.

"We tie a bow around it," she repeated.

Roarke took one last disgusted look at the paintings. "I'm more than pleased to help fluff that ribbon."

Peabody walked over. "Pine's changing into his own clothes. He gave me the cash — he had it on him. It's bagged. I gave him a receipt. I've called a cruiser to take him home."

"We should be able to give the money back to him at some point. It was payment for services."

"Got the drugs, Dallas." Baxter held up two bottles "Prescription barbs, pill form. Two different kinds, two different doctors. Both stored here inside a locked drawer behind the bar. Neither one's full. Got some uppers here, too. I'm guessing personal use. And a third doctor."

Eve smiled. "I'm liking the shine on this ribbon. Flag for the lab. They'll match it. Peabody, go ahead and contact the sweepers. There's no rush, but we'll want them to process when we're done with the initial search."

"It's nice not to have to contact the morgue."

"Yeah. Aaron." Eve stepped to him when he came out of the dressing area. "We have your transportation downstairs."

"Thanks. Really. It looks like you saved my life, so thanks."

"You helped. Nice backfist."

He smiled a little, rubbed his face where the spirit gum had stuck a little too well. "You shouldn't work the stroll if you can't defend yourself."

"Good thinking. Detective, why don't you escort him out? I'll contact the sweepers."

"Come on, Aaron, let's get you home."

As Eve pulled out her 'link, Roarke came back. "You may want to have a look. I found more costumes, wigs, props, in one of the bedrooms, stored in garment bags."

"Can you ID the paintings?"

"I believe so, yes."

"Baxter, Trueheart, carry on."

She went with Roarke, started down to the second floor. "He won't kill again. He won't even start those paintings."

"I'm over it," he told her, and because he felt she'd tolerate it, just this once, brushed his lips over the top of her head. "I'm well satisfied to help tie this bow around him."

She glanced at her wrist unit. "Right about now, if Mira's right, he's going to be demanding his call, and that's going to be to his mother, because Mira doesn't miss. His mother will call in a fucking battalion of lawyers.

"So." She took a breath. "Let's tie that bow real pretty."

Chapter Twenty

In the end, Eve decided they needed a very, very long ribbon. Considering himself invulnerable in his glossy urban castle, Jonathan left behind a mountain range of evidence.

The paintings, of course, and the costumes — those worn and those waiting to be filled. The drugs he'd used to render his victims unconscious before killing them.

They found the wire, the glue, boards identical to what he'd used on the second victim. He'd painted the background for the third victim, which he'd decided not to use, and yet another — so much red — for Aaron Pine.

He'd taken photographs of his victims, in the costumes, in the pose he'd directed. He'd taken more of those victims, and the others he'd chosen, on the street. He'd labeled them with their location, and the painting he'd planned to create.

He hadn't bothered to dispose of their clothes, instead storing them, in an orderly fashion, in the closet of another guest room.

Between them, Feeney and McNab found an ocean of digital evidence. Various files contained data on each painting — those begun, those planned — with contacts for the fabrics, the costumers, the tatters in Ireland, the dates of his travel and appointments. Each separate file contained his extensive research on the individual painting, the pigments employed, the techniques, the history of the artist, and anything known of the model.

He had files on the galleries, the managers, the owners that included his personal notes raging against them. And more damning, the name of the painting assigned to each.

He'd opened another for media reports of the murders.

In yet one more, he'd started to write his autobiography. He'd titled it:

The Artist
The Gifted Life of
Jonathan Harper Ebersole

Though he'd yet to reach beyond his own childhood, he'd written his own foreword.

I was born to create art, to realize my vision with pigment and brush. This is both my gift, and my curse. To be filled with this vision, this talent, this purpose, demands sacrifice, even suffering.

Every true artist faces the brutality of rejection, the cruelty of criticism. And worse than these, more brutal, more cruel, apathy.

How many of the gifted, through the ages, have been driven to suicide by the apathetic, by those who blithely consider themselves lovers of art?

While I sacrificed, while I suffered, while the blades of apathy cut deep, I determined this would not be my fate.

I would live. I would paint. I would humble those who turned their backs on my gift.

Some will condemn my methods, but they are less than nothing to me. Those who truly understand greatness know the power of art supersedes all else.

With my gift, with my art, I have bestowed immortality on those who were no one. Their life beats its pulse in the series I call *The New Master Emerges.*

While my greatest works to date, these will not be the last. In the following pages, I will take you on the journey of a life dedicated, above all else, to the god of art.

When, at last, Roarke drove home, she sent memos to Reo, Mira, Whitney.

"I need Mira to observe, but right now, I'm coming down solid on legally sane. Crazy, oh, fuck yeah, but not over the legal line. He knows right from wrong, he just doesn't give a damn. He used an alias on a cash receipt. His actions throughout? Carefully, systematically planned. He chose LCs because he considers them no one, and easy to lure, and he considers himself above the law. He sought to humble — his words — people who'd said no to him."

"I'd lay a healthy wager he's rarely heard the word *no.*"

"You'd win that bet." Eve scrubbed her hands over her face. "I get some satisfaction at knowing he'll spend the night in a cell, waiting for someone to ride to his rescue. Next step's tomorrow. I need verification from the lab on the drug, on the fibers from the back of the AT, on the victims' clothes."

Now she rubbed the tension in the back

of her neck.

"I think he kept their clothes to use later."

"To use?"

"Yeah. Costumes. Besides the ones he had made, he had other stuff. The shawl-type things, hats, fake jewelry, a couple of fancy dresses, and all that. We saw some of it in his other paintings around the house, in the studio."

"And in those works, those previous works, there was at least a dull glimmer of talent."

"Pedestrian."

"Yes, at best. But the ones he killed for? No glimmer at all."

He drove through the gates.

"You were right about the costumes — the paintings he planned to copy with them. It's all written out."

"Yet you worry. You have all the evidence, you have evidence in his own words. He held a weapon — such as it was — to his intended victim's throat, then tried to attack you with it. And yet you worry."

"Yeah, I do." She got out of the car, walked to the door with him. "He'll have money, influence, and power behind him. Hell, surrounding him. If you read his data, it's clear he's never done a single hard day's work in his life, never earned his own way on anything."

She looked over at him as she walked into the house. "He grew up exactly the opposite of us. Pampered, indulged, spoiled. Plenty of others are, and don't turn into psychopaths, but it's a factor in his pathology."

He slid an arm around her waist as they started up the stairs. "You worry he'll wiggle out on an insanity defense?"

"Some, yeah, but I'd take it. He'll still be locked up. As plush as the Harpers could manage, but locked up. Nobody else dies. It wouldn't be just, and still, I'd take it. I worry because I know they'll throw everything they've got at getting him out, getting him off."

"Eve, I can't believe even with the depths of the Harper Group's pockets, they can overcome the amount of evidence you've compiled against him. Add what's on your recorder during the arrest."

"He was shocked. People broke into his house, had weapons. He snapped, he panicked. They'll try that."

"And you'll counter it. I'll place another wager then, won't I? And it's all on you."

She leaned against him a moment as they walked into the bedroom.

"It's still step-by-step. I can get a confession out of him, but I can't get a confession out of him if the lawyers zip him up. And they will. They'll try anyway. We'll have to work through them to get to him. I'll need Reo there."

"You'll have her, and Mira, and a bloody Mount Kilimanjaro of evidence. Add an egoist, a malignant one at that, and one you'll skillfully goad into bragging about everything he's done and planned to do."

He slipped the jacket off her shoulders, laid it aside, then rubbed at the knots.

Because it helped to hear it, she nodded. "I know what buttons to push if I can get to them."

After removing her weapon harness, she sat to pull off her boots.

"You'll get to them."

"They'll delay, toss up obstacles."

"And still."

She rose, began to undress as he did.

"Summer's nearly over, right?"

"You wouldn't know it by the weather, but it's waning, yes."

"Let's have a barbecue thing."

He turned, studied her. "You're very tired, aren't you now? Not altogether lucid."

"Actually, worrying's got me . . . I don't

know what. But I mean it. Or right now I do. They all dived right in. Put in a full day, but dived right in. Including you. He's off the street because they did, you did. I know in my gut I'd've gotten him eventually, but it might not have been tonight. Without the help, I might be going to the morgue again in the morning. I'd be briefing the feds tomorrow."

"So we'll have a barbecue."

She shrugged. "You like them, they like them, summer's almost over. And tonight, Jonathan Harper Ebersole sleeps in a cage."

"We'll plan for Saturday then, or Sunday if that works best. Including the Miras, the Whitneys?"

"Yeah, yeah." She slid into bed with him. Galahad rolled over from his sprawl and curled at the small of her back.

"Nadine and Jake. And we haven't seen much of Charles and Louise of late so we'll see if they're free. Mavis and family, of course."

"See, this is what happens. You decide to do something nice, and it balloons on you. Then the balloon pops and all the gunk inside spills all over you."

"Let me worry about all that. I'll enjoy it."

He would, she thought, which was part of the why she'd said it. She'd be okay with it, but he'd love it.

As the cat curled against her, she curled against Roarke.

He brushed his lips over her forehead and he stroked her back as he often did when trying to soothe her into sleep.

But her mind wouldn't rest.

She lifted her mouth to his.

"Help me out, will you, pal? I don't want to dream tonight."

So his mouth took hers again, gently, while his hands stroked her back. And murmured to her as those hands slid under the nightshirt she'd tossed on.

She heard the cat give a kind of annoyed grunt before he rolled away.

"If you dream, dream of me. Dream of us. Dream of this," he said, and took her mouth again. Again tender, so tender and so warm.

She laid a hand on his cheek. His hands, his lips didn't just stir desire, but beat in her heart as well. Worry began to fade in wonder. That he was hers, that he wanted to be hers.

She answered tenderness with tenderness, understanding, as she never had before him, that when love surrounded desire, it meant everything.

With him, she had everything.

He felt the tension fade away as she softened against him. His fierce cop let go for him, let the day, the night, all that came before this moment go.

He took his time, hands gliding rather than demanding so she could drift, just drift before the rise.

And he, lost in her, could drift with her.

She allowed herself to surrender, needed to surrender, could surrender because she knew he would cherish.

And with surrender, she found peace. With peace, she found pleasure. All tangled together in a slow, quiet blooming.

He soothed and seduced, tending to her body, inch by inch. Drawing out her emotions to join with his, patiently, so patiently layering sensations that she slid to peak, slid over like water poured from a cup.

Then he was with her, inside her, bodies joined in a slow, easy rhythm that spun out time. So slow, slow and sweet, they climbed to peak and spilled over together.

She didn't dream.

And when she woke, felt incredibly grateful for that single, simple fact. More gratitude filled her when she saw Roarke in his perfect dark suit, with his perfectly knotted tie, in the sitting area with the cat across his lap and the stock figures scrolling by on the muted screen.

The familiarity of it, the quiet routine of it kept worry at bay another few minutes. It wouldn't be an easy day, she knew. She had to prepare for long, for hard, but to have this to start that long, hard day?

A gift.

"You slept well," he said without looking over.

"I haven't moved a muscle. How do you know I'm awake?"

"I can hear your brain working."

"You know that's not possible."

"And yet." Now he looked over, smiled that smile of his. "And as your brain's working, I'll suggest you wear something formidable today. Black if you must, but with punch."

"My brain can't worry about clothes before coffee."

She rolled out of bed and went straight for coffee. Drinking that first life-saving sip, she studied him.

"You helped me out last night."

"I reaped considerable benefits."

"Damn right, but. I'm going to give you a little payback anyway. You pick out the formidable. I expect to deal with the obscenely rich. You qualify there, too. Just add intimidating to formidable."

"First a barbecue and now this." His clever fingers scratched at the cat as he studied her. "Where is my wife?"

"She's right here, so don't get used to it, Ace."

With that she went in to shower.

More routine, and exactly what she needed to fortify for the day ahead. Hot jets, steam rising. Then warm air swirling, all giving her time to think, to begin to strategize.

When she came out, he'd laid clothes on the bed, had two domes on the table.

He hadn't gone for black, she noted, but the dark gray of an angry thundercloud in the trousers, the jacket. He'd paired that with a thundercloud vest with thin lines of dark, deep bronze. A simple T-shirt and the buckle of the gray belt picked up the bronze. As did the three chunky buckles on the over-the-ankle gray boots.

"Formidable?"

"With you in it, oh yes, indeed. Take off the jacket when you're in Central. Show them your weapon and those well-toned arms. Show them who you are."

"Okay then."

"The diamond studs — the small ones." He nodded toward the dresser.

"Oh, but —"

"The obscenely rich will recognize the quality. You'll forget you're wearing them. They won't."

She'd think about it, she decided, and walked over to join him.

With the cat now stretched on the floor, Roarke took the domes off.

"Waffles! Never wrong."

Waffles and berries and bacon. Add more coffee and the day began perfectly.

She drowned the waffles in syrup.

"Do you have a plan of attack?"

"I'm juggling plans, since I don't know how they'll push on defense. I do figure they can keep him quiet for a while. That doesn't mean I can't bring him into the box with his attorneys present. They'll file briefs, but that's Reo's deal. I can goad and insult him all I want. He might stay silent through a round of that. Then it's back to the cell. He'll have to sit through arraignment, and take what Reo throws out."

"It'll wear on him."

"That's just right. Maybe it'll take another round, maybe two, I'd say three at the outside. Add a second night in a cell? He'll break."

She ate waffles, switched to bacon.

"He'll break," she repeated. "I just have to get to the buttons and keep pressing them. If I'm pressing the wrong ones, Mira will tell me. I don't care how much they pay the lawyers, how good they are, nobody will be able to shut him down once I punch the first crack in the wall."

"As I said before, my money's on you."

She looked over at the clothes on the bed. "Pretty much literally." Eating, she considered. "What would you do if I started shopping for my own clothes?"

"After I'd been treated for shock? I'd implore Louise to give you a full medical workup, including a brain scan."

"Ha ha. I used to shop for my own clothes."

He leaned over, kissed her cheek. "I'd say it was more bought them than shopped for. And I do treasure the button that fell off the hideous suit you wore the day we met."

"Sap. A smartass and a sap. Well, I'm going to go put on your money, get a little jump on the day. I'll wake Reo up, if she's not already up, on my way downtown. I think we need to meet before it all starts."

She got up to dress.

"I'm figuring the legal wrangles may take a couple of days. If he has to spend the weekend in jail, he'll crack like an egg on Monday. If he lasts that long."

As she put on the trousers, pulled on the T-shirt, Roarke carried the plates and domes into his closet.

Amused, she watched him come out, firmly close the door as she buttoned on the vest.

"Really?"

"He needs to learn not to lap at dishes."

"Next, you'll put the breakfast stuff in your closet safe."

"If needs be."

She strapped on her weapon harness, frowned at the small studs. "I want to say cops don't wear diamonds, but I've got a big-ass one under my shirt."

"The studs are a subtle statement, and won't go unnoticed if you deal with any of Ebersole's family today."

"I expect to. Someone's going to come to

protect the baby boy against the big bad cop."

She put them on, and decided to do exactly what Roarke had told her she would. Forget she wore them. So she sat, pulled on her boots. And from her vantage point, watched the cat manage to open the closet just enough to squeeze his bulk through.

"Roarke."

He glanced over where she nodded.

"Well, fuck me." He marched to the closet, came back out with a disappointed Galahad. "Banishment it is then."

As he put the cat out of the room, Eve's 'link signaled.

"Looks like Reo's tagging me first," she said as she picked it up. "Dallas."

"How soon can you get to the courthouse?"

"I'm leaving here in a minute. Why?"

"Jonathan Ebersole has Kopeckne, Addison, Wright, and Wu as his counsel."

"Which means?"

"They're who defense attorneys want to be when they grow up," On-screen, Reo used both hands to somehow pull her fluffy hair into a smooth twist. "And he's got a bail hearing at nine."

"What? Nobody works that fast."

"They do. Arraignment and bail hearing at nine."

"He won't make bail." She worried there, but . . . "Not with these charges, he won't. He's a flight risk."

"Dallas, they maneuvered somehow, and got Judge McEnroy."

"Shit. Shit. I'm on my way."

"Tell me what it means," Roarke asked as she grabbed her jacket.

"It means they managed to get the judge most likely to set bail. Not a slam dunk, not with these charges, not with Ebersole's money and connections that scream flight risk, but not impossible. It should be. It should be impossible. If he gets out for five damn minutes, he'll run. His family will get him out of the country, set him up, and . . ."

She had to take a minute, and a long breath with it. "They'll put a tracker on him. McEnroy's big on trackers, but . . . I need a favor."

"Of course."

Ten minutes later, she jogged down the steps. Roarke went with her, stopped her at the door by taking her shoulders.

"I expect you to take care of my cop and keep me updated."

"I'll do both. Thanks. Maybe I won't need the insurance, but I'm not going to gamble."

She kissed him, then dashed to the car. As she sped toward the gates, she hit lights and sirens.

She flicked her wrist unit to contact Peabody.

"Get to the courthouse. Fifteenth floor. Ebersole's being arraigned at nine, and there's a bail hearing."

"At nine? How did they —"

"Money, Peabody. Get there."

When Eve spotted a knot in traffic ahead, she punched vertical. She didn't have time to waste.

Her in-dash signaled. She nearly ignored it when the readout told her Nadine Furst. Then she calculated.

"I'm on my way to the courthouse."

"So am I. Or will be in three minutes."

"If you want a one-on-one, you've got it, but it has to be fast."

"Make that a minute and a half," Nadine said, and clicked off.

APA Cher Reo didn't allow herself to pace outside the courtroom. Pacing here would make her look weak and nervous.

She was, by God, not weak. But plenty

nervous.

She had no doubt in her mind, with the evidence in hand — and whatever else could be gathered — she'd get a conviction. For Christ's sake, the NYPSD had caught him with his next victim, one he'd threatened to kill — on record. They had the paintings, the costumes, his own words, the drugs used, the wire, the damn glue.

They had it all.

And none would matter if he got out, got away, riding and hiding on Harper Group money.

She'd make that case, and she'd push it hard.

But, but, but.

She sprang up from her bench, shoving files aside as she spotted Peabody.

"Where's Dallas?"

"She was on her way when she made contact. I'm closer, but she'll be here. How the hell did this happen so fast?"

"They pulled all the aces from the deck — including getting Judge McEnroy on the bench."

"That's not good. But still, bail's not going to happen."

"I want the judge to see NYPSD in the courtroom. I want, if I can wrangle it, a chance for him to hear the arresting officer's statement on that arrest. I've barely had time to prepare. They got the jump on me.

"And here they come."

Peabody glanced back to see four people striding down the wide hall. Two men in suits, one woman in a suit. And a second woman she recognized as Phoebe Harper.

She thought the three lawyers looked just like a vid version of slick and successful attorneys.

On the other hand, Phoebe Harper looked quietly elegant in a long-sleeved black dress, her golden brown hair waving to just above her shoulders.

She was thin and petite, makeup subtle, jewelry understated. And she looked, Peabody gauged, about a dozen years younger than sixty-seven.

The tallest of the lawyers, the one with silvery hair that formed wings at his temples, leaned down toward her, murmured something.

Peabody watched Phoebe's gaze shift, and as they zeroed in on her and Reo, deep, dark blue eyes like her son's went hard.

The female lawyer guided her to a bench on the other side of the courtroom door.

She sat, crossed her legs, folded her hands in her lap, and stared straight ahead.

The tall man walked to Reo, held out a hand. "Ms. Reo."

"Mr. Kopeckne."

"My co-counsels Alan Addison and Carleen Hammott. I don't believe we've met before."

"No, we haven't."

"I know you by reputation, of course." He smiled, charmingly.

"I can say the same. You've traveled a long way in a short time."

"The flight from California gave us time to begin to review the case against our client."

He went into the courtroom, followed by his associates. Hammott accompanied Phoebe inside.

"Where the hell is Dallas?" Reo muttered. "I've got to get in there."

"Look, I'll tag her, get an ETA."

As Peabody started to, she saw her partner exiting the elevator.

Reo strode straight to her. "What took you so long? We have to go in."

"I had to make a stop. I'm here now. The lab's putting a rush on the drugs, the wire, glue, all of it."

"We've got to go in now. I want both of you seated right behind my table. Ebersole's got three attorneys at his, and his mother will be right behind them."

"His mother. Mira scores again."

"They'll point out his family support."

"I don't see that as a weight on his side."

"And I'll turn it around. They'll also use the fact he has no record, no violence. I've got ammo, Dallas, but if the court springs him, I need him under watch."

"Trust me, already set up."

Reo nodded. "It just had to be McEnroy," she mumbled, then went into court.

"You didn't say anything about making a stop," Peabody said.

"Some insurance, just in case. I'll explain if we need to use it."

They went inside, sat, and Eve took the opportunity to study Phoebe Harper.

Some resemblance, she thought, in the coloring, but where Jonathan's face had a kind of bland softness to it, his mother's was honed. Maybe from DNA, maybe from what money could buy, but either way, she had a sharp, striking look about her.

And when the woman turned her head, met Eve's steady gaze, Eve saw the cold, hard steel under the striking.

Used to having her own way, too, Eve decided. And damn determined to have it regarding her son.

And damned if she didn't see Phoebe's glance flick to the earrings.

Roarke scored again.

Though amused, Eve kept her face impassive, her gaze steady, a way of letting the woman know she was equally determined justice got its way.

Phoebe looked away first as they escorted Jonathan into the courtroom.

His mother had brought him fresh clothes, she noted, the suit, the crisp shirt, the tie, the shined shoes. He'd knotted his hair up.

He gave his mother a look of sorrow with just a hint of tears.

She touched her hand to her lips, then extended it to him.

Moments later, the bailiff ordered all to rise.

Chapter Twenty-One

Judge Gerald McEnroy entered, beefy in his black robes, his hair tightly curled around his wide, deep brown face.

Eve let the preliminaries go by, focused on the defendant and his mother.

She studied Jonathan's profile, his body language as McEnroy informed him of his trial rights.

Not nervous, Eve concluded. Pretending to be, a little, but not nervous.

Smug. To her eye, he came off smug.

His mother kept her hands clasped together tightly on the knee of her crossed legs. Some nerves there, Eve thought. She carried them for her baby boy.

Jonathan's shoulders hunched a bit when they read the charges against him, outlined the probable cause.

But not nerves, Eve concluded. Insult.

"Mr. Ebersole, do you understand the

charges against you?"

He started to speak, then the lawyer with the silver hair leaned toward him, whispered something.

Jonathan rose politely. "Yes, Your Honor."

"How do you plead?"

"Not guilty, Your Honor. Thank you." And sat.

Reo rose. "Your Honor, the prosecution believes the charges against the defendant are heinous and show a disregard for human life. We contend, and have substantial evidence to prove, that Jonathan Harper Ebersole intended and planned to continue his killing spree.

"In addition, the defendant has access to great wealth. His family owns property and homes in several countries. He has access to private shuttles, and poses a serious flight risk. We request he be remanded until trial."

"Your Honor." Kopeckne rose. "The defense contends denying bail until the trial is concluded would be undo punishment. It will take several weeks for his legal representatives to mount a defense given the unwieldy and circular route law enforcement employed to the arrest of my client."

"Your client took an unwieldy and circular route to murdering three people and attempting to murder another," Reo snapped back.

"We're not trying the case today, Ms. Reo."

"Your Honor, the Harper Group is a multibillion-dollar company with global arms. The record of the arrest clearly shows the defendant threatened Aaron Pine with a weapon, the same weapon he attempted to attack Lieutenant Eve Dallas with in his attempt to escape arrest. This shows a propensity for violencc."

"It shows," Kopeckne argued, "a young man shocked and frightened when his home is invaded." He held up a hand. "Or so he believed in the moment. He has never exhibited violent behavior. He has no criminal record. He has his family's emotional support, and deep ties to New York."

"Your Honor —"

McEnroy slapped his gavel. "Just hold on, both of you. I repeat, we're not trying this case today. This is a hearing regarding bail. The defense is entitled to build that defense. Due to that, and the court calendar, this trial would begin . . ." He checked his calendar, nodding, frowning. "On February eighteenth of next year."

He sat back. "While I understand the

prosecutor's desire for remand, I am disinclined to incarcerate a defendant for six months before that defense can be given.

"Ms. Reo." McEnroy held up a finger before she could protest. "During this period, and throughout the trial, the defendant will be confined to his home. He is not to step foot outside those walls, and will submit to wearing a tracker to ensure same. He will surrender his passport. Bail will be set at fifty million dollars."

"Your Honor, that's an egregious sum."

McEnroy lifted his eyebrows at Kopeckne. "I believe it's well within the means of the defendant to post, and will serve as a deterrent against flight. Mr. Ebersole, do you understand the terms of your release on bond, and that said bond will be revoked, and you remanded to jail if you break those terms?"

"I . . . I . . . Yes, Your Honor. Thank you."

"The prosecution could not object more strongly."

"Understood, Ms. Reo. But we are still a court that adheres to innocent until proven guilty."

"In addition, the residence in which the defendant lives, rent free, where the prosecution and the evidence contends Mr. Ebersole murdered three people, is still being processed. It's not possible for him to enter those premises."

"Your Honor, the defendant's family owns another property in New York. An apartment in a secure building, which the defendant may use until his own home is cleared."

"Very well. State the address for the record."

McEnroy nodded his way through that. "Mr. Ebersole, do you agree to the terms of house arrest at this location?"

"Yes, sir. Yes, Your Honor."

"So ordered. This hearing is adjourned."

"All rise," the bailiff announced.

Jonathan sprang up and all but fell into his mother's arms.

Eve heard him say, "Mommy." And though he made sobbing noises on her shoulder, he sent Eve a smug smile.

Gonna wipe that off your face, she thought. And real soon.

She didn't speak until she and Peabody left the courtroom.

"It'll take time to post the bond, then he'll need to go to Central, pick up his personal effects. We'll have him tailed until he gets to his new home."

"Jesus, Dallas, you know he's going to run."

"Yes, I do."

She waited for Reo, who came out steaming.

"Goddamn it, I hope McEnroy can live with it when that murdering asshole gets somewhere we can't touch him. I hope he can live with it when he kills someone else. Fuck that, no I don't. I hope he can't live with it."

"Nadine's going to be outside, on the steps. She'll want to talk to me. She'll want you, too."

"Just what I need."

"After she does what she does, I need you in my office."

"Dallas, I don't have time to —"

"Yes, you do. I figure at least two hours, maybe more. Peabody, book a conference room. There's not enough space in my office. Let's get going. It'll take me a chunk of that two or three hours to explain."

"Start now," Reo demanded as they walked to the elevator.

"No. Stay pissed. It's a good look."

"I don't know what the hell you plan to pull out of your sleeve, out of your hat, or out of your ass, Dallas, but it better be good."

"It's the best I've got." As they rode down, Eve turned to Reo again. "Tell me this. If he breaks the terms of his bail, will Kopeckne's firm still represent him?"

"I don't know." Weary, Reo ran a hand over her hair. "Their rep is sterling. I can't see them being any part in aiding him to rabbit on this. And I think if he does — and he damn well will — they'll be as pissed then as I am now."

"Good. Mommy's going to have to find new fancy lawyers."

As expected, Nadine waited on the courthouse steps. Not alone, Eve noted. Plenty of other reporters lined the way.

Ignoring them, she walked to Nadine.

"I heard. Tough one," she said to Reo.

"You've got five minutes," Eve said. "Five with me, five with Reo."

"Hey."

"Then you need to stay ready."

Nadine's cat's eyes narrowed. "For what?"

"Keep your camera on call" was Eve's answer. "Make sure you have good transportation. And be ready. Take your five."

Nadine signaled to her camera, rolled her

shoulders, brushed at her camera-perfect hair.

"This is Nadine Furst on the steps of the New York City Criminal Court. I'm speaking to Lieutenant Eve Dallas, the arresting officer of Jonathan Harper Ebersole. Mr. Ebersole is charged with three counts of murder in the first, as well as other charges. Lieutenant Dallas, how do you feel about Judge McEnroy's decision to set bail at fifty million, and ordering Mr. Ebersole to house arrest?"

"The New York City Police and Security Department gathered substantial evidence, which led to Ebersole's arrest last night for the premeditated murder of three people, and on record, the attempted murder of another individual. We believe we took a dangerous and violent man off the streets. My personal feelings regarding Judge McEnroy's ruling don't matter. We did our job, and will continue to protect and serve the people and the city of New York."

She answered more questions, keeping it dispassionate and very restrained, before stepping aside. Reo's responses held a great deal more passion and fire, and Eve thought that was just fine.

Eve checked her wrist unit.

"That wraps it. Reo, you should ride with us. Nadine, stay ready. Keep your camera on call," she repeated.

"Tell me something," Reo insisted as they walked down to the sidewalk. "I need to tell the boss something."

"I'm going to go through it once, all together. But I'll tell you, I'm not letting that sniveling, slimy, snickering son of a bitch out of New York. Not today, not tomorrow. Not until he's on his way off-planet to Omega."

She waited until she got into the car, got behind the wheel.

Then banged her fists on the wheel.

"The judge is a fucking moron!"

In the back seat, Reo threw up her hands. "Finally!"

"And he's going to look like one. The Harper Group could piss fifty million in a bucket and not miss it. She won't wait. She'll make her move today. She'll already have everything sct up."

"Who?"

"Mommy," Eve said, and pulled away from the curb.

"I really want to hear this." Then Peabody grabbed the chicken stick as Eve hit lights and sirens again.

■ ■ ■ ■

In the garage, Eve didn't bother with the elevator, but headed straight up the steps, then out to the glides.

"How about a hint?" Peabody asked. "A clue?"

"You'll get the whole shot in a few minutes. Tag Feeney. I need an e-man, and now. Bullpen."

As Peabody made contact, Eve stuck her hands in her pockets.

She believed in the system, but sometimes the system needed a kick in the ass.

"It'll take some time for them to deal with the paperwork, then he'll need to come here, get his stuff, then get to the penthouse. She'll be with him every step for that."

"If she's going to help him run, why go to the penthouse at all? And yeah, she's going to help him run," Peabody added. "But they'll have to ditch the tracker."

"That's why the penthouse first."

"I won't say they're a hundred percent effective," Reo began. "Nothing is. But they're damn close."

"That much money buys expertise. How about the lawyers? Would they conspire on this for a big, fat payday?"

Reo didn't hesitate. "Absolutely not. They've earned their reputation, and this would ruin them."

"Good. I didn't think so."

She hopped off the glides and strode straight into the bullpen.

"Court," Baxter said, gesturing at Jenkinson and Reineke's empty desk. Then at Carmichael's and Santiago's. "Follow-up. On their way back."

She decided the hell with a conference room.

"You and Trueheart, soft clothes. Officer Carmichael! Pick two officers. I want you and them on surveillance. Visibly on surveillance. Peabody, give them printouts of Ebersole and Harper's ID shots. I want you seen. I want you obvious."

"Yes, sir."

"The woman comes and goes as she pleases. If you spot or believe you spot Ebersole leaving the building, contact me. Do not move on him."

"How's he going anywhere?" Baxter demanded. "He's in custody."

"He made bail."

"What the —"

She cut Baxter off with a look. "Soft

clothes," she repeated. "I don't want you seen. You're fucking invisible. If you see or believe you see Ebersole, contact me. Do not move in. Follow. Be prepared to follow a vehicle."

"Sir, Lieutenant," Trueheart said. "They didn't let him out without a tracker. I mean, with all we had."

"They didn't, but he won't be wearing it when he leaves the building. And he will leave the building. If they have to exit the building on foot, they won't leave together — she'll go out first. He'll be disguised. He'll either have a car waiting, or walk a short distance to where a car's waiting — with her in it."

She shook her head. "Watch for that, but they'll have a better way."

When Feeney walked in, face stony with anger, she nodded. "I feel the same, but we need to set this up fast. Use Peabody's unit, and get this on-screen."

She handed him a disc.

"The better way. The building has underground parking. The slickest way out for him, use the penthouse's private elevator all the way down to the waiting car. Has to be a car, as the building doesn't have roof access for air vehicles."

"How'd you get all this so fast?" Feeney asked as he studied the blueprints on-screen.

"Some help from the consultant. I'd like McNab, or whoever you assign, to ride with Baxter. I want to know how many people are in the penthouse at all times."

"I'll get you McNab."

"Good. The Harpers have a private airstrip in their compound upstate, but that's a long way to go, and they're in a hurry. We factor for that, and we have a jet-copter and pilot on call, but best bet is private shuttle. Bring up the map on there, Feeney."

When they had, Eve used her pointer. "Here are their options. Facilities for private, long-distance shuttles. The Harpers have their own private shuttles. They have six of them. One, the one Phoebe Harper used to travel last night, is already here. They won't use that, too easy to trace, but we factor. This station."

She highlighted another. "It's the closest to the penthouse."

"Bring another in, have it ready to go." Feeney nodded. "A lot of options to cover, kid, and if he's managed to ditch the tracker, no way to be sure. You're going to need more men."

"He won't be wearing the tracker, but he'll be carrying one. The consultant had one on hand, one used in covert ops."

Feeney's face began to light up. "Damn right he did."

"I made a stop on the way to court. She may have bought him some new ID — though he won't need it, since she'll take him somewhere without extradition. He's got a real nice wallet to carry it in if so."

"You put the tracker in the wallet." Now Feeney grinned at her.

"It's small, thin, almost transparent. I've got the code to activate. She'll have gotten him a new 'link, the new ID most likely, a new passport, but why would she buy him a new wallet when he's already got one with his initials engraved on it?"

"She had to work most of the night on all this," Reo put in. "And I agree, a new wallet wouldn't be a priority. It had to take hours and an extraordinary amount of money to do what you think she's done since his arrest."

"He's her baby boy. Whether she ruined him or he came out ruined, the result's the same. Three people are dead, and with this? She's as responsible as he is."

Eve thought of the long, measuring stare

they'd shared in court.

"We'll be making two arrests today."

She checked her wrist unit. "Surveillance teams, get moving — pick up McNab and get me how many bodies are up there. Feeney, you're going to need a portable. The van's too slow. You'll ride with me and Peabody."

"So will I," Reo said. "I need to update my boss."

"So do I. Let's make it fast. Peabody, while I report to the commander, inform Mira that her presence in Observation is vital when we bring Ebersole back in."

She watched the clock as she reported to Whitney. Gauged the time as she tagged Nadine.

She would, she swore it, sew Jonathan Harper Ebersole and his mother up, and sew them up together.

And add another big, shiny bow.

She waited until Baxter checked in.

"Ebersole and Harper just arrived. They're going into the building. McNab reports two other people already in there."

"Stay invisible. Stay ready."

She walked out to the bullpen. "Suspects entering the building. Two others already in the penthouse. We're moving."

"Already tracking him." Feeney tapped his portable. "Signal's clear and strong."

"Let's keep it that way."

Since Santiago and Carmichael were back at their desks, she nodded to them. "Mind the store."

She glanced at the elevators, then at Feeney.

"Can you make it go straight down, no stops?"

"Not supposed to, but in this case." Inside, he used a swipe, then keyed in a code.

"We'll set up close," Eve continued. "Not too close, but close enough. People already in there, waiting for them. If he doesn't move inside two hours . . ." She shook her head. "We've lost him."

"We're not going to lose him." Feeney stood, resolute in his baggy shit-brown suit. "We're the long arm of the fucking law."

"Why is it one arm? You need both to be long, or at least the same length."

"It only takes one to grab some asshole doing the crime. Then you don't need long to cuff 'em."

"You know what would be frosty?" Peabody held out her arms. "If cops could stretch their arms like Mr. Fantastic."

"Who the hell is that?"

"The Fantastic Four, Dallas. Superheroes. But what would be even more iced? Having invisible capabilities. Like right now, Baxter and Trueheart could literally be invisible. Then they could stand right outside the penthouse door, follow Ebersole out, down to the car."

"I'd rather have super speed. The older you get," Feeney told them, "the more you appreciate super speed."

"Like the Flash. He's not one of the Fantastic Four," Peabody explained.

"I'll make a note of that." Eve got out of the elevator.

"I'd be Wonder Woman." Reo shrugged when Eve gave her a baffled look.

"She has an invisible plane," Peabody pointed out.

"I wouldn't care about that. I'd want the Lasso of Truth. And the outfit. And the body to rock that outfit. But the lasso would be priority."

Reo settled in the back with Feeney. "I don't get to go on busts with the long arms of the law often enough. But if I did, I'd bring my lasso."

"Feeney."

"I've got him, Dallas. He's in the penthouse. Tracker's moving around a lot, but in that area. He's inside. I might shoot for the web-slinger."

"Oh, Spider-Man!" In the front, Peabody shifted, looked back at Feeney. "I had a serious crush on Peter Parker when I was a little girl. And now, come to think, I've got my own sort of Peter Parker. I might try for Black Widow. The outfit and body again. No superpowers, but a totally mag ass-kicker."

"Wouldn't you have to kill Peter Parker first to make widow?" The minute she asked, Eve ass-kicked herself for letting them suck her in.

"She's not that kind of widow. It's a code name, like the poisonous spider. You should probably take her, Dallas, you'd fit. I could go with the Scarlet Witch."

"That one's got some issues," Feeney reminded her.

"Yeah, but I'd overcome them. I'd make a totally extra Scarlet Witch."

"Now that that's settled, maybe we can all focus on stopping the evil villain and his mommy from escaping to Planet Zero. Peabody, keep tabs on the court-ordered tracker. I suggest using technology rather than your imaginary superpowers."

"I've got him."

"Wallet tracker's still moving around," Feeney added.

"So's the original."

Eve pulled into a loading zone a block from the apartment building. "Baxter, Officer Carmichael, we're in position. McNab?"

"Still four heat sources."

"Okay, okay, wallet tracker's holding steady now."

"So's the original. Like he's maybe sitting down or at least standing still."

"Sitting," McNab said. "Looks like sitting from here. One source beside him, very close. One across from him. One . . . looking on, I'd say."

"They're starting work on the tracker," Eve muttered. "Roarke said it would be slow, tedious work to do it right, to keep it going and remove it, undamaged, at the same time." She flicked a glance in the rearview at Feeney. "Estimate thirty to forty minutes."

"For Roarke?" Feeney smirked, just a little.

"For an exceptional e-man who could bypass it. Either one already on the Harper payroll or a freelancer. One who's also willing to face prison time. Aiding and abetting, accessory after the fact."

"Works for her already if he knows the score," Feeney concluded. "Freelancer if she didn't want the tie-in. Still holding steady."

"Some loyalty, maybe. And a big fat fee either way, add an escape plan to anywhere the e-man wants to go. That's not going to happen.

"McNab, when Ebersole and his mother move out, you switch and stick with Officer Carmichael's team. I want you on the two others. Do not arrest. Don't move in until we have Ebersole. I'm getting you backup. Don't lose them."

"You're sure they'll leave first?" Reo asked.

"No. Playing the odds. She wants her baby boy safe. The court tracker needs a heat source and pulse to monitor. One of the other two have to wear it until they're away. Otherwise, hell, just cut it off and go."

"Can't risk that with cops very visibly watching the building."

"That's right. She'd never risk that anyway. She'd want time to get him out of the building, into the shuttle, and gone."

"Even if he got away, we'd have her." Reo shook her head. "We'd trace all this afterward, and we'd have her."

"Maybe she's willing to go to prison for him, maybe she figures she has enough money to beat the charges. Or the desperate mother defense will hold up."

"I can promise you it wouldn't. Juries don't like people who use their billions to escape justice. She'd do time. One way or the other."

"It's going to be one way. And that's our way."

Thirty minutes crawled by, then five more.

At thirty-eight minutes, Peabody said, "Wait! There was a flicker. Just a flicker. I wouldn't have noticed if I hadn't been looking right at it. The dot — the court tracker — just flickered for a few seconds."

"He got it off."

"All heat sources standing," McNab reported.

"Wallet monitor moving."

"All heat sources moving. Three separating, same direction. One remaining."

"The court monitor's remaining, Dallas."

"And the wallet's heading down. Elevator."

"McNab, keep on the penthouse. Switch to Officer Carmichael's team. Baxter, Trueheart, follow, but keep your distance. We're monitoring. We'll direct you. Feeney, you're the navigator."

"Copy that. Still heading down. And . . . just passed street level. Parking garage it is. Out of the elevator now, walking, walking. Holding, holding. Moving, faster. In a vehicle now, heading toward the exit. Pausing . . . exiting. Coming out on the street."

"We see him," Trueheart reported. "Black town car, New York license three-five-six-Kilo-Papa-Echo."

"Give them a block. I'm moving. McNab?"

"Heat source still in the penthouse. I'm going to guess? He's having a drink."

"Car's moving steady west."

"Stay invisible. Peabody, coordinate with McNab. Give him the go when I tell you."

"Turning north on Eighth," Feeney said.

"North. Eighth." Eve brought the map back into her head. Then because she didn't want to risk a mistake, tossed it up on the windshield.

"Closest for private shuttles, long-range. Got it. Baxter, continue to follow. I'm moving ahead."

She went vertical, punched it. And heard Reo's "Oh, sweet Baby Jesus."

As she flew, Eve tagged Roarke.

"Lieutenant."

"West Side Shuttle Station. I need you to clear me, then Baxter's vehicle right through the gate for the privates and tag Nadine."

"Consider it done."

"We're kind of busy here, so can you find out what private's geared up for takeoff to one on the list of locations I gave you this morning?"

"Two minutes on that. Take them down."

"Can I ask how he can clear you through like that?"

Now she flicked a glance at Reo. "He keeps a couple of privates there." She muttered the rest. "And he might actually own the station."

"That would do it."

"Heat source and monitor still holding at the penthouse location," Peabody reported.

"We hold there, too. Baxter, when you get through the gate, lock it down, then back us up."

"They're a couple blocks behind us now, kid."

"We want more room than that."

"How long can this thing stay up here?" Reo wondered.

"As long as I need it to." Eve hoped.

"You got three blocks now. This is where they're going, and you've got three blocks on them."

"One more," Eve murmured, and pushed for it before she dropped down, and answered Roarke's tag.

"Venezuela, specifically Caracas. The shuttle's on the tarmac outside hangar 303. It's a Harper Group shuttle, a JZ 15, tail number Delta-Echo-five-four-nine-one. Would you like me to delay the takeoff?"

"No need, arriving there now. I'll get back to you."

She drove into the station, swung toward the private gates, and barely slowed before they opened for her.

"Box them in," she murmured. "Reo, you keep covered. The driver may, and probably does, serve as a bodyguard. He may be armed."

"You don't really think —"

"No chances. There's the shuttle."

"Dallas, McNab says the source in the penthouse looks like he's kicked back and watching some screen. Kicked back anyway."

"Not for long."

She drove straight into the hangar, and

had the startled pilot running in after them.

The woman wore a formal uniform and moved fast.

"You can't —" She stopped, frowned at Eve's badge.

"What's the problem? I've got passengers coming in."

"Who's on the shuttle?"

Reo stepped out, held up her ID. "APA Cher Reo, you really want to answer the lieutenant's question and quickly or be charged with obstruction."

"Well, Jesus, I just fly the shuttle. Ms. Harper. Phoebe Harper and Marcus Solo. They're bound for Caracas."

"They're bound for prison, and you'll want to stay out of the way."

"Listen, I just fly the shuttle."

Holding up her hands, the woman backed away.

"Feeney, give the portable to Reo. Reo, stay out of the way."

"I have no problem with that."

"They're through the gate," Feeney said as he handed the portable to Reo.

"Move in, McNab. Block the gate, Baxter. And let's give mother and son an NYPSD welcome."

From the hangar, she watched the car pull up beside the shuttle. When the driver got out, opened the rear door, she stepped out, flanked by Peabody and Feeney.

"This is the police. Put your hands where I can see them. Reach under that jacket, pal, and you're down."

The driver put his hands up.

"Thinking about running, Jonathan? Nowhere to go, but I'll be more than happy to stun your ass if you try."

"Mommy, do something!"

"How dare you threaten my son! Jonathan, get on the shuttle."

"It's not going to Caracas, or anywhere else. But try it, and you're down."

Phoebe's jaw hardened. "Get on board, darling. I'll handle this."

Instead, he did exactly what Eve expected. He ran.

"Got her, Peabody?"

"Yeah."

"I've got the driver. Go, kid."

As she raced forward, Phoebe rushed to block her path. Eve just knocked her aside.

He ran fairly well, Eve noted. Not well enough, but not bad. She calculated overtaking him in about thirty seconds, then called out one more warning.

“Stop. Or I will deploy my weapon.”

When he didn’t stop, she kept her word.

His body jiggled, danced. From behind her, she heard his mother scream. She glanced back long enough to see Peabody restrain her, Baxter assisting. Trueheart broke off and raced after Eve.

Jonathan dropped, shook, then as she stood over him, lay shuddering.

“Hey, Jonathan.” She pulled him up to sitting, snapped the cuffs on him. “Nice to see you again.”

His nervous system still jolted by the stun caused the word to garble some, but she recognized it. “Mommy.”

“I’m your mommy now, and you’re grounded for the next few lifetimes.”

Chapter Twenty-Two

While Trueheart dealt with Jonathan, Eve walked back to Phoebe, glanced over at the raw scratches on Peabody's throat.

"Give you some trouble, Detective?"

"I gave her more, sir."

Due to the struggle, Phoebe had more than a few hairs out of place now. And the cold look in her eye had gone to blazing fury.

"You think you can attack my son, manhandle me, and walk away from it? My attorneys will destroy you, all of you."

"I bet not. Not only is this entire arrest on record" — she tapped her lapel — "but —" And pointed up.

"See that chopper? See the Channel Seventy-Five in big letters on it? They're live. Your son's attempted escape, with your assistance, broadcast as it happened. On-screen, on their website, on all their social media."

"The boy's got the e-man," Feeney added.

"And your tech who removed the court-ordered monitor? In custody. I bet he'll trade some time off his sentence for telling us how you hired him, how much you paid him. Doesn't matter either way, you're done."

And it felt incredibly satisfying.

"Phoebe Harper, you're under arrest for aiding and abetting a fugitive from justice. For conspiring to facilitate his escape, for conspiring to remove a court-ordered monitor, for obstruction of justice, for assault on police officers, for resisting arrest.

"We'll be adding creating and/or procuring false identification, arranging for international transportation using same. And the icing I really think I'll have a chance to enjoy? Accessory to murder, after the fact."

"You have no idea who you're dealing with."

"Funny that your dumb-fuck son said the same thing to me. Here's the same answer. I do. I really do. And you're dealing with me now. You have the right to remain silent."

When she finished reading Phoebe her

rights, she sent them to Booking in separate cars.

Reo strolled over. "Well, that was exciting. And you may enjoy knowing that Kopeckne saw the live feed. A little bird tells me he's already filed for withdrawal as counsel. He won't touch this. His firm won't touch this."

"She'll get another."

"Yes, but not of that caliber, Dallas. It matters. She won't be able to get representation at that level, not after this. Having Nadine record this, broadcast it live? Genius," she said, and held up a hand for a high five.

"Another layer of insurance. Peabody, get a picture of those cat scratches before you use a healing wand. And let's go roast their asses."

On the way to the car, she contacted Roarke. "They're in custody. Thanks for the help."

"Delighted. Will you interview soon?"

"In a few hours. They need to be booked, processed. I want to write it all up, nice and pretty. We'll take the low-hanging first — bodyguard, the e-guy. Then I need Mira, and I'm going to toggle between them if necessary. Hit him first. He's weaker."

"If I can, I'll come in to watch. It's been a

long week and I could use some fun."

"See you if I see you." She pocketed the 'link. "Reo! We're heading out."

"I can write it up nice and pretty," Peabody said as they got in the car.

"Yeah, you can, but I want this one. You write up your part, including those scratches."

"They really sting."

"Been there." Eve rolled her shoulders. And thought it amazing just how much weight had dropped away. "How about you run that low-hanging fruit so we see what we've got?"

"I've got the bodyguard already. Mikah Jessup, age forty. He's head of Phoebe Harper's personal security team, and has been for nine years. Fifteen years with the company altogether. No criminal. Divorced, no offspring."

"Loyalty. How about the tech?"

"McNab reports Shaun Ye — I'm running now. Okay, age twenty-six, freelance tech — he's done some work for the Harper Group, as a subcontractor. Single. A few minor bumps here."

"Money. He'll flip and fast. Jessup will stick. We'll take money first. Your lead."

"Hot dog!"

"What'll you offer him, Reo?"

"He's more windfall than low-hanging fruit. Dump it down to misdemeanor, six months. Immunity's possible, depending. We want the payment to wrap around Harper. We want her instructions and so on wrapped, too."

"I can live with either," Eve decided. "He's nothing. A tool, nothing more."

"Agree. With the bodyguard, I also agree he'll be stickier. If he flips, gives a full statement, testifies, three to five years. If he sticks?" Calculating, Reo lifted her shoulders. "He'll do twice that. If he had a part in hiring the tech or in procuring the ID? Twenty to twenty-five."

"What about Harper?"

"Well, doing some math, adding up the charges?" Smiling, Reo ticked off on her fingers. "Let's call it fifty. Yes, I believe fifty works well, though I'll start off higher considering the heinous nature of her son's crimes. If she gets a really good lawyer, we might deal that down to twenty, but I'm not inclined there. And she won't get bail, not after this. She also forfeits the fifty million she posted for her son."

"I can live with fifty inside." Eve answered her in-dash. "Commander Whitney."

"Lieutenant. Good work. I need you to meet with Kyung for a media conference in one hour."

"Sir, I have APA Reo with me. We're strategizing before the interviews. We have four to —"

"The live feed from Channel Seventy-Five was a thing of beauty. Beauty costs, and that cost is full media access at this point. One hour."

"Yes, sir." She waited until she ended the call. "Fuck it! 'Good work. Here's your punishment.' Fuck it. You don't need me in the box with the first two."

"Oh, what?" Peabody lost all color. "You want me to go solo? But why do I get punished?"

"I could say because, but take McNab in for the tech. They speak the same weird language. You can pull Jenkinson for the guard. If he's not available, Baxter."

"I don't get to be bad cop, do I?"

"Use your bad cop on the tech. McNab's more sympathetic — same language," she repeated. "For the guard you want to sympathize and relate to his sense of loyalty and service. He won't break for bad cop. Jenkinson will know that, and play it so you can contrast. Loyalty and service are your strengths. Use them."

She pulled into Central's garage, just sat a minute. "And I was feeling pretty damn good."

"It was still genius, Dallas." Reo gave Eve a pat on the shoulder before she slid out of the back. "That feed in court? Private shuttle waiting. Ebersole running, Harper trying to stop you, swiping at Peabody? It's diamonds and gold. And I'm betting Nadine's commentary added more shine and sparkle."

"Blah, blah, bollocks, blah."

She went straight to her office, and with coffee, wrote up her report — nice and pretty.

Peabody stepped in. "They're bringing up Shaun Ye. Any advice?"

"Hit him out of the gate. Aiding and abetting a serial killer in an escape. There's precedent for one who aids and abets receiving the same sentence as the accused. Three terms of life, no parole, off-planet. Put that thought in his head, he'll give you everything you need, and it'll save time."

Eve pushed up. "Get every single detail. How she contacted him, what she paid, what she offered, what she told him. What they discussed in the penthouse. You're tying her up more than him."

"I've got that. I've got this."

"Yeah, you do."

Instead of hearing those details firsthand, Eve went up to meet Kyung.

Tall, smooth, and elegant, the media liaison extended a hand. "Congratulations, Lieutenant, on a virtually surgical bust. Two, actually, considering last night. I understand you have important work yet, but a name like Phoebe Harper draws ratings and clicks. As does preventing the escape of an alleged serial killer — who happens to be her son."

Blah, blah, bollocks, blah, Eve thought again.

"I want to keep this brief."

"Also understood. May I say you look particularly well today?"

She gave him a narrow-eyed stare. "I've always thought you're not an asshole, Kyung. Don't make me change my mind."

He just smiled at her, then gestured her out to the packed media room.

She got through it, but could only think she'd never get that twenty minutes back. Still, since he'd kept it to twenty despite more shouted, repetitive, and often — to her mind — stupid questions, Kyung retained his status of not an asshole.

She swung into Observation, noted Reo had joined the interview. Which meant they'd made a deal. She listened briefly as the tech and McNab spoke in their native tongue.

She went back to her office, and thinking of Roarke's morning advice, took off her jacket. At her desk, she did deeper runs on Mikah Jessup, then Phoebe Harper.

When Peabody came in, she glowed.

"We got reams of details. She contacted him personally, told him his previous work for her company had been exemplary, and she needed just that again, and immediately. He claims she gave him a whole line about persecution, false imprisonment, planted evidence. He admitted he didn't much care either way. Because she transferred five million into an account for him — up front. And he'd get another five after, along with a private shuttle to his choice of Palawan."

"Where?"

"Palawan. I had to look it up. It's an archipelago in the Philippines. The ten million and island life — she also promised him a villa — seemed like a mag idea. Reo ended up giving him the six months. He has the receipts, Dallas. He was to stay in the penthouse, with the monitor, until she contacted him to say they were in the air. He listened to conversations in the penthouse, how they checked the plans, arranged for the shuttle, how Jessup was to drive back after they took off, park in the garage, leave the car.

"He saw Harper give Ebersole the new ID — including the passport. She already had a bag packed for him. She gave him a new 'link, promised to stay with him until he settled in Caracas, and quizzed him on his new background and name.

"She'd already opened an account for him in Caracas under that name. Seeded it with a hundred million. You know, just to get him started."

Peabody took a breath. "Dallas, she told him she was buying him his own gallery, along with the villa."

"And she expected to get away with all of it, just go back and pick up her life as usual. Some people have too much money, and I know how that sounds coming from me."

"No. Roarke's the most generous person I know. He's not selfish, self-serving, and he, well, screw it, he has honor. Phoebe Harper just doesn't have honor."

"No, she doesn't."

"She has to know, Dallas. She has to know Ebersole killed three people, planned to kill more. But she'd set him loose. Not get him help, but set him loose, set him up like a fucking king.

"Those people." Not glowing now, but fired up, Peabody pointed at the board. "Their lives are nothing to her. She's worse than her son. She's worse."

"You're right. She's worse. Do what you can with Jessup, then we'll take Ebersole. Do you know if they've lawyered?"

"The last we heard, Harper's working on it — or has her husband working on it. Reo was right. A lot of top firms won't touch this, especially with the live feed out there. Jenkinson's with me. McNab's writing the tech interview up. I can follow most of the geek speak, but some of this went over my skill set."

Eve gave it an hour, then took a turn in Observation. Jessup sat without counsel, and sat resolute to her eye. Not going to break.

Jenkinson hit hard. He had crime scene photos of the victims on the table, he used their names. He pushed, snarled, and looked fierce despite the mutant, bug-eyed fish swimming over his tie.

In contrast, Peabody spoke of loyalty, of how it could be misplaced and exploited. Of the victims as people with hopes and dreams.

Reo stepped in, watched with her.

"He'll do the twenty."

Eve nodded. "Yeah, he will."

"Good look," Reo added after a quick up-and-down study of Eve. "Damn good look. Weapon on your side, biceps cut, and glorious little diamonds in your ears."

"I was going for formidable."

"Oh, you passed formidable, cruised by intimidating, and hit dead-on scary."

"Even better."

Eve used her communicator, texted Peabody.

Wrap it. He won't budge. We can try again after we interview Harper, but he's Reo's now.

"I'm sending for Ebersole."

"Good. He's still without counsel. Not only has word gotten out, but that feed. They'll have to settle for someone hungry enough for the fee. My impression is they've been advised to work a deal, but so far, she's not willing."

"That's why he's first." Eve rolled her shoulders, circled her neck muscles. "I can break him."

"Counting on it. I'll be here, wishing I had popcorn. Mira?"

"She'll be here."

Once Jessup was taken back to a cell, Eve met Jenkinson and Peabody.

"He's got a thing for Phoebe Harper," Jenkinson told her. "I think a mom thing, not a sex thing. Sex thing we could crack. But a mom thing?" He shook his head. "It's a tougher nut."

"We don't need him, and he earned the twenty he'll do inside. Just one more life in the shitter."

"I'll write it up. Hey, I heard we're having a cookout at your place Saturday."

"Correct, and it's casual. No ties."

He just grinned. "I got a shirt that's killer."

She couldn't imagine it, and decided as he strolled back to the bullpen, she didn't want to.

"Ebersole and Mira, both on the way. Do you want a break?"

"No. I'm rolling."

"Coffee, my office. I'll tell you how I think we play this."

■ ■ ■ ■

They'd put him in an orange jumpsuit. In addition, he wore restraints on his wrists and ankles.

Eve saw fear, and could smell it. But he covered it with arrogance.

"Dallas, Lieutenant Eve, Peabody, Detective Delia, entering Interview with Ebersole, Jonathan."

She read off the various files, including those pertaining to the aborted escape.

Then she sat, smiled. "Well, Jonathan, you're completely fucked."

"I don't have to talk to you. I have nothing to say to you. I want to speak with my mother."

"No, you don't have to talk to us. Detective, remind me. Is speaking to Mommy included in the prisoner's rights?"

"No, sir, it's not."

"I didn't think so. Your mother's in a cell, Jonathan, and she's going to stay in one for about a half century."

He smirked. "No, she won't. When our lawyers get here, we're out. You might end up in one though."

"You understand your bail's been revoked?

You're now remanded into custody until your trial, through your trial, and with what we have, for multiple lifetimes thereafter."

He pressed his lips together, but tried a careless shrug. "We'll pay another bond. You won't keep me in here."

As if surprised, Eve sat back. "You actually believe that. Let me tell you something Mommy won't. You removed a court-ordered monitor, accessed false identification, arranged for a flight to a country without extradition to the United States, and were, when recaptured, about to board a private shuttle in order to escape . . ."

She couldn't help herself.

"The long arm of the law. Those actions negate any possibility — I mean *any* — for a reinstatement of bond in any amount."

"Whatever it is, my mother will pay."

"Jonathan." Now she leaned forward. "Listen to the words. There will be no bail hearing. You have forfeited the right to any consideration thereof. You have added a whole new list of charges. Serious charges. Your mother also faces a list of serious charges, and as she has proven herself to be a flight risk with the means to procure what she needs to do so, there will be no bail for her, in any amount. Mommy will very likely die in prison."

"You don't know her. She'll beat you. She always wins."

"Your lawyer has withdrawn from your case, and she's unable, so far, to find a replacement. I'm already winning."

She opened the box she'd brought in. "Fake ID, including passport." She tossed them on the table. "A new 'link, registered to the fake ID with Mommy's private numbers already loaded in. Cash, ten thousand in Venezuelan bolivars, the documentation to your bank account in Caracas under your fake name, containing a hundred million. You've got a hotel suite booked, under the fake ID. Just until the sale's completed on the villa she bought for you.

"Oh, and here's the monitor she paid to have removed. Shaun Ye's been very cooperative. All this is cut-and-dried, Jonathan. You're both going down. Does it bother you, at all, to know your mother's going to spend the rest of her life in a cage?"

On a sniff, he looked away. "I don't have to talk to you."

"I think it doesn't, not really. Because you first, right? Always you first."

As Jenkinson had in the last interview, she tossed the crime scene shots on the table.

Slowly in this case, one at a time.

And she watched the pride and excitement light in Jonathan's dark blue eyes.

"I guess it's not much to worry about when you'll already be caged for taking the lives of these human beings."

He sat back, tried to cross his arms. When the restraints stopped him, a bit of panic flickered. Then he shrugged.

"Peabody, why don't you do the honors this time?"

"Happy to." Peabody began to unload a second box. "We have the barbiturates used to dose Leesa Culver, Bobby Ren, Janette Whithers."

"Those are my prescribed medications for anxiety."

Oh, he couldn't help but talk, Eve thought.

"They're also what you used to incapacitate the three people you killed," Peabody said, and continued. "We have the wire you used to pose their bodies after you strangled them."

"Wire? I'm an artist! It's wire to hang paintings."

"Glue, used, again, on the bodies of your victims."

"Please." He let out a snort of a laugh. "What household doesn't have glue?"

"These were taken from your residence."

"So what?"

"And they match — exactly — what you used on the victims. We have these, the clothing, the other personal effects of those three victims, also found in your apartment."

"Planted, by you."

"Not only was the entire search recorded, but how the hell did we get the clothing each victim wore on the night they were killed?" Peabody demanded.

"I'm sure my lawyer will figure that out."

"We have documentation for your travel to France, the Netherlands, Italy, England."

"I enjoy traveling." He stared up at the ceiling as if bored. "It inspires my art."

"Where you purchased the fabrics and engaged costumers to create the costumes you had your victims wear — as well as costumes you planned for others."

"Prove it!"

"For Christ's sake," Eve exploded. "We found several in your residence. *Woman with a Parasol* — Monet. *Self-Portrait with Grey Felt Hat* — Van Gogh. *The Crystal Ball* — Waterhouse. *The Desperate Man* — Courbet."

"You know some art," Jonathan interrupted. "How surprising, considering. I often provide costumes for my models."

"We have your own words," Peabody continued, "your autobiography in process, your own documentation of the victims, when and where you selected them. Where you decided to leave the bodies and why."

"I'm an artist," he said again. "I've been toying with adding fiction writing to my scope. Writing about an artist. And I often walk around the city, looking for inspiration. All of this is clearly circumstantial."

"Now he's a lawyer, too." Eve sat back. "We have your paintings, Jonathan. Paintings of the three victims dressed and posed in the costumes they died and were dumped in. *Girl with a Pearl Earring,* Leesa Culver," Eve said as Peabody laid down photos of the paintings. "*The Blue Boy,* Bobby Ren. *Self-Portrait in a Straw Hat* — Janette Whithers."

"Painted purely from my own imagination."

"That won't fly, Jonathan. I mean, look at them. Sure, the photos don't show the real light, the exceptional detail. If you hope to go that route, you shouldn't have painted them with such skill. I've seen the portraits, and the fact is, I'm fortunate enough to have married into an amazing art collection. I do know art."

He didn't look bored now, Eve thought. But riveted. She kept pushing the buttons.

"I can recognize great art when I see it. You have far too many details of your models to claim you just" — she flicked her fingers — "made them up. Those paintings are alive, so maybe I get, to some extent, what you decided to prove to the critics. I get why you needed to prove you could not only match the masters but exceed them."

"They are extraordinary." With a fingertip, he pulled Leesa Culver's portrait closer. "Of course, they're not finished. But this one, this is nearly. You can see the brilliance. I put my heart and soul into this work."

He looked at Eve now, with those eyes that weren't quite right. "As an art collector, you have some sense of the sacrifice the artist makes to create. But unless you're the creator, you only have a glimmer."

"Years of study," Eve said, "of practice, of dedication, the pain of rejection, the insult of criticism by those who won't ever understand, won't ever suffer, won't ever create. You needed to show them, and you have. You did. You can't betray yourself now by refuting your work, the brilliance of it. How you planned out every detail, down to the smallest point to create masterpieces. To make these people immortal."

"Yes!" Tears of joy sprang to his eyes. "Yes, yes, you see! At last. They were nothing, common whores. I made them icons who'll live forever. With my own hands, I took their light, their life, and with my own hands I poured that into my work. I had a duty to my art. I had a vision that couldn't be denied. I was entitled to take what I needed, and to give it to the world."

"And you have. Tell us how. The world needs to know every detail of how you went from concept to execution."

So he told them. Every detail.

When they had it all, Eve took the next step.

"Why did you deny all of this? Why did you hide your process?"

"To avoid all this. To keep some law that cares nothing about art from stopping me, punishing me. I refuse to go to prison because some judge, some jury puts the lives of nobodies above me and my art."

"So you ran."

"I knew my mother would take care of it all. She always does. And she will. She'll take care of all of this nonsense."

"Of course. If you'd made it to Caracas, what then? Obviously, you'd continue to paint. Would you continue to kill? To create the immortal?"

"Genius does what it must. It's above common laws and mores. I won't be restricted in what I need to create. My mother understands this, supports this as no one ever has until now, with you."

Eve took an extra beat for the unexpected gift. "You explained all this to your mother?"

"Yes, I felt I must. I'd always intended to tell her when I'd completed the series of eight so that she could arrange things."

"What things?"

"A show in New York, whatever legal fees required to circumvent any legal matters. The show itself would, no question, supersede those matters, but people had to see the art first.

"I'm an artist, but she is a businesswoman, and would know what to do to protect me, who to pay off, and so on."

"You told her, as you've told us, you killed Leesa Culver, Bobby Ren, Janette Whithers, had planned to kill Aaron Pine, and four others."

"I don't remember their names, for God's

sake. Why would I?"

"Why would you?" Eve agreed. "But you told your mother you'd killed three people and had planned to kill others."

"Yes, I told her the method I'd found to lift my work up. She told me not to speak of it. No one would understand, and she'd fix everything so I could live free."

"And continue your work. Your art."

"Of course continue. How could I go back now that I know what I need? I took their lives with my hands, and with my hands transferred that life to the portraits. I gave them immortality and created brilliance.

"Now that you understand and appreciate, I want to talk to my mother. I expect the lawyers will work out some sort of deal, and we can all go back to our work."

"Jonathan, in the beginning of this interview, I explained to you what would happen, and what wouldn't."

"But that was before I explained, before I knew you fully appreciated and understood my work."

"And now that you've explained, I can promise you'll spend the rest of your life in a concrete cage, off-planet. Your mother may, probably will, serve out her life on-planet, but she'll have a cage, too."

"You can't mean that! Look! Look!"

When he pushed at the photos of the paintings, Eve rose. "Yes, I see. I see three people you killed, with your bare hands after you rendered them unconscious, so you could try to copy great art, and all for your own ego, your own sense of importance. Because you think money, money you never earned, makes you better.

"And your art, Jonathan? Is crap. It barely reaches the level of crap. Interview end. Peabody, see that this piece of shit is taken back to his cell."

"With pleasure."

"You can't do this! I want my mother. I want my mother now!"

"Fuck you and your mother," Eve muttered after she stepped out.

Epilogue

Mira stepped out of Observation, and before Eve saw it coming, took both of Eve's hands.

"It takes a lot to chill people in our line of work. He managed." She squeezed Eve's hands. "Well done. Very, very well done."

"He wanted someone besides his mother to tell him what a genius he is. That's all I had to do. Tell me he's legally sane."

"I can and will tell you just that. You worked that out of him as well. He knew right from wrong. He considers himself above all that. Ego doesn't make him legally insane. He's a malignant egoist who's been pampered and indulged and given whatever he likes so he believes he's entitled to take what he likes. Including lives."

"I'm taking his mother next. I'm taking her now."

"I'll stay for that. She created him."

Eve glanced over as Roarke stepped out. "Reo's on her 'link with the attorney Phoebe Harper's just managed to engage. Lieutenant, while his work is crap, yours rises to genius. I was here from about halfway through that."

"He'd have kept killing. She knew that. He couldn't have stopped, wouldn't have stopped, and she knew it."

Mira moved aside so Roarke took Eve's hands. "She thinks, as he does, her money, her position will buy them both out of this. You'll prove her wrong."

Reo came out. "Decent firm, nothing special. Solid enough to understand their clients are in a hell of a fix. They want to talk deal. Ten years for him, in a facility — a nice plush one — for therapy and treatment. Two years of community service for her, and a ten-million-dollar fine."

"And you said."

"How about no? Absolutely, unequivocally no. I'd've dealt on her, to a point, until I heard that last bit. He told her everything. She knew he'd killed and intended to continue. She intended to get him away despite that. Not even for help, but so he could do as he pleased."

"Hold that line, Reo."

"You hold yours." Reo gave Eve a decisive nod. "I'll hold mine."

"I'm bringing her up. Let her attorney know."

"I'm begging for coffee."

"I'll see to it," Roarke told her. "Charlotte, coffee or tea?"

"I'll go for the coffee, and thanks."

As Roarke started toward Eve's office, Whitney stepped off the elevator. They exchanged a few words before Whitney continued to Eve.

"Interview end?"

"Yes, sir. We got a full, detailed confession. He also implicated his mother as accessory after the fact."

"I've just gotten off the 'link with the governor." His eyebrows lifted when he saw Eve's eyes go flat. "Relax, Dallas. Yes, they've gone to him, the Harper family — which he tells me didn't include the senator. He also viewed the live feed. He'll take no part in this, and wanted to assure me of same.

"Dallas." He laid a hand on her shoulder. "I'm going to apologize in advance, but when you've completed your work here, you'll need to address the media again."

"Well, Christ. Sir."

He laughed at that. "A sincere apology. If it helps, I'll have to address them as well."

"It really doesn't."

Roarke and Trueheart came down the hall, both of them carrying coffee.

Which told Eve he'd probably provided coffee for the whole damn bullpen.

"I'm going to have a quick sit-down with Harper's attorney. It's Malory Felds, Dallas. Solid, but no Kopeckne. And I'll hold the line. Ten minutes should do it," Reo said.

"Peabody, my office."

She went straight there, straight to the window. She opened it, leaned out. Breathed.

"No sympathy for her. None."

"I don't feel any."

"Good. She doesn't deserve it. What would your mother do if you killed someone in cold blood, and had no problem doing so again?"

"She'd do everything she could to get me help. She'd visit me as often as possible in prison. I would've broken her heart, but she'd tell me she loved me, and visit me."

"And if she had more money than God?"

"Exactly the same thing."

"That's exactly it. This isn't love, it's obsession. It's a sick kind of pride. We don't give her an inch."

"Two bad cops."

"Two damn good, pissed-off cops. For them." She pointed at the board. "She's as responsible as he is. We stand for them, and we take her down."

"Do you think we can break her?"

"She's already broken, so it doesn't matter. Confession, no confession, it really doesn't matter. What we're doing?" Eve closed the window, turned. "We're spitting in her eye."

"For them."

"For them. Let's go spit in her eye."

Eve didn't see fear this time, but absolute arrogance. Though they hadn't shackled her, they'd exchanged her designer dress for inmate orange.

Beside her, her attorney wore a dark suit, had her glossy brown hair in a twist smooth like Reo's. Rather than confidence or nerves there, Eve thought she sensed resignation.

"Record on. Dallas, Lieutenant Eve, Peabody, Detective Delia, Reo, APA Cher, entering Interview with Harper, Phoebe, and her counsel of record, Felds, Malory."

Eve recited the rest, then sat. "Ms. Felds, you'll state for the record that your client has been read her rights and obligations in these matters and fully understands them?"

"I will."

"Ms. Harper, you engaged the services of one Shaun Ye, a freelance technician, and agreed to pay him ten million dollars — half on agreement, half on completion. You further contracted to provide him with transportation to the Philippines, and purchase a home there for him. In exchange, he would undermine and remove from your son, Jonathan Harper Ebersole, the court-ordered monitor he was charged to wear as a condition of his release on house restriction pending trial for three counts of first-degree murder and other related charges. Is this true?"

"Lieutenant, my client does not deny those actions. In an emotional state after her only son's arrest, my client led with those emotions in an attempt to protect her child."

"He's twenty-eight, shortly to be twenty-nine. He's not a child. Ms. Harper, did you access false identification, including a passport for Jonathan Harper Ebersole in the name of Marcus Solo?"

"Lieutenant, as I said, Ms. Harper will not refute these charges. Her maternal instincts —"

Eve whipped her head around to Felds. "I will have the charges and her statement verifying them on this record, Counselor.

"Did you provide Jonathan Harper Ebersole, arrested and arraigned for three counts of murder in the first degree and related charges, with transportation to Caracas, which has no extradition treaty with the United States? Did you additionally provide him with lodging in Caracas, with funds in cash and in an account under his false identification?"

"Do you have a son, Lieutenant Dallas?" Phoebe demanded.

Not children, Eve noted. A son. "No."

"Then you'd hardly understand the need, the duty I felt and feel to protect my son."

"Is that a yes to the question?"

"Yes! I did what needed to be done to protect my son, to get him to safety."

"That would include assaulting two police officers, and inflicting harm on a police officer."

Appearing completely composed, Phoebe folded her hands on the table. "For a mother guided by a mother's love, her child comes first, and no true mother would fault me for it."

"You really think you can get off with

that?" Eve glanced at Reo, who just smiled slightly, shook her head.

"Your head of security, whom you dragged into this, will do twenty years in prison. He doesn't matter to you either."

"He's a grown man. He made his choice."

"Jonathan's a grown man, and made his."

"We will submit to the court that my client took action in a desperate and emotional state. That she —"

"She got a hell of a lot done in a desperate and emotional state," Reo said. "You can try it, Ms. Felds, but we both know the chances are slim. Maybe I don't get the full fifty, but I'd lay odds on a minimum of thirty. And that's not all.

"Lieutenant."

"Did Jonathan Ebersole confess to you that he had killed three people, people he lured to his studio with the promise of payment for modeling?"

She saw it then, that first flicker. Not of fear, not really fear, but anger.

"Did Jonathan Ebersole explain to you his motives for doing so? To bring their life into his art, as that art had been rejected over and over as ordinary. At best. Did he explain that he needed to take lives to continue to create his art?"

"My client won't answer that question. It's purely speculative."

"It's not. It's fact. He told us, Phoebe. He couldn't help himself. You've made him believe he's too important to be denied anything. He told us he explained it all to you. You told him not to discuss it. You told him you'd protect him, get him away where he could live free and do whatever he needed to do."

"My client will not respond to —"

Eve rose, leaned in. "You knew. You knew what he'd done, why he'd done it. You know what he is, you knew what he'd continue to do. If things got too sticky in Caracas, you'd just move him somewhere else. Lives taken? They didn't matter. Only he matters."

"He's my son. He's my child."

"He's your monster. Created by you, nurtured by you."

"You shut your mouth about my boy." Phoebe rose, leaned in so they were all but nose to nose.

"Ms. Harper, please sit. Please leave this to me. This interview is over."

"You're not in charge here, Phoebe. You're never going to be in charge again. Your baby boy's going to prison, off-planet, forever."

"He won't serve a day. I'll destroy you if

you try. You think because you wear diamonds with your weapon it puts you on *my* level? I'll ruin you for what you've done to my son."

"Give it a shot. You? You're never getting out of a cage either. Your baby boy made sure of it."

"You coerced him. You've twisted his words."

"Didn't have to. All I had to do was play you. Tell him he was a genius, that his art was masterful. When you know as well as I do it's crap."

Eve saw the slap coming, let it land.

"And there's one more," she said as the attorney sprang up, tried to control her client. "Assault of an officer, on record. You made him what he is, Phoebe, now you have to live with it. So do your two daughters, whom you haven't mentioned once. For your knowledge of Jonathan Ebersole's actions, for your knowledge of his intentions to continue his murderous spree, you are additionally charged with accessory to murder after the fact, and conspiracy to murder before the fact. How long there, Reo?"

"She'll get life, no parole. I'll give you on-planet, Counselor. That's it."

Now Felds looked more desperate than resigned. "We will take this to trial."

"I look forward to it. As a proven flight risk, we both know your client will be remanded."

"If this is the best you can do," Phoebe snapped, "you're fired. I'll engage more competent counsel."

"Ms. Harper — I need to consult with my client."

"The one who just fired you?" Eve asked. "Enjoy. You?" She looked back at Phoebe. "No, you'll never be in charge again, and that goes down as one of the biggest accomplishments of my life so far. Peabody, arrange for an officer to wait outside and escort the prisoner back to her cell after she speaks to her former attorney.

"Now, interview end."

"You think because you married wealth and power you understand what it can and will do?"

Eve paused at the door, glanced back. "I think because I've spent my career dealing with monsters, some who make even you look small, I know what I'll do to stop them.

"And I've done it."

Stepping out, Eve shoved both hands through her hair.

"She clocked you pretty good," Peabody told her. "Your cheek's still red."

"On record. Will she get life, Reo?"

"I'm going to promise you that, and I don't make that kind of promise lightly. She's wrong about a jury. Any true mother will see what she is. You wrapped her for me, Dallas. I'll tie the bow."

She waited for the rest to come out of Observation. Mira laid a cool hand on her hot cheek. "You baited her."

"It didn't take much."

"No, it wouldn't. At first pass, I'd call it borderline personality disorder. She can't be wrong. Must be the center. Her son has all her love, as to give it to others takes from him. He, at least, gives her the pretense that she's the center for him. I think she'll continue to believe, for some time, that her money and position will override all of this, and she and her son will walk free."

"She won't," Reo said. "She will, most likely, insist on a trial, and why not, since we won't entertain a plea that lets her out in this lifetime. But at trial? We'll bury her, I swear it.

"I need to update my boss. See you Saturday. I trust you'll have plenty of wine."

"You closed the lid," Whitney told her,

then surprised Eve by giving her a light punch on the shoulder. "She swung for the fences. You didn't even flinch."

"Well, I saw it coming."

"Didn't even flinch," he repeated, and smiling, walked away.

"Saturday." Mira touched her lips to Eve's cheek. "We'll drink plenty of that wine."

"I could use some now," Eve murmured when Mira left them.

"You'll want to write it up first."

Eve nodded at Roarke. "I want to close it out. Lid's on, yeah, but I'm going to lock it down. Peabody, go home. Go bask in your happy kitchen, bake something, build a sofa, play with the kid, whatever."

"No, sir. I'm locking my own lid first. He took the lives, but . . ."

"She's worse," Eve finished. She started to her office.

Peabody peeled off at her desk.

"Under an hour," Eve told Roarke.

"Take the time you need." Like Mira, he laid his lips on her cheek. "I saw it coming as well. I believe I flinched."

Since that made her laugh, she hugged him. "Under an hour. Close it down, lock it up."

"Then we'll go home, take a walk to the pond, have some wine."

Since she'd taken off her jacket as he'd suggested that morning, he tapped her weapon harness.

"You did look formidable, Lieutenant. Every inch of formidable. Tag me when you're ready."

"Roarke?"

He paused at her doorway.

"I'm glad you were here for the end of it. Now we don't have to talk about it tonight. We don't have to give them a minute's more time once we walk out of Central."

"Just you, me, and the cat for the evening."

"Sounds good. Real good."

When he left, she stood a moment, rolled her shoulders. As before, she marveled at the weight lessened.

Duty done, justice served, she thought.

Then she sat to close it out and lock it up.

ABOUT THE AUTHOR

J. D. Robb is the pseudonym for #1 *New York Times* bestselling author Nora Roberts. She is the author of more than 250 novels, including the futuristic suspense In Death series. There are more than 500 million copies of her books in print.

www.ingramcontent.com/pod-product-compliance
Lightning Source LLC
Jackson TN
JSHW070220150826
106630JS00002B/2